Christmasville

Merry Christmasville!

[signature]

September 25, 2009

Christmasville

A NOVEL

By

Michael Dutton

Linden Park Publishers, Ltd.
51 Bateman Avenue
Newport, Rhode Island 08401

Published by Linden Park Publishers, Ltd.
51 Bateman Avenue
Newport, RI 02840
U.S.A.
www.lindenparkpublishers.com

First published in 2007 by Linden Park Publishers, Ltd.

Copyright © 2007 Michael M. Dutton
All rights reserved

ISBN 0-9786655-0-3
ISBN 978-0-9786655-0-0
LCCN 2006906693
SAN 851-2205

Printed and bound in the United States of America
Text set in Baskersville

Dust jacket design by Alison van Dam
Dust jacket photographs by Katelin Dutton

This book is a work of fiction. Any references to historical events; to real people, living or dead; or to actual locations are intended solely for the purpose of seating the work of fiction in a historical reality. Other names, characters, places and incidents either are the product of the author's imagination or are used fictitiously, and their resemblance, if any, to real-life counterparts is entirely coincidental.

ATTENTION UNIVERSITIES, COLLEGES AND PROFESSIONAL ORGANIZATIONS:
Quantity discounts are available for educational and gift purposes.
For information, please contact Linden Park Publishers, Ltd., 51 Bateman Avenue, Newport, RI 02840

Dedication

To Katherine M. Dutton –

"me mum" of course –

who taught me what was important,

what was not important

and

the wisdom to recognize

the sometimes subtle comma that separates them.

Acknowledgments

Time – that most precious of commodities – is a gift that should always be carefully considered when one gives it away, a genuine luxury when one is so fortunate as to receive it from others.

In varying increments, my family and friends have graciously presented me with that most precious of commodities. I am gratefully indebted for the time, and the services, which they have generously afforded me.

I would like to thank:

Alan Bernstein,
Jack Casey,
Dan Dutton,
Cheryl Glennon,
Mariann Maida,
and
Diane Tholin.

My brother, Dan, and Mariann, were particularly incisive and scrupulous in their editing and proofreading efforts – the slash of the red pen etched across the pages with relentless precision (signs of wounded language, in need of repair).

Cheryl Glennon – the persistence of her enthusiasm, regarding the publication of *Christmasville*, is fondly noted.

I would also like to thank my wife, Carol, my daughters, Meg and Kate, and my stepdaughter, Cheryl Lewis – not only for their input and commentary but for their unswerving support.

Of course, lastly, I would thank you, my reader, who has been so bold as to select this book, among many, investing your "most precious of commodities" into what, hopefully, will be a memorable, magical experience.

Christmasville

Prologue
She Bites into a Cookie, Swallows a Mouthful of Milk and Begins

Chapter 1 . . . . Christmasville

Chapter 2 . . . . A Snowman from China

Chapter 3 . . . . Faith

Chapter 4 . . . . The Constant Nuance of Trees

Chapter 5 . . . . A Game of Checkers

Chapter 6 . . . . The Eve of St. Nick

Chapter 7 . . . . First Night

Chapter 8 . . . . Maiden Journey

Chapter 9 . . . . Thirty-Two Degrees of Illumination

Chapter 10 . . . . What The Iceman Said

Chapter 11 . . . . The House at the End of the World

Chapter 12 . . . . Elastic Plastic

Epilogue
A Remarkable Discovery

Prologue

She Bites into a Cookie, Swallows a Mouthful of Milk and Begins

"Ready to get started?"

"Ready," Madeleine replies.

In the upper hallway of their split-level house, he reaches up and grabs the short, knotted rope that hangs down from the wooden flap of the attic entry. Swinging it downward, springs groan and metal hinges creak in dryness as he unfolds the ladder and positions its legs securely on the floor. Madeleine hands him the flashlight, stepping back to watch her father ascend the ladder into the attic.

About halfway up the steps, he reaches up and spins the light bulb around in its fixture because the pull-chain is broken and he has neither time nor inclination to repair it. Besides, it works fine the way it is anyway. When the bulb is illuminated, light splashes across rafters and floorboards, shaping shadows as it spills around a pair of old table lamps, a rocking chair, a nightstand, a mattress and crib that's been disassembled, an ivory bassinet, a pine highchair laid flat on its back.

Continuing up the steps, he climbs onto the wooden floorboards that extend the length of the center aisle through the attic. He moves about on his hands and knees because, at its highest point, the distance between the floorboards and the rafters that support the slope of the roof is less than four feet. To the right and left of the center aisle, exposed floor joists segregate row upon row of silver-foiled insulation.

At the base of the ladder, with lollipop in hand, Madeleine watches her father disappear. Smears of cherry-flavored sugar are pulled like quotation marks from the corners of her mouth, across the creamy complexion of her cheeks.

Stacked randomly between the furniture are boxes of summer clothes, curtains, photographs and record albums, baby toys, ice skates, mittens and earmuffs, decorations labeled "Easter" and "Halloween".

It occurs to him that the attic, though infrequently visited, is a calendar that documents the seasons of his life.

Dust. It lies across furniture and boxes like a fine gray snow. It swirls up as he crawls along floorboards, drifts about in the beam of his flashlight. It sticks to the sweat which beads up along his forehead, curls into his nose and mouth as he breathes. It has a dry, stale taste to it.

As he maneuvers between the crib and the mattress, around the bassinet, he bumps into a wooden plant stand. It rocks once and then quickly falls over because, poorly placed on top of the stand – making it top-heavy – was an iron disc that he once used for weight-lifting.

"Daddy?" Madeleine calls, switching the lollipop to the other side of her mouth. "Are you all right, daddy?"

"I'm all right, Maddy," her father replies.

Shining the flashlight down, he grimaces. Having fallen in the slit between floor joist and insulation, the weight is so heavy that it has punctured the ceiling of the room below. Wedged into the sheet rock, he has difficulty removing it.

'It must be a ten pounder,' he says to himself, after putting the flashlight down and pulling the weight out with both hands. Laying it down – in a secure place this time – he grabs the flashlight and inspects the damage that he has caused.

"What happened, daddy?" Madeleine asks from below.

"I knocked something over."

"Do you want me to come up and help you?"

"No," he replies. "You stay put, Maddy. It's much too dirty up here. OK?"

Through the gash in the ceiling, he observes below the closet of Madeleine's bedroom.

'Another project for daddy to do,' he thinks, turning away to move down the center aisle, through the rising flurry of dust, toward another season of the calendar.

Twenty-two boxes – that's what she counted after her father had carried them down, one at a time, and stacked them on the floor of the hallway. There were eleven wooden wine crates, seven cardboard boxes that once contained canned vegetables, two large plastic containers and two shoeboxes.

"All there, Maddy?"

"Yep. They're all here, daddy."

Folding the ladder up, he pushes the wooden flap of the attic back into place. Madeleine goes to the bathroom nearby to discard the stick from her lollipop and to wash the stickiness from her hands and face. The rope that hangs down from the flap of the attic swings back and forth like a silent metronome.

Two at a time, he carries the wine crates down from the hallway to the dining room table that has been cleared of tablecloth and candlesticks. With a box cutter, he slices the plastic packing tape that secures the wooden lids to each of the crates. He peels the tape back and around, rolling it into balls that he sticks to the top of a chair. Removing the lids, he stacks the boxes near the chair at the end of the table where Madeleine sits. She has carried the two shoeboxes down – because they were light and manageable – and because they contained the chalkware figures of the Nativity set that she was fond of unwrapping from their tissue paper cocoons, that she was only too happy to arrange – and to re-arrange – on the mantle over the fireplace, on the piano in the living room, on a far corner of the train platform until she was content that she had found the perfect spot.

A king, an angel, a donkey, a cow. The little shepherd boy with the lamb on his shoulders. A king, an angel, a dog, a camel. The Virgin Mary in her pale blue robe and Joseph with his broken hand. A king, an angel, another cow and a second camel ...

"I made you some cookies," her mother says, arriving from the kitchen with a plate of tollhouse and a glass of milk.

Her mother has dark brown hair, like the chocolate inside the cookies, and is beautiful and big in front because her body is busy making babies. Not one baby, but two.

"Thank you, mommy," she says, after turning to look directly at her mother.

She wants to be sure that her mother can see her lips move when she speaks.

"I'll make you a manger," Madeleine says, before turning to unwrap the little babe, Jesus, nestled in a sky blue blanket.

"Could you make me a little brown one with a straw roof?" asks her mother, peeking into the crate on the floor near Madeleine.

When Madeleine turns, she spots the crate with the disassembled manger inside. Her father had made it in his woodshop – three walls that slid together through slits, a floor and a roof with strands of broom straw glued to the top of it.

"A fine wooden one with a fence for the animals and a tiny light inside," she says, after turning to look at her mother.

"That'll do nicely," her mother says, leaning down to kiss Madeleine on her forehead, to run the palm of her hand across her hair and neck.

When her father arrives, he puts the last of the cardboard boxes on the floor near Madeleine, pulling the flaps open to expose their contents.

"I'll be in the sunroom, working on the train platform" he says, looking directly at Madeleine's mother.

"Would you like me to make you your lunch now?" she asks. "There's plenty of turkey left over from Thanksgiving – I could make you a sandwich."

"That would be nice," he says, smiling at her before leaning across the table to grab a tollhouse.

"And I'll bring you some cookies, too," she adds, pulling the balls of tape from the top of the chair and returning to the kitchen.

Her father climbs the steps to the upper hallway, fetching the plastic containers with the train sets inside. He goes into the sunroom to work on the platform.

Madeleine bites into a cookie, swallows a mouthful of milk and begins – pulling the parts of the manger out, sliding its walls together.

Christmasville

The police station used to be across the street from our house but it's not there anymore. At the end of Maple Street were the bank and the firehouse but they're on Juniper Street now. The bank sits back away from the street, which is much better because they put a little park out front so we have a place to sit on Friday nights, after we're done sledding, to drink hot cocoa and to watch the weekly fire drill. The fire chief stands in the middle of the street, holding up traffic as he directs the trucks from their berths in the firehouse. Tucker, the chief's Dalmatian, sits obediently nearby until the signal is given and he jumps on engine # 2 with the chief just in the nick of time before it races away. He's a good dog but he doesn't like anyone to pet him unless you give him a treat first.

On the other side of the bank, where Poplar Street runs into Juniper, is the police station. The Thompson family used to live there in a red and white, two-story house but they're our neighbors now, which is a lot more convenient because Emily Thompson is my best friend. We live on Caterson's Hill, at the very end of Maple Street.

Directly across from the bank and the firehouse are city hall, the public school and the municipal hospital. They're the biggest buildings in town, I suppose. They were on Caterson's Hill last year – by "dead man's curve" on Maple Street – but I like them better on Juniper because it makes our town look more like a city. I don't know why they call it "dead man's curve." Somebody said that an ambulance once plummeted off the steep embankment in a snowstorm, crashing into an oak tree by Wright's Produce Stand below. The driver suffered a broken ankle but the only thing that died was the tree. So maybe they should call it something else then. I don't know – something like "croaked oak curve" or something like that.

Wright's Produce Stand is on Mulberry Street now, next to the Christmasville Inn.

I know this all sounds confusing but what I'm trying to say is this: each year – between the last night of January and the morning of December 1st – all the buildings in Christmasville are moved somewhere else. It's not that they were demolished and re-built on their present sites because they had become damaged or dilapidated. It's not that they were changed in any way – renovated or expanded because of a higher crime rate, a rise in fire alarms, a surge in the number of students in school, an upswing in accidents or an increase in the population of people who suddenly decided to become vegetarians. Each year all of the buildings in Christmasville are identical in every way except for their location. It's like someone had played a game of checkers, picking up each building throughout the course of the game and setting it down somewhere else. It's a game of checkers that nobody knows anything about. Nobody except me.

It's kind of … well, it's kind of crazy but every year – as soon as I wake up on December 1st – I find my way in the snow down to the gas station, wherever it's been re-situated, and get myself a map. The gas station is clear across town this year. But studying the map is the only way that I can sort out all the changes to Christmasville. Or the *change*, I should say, since it's the only thing that really happens in Christmasville, anything of consequence anyway.

There was a time when I would point out the transformation of our town to Mr. Mason, our neighbor, who is no longer our neighbor, or Mr. Cauldwell, the manager of the supermarket, or Tommy Burks, the boy who once lived across from us when we lived on Willow Street. But I don't talk about it any more because they would look at me as if I was an alien from another planet, telling them a joke without a punch line.

I remember Mr. Mason, leaning against his car with a snow shovel in one hand and a cup of hot cocoa in the other. He was taking a break between clearing the driveway and the front walk.

"What's the matter, Mary Jane? You don't seem to be yourself these days," he said, as I trudged down the street in the snow, dragging my new sled behind.

When I explained to him what was bothering me, he listened patiently, nodding his head every now and then to show that he was interested. But the further that I got into it, the more uncomfortable he became because by the time that I had finished, he was staring into his cup of cocoa rather than looking directly at me.

"I'm sure there's an explanation," he said, turning away to shovel snow even before he had finished his cocoa. "Maybe you should talk to Father Conover about it."

But what he really meant to say was maybe I should talk to Doctor Sperry, the school psychiatrist, because a couple of days later I heard him speaking to my father on the sidewalk out front and the notion of "emotionally challenged" was mentioned twice.

At the supermarket, I got the same reaction from Mr. Cauldwell. "Sure, Mary Jane," he said, scratching his head before turning away to stamp cans of mixed nuts with his price gun. "And I'm sure that the world's flat too, huh?" he added, anxious to change the subject, to move on with his work.

Mr. Cauldwell always gets nervous and sarcastic whenever the topic of conversation becomes kind of abstract and intangible – as if it were a powerful force, like gravity, pulling him away from the comfortable orbit of his routines.

Tommy Burks got into trouble because he was caught writing, *"Mary Jane Higgins is a fat fruitcake"*, with spray paint on the back of the Union Train Station. He had scribbled it at least a dozen times on buildings, sidewalks, bridges throughout town but it was Mr. Bachmann, the stationmaster, who caught him red-handed, the green paint smeared across the front of his jacket. Tommy was released to the custody of his parents and had to perform community service as a result of his mischief: eradicating his handiwork with wire brush and mineral spirits until every trace of it was gone. My sentence was much stiffer though – meeting with Doctor Sperry every Tuesday and Friday afternoon, forfeiting my home economics class.

And I am *not* fat.

But anyway, the sessions with the psychiatrist weren't too bad because, every now and then, he would give me a candy cane or a chocolate soldier to eat during the therapy sessions. Enticement is a trick of his that works real well – I get the candy and he gets to hear what he wants. It's what you call a "reciprocating relationship", to use a psychiatric term.

"Why don't we start at the beginning, Mary Jane," the psychiatrist started. "When did you first imagine that our town was being transformed into something other than what it is?"

I was naïve at first. I thought that everyone else ... I thought that they *sensed* the transformation like I did. I thought that everyone else at least suspected that something ... something was different about Christmasville, year after year. And beyond – beyond the town limits, didn't anyone ... *anyone* ... didn't they have that strange feeling that there was more to it than what met the eye, or the ear, or the nose? – Fleeting shadows passing through the night sky, sounds on the threshold of being heard, foreign odors carried by the wind, barely detectable.

"And didn't anyone else dream? – Didn't they dream about spring showers and summer vacations and autumn leaves?" I asked the psychiatrist.

But it really floored me when he replied: " *'Spring showers and summer vacations?'* What does *'autumn'* mean? – I'm not familiar with that word."

I guess I'm going to have to explain about that now. And I will – that is, I'll try to explain but the problem is the same as it was with Doctor Sperry – where do I begin?

My name is Mary Jane Higgins and I'm fourteen years old. *I'm always fourteen years old.* I live in a gray and white split-level house but this year it's on Maple Street. Last year, we lived in the same house but it was on Willow. My father works in the lumberyard and my mother is a cashier at Cauldwell's Supermarket. I have two younger brothers – twins – which is a real problem because, like me, they never get any older. But of course, just like everyone else in Christmasville, they don't know that. The notion of living out eternity with Roger and Todd never graduating from their juvenile phase is something that would drive anyone to the brink of ... of "emotionally challenged".

Autumn. Autumn is a season between summer and winter. It's when some of the trees shed their leaves, preparing themselves for the long sleep of winter. They're those big, brown, brittle flakes – the leaves – that you might find at the bottom of the snow. I never found any though.

I don't know how I know all this but I do. It's because I dream a lot, I suppose. At first, my mother and father said that I was "precocious" and "creative", especially after I told them about some of my dreams. But they don't say that about me any more. They say something else.

Anyway, it never occurred to me before, but maybe everybody in Christmasville ... maybe they're like leaves ... – No, maybe we're all like trees and we go to sleep for a long time but we don't realize it because ... because we're asleep. Like oak trees and maples – trees that, for some reason or other, shed their leaves before winter arrives.

Maybe there's more to the year than just December and January. Maybe what happens is, on the last night in January, we climb into our beds like we normally do but, instead of waking up the next morning in December ... maybe there's a long string of nights ... nights and days – whole months in between – two months for spring, two for summer, two for autumn and ...

I know that doesn't sound "precocious" or "creative". It just sounds crazy. But I don't know any other way to explain what I sense, what I suspect, what I dream.

I never told Doctor Sperry anything more than what "autumn" is. I let him "convince" me that I was an impressionable child, overly influenced by weird dreams – "nightmares", he said. And that's all fine and well because I had to get back into home economics class. It was already the end of January and I needed to finish the woolen hat and scarf that I was making for mom before Christmas. And besides, if I was going to find out about … about trees, then I couldn't waste my time with any school psychiatrist.

It's a good plan. At least I think it's a good plan. I decided that on the last day of January, I'll pretend that I'm sick so I can stay home from school and sleep the whole day away. When I get up, I'll drink tons of coffee so I won't fall asleep through the night. After everyone else is in bed, I'll sneak out of the house and make my way down to the train station and buy a ticket. If I'm on the train … If I'm on the train and I'm awake and I travel to another place and return the following morning, then I'll find out what really happens between the last day of January and the 1st of December. And I can see what else is out there too, what towns or cities – whatever it is that lay beyond the ends of Christmasville. Or maybe I'll find out that I need to talk to Doctor Sperry again in more detail. At any rate, I guess I'll find out soon enough because that's where I am right now. It's the night of January 31st.

At ten o'clock, mom and dad come into my room but I pretend that I'm already asleep. Mom holds the palm of her hand against my forehead to see if I'm running a fever. Her hand is so soft and warm that sometimes I wish that she would just leave it there all night long. But she pulls it away to push my hair back away from my face, kissing me on the forehead. Dad leans down like he always does and kisses my cheek before whispering, "sweet dreams, princess". I'm fourteen but I guess I'll always be his princess. And that's OK.

By ten thirty, my parents are fast asleep. Maybe they're dreaming – I don't know if they dream. Not like I do. The twins went to bed at nine – they were put to bed, that is, because if they had their way, they wouldn't go to bed at all. Once mom's decided whether it's Roger or Todd who gets the top bunk for the night, they climb into their beds, exchanging a few nasty words to each other because the twin whose been assigned to the bottom bunk is disgruntled by mom's decision. And then it's their prayers and lights out, sending them both into worlds where, I'm sure, they'll concoct new ways of terrorizing their older sister once they're awake the following morning.

But I won't be here, will I.

At ten forty-five, lying in bed, I hear the train whistle. It's the long, lonely whistle of the passenger train as it approaches the Oak Street Station in south Christmasville. It'll sit there for at least forty-five minutes because that's where it gets its coal. Then the conductor will start up the engine again, moving the train slowly northward until it arrives at Union Station.

The sound of the train whistle is the signal for me to get up from my bed and to set out on my journey. I put my long johns on beneath my corduroy pants and my woolen sweater. Then it's my ski leggings and coat, my hat and gloves. When I see myself in the mirror on the back of my bedroom door, it pretty much sums up the way that I feel – like a stuffed turkey, dressed for the holidays. For a moment I think about … about Tommy Burks and about what he wrote, but he won't see me because the dumb jerk's asleep in his bed.

From the floor of my closet, I drag out my backpack. It's got all my supplies inside – peanut butter and jelly sandwiches, shortbread cookies, chocolate bars and the thermos of hot cocoa that I made earlier in the day. I've got dad's big flashlight, fresh batteries, some extra clothes and two books that I can read along the way because … I don't know how long it's going to take me to get to wherever it is that I'm going. In my little red purse is eighty-seven dollars and fifty-three cents.

When I sneak outside onto the front porch, it is so still and crisp that I just stand there for a moment, breathing in the air. It is cold and clean and carries the heavy perfume of spruce trees and pinecones. In the sky above, stars twinkle like lights draped across the invisible branches of a huge Christmas tree.

Because we live on Maple Street this year – on Caterson's Hill – I can see all of Christmasville from our front porch. Looking out over the roofs of the buildings below, West Juniper Street shoots south, past the Church of St. Mary's, its towering steeple, a finger that points toward the heavens, reminding us always of grace and goodness and things far more lasting than the memory of Christmas gifts. It's something that mom and dad try to point out to the twins as much as possible but it hasn't had any impact yet. I don't know if it ever will.

Beyond the church, Juniper Street slides beneath Beech Boulevard, which is under continuous construction day after day, year after year, the dump trucks hauling in the same loads of asphalt, the steamrollers paving and re-paving, the snow plows persistent in removing the same snowfalls. I remember that last year Beech Boulevard was being built near Pine Street. And the year before, it was next to Mulberry, near Wakefield Bridge.

As Juniper Street exits the underpass beneath the boulevard, it winds through farmlands, skirts the gas station and runs zigzag near the train trestles that support the Overland Freight Express. The freight train whizzes through town once or twice or maybe a half dozen times a day though I don't remember it ever stopping. The other rail line – the one that carries passengers and stops at both the Union and the Oak Street Stations – runs parallel to Juniper Street before it swings into the tunnel that's burrowed into Caterson's Hill beneath our house.

From the porch I can look down onto the roof of Union Station and its two platforms. That's where I'll be going. It's between the diner and the power station, which houses the giant transformers that make electricity, that hum gently in the peace and stillness of the Christmasville night.

Startled by an icicle that falls from the roof of our house and crashes to the porch behind me, I turn about. From the corner of my eye, I catch a flash of light from one of the windows of our neighbor's house. This really makes me nervous because if Mr. or Mrs. Thompson have discovered me on the porch at this time of night …

But it's all right because after the curtains move, I recognize Emily, who is standing at her bedroom window. She waves at me before sliding the window open a couple of inches so she can lean down and speak through the opening.

"I'll be right down," she whispers loudly, shutting the window afterwards.

Emily Thompson is the only person in Christmasville that I told about my plan. She doesn't dream like I do but … but she believes. And that means a lot more than what any psychiatrist or doctor or anybody else says for that matter. Maybe it's Emily's believing that gives me the courage to do what I have to do.

Trudging in the snow from the back of her house to the front of mine, Emily meets me on the sidewalk.

"What are you doing, Emily?" I say, surprised because she's fully dressed in her coat and leggings and the snow boots that she got for Christmas.

"I'm trying to pull my hood up so I can tie it," she says, turning her back to me. "Can you pull it up for me, Mary Jane?"

A flap of the hood is caught beneath one of the shoulder straps of her backpack.

"You can't go with me, Emily," I say, pulling the flap free and lifting the hood around her head.

"Sure I can. I've got all my stuff. I made sandwiches and cocoa. And I've got my own money for the train ticket. Besides," she adds, trying to tie the strings of her hood with her gloves on, "I want to find out about summer vacations even more than you do. I hate school."

"But it might be a long trip," I say, taking my gloves off so I can tie her hood. "It could even be dangerous. I mean, I don't know what's going to happen, Emily. I don't know what it'll be like when I get where I'm going. Or when I get back."

"If it's a long trip, I can help you stay awake. Or we can take turns sleeping while one of us keeps watch. You know what I mean? It'll be much better with the two of us, Mary Jane. Besides, I've already made up my mind."

Emily is thirteen – almost a year younger than me – but once she's determined to do something, there's nothing that can be said or done to prevent her from doing it.

"OK," I say, giving in. "But first we better fix Harry up. I don't want the train conductor to think that we're little kids or something, too young to travel without our parents."

I go around to the back of Emily where Harry, her teddy bear, peers out from the top of her backpack. Loosening the flap, I tuck him down inside.

Although Union Station is right below us, near the bottom of the hill, it's too treacherous to climb down along the icy rock ledges to get to it. We have to go the long way around, following Maple Street along "dead man's curve" and passed St. Nick's where it swings down to meet East Juniper Street below. The Church of St. Nick's glows warmly in the night, the light spilling through the stained-glass angels that guard the big, white doors of the entrance.

"Can you tell me about summertime, Mary Jane? And about the ocean? Tell me about beach sand again," she asks, fascinated by the description of warm, white granules that run through your fingers like water.

When we get around "dead man's curve" and passed the church, we have two options for getting down the hill. There is the slow way – the long, metal staircase that winds down from platform to platform alongside the street and which deposits you safely at the bottom of the hill. It's the option that our parents insist upon taking. Or, there's the fast and fun way down – the mode preferred by every kid in Christmasville.

Lying on our backs on the top of the hill, in the middle of the street, our backpacks are held tightly against our stomachs. There isn't any need to push. It's a matter of gravity, coupled with the almost frictionless fabric of our coats and leggings against the icy surface of the street.

"OK to go!" I say, after insuring that no cars or trucks have turned from Juniper onto Maple Street, attempting to make their way up the steep, circular incline of the hill.

Because I'm bigger and heavier than Emily, I grab her by the hand as we shoot down the hill, our bodies wanting to spin and turn, bobbing and bouncing across the uneven patches of ice, picking up speed as we glide. Emily screams once because the weight of my body propels her faster than if she were "body-sledding" by herself. And then, before we know it, it's the big snow bank at the bottom of the hill – sometimes, when you slam into it, it finds arms that suddenly wrap around you and that pull you inside, jolting you to a screechless stop. Or, at other times – this time – the snow bank slings you up and over so that you fly through the cold air, limbs flailing, to somersault through the powdery splash of new fallen snow.

It takes us a couple of minutes to find Emily's backpack in the snow before we continue on our way.

I never fully realized how beautiful Christmasville is, especially in the stillness of night. All the houses and buildings are alit, casting pools of blue and orange, of green and red, against fields of snow that flow across lawns and parks, that snuggle around trees and shrubs and cars, sleeping. Even the white ice that is molded by traffic to the surface of Juniper Street captures the glimmers of lights, shooting them out like sparks as we move down the street.

"That used to be where the radio station was," I say to Emily, pointing at Jack's Toy Store, next to the firehouse.

"I don't remember," she replies, taking a bar of chocolate from her coat and snapping it in half to share.

Emily shivers in the cold that has seeped into her coat and leggings. It occurs to me that she is eating the chocolate to prevent her lips from trembling – or to prevent me from seeing that her lips are trembling.

"We haven't much further to go, Emily. Are you OK?"

She nods her head, biting another mouthful from her chocolate bar.

In the air is the smell of oak and elm and apple wood burning, the smoke rising from chimneys or spiraling downward in a sudden flurry of wind.

Between the school ahead and the trees along the curve in Juniper, past the junction at Poplar Street, I see a pickup truck moving toward the diner. Its headlights carve a funnel that the truck chases but never catches.

Pulling into the parking lot beside the diner, Joe Matthieson gets out of his pickup and dashes inside, out of the cold. It's supposed to be a big secret but everybody in town knows about Joe and Doris Caterson. She's a waitress and every night he stops in to help her clean up and to close down the diner at midnight. He says that he doesn't want Doris to drive in the snow so he picks her up because he's her boy friend. But sometimes – and this is the secret part – he doesn't take her home. He takes her back to his apartment.

Instead of turning from Juniper onto Poplar Street, Emily and I move along the deep snow banks that have been plowed to let cars in and out of the bank parking lot. That way, we won't be spotted by a policeman who might step outside of the station to get a breath of fresh air or a quick bite to eat from the diner nearby before it closes.

"What's grass like, Mary Jane? – I know you said that it's green and that it grows ... Is it like hair?"

"It's thicker than hair," I reply, helping Emily climb up and over the steep snow bank and move toward the train station. She is cold and tiring, her small frame having difficulty clambering through the deep snow in the field between the station and the powerhouse.

The giant transformers that make all the power for Christmasville are humming really loud. Maybe it's because we're so close to them. Or because everything else is so quiet. Maybe it's because of the bitter cold and they have to work harder than they normally would, pumping out extra power to keep all the houses and buildings warm and alit.

When the terminals on one of the transformers suddenly arc in a brilliant display of yellow and blue, the sound is terrifying. It crackles and sputters, the jagged jump of electrical energy scribbling a lightning bolt against the dark sky. Huge sparks – the size of snowballs – shoot from the terminals. Most of them vaporize in the air as they fall but a few of them float down, fizzling in the snow before drowning.

Emily is too frightened to move. She stands perfectly still behind me, mouth open, gaping at the fireworks.

As I pull her along in the snow and drag her towards the train station, I realize that it was a mistake to bring Emily along. Although she's my best friend, she's too young and fragile for this kind of adventure. It's not her fault that she's unprepared for the unexpected.

The station is empty, which is a good sign. I sit Emily down on a bench near the woodstove and pour her some hot cocoa from my thermos so she can get herself warmed up. Lowering her hood, I pull her gloves off and hand her the cup.

"Are you OK now?" I ask.

She nods her head and sips.

"Good," I say. "Now listen, you wait here while I find out about the tickets. OK? – Don't go anywhere."

As I approach the ticket booth, I go over the story in my head. The original one – the story that I had planned to tell the stationmaster so I wouldn't arouse any suspicions about buying train tickets, without my parents, and so late at night – had to be amended because of Emily. I know that I shouldn't lie but it's only a snowy white lie.

I can't see Mr. Bachmann behind the metal bars of the ticket counter. I don't see anyone.

"Hello?" I say. "Mr. Bachmann?"

There's a metal bell on the counter so I give the ringer a couple of punches with my finger. On the wall the clock reads, eleven twenty-two.

"Mr. Bachmann?"

As he comes from his office in the back, he rubs his eyes with his hands as if he's been sleeping. He puts his glasses on.

"Mary Jane?" he says, surprised to see me.

"Hello, Mr. Bachmann," I reply. "I would like to purchase train tickets, please."

I said it that way on purpose, deliberately substituting 'buy' with 'purchase' because it sounded more like a grown-up would say it.

"Tickets? – Tickets at this time of … at this time of night?" he says.

"Yes", I reply. "I would like to purchase two tickets for Emily Thompson and myself. We're going to visit my grandma because she's not feeling very well. Mom and dad said that it would be a good idea for me ... – for *us*," I say, modifying what I had memorized, "for Emily and I to visit grandma so we could check up on her. You know – to make sure that everything's all right."

"I see," Mr. Bachmann says, scratching his head. "I'm sorry to hear that grandma's ill – I hope it's not something serious."

"Serious? – Oh, no. Grandma only has a bad cold but she can't go out of the house to get her medicine for herself. So mom had a prescription filled here, in Christmasville, and I'm to deliver it. See?" I say, taking the vial out of my pocket and holding it up as proof.

At the beginning of December the twins had gotten bronchitis. They got over it ("unfortunately", I would say if I were mean) so I took the vial that their medicine came in, emptied out the few remaining tablets and filled it up with little white mints. I typed up a new label at school, with grandma's name on it. But the name of the twins' medicine didn't sound medical enough. I changed it to read something more serious and appropriate for grandma's "condition", adding a couple of warnings to boot – "May cause drowsiness" and "Do not drive or operate any machines when you take this".

Mr. Bachmann lifts his glasses, squints his eyes as he reads the label.

"Placebo of Pallantinius," he says aloud. "Sounds like pretty strong medicine to me."

"It is," I reply, improvising as I go. "Grandma has a slight heart murmur so they have to be careful what they give her so it doesn't … you know, so it doesn't aggravate her heart murmur."

"I can understand that," he agrees, handing me back the vial.

The eleven-forty passenger train whistles once, twice, three times as it announces its departure from the coaling station and moves northward. Although it runs late sometimes – depending upon how much coal needs to be loaded – tonight it's running on time.

"OK, Mary Jane. Two tickets for you and Emily Thompson – I'm sure that you'll be wanting round trip tickets, right?"

"Yes … round trip," I answer, a bit surprised because it's moving along so easily.

"And that'll be to … I'm sorry – what town is it that grandma lives in?"

I'm looking directly at Mr. Bachmann but trying to conceal the sudden panic that makes my head swim. I'd been so concerned about *leaving* Christmasville, and returning, that I never bothered to figure out where I was *going*.

"Mary Jane?" the stationmaster asks. "Where does grandmother live?"

"Oh … yes," I reply, stalling for time. "Grandma lives in … in … She lives in St. Valentine's," I say, after stealing a glance at the schedule of arrivals and departures on the wall behind Mr. Bachmann. "Sorry – we've all been so worried about grandma that I couldn't remember it for a second."

"That's understandable," he says. "St. Valentine's is a lovely town, I hear. Not quite so large or busy as Easterville, but lovely and quaint."

"You've been there, Mr. Bachmann? – To St. Valentine's and Easterville?"

"Well, no, not exactly. I've heard people talk," he replies. "I'm sorry – how long did you say that you'll be staying with grandma, Mary Jane?"

It's another question that I'm unprepared to answer.

"Um … probably only for the night," I say with hesitation. "But it could be for a couple of nights – it depends. It depends on how long grandma will need us to stay with her. Is that important?"

"No. I'll just make your return tickets valid for the next seven days. If you think that you'll be staying with grandma for longer than a week, then just bring them into the train station at St. Valentine's and have them extended. Do you understand that, Mary Jane?"

"I understand," I answer, nodding my head.

As Mr. Bachmann finishes making up our tickets, I try to anticipate any other questions that he might raise. But he stamps each of the tickets with a hand-stamp, puts them in envelopes and slides them across the counter, saying: "That'll be thirty-two dollars and forty-six cents."

I take the money from my purse and hand it to Mr. Bachmann, elated because the tickets were much cheaper than I had expected. I didn't know – I never traveled by train before; I never ever traveled out of Christmasville before – period – so I had no idea if the tickets would be ten dollars or a hundred.

"You and Emily have a safe journey, Mary Jane," Mr. Bachmann offers as I stuff my tickets and purse into my backpack.

"Thanks," I reply, turning from the counter to leave. "Have a good night, Mr. Bachmann."

"Oh – Mary Jane?"

It was too good to be true, I think, stopping in my tracks and turning about to face the stationmaster again.

"Yes?"

"I do hope that grandma has a speedy recovery."

I never knew that girls could snore. But when I return to Emily by the woodstove, she is laid out across the bench and snoring so hard that I swear, were she facing the iron furnace next to her, she would extinguish its yellow and bluish flames in a single blast.

She looks like a little kid lost, bundled up in her coat and leggings and scarf, her small arm wrapped securely around Harry, her teddy bear. I don't want to wake her but I don't know what to do with her either. The train for St. Valentine's is rapidly approaching, the tracks rattling, the sound of its whistle announcing its arrival.

Quickly, I take a pencil and the train tickets from my backpack. After removing Emily's tickets from the envelope and slipping them in with mine, I jot her a note on the front of the empty envelope, explaining as best I can that it's better this way. It's better because she's a little kid – though I don't write that. I write instead that I don't want to get her into trouble or to put her in danger because she's my best friend and because she's the only one who believes in me.

When I finish writing the note, I put some money in the envelope so she can take the taxicab home. I write "Emily" on the back of it and take a clip from my hair so I can attach the note to the front of her coat.

The big, black-and-silver locomotive reminds me of a wild animal, grunting and growling, breathing out jets of steam and puffs of smoke as it passes the station. There's over half a dozen cars attached to the end of it. On the tracks ahead, the engine slows, letting out a loud "hissssssss" as it settles to a stop.

Leaning down, I push Emily's hair away from her face, tucking it back behind her ear. I swing my backpack over my shoulder and leave, turning back twice to make sure that she's still asleep. When I go out on the platform, I can see the locomotive near the mouth of the tunnel that winds through the ridge of Caterson's Hill. There is still steam and smoke coming from the engine but gently so, as if it were catching its breath before its lunge forward, into the tunnel. The conductor steps from the engine with his brass lantern and looks back along the length of the train. He is a tall man in a black cap and uniform.

"All aboard!" he shouts, his deep, loud voice, a cannon burst that shoots across the platform and down the track, well beyond the end of the train.

The car in front of me is called a club car. I don't know exactly what that means but I climb up the steps and go inside anyway. It reminds me of the school cafeteria, which is really great because I can eat my peanut butter and jelly sandwiches and drink hot cocoa while I read my book. And since no one else seems to prefer the luxury of the club car, I can sit wherever I choose.

No sooner am I settled in than the whistle blows from the engine ahead and the train jolts forward. I have my book out but I want to watch our sleeping town – Christmasville – as we pull away, the brightly illuminated houses, the warm glow of snowfall blanketed across parks and fields or nestled in the evergreen embraces of pines and spruces, cedars and firs. The last thing that I see before the club car slips into the tunnel is my home on the hill … and below, the brilliant flash and spark of electrical arcs, dancing wildly from the transformers of the power station.

It's silly, and childish too, but before I realize it, a tear swells on my lower eyelid, slides down along the bridge of my cheek.

Less than a minute elapses before the lights inside the club car begin to flicker. It's pretty scary, actually, because inside the car, in the tunnel, it gets black as licorice in the few seconds or so that the lights are out. And the train – it seems to sway and rattle so much more so in the darkness.

The lights continue to flicker and now they're out without coming back on. At the same time, there's a sort of whirling sound that starts out in a high pitch but gets lower and lower and I know that something is wrong or broken because as the sound winds down, the train slows until it lurches to a complete stop.

I can't see anything. I hear nothing. My mouth is dry but I don't want to pour the hot cocoa out of my thermos because I might spill it all over. I'm scared but I don't want to act like a baby and start balling my eyes out.

After what seems like forever, I hear sounds coming from the front of the train. At first, I think that somebody is working on the engine, trying to fix it. Then I think that maybe some of the other passengers are moving through the train, from car to car, trying to figure out what's going on. Before I know it, the door at the front of the club car swings open and I see a light – a flashlight – and then I recognize the uniform of the train conductor.

"Don't be alarmed, Mary Jane. This happens all the time," he says, moving toward the area where someone would sell food and drinks to the passengers. "We've lost our power."

I'm not so much alarmed as surprised, mostly because the train conductor knows my name.

"How long does it take for the power to come back on?" I ask.

He's shines his flashlight on an electrical panel on the wall by a refrigerator.

"It could be a couple of minutes," he replies, swinging the gray metal door of the panel open. "But usually it's longer. There," he says, flicking a switch that enables a series of backup lights to dimly illuminate the club car.

"Where is your friend?" he asks, closing the door to the panel and fussing around with a pan by the stove. "Where's Emily?"

"She fell asleep at the station," I reply. "How do you know our names?"

"Because I'm the conductor," he says, laughing. "It's my job to know the names of my passengers. It's Mr. Bachmann's job to make sure that he gives me the passenger list before we leave his station."

He pours water into the pan and sets it upon the stove, lighting the gas pilot with a match. "I'm making us a pot of tea, in case you're curious. It'll keep us warm, especially if the power's out for more than a hour. It can get mighty cold in here when the wind starts to race through the tunnel."

"But … but how do you know that my name's Mary Jane and not Meg or Kate or one of the names of your other passengers on the list?" I ask, insisting upon a better explanation.

"Oh, that's easy to figure out," he says, laughing even louder than before, "because you, Mary Jane, are our only passenger!"

The tea feels warm and relaxing as it runs through my body. It's a mixture of things – chamomile and ginger root, jasmine and hibiscus – things that I never heard of before. It tastes especially good with a little honey stirred in.

"Aren't you having any tea?" I say to the conductor, who has returned to the area by the stove to fiddle around with pipes and valves.

"Shortly," he replies.

It's twelve o'clock. It's twelve o'clock because, between the blasts of wind that rush through the tunnel, I can hear the bells of St. Mary's – the train of its tolls repeated by the mouth of the tunnel and whispered along the rocky curves that wind through the hillside. The bells are a soothing sound that reminds me of home, of mom and dad, of my warm and empty bed tucked away inside my home.

"Do you think you'll be all right if I leave you for a little while, Mary Jane? – I should be making my rounds."

"Your rounds?" I say, lifting my hand up to cover a big yawn.

"Yes," he answers, approaching the booth where I'm sitting, dangling his flashlight as he moves. "I should make sure that the generators in the other cars are in proper working order. Will you be all right if I leave you alone for a bit?"

In the dim light of the club car, I can see now the black nametag that is pinned to the pocket of his uniform.

"Yes … Yes, I'll be fine, Mr. … Mr. Lionel," I reply.

I picture the wheels of a locomotive starting up; the bursts of steam making them turn and grind against the metal track, spinning them faster and faster. But when I open my eyes, I see the twins – Roger and Todd – one of them on either side of me. They're giggling as they jump, up and down, higher and higher, jolting me from left to right as each one lands and then launches himself from the mattress of my bed.

"Get out of my room, brats!" I shout, sitting up.

"Mary Jane's a fruitcake! Mary Jane's a fruitcake!" they sing in unison, jumping from my bed and scrambling from the room before I throw something at them.

Todd peeks into the room after my pillow strikes the door and falls to the floor.

"Daddy says you have to get up, Mary Jane," he says, sticking his tongue out.

Roger leans down and picks up the pillow, bravely running into the room to throw it back at me before quickly retreating.

"Get up, Mary Jane! Daddy wants to tag the Christmas tree before lunchtime."

I jump from my bed but they run away, slamming the door as they leave.

"Mary Jane's a fruitcake! Mary Jane's a fruitcake!" they shout, running down the hallway.

Climbing into my robe and slippers, I look out the window. A fresh blanket of snow has fallen through the night. On the other side of the street I see Mr. Caterson shoveling snow from his driveway. He stops to talk with Wally, the mailman. Next door, in front of the lumberyard where dad works, a bunch of kids are having a snowball fight that moves down the street as one side presses on toward the other. Tommy Burks – the dumb jerk – he gets one right on the kisser.

"Serves him right," I say, laughing to myself.

On top of the hill, beyond the street, the public bus rounds "dead man's curve", passing Link's Pharmacy and the Five & Dime before stopping to pick up a group of passengers.

"How's my princess feeling this morning?" dad says, coming into the room and kissing my cheek. "You certainly had a good night's sleep, Mary Jane."

I didn't realize it, but it's almost eleven o'clock.

"Aren't you working today, dad?" I say, yawning and confused because I had slept so late but was feeling so tired.

"It's Saturday, princess. We're tagging the tree today – remember?"

"Oh, yes ... the tree," I reply, without remembering.

"Why don't you get some breakfast first and then get ready. OK?" he says, starting to leave. "Oh – I nearly forget – Emily's here to see you."

When she comes into my room, she looks pale and tired. Without saying anything, she removes her hat and gloves and shuts the bedroom door behind her.

"What's the matter, Emily? You look like you saw a ghost."

Reaching into the pocket of her coat, she takes out a note that is written on the back of an envelope and hands it to me.

I turn toward the window, suddenly realizing that it's December 1st. I wonder where the gas station is this year.

A Snowman From China

"Nobody ever asks for one," Mr. Carson remarks, looking through all the drawers and the cabinets beneath the counter and the cash register. "But I thought I saw a box of them on the floor somewhere," he says, scratching his head, trying to remember where he had last seen one. "Let me see if there's any in the supply closet. I'll be right back."

Through the picture window, Emily and I watch a yellow snowplow swing around the curve on Mulberry Street, spinning a wave of snow and ice and slinging it against the snow bank on the other side. The metal plow makes a loud, grating sound as it scrapes the surface of the asphalt and moves on.

"What'll we do if he doesn't find one?" Emily says, taking a strand of her hair and twirling it around her finger.

"What'll we do if he does?" I reply.

Outside, in the windless afternoon sky, giant snowflakes fall in a gentle, zigzag pattern.

"Here you are, Mary Jane," says Mr. Carson. "I found the box on a shelf in the closet. I guess one of the boys put it there when he was mopping up."

"Thanks," I reply, taking the map from the tall flagpole of a man behind the counter and tucking it into the pocket of my coat. "Can Emily have one too?"

"Sure", he says, removing another map from the pile that he had put beneath the register and handing it to her. "What do you need the maps for anyways?"

I glance at Emily. That fast, she's engrossed in the picture of St. Nick's on the cover of the map, scrutinizing the bold application of color that highlights the stained glass windows of the church.

"It's a project that we're working on. You know – for school."

"Oh," says the gas station manager. "For geography?"

"No. It's a project for civics class. It's about city planning and zoning – stuff like that."

"It sounds like it might be fun," he remarks, climbing onto his stool behind the counter. "But I thought that you and Emily were in different grades?"

"Yes … Yes, we are," I reply, knowing what direction he's taking. "Emily's only helping me with the project. Aren't you helping me, Emily?" I ask, nudging her so that maybe, just maybe, she'll pitch in and help me to get past this unexpected crossroad with Mr. Carson.

"I'm helping Mary Jane," she says curtly, adding nothing more.

"It's because Emily's father is the mayor," I continue – without assistance. "He's always talking about city planning and city development and zoning things differently so that we don't have some of the … some of the problems that we have in Christmasville."

"Problems? What kind of problems?" Mr. Carson insists, showing an even greater interest than he had initially. "I wasn't aware that Mayor Thompson thought that there were any problems with our zoning ordinances."

Emily flips her map over, reading the advertisements on the back.

"No! – That's … that's not what I meant," I reply, trying to think of a way to get off of this dead-end street that I had steered myself onto.

Luckily, the telephone rings. Mr. Carson snaps it up though I know he's got more questions that he wants to ask us before we leave. I don't know why he's so interested about us having the maps. I mean, I know he can really be nosy but, in the years before, when I came in to ask him for one, he never so much as raised an eyebrow. He just handed it over with a simple, "Here you are, Mary Jane", before going back to doing what he does best – sitting on his stool and reading his newspaper or watching the cars pull in and out of the pumps while his two boys, Billy and Pete, filled tanks with gas, checked oil levels, cleaned dirty windshields.

"Well, thanks for the maps, Mr. Carson," I say, seizing the opportunity to grab Emily by the arm and to vacate the premises of the gas station before he hangs up the phone.

"You could have helped me out, you know," I point out to Emily as I pull my hood up and slip my hands into my gloves.

"Helped you out with what, Mary Jane?" she replies, folding the map and putting it into her pocket.

And it wasn't a fib that I told Mr. Carson either – I really do have a project that I'm working on for civics class. I just haven't figured out how the map fits into it yet.

Trekking through the falling snow, we cross Mulberry Street and climb the snow bank onto the sidewalk. Although it's been shoveled clear, a white veneer – already a half inch deep – blankets the pavement. As we pass in front of Hartmann's Apartment House, we can see that someone is stringing new Christmas lights across the top of the building. We can't see who it is exactly because the tall holly trees in the front yard prevent us from seeing the top of the ladder, where the person is pulling the long string of lights up from the ground.

"Where're we going?" Emily asks, kicking a boulder of snow that the plow has deposited on the sidewalk.

"I thought we'd go to the diner and get a big plate of French fries. I don't know about you, Emily, but I'm starving," I add, feeling my stomach growl though I already ate lunch less than two hours ago. "If we sit in a booth in the back, nobody will bother us while I try and figure everything out. You remembered to bring the paper and pencil, didn't …"

When I turn to the side, it's like I'm talking to my shadow because Emily has stopped dead in her tracks, about five yards behind me.

"What are you doing, Emily?"

"What are you doing, Mary Jane?"

"Don't you want to go to the diner and get some French fries?" I ask.

"Sure," she replies. "But why are we going this way? The diner's the other way – on Jenkins' Hill."

Without saying anything, I start the other way with Emily.

Sometimes it's really confusing, especially before I've had the opportunity to sit down with a map of Christmasville and learn all the changes that have occurred between January

31st and today, the first of December. Emily is a big help though. If I have a question about where the supermarket or the hospital are, the police station or the firehouse, then she tells me exactly where they're situated while I draw boxes on the map and label them. Emily has a real good memory ... I suppose she has a real good memory – that's something that I'll have to think about. Anyway, at least she remembers where everything is. I only remember where everything was.

"Did you bring the paper and pencil, Emily?"

"I remembered them but I didn't bring any money," she replies.

"I've got plenty of money for both of us," I say.

I have exactly *eighty-seven dollars and fifty-three cents.* I know because I counted it out twice this morning before I went out with dad and mom and the two brats to tag our Christmas tree. It should have been only ... fifty- ... fifty-some dollars and cents because ... – Was it *last night* or was it *nearly* a year ago that Emily and I went down to Union Station to buy – to "purchase" – the tickets for the train? And where did *they* go? – The train tickets? Was it Mr. Lionel who had taken them from my backpack as I slept, replacing them with the money? Or was it Mr. Bachmann? And why did Emily still have the ticket envelope that I wrote the note on? How did Emily and I wind up back in our beds, as if nothing had happened at all? I have so many questions – so many questions without answers.

Emily says that she remembers, that she vaguely recalls the journey through the snow, the bitter cold, the night sky spread starry and velvet above us. I'm not sure if she really remembers anything about it but then, out-of-the-blue:

"Can I have one of your mints?" Emily asks as we shuffle through the snow.

"What mints?"

"The ones in your pocket," she says.

I dig my hands into my coat. When I take out the plastic vial that contains grandma's "medicine", I laugh so hard that my eyes start weeping.

"What's so funny?" asks Emily, feeling left out.

"It's funny because ... because ..." I reply, catching my breath. "It's funny because you remembered what was. You remembered what I had forgotten all about."

I guess it's things like this – the mints – that make me feel better. It makes me think that I'm not as nutty as a fruitcake after all. It really did happen – the journey through the snow, the train, Mr. Lionel. But there's something else too. There's a kind of ominous feeling because wouldn't it be better if I was crazy after all, if I only dreamed or imagined that there was more to Christmasville than just Christmasville? Sometimes – a lot of times – I ask myself that.

"Why do they call them *French* fries?" Emily asks.

"I don't know," I answer. "Maybe it's the way that they make them."

She leans down to grab a handful of snow, forming it into a ball.

"Why do they call *French* doors, *French*?"

"I don't know that either, Emily," wondering why Emily always asks 'why'.

She tosses the snowball toward a fire hydrant but misses.

When we get to the end of Mulberry Street, instead of going down Juniper and walking in front of our school, we continue onto Elm Street for a bit so we can cut through the parking lot and the playground between the back of the school and city hall. It's not that it's faster because we'll have to trudge through the snow on the other side of the lot. It's just that … well – I don't want to pass in front of the school because they've already started the snowman contest. There's a bunch of kids, laughing and shouting as they roll balls of snow across the front yard of the school until they're so big that they can't push them any further. That's where they stop, each team shaving the ball with their hands to make it rounder and using the excess snow to anchor the large ball in place. Only then do they start on the next one – the middle ball, the one that will become the snowman's belly.

Huddled together on the steps of the school, drinking coffee or cocoa and probably wishing that they were somewhere else on this cold and snowy Saturday afternoon, are a half dozen teachers and administrators. They're supposed to be supervising the event, insuring that all the rules of the contest are followed to the letter, before they wind through the frozen figures, with clipboards and pencils in hand, judging which snowman – or snowperson, I should say, since there's usually at least one snowwoman – is the very best of the year. But, honestly, if I had to judge how well any of them were supervising, it wouldn't be an easy task because none of them had seen Tommy Burks drop snow down the back of Debbie Lister's parka or Zack Foster when he kicked a big chunk of snow from another team's bottom ball when they weren't looking. Maybe if I judge them in reverse order – picking out which teacher or administrator is the biggest loser – then it would be easier. At the top of the list … well, it would have to be a tie between Mr. Marshfield, our school principal, and Doctor Sperry, the school psychiatrist. Neither one of them could take their eyes off of Miss Perkins, the biology teacher, who, it was said, was the only girl in the history of the "Miss Christmasville Beauty Pageant" to have won two years in a row.

Anyway, maybe it's better that the principal and the psychiatrist are pre-occupied because if either one of them saw me:

'Aren't you and Emily competing this year?' Mr. Marshfield would ask, furling his bushy eyebrows just long enough to make us feel guilty.

'Do you think maybe there's another reason, Mary Jane, why you don't want to build a snowperson?' Doctor Sperry would pose, deliberately trying to confuse me as he holds out a piece of chocolate.

And who knows what nasty things Tommy Burks would say. Moving around the public library toward the corner of East Juniper and Maple, I look back and see him – the dumb jerk – him and Ricky Caterson are rolling the second ball for their snowman. I hope Tommy …

But I don't say it because it's not good to wish for something bad.

When Emily and I get to the metal contraption that is built into the rocky ledges of Jenkins' Hill, we both look up at the winding configuration of stairs and platforms. The thing about hills is this: first, every town should have at least one of them, the steeper and longer the better; and, second, while somebody already invented the best way to get down from a hill – the sled – somebody needs to invent a much better way to get back up again. Maybe Mr. Wright, the owner of the produce stand, could come up with something. He likes tinkering around with inventions. Maybe if somebody dropped him a hint, then he could invent something that was actually good for everybody, something that people would actually find useful and practical.

As Emily and I climb the stairway, we stop at each landing so I can look out over

Christmasville and start getting a rough idea of where everything is situated this year. Re-situated, that is. The school, of course, since we already passed it, was moved from the long stretch of West Juniper Street to East Juniper, at the junction of Mulberry and Elm. On the north side of the school, where Juniper Street turns west and Maple Street begins its sharp, rising arc up Caterson's ... I mean, Jenkins' – Jenkins' Hill – is the public library, which we passed as well. But I don't think that it's the best place for the library to be located. I can imagine myself sitting in one of the reading rooms at the front of the library and trying to read a book, but looking up every time a car or truck comes sliding down Maple Street and skids to a stop. It occurs to me that just one of these times, maybe it won't stop at all, the vehicle sliding on the ice, passing the stop sign and running over the curb and sidewalk toward the library. But then the good thing is – if a driver does lose control and ends up smashing into the front reading room of the library, then he won't have to go very far to find out how to repair his car. Because that's where the "A" section is, where the books that come under "automotive" are.

Behind the school, facing Elm Street is city hall. It's red brick bell tower pokes through all the trees that surround it. That's where Emily's father, the mayor, works. Across the street from city hall is the hospital, which used to be where the public library is now. And now that I think about it, that made a lot more sense having the hospital where it was before because if a vehicle came down Maple Street and did slide out of control, and did crash into a building, wouldn't it be better if it was the emergency room of the hospital?

Behind city hall, next to the library, is the Church of St. Ives. It used to be at the southern tip of town, near the Oak Street Train Station. Of all the churches in Christmasville – there are three of them – St. Ives was always the warmest and coziest, the stained glass angels and saints looking down at you with kind, almost human, eyes.

On the far side of city hall, facing Elm Street but girdled by West Juniper, is the post office. From where I'm standing I can just about make it out. Directly behind it, beside the Church of St. Ives, is The Christmasville Courier building. That's where I want to work – I want to be a reporter for *The Courier* when I ... if ever I ... if ever I grow up, that is.

"Is it a lot different than it was last year, Mary Jane?" asks Emily, stopping on the landing before the last flight of stairs to the top of the hill.

"Everything except the train stations and the power station – they're always in the same place every year. Maybe they can't move them around like everything else. And all the streets are the same, except for Beech Boulevard – it's always in a different place."

Running parallel to the elevated trestles of the freight train is the never-completed, almost-finished highway of Beech Boulevard. It stretches south, by Wakefield Lake, toward the farmlands on the outskirts of town.

"It looks like they're trying to hook up the boulevard with Maple Street this year," I say to Emily, pointing at the tractors and the workmen below as an elevated support is moved into place.

"Then we'll have another hill to sled down," Emily says.

"I wouldn't count on it, Emily," I reply skeptically, knowing that the highway will never be completed.

As Emily and I walk along Maple Street, the "plan" for this year's Christmasville starts sinking in. That's what I call it – the "plan" – because each year that our little town is re-situated, there's always some kind of scheme that makes it all kind of make sense. For example, this year the public service buildings – city hall and the post office, the library and the hospital, the newspaper and our school – are grouped together, more or less, in the center of town. And Maple Street used to be a residential neighborhood. It was where Emily and I lived yester… where we lived last January. But I really like it now because this year, starting with Jack's Toy Store, it makes up the bustling shopping district.

"Look at that!" Emily says, pointing at the huge dollhouse in the first display window of Jack's. "That's what I want for Christmas!"

Even though Emily is thirteen, she still likes to play with her dolls. She must have at least a hundred of them, in all shapes and sizes. I have to pry her nose away from the window because she would stand there like that, scrutinizing every little detail of the house and the furniture and the family of dolls until she had it completely memorized – or her nose froze firmly to the window – whichever came first.

"Come on, Emily," I say tugging on the sleeve of her coat.

"But I want to see it," she says, moving along but not without relinquishing her gaze until the next window comes into view.

Mr. Rausch – that's Jack and he owns the toy store – is stepping from the next window case onto a service ladder. He almost loses his balance and falls back because he has a bunch of empty boxes in his hand. Catching himself at the last minute, he carefully descends the two steps to the floor. He's an older man with glasses that are so thick that it looks like two magnifying glasses are glued into the frames. When he looks up and sees Emily and I outside the window, I clap my hands together as if to signify, "Good job!"

He smiles. It's a beautiful smile that has to work extra hard to materialize because Mr. Rausch has a deceptively stern face with deeply etched wrinkles and wild, woolly eyebrows that otherwise make him look mean if you didn't know him very well.

When he puts the boxes down on the floor, he holds a finger up as if he wants us to wait a minute. He moves off to the side and we're not sure why he wants us to wait but then – he must have thrown a switch because the whole window is suddenly illuminated in Christmas lights. At the same time, a toy train, with Santa Claus as the conductor, begins to race through tunnels and across bridges, circling the snowy village again and again. Smoke streams from the engine. Through the display window, we can hear a whistle that goes off every time the train passes the station. An electric gate rises and falls as the black-and-silver locomotive approaches a street junction. In the four train cars that follow the engine and the coal tender are a dozen foiled-covered, chocolate soldiers that stand guard over what must be a hundred Christmas packages, each of them wrapped in ribbons and bows that are so tiny that you wonder how they can make them so small.

After about a couple dozen laps, my stomach growls so loud that I glance at Emily to see if she hears it.

"Let's get something to eat," I say, pulling her away from the window.

We pass in front of Clauson's Department Store. Emily is pokey again because she wants to see, to inspect, to memorize everything that's in the display windows and I have to move her along again. Where Maple Street turns west – into that treacherous arc of "dead man's curve" – is Cauldwell's Food Market. I can see mom inside, toward the back of the store. She's writing down numbers on a clipboard as Mr. Cauldwell counts canned goods on the shelf in front of him. I don't want to bother her because she's busy with inventory and because ... well, because I'm hungry and if I tell her that we're going to the diner, she'll lecture me on spoiling my dinner.

Next, it's Grubbs' Hardware Store, followed by Link's Pharmacy and Luncheonette. That's where we see Wally, the postman, who gives us both candy canes. Emily puts hers in her pocket but I rip off the plastic wrapper and start eating mine right away. It'll hold me over.

"Mary Jane?" whispers Emily in front of the Five & Dime. "I have to go to the bathroom."

She clenches her teeth and distorts her face into a grotesque expression as if the notion of relieving herself is something that causes her immeasurable agony.

While I wait for Emily, I lean against the bottom ledge of a display window and watch the cars go by. Joe Matthieson speeds by in his Ford pickup. He looks kind of mad and I wonder if he had an argument with his girlfriend, Doris. Mr. Thompson – Emily's father – drives by, beeping his horn and waving. He's always driving around town, stopping here and there to talk with whomever it is that makes up his "constit ...," his "con-stit-u-ency", he calls it. I guess that's what a mayor is supposed to do.

Across the street – beyond the ledge where the hill drops down in a stippled wall of rock and ice – I see the Overland Freight Express as it slowly winds its way along the trestles that elevate the train over the lower part of Christmasville. It looks like it's going to crash right into the side of the hill before it veers off to the west and moves away, announcing its passage with two blasts of its whistle. For a moment, I think about the toy train in Jack's Toy Store, expecting on a silly whim to see Santa Claus as the conductor, leaning out of the locomotive to wave and to shout "Ho! Ho! Ho!" as he ...

"Good afternoon, Mary Jane."

"Oh, hello ... Hello, Mrs. Franklin," I reply to my civics teacher, snapping out of my daydream and spinning my head around.

"How's our project coming along?" she asks, adjusting her two bags of groceries.

"Project? – Oh, yes, I'm doing really well with it," I say, stretching the truth because the only thing that I've done so far is to pick up the map of Christmasville. And of course I haven't figured out yet how that actually fits into it.

"Good," she says, moving along in baby steps, trying not to slip on the snow in her rubber boots.

When I finish my candy cane and lick my fingers clean, I turn around and peek into the Five & Dime, wondering what's taking Emily so long. I guess I should have known better because there she is, looking at colored pencils and fingering through a book of word puzzles.

"Emily?" I say, after going in to get her moving.

But before she will leave, I have to lend her the money to buy the pencils and the book.

Moving along the sidewalk, we pass the police station. Through the front door I can see Sergeant Myers doing the crossword puzzle in The Courier. He's nibbling on the end of his pencil because he's stuck on a word again. He nibbles a lot, rotating pencils every few days or so. Except for the police chief's 50th birthday celebration, which always happens on the 17th of December, it's never very busy at the station. That's probably a good sign because it means that nobody was arrested or brought in for questioning. Although it might be interesting – just once in a while – if somebody … but no, I suppose not.

As we approach the firehouse, I hear Tucker, the Dalmatian, bark twice toward the back of the building. He's probably announcing to the firemen upstairs, who are playing cards or listening to the radio or taking catnaps, that he needs to be let out so he can do his business in the fenced-in yard out back.

Because it's almost three o'clock, a lot of people are going in and out of the bank before it closes. Throughout the month of December, the bank opens up on Saturdays so that everyone can take their money out of their Christmas clubs and spend it shopping. Emily and I have to watch ourselves as we cross the icy lot to the diner next door because cars are constantly moving in and out to park or to enter or exit the long line of vehicles at the drive-up window of the bank.

Inside the diner it's warm and toasty, the heat flowing from the coal stove and down the long aisle of the service counter, filling into the pockets of the booths like maple syrup spreading itself across Belgian waffles.

'*Belgian* waffles?' – I have to think about that. 'What does *Belgian* mean anyway? Is there such a thing as *Belgian* fries? How about *French* waffles?'

Brett Tolliver, who is in my social studies class, and his mother, are sitting in the second booth eating ice cream sundaes. As Emily and I move down the aisle, he turns his head the other way, looking out the window and pretending that he doesn't seen us. Like most boys, he's embarrassed because he's with his mother so we just ignore him and head toward the last booth in the corner. Mrs. Tolliver is so intent in her attack of the ice cream sundae that she doesn't even look up.

Everyone else in the diner is sitting at the counter, joking around with Doris, the waitress, or with Clyde Bonner, the cook, who pokes his head out from the kitchen just long enough to say something to somebody before disappearing again. He reminds me of a turtle sticking its head out of its shell when he does that.

At the last booth, Emily and I slide into the red, vinyl seats and take our gloves off. We hold our hands up around our mouths and breathe into them, to warm them up.

"Would you girls like to see the menu?" asks Doris as she deposits two glasses of ice water on the table in front of us. "Or do you already know what you want to order?" she adds, removing her pad and pencil – presumptuously – from the pocket of her apron.

"I'd like the big plate of French fries, please," I answer. "And hot cocoa."

Emily plops her elbows on the table and cups her chin in the palms of her hands. She bites her lower lip, moves her eyes around at different points on the ceiling indecisively.

Doris taps her order pad with her pencil.

"Emily?" I say.

"I'm thinking about what I want," she replies.

Doris looks back toward the counter where Mr. Wright is pointing at his empty coffee cup.

"Just bring us the menus, please," I say to Doris.

"Emily – you've had at least a half hour to decide what you want to eat."

"I know," she whines. "But I don't want to eat too much because we're having Chicken

Teriyaki for dinner tonight."

The notion strikes me again. 'Chicken *Teriyaki*? – What does that mean? Does *Teriyaki* have something to do with the way it's made? Like *Belgian* waffles and *French* fries? Or is *Teriyaki* the name of the chef who invented the recipe for it? And what kind of name is that? – *Teriyaki*? Maybe it's *Terry Yaki*, but shortened, like they do with "nite" and "lite" in advertisements in the newspapers.'

When Doris brings us the menus, I open mine up though I know that I'm going to order the French fries.

'*Texas* toast?'

'*Philadelphia* cream cheese?'

'*Canadian* bacon? What makes bacon, *Canadian*?'

"Can I have some of your French fries, Mary Jane, if I just get a hot cocoa?" Emily unzippers her coat and wrestles with a sleeve, trying to get her arm free.

"Sure you can," I reply, burying myself in the menu again.

"You're getting the *big* plate of fries, right?" she asks.

"Yes," I say, moving from the breakfast section of the menu to lunch and dinner. '*Russian* dressing? And *French* dressing? – How can you make salad dressing the same way that you make deep-fried potatoes? It doesn't make any sense.'

'*New York* strip steaks?'

'*Italian* and *Swedish* meatballs? What makes them *Italian*? Or *Swedish*?'

'How do you brussel *Brussels* sprouts?'

'And why is it Boston cream pie and not just cream pie with chocolate frosting? And why *frosting*? Or *icing*? Neither one of them are cold when you spread them on top of the cake or pie. They're always at room temperature.'

'*New York* style cheesecake? How do you explain *New York*? And how is there any connection between strip steaks and cheesecakes? – Aside from the fact that you eat them ... and that they rhyme.'

"Are you ignoring me?" Emily asks.

I peek at her over the top of the menu. "No. I was just thinking about things."

"Thinking about what?"

"The map," I reply, reaching into the pocket of my coat and pulling it out. "I was thinking about the map. Do you have the paper and pencil?"

Emily digs her hand into the inside of her coat and removes them from what she calls her 'secret pocket'. "Here," she says, passing them over before wiping the fog off the window to peer outside.

"Are you girls ready yet?" Doris asks, approaching our booth, tapping her pencil against her pad.

"Yes," I reply, reciting the things that we want.

She pushes a curl of hair away from her eye and scribbles the order on her pad.

"Doris?" I say, seeing that she is about to leave. "Why do they call French fries, *French*?"

She thinks a minute, tapping her pencil on her pad. "I think it's the way that they make them, honey – fried in oil."

"Then why do they call French dressing, *French*? – It's not fried."

Doris looks up at the ceiling with a serious, quizzical expression. "You know? – I don't really know," she says. "Maybe it's because oil is used to make both of them. French fries are fried in oil and French dressing is made by mixing up oil with other ingredients. I'll ask Clyde. Maybe he knows," she says, gathering up our menus and moving toward the kitchen.

I move the silverware and the glass of water off to the side and open up the map on the table. With Emily's pencil, I draw boxes along Maple Street and label each one until all the buildings are lined up according to the new "plan" of things. On Pine Street I draw my house and some of the other houses that surround it. Next, it's Emily's house. Although she lives on Juniper Street now, facing The Christmasville Courier building, our backyards are almost next to each other so we're still neighbors and don't have to go very far to get to each other's houses.

As I continue to put boxes and labels on the map, filling it up with the new configuration of Christmasville, I write things down on the piece of paper that Emily brought. These are the things that I have to do before ... before January 31st ... before I decide exactly what it is that I'm going to do if I want to resolve once and for all this whole issue of Christmasville. I put them into a list:

Pick up train schedule.
Are there maps of St. Valentine's and Easterville? Where do I get them?
If you can – find some leaves under the snow to explain "autumn".
Where does Mr. Lionel live?
Besides the train, what other ways ...

When I peek up, I see that Emily is engrossed in a puzzle in her new book. It's a word search and I have to smile because she always sticks her tongue out the side of her mouth when she's concentrating on getting something done. What's funny too is that she picks out a different colored pencil for each word that she circles – like right now, she's using a bright red one to circle the word, "firehouse".

Behind Emily, I see Doris talking with Clyde. Mr. Wright must have overheard what they're talking about because he says something to the two of them, causing Doris to snap her head around and to reply. She looks over toward Emily and I, but I can only lip-read a single word that she says: "*French*". Quickly I look down at the map as if I wasn't paying any attention.

"Emily? Where does Tommy Burks live this year?" I ask, finishing up the central block of Christmasville with city hall and the post office.

"On the corner of Elm and Mulberry, across from the school."

"Zack Foster?"

"On Oak Street near the radio station."

When Doris arrives with our order, I turn the paper over so she can't read anything that I've written down. Doris is a nice person but, like Mr. Carson at the gas station, she can really be nosy.

"Clyde says that the word, '*French*', refers to the way that food is prepared – with oil. And I guess that's right," she explains, "because Clyde took cooking classes."

She puts the cups of cocoa down in front of Emily and I, and then, between us, the sizzling plate of French fries. I want to ask her about *Teriyaki* and *New York* and *Canadian* but I think better of it and say nothing except, "Thanks, Doris".

"What are you doing with the map, Mary Jane?" she asks, turning her head as she tries to read the labels that I had written.

Like I said: Doris can really be nosy.

"It's a project for school," I reply, folding the map and paper up and tucking them away in the pocket of my coat.

"Oh," she says curtly, turning away but almost walking right into Mr. Wright, who has come up behind her.

He's a big, burly man with a plaid shirt and green suspenders.

"Mary Jane?" he says.

Doris rolls her eyes as she steps around him to leave. "Really, Otis, you're not going to fill the girl's heads up with some of your crazy ideas, are you?"

"Crazy ideas?" he says, laughing. "Maybe unusual, and different, but certainly not crazy," he says, lifting his mug of coffee up and drinking. "The problem with you, Doris, is that you haven't any imagination."

Doris shrugs it off and disappears into the kitchen.

"Anyway, Mary Jane, regardless of what Doris – and, Clyde, for that matter – think about the topic of *French*, I don't think it has anything to do with that nonsense about oil or the way that some foods are prepared."

"You don't, Mr. Wright?" I say, sprinkling salt on the fries. "What do you think it means?"

He scratches his ear, shifts his weight from one leg to the other. "Well, between the three of us," he says, acknowledging Emily and lowering his voice, "I think it has something to do with where it's *from*."

I consider telling Mr. Wright about some of my weird dreams, about "autumn" and about what happened with Emily and I at the train station, but I decide otherwise and just listen. I tried to tell other people in the past but all that ever got me was a lot of wasted time with Doctor Sperry. And that's something that I don't want to repeat.

When we leave the diner for home, I have to drag Emily along. Of course, it's the windows again – with Emily stopping every so often along Maple Street to gaze at something that catches her fancy, inspecting things that aren't even specifically for a kid her age, like ironing boards in the Five & Dime and pots and pans in the hardware store. And of course she's sluggish because, even though she had said that she didn't want to spoil her dinner, she had eaten far more French fries than I. At the time, I guess I was more pre-occupied by what Mr. Wright had to say about French than I was with the fries.

He said that the word, "*French*", in his opinion, referred to something that was made in a faraway place – "*Frenchland*" – he suggested, a place far beyond the limits of Christmas-ville. When I asked him about Russian dressing and Canadian bacon and Chicken Teri-yaki, he said the same thing – that maybe they were things that originated in other places.

"Maybe there are places called *Russianville* and *Canadiandale* and *Teriyakitown*," he replied with a dead seriousness.

Except for towns that were listed on the schedule at the train station – "St. Valentine's" and "Easterville" – it was the first and only time that anyone – and I do mean anyone – ever suggested that there were places beyond Christmasville. And that by itself gave me plenty of food for thought.

"How do you want to go down?" Emily asks.

We're at that part of Maple Street that swings down toward Juniper.

"We better take the stairs," I reply, noting all the traffic that's going up and down the hill and the darkness that is slowly covering our town like a woolen blanket.

At the bottom of the stairway, we would have gone down Juniper Street toward Emily's house were it not for the streetlights that shine through the trees on the front yard of our school. In patches of light and shadow, we can see them. Like friendly sentinels, the snowmen are poised in different positions throughout the schoolyard, their individual personalities expressed in a variety of buttons; mixed wardrobes of hats, knitted scarves, mittens that don't match; cashew teeth and carrot noses and gnarled limbs of oak or maple branches that point skyward or downward or, as in the first snowman that Emily and I encounter, arranged in such a way that he looks like he's scratching his butt.

Emily giggles as she marches around the back of the snowman to read the names of his makers on the cardboard placard: " 'Susan Wilson and Linda Cauldwell' – They got an 'Honorable Mention'," she adds.

If you didn't win First or Second or Third Prize, then you could always count on an "Honorable Mention" since, as Mr. Marshfield was accustomed to saying, to repeat again and again: "There's never any losers when everyone competes on the same playing field."

Mr. Marshfield is fond of comparing every activity under the sun to a game of sports.

"This one's the best," Emily says, having scurried over to the next snowman.

Elegantly dressed in top hat and bow tie, wooden cane and monocle, rhinestone buttons that sparkle in the streetlamp and gloves instead of mittens, is a dapper snowman that looks like he's stepping out for a night on the town.

"First Prize!" Emily announces from the back of the snowman. "The Lisa Jenkins Dream Team."

She's like that, of course – Lisa Jenkins – a spoiled brat who always takes credit for something that probably somebody else did all the work for.

Second Prize is a tie between a snowman in the trappings of a hockey player and a snowwoman – a tiny ballerina with a pink tutu. She is no taller than Emily, meticulously carved and, in my estimation, the best of the lot.

"Oh my God!" Emily exclaims.

When I move around to the front of the next snowman, I realize why Emily is so shocked. Somebody had taken its carrot nose and put it where it oughtn't be.

"I bet I know whose snowman this one is," I say, walking around to the back and reading: "Tommy Burks and Zack Foster."

I feel like writing "dis" in front of "Honorable Mention" but instead fix the snowman up by pulling the carrot out and making it his nose again. Being the coward that is, Tommy probably put it there after the contest was over.

By the time Emily and I look at all the snowmen – and snow*women* (there are two of them this year) – it's completely dark. Emily yawns, rubbing her eyes with her mittens.

"Ready to go, Emily?" I ask, turning toward home.

From the corner of my eye, an iridescent glimmer sparkles like magic from the side yard of the school. It's another snowman – but a really big snowman that's perfectly formed.

"Look at that!" I say, pointing it out to Emily.

Slowly, we trudge through the snow toward it.

"It must be ten feet tall," I note as we approach. "Somebody must have used a ladder to make a snowman that big."

"I never saw one that big," says Emily, her widened eyes expressing her astonishment.

When we arrive in front of the huge snowman, we take a moment to sort of digest the height and girth of him, the strange sparkle that emanates from the white veneer of his body. Although he's gaily dressed in top hat and scarf, a tartan necktie and belt, the black buttons that compose his face make him look wistful and melancholic – like he's thinking about something from long ago, something that he's fond of but misses, something that makes him happy but also kind of sad.

"Who made him, Mary Jane?" says Emily, glancing at me as I move around to the back of the snowman to read the cardboard placard.

"Mary Jane? – Who made him?"

But there isn't any sign – there's just an inscription that's carved near the very bottom of the snowman. It's partially covered with snow so I lean down to brush it away and then step back, trying to read what the inscription says.

"It doesn't say who made him," I reply to Emily, a cold shiver running through my bones as I begin to understand – to try to understand – the meaning of the script. "It says: Made in China."

"China?" Emily says with a screwed-up face. "What does that mean?"

"I think it means that he's not from Christmasville," I reply. "I think it means that he's from somewhere else … somewhere beyond."

Warily, Emily steps backward three or four steps until she trips on a fallen branch and plunks down on her backside. Sitting in the snow, the ovals of her eyes approximate the size of her open mouth as she gapes at the enormous snowman in front of her, studying each detail from its base to its head.

"An alien," she says, her voice mixed with equal measures of wonder and trepidation.

Faith

From the window of the classroom, I count six yellow buses as they swing from Elm Street into the parking lot behind the school, lining up near the exit.

Behind me, somebody coughs three times, asks the teacher to be excused to the lavatory. There is the rubbery squeak of footsteps on tile, the creak of the door opening and closing at the back of the classroom.

Outside, the mail van rounds the corner from East Juniper onto Elm and scurries by like a fat squirrel, kicking up chucks of ice and snow in its wake. Wally, the postman, is running behind schedule again. He always runs late in the afternoon because he plays chess with Mr. Mason, the milkman, at the diner. Seated at a booth, his empty soup bowl and half-eaten sandwich pushed off to the side, Wally moves his plastic pieces quickly across the board since it's his lunch break and he has to get back to work. Opposite him, Mr. Mason studies every move, carefully developing his game strategy because, for him, it's nearly the dinner hour – his workday is already over and done with. That's why he usually wins and why Wally is sometimes a bit grumpy in the afternoon.

Behind me, a book falls to the checkered floor – another crack in the porcelain silence that has descended upon the classroom since we started our algebra exercise.

Outside, in a corner of the schoolyard, an old pine tree reels in a sudden gust of wind and then settles down, relaxing its crusted, aged limbs before the next burst arrives. I can almost hear the creaking of its branches as it wrestles with the wind, and I wonder: do trees get arthritis like people do?

At the front of the classroom, Mrs. Kelly begins to explain algebraic equations on the blackboard. She writes them out with a stick of green chalk, speaking as she writes, enunciating each word with the polished precision of someone who has devoted herself to the profession of teaching.

I sit at my desk and look through the window. I can't concentrate on my studies because all the week long was it the invariable distraction of the snowman that was *Made in China*, the strange algebra of his unexpected appearance – the "x" in the equation you could say; and then later, the next day in fact, the unforeseen surprise of his inexplicable *dis*appearance – what you might call the "y" variable. I think to myself: 'x – y = … z? 'Z' as in 'zero'? But if it does equal zero, what does it all mean then? What does any of it mean?

Last Sunday morning, after church, I was determined to find Mr. Marshfield and Doctor Sperry and pull them by the sleeves of their coats to the site of the snowman and say: "Isn't this something? – A snowman that was *Made in China*." I wanted to watch the look on their faces as they tried to explain what they would not be able to explain. "*China?* – I wonder where that is exactly," I would pose, watching the school principal and the psychiatrist stand there – one dumbfounded and the other flabbergasted – squirming like a couple of worms as they looked at each other, groping for an explanation.

But it's a good thing that I learn from my mistakes, taking the extra precaution of going to the schoolyard first because the snowman wasn't there any more. The only sign that remained of his mysterious existence was the round impression, left in the snow by his enormous weight. And that, too, is almost gone now, the saucer-shaped impression of his lower torso nearly completely erased by the wind and the snow.

Somebody must have moved him.

"Mary Jane?"

It's the only explanation. He couldn't have been knocked down by a Tommy Burks or a Zack Foster because, as gruesome as it sounds, there would have been parts of him lying around in the schoolyard. He couldn't have melted away that fast because the other snowmen – and snow*women* – though slightly disfigured by the dip in temperature last Saturday night and Sunday, had stood their ground in front of the school. Oh, a limb or two had fallen to the ground; a carrot nose had leaned lower and lower before tumbling down; a hat had blown away; mittens had slipped from crooked stick-fingers and a number of buttons had become unfastened and lost in the snow. But each of the snow- ... each of the snowpersons had remained reasonably intact, weathering the warmth and the wind in their respective fashion.

Somebody must have moved him.

"Mary Jane?"

After all, it does kind of fit into the "plan" of things – the process of re-situating houses and buildings throughout Christmasville between the last day of January and the first of December. But the thing is, it's ... it's December which means that things can still be shifted around, which means that the snowman might be discovered someplace else – in somebody's backyard or behind a barn or beside the lake, which means that other things ...

'Why are houses moved from one place to another year after year? Why does a snowman suddenly appear only to disappear a short time later? Why is there a "plan" at all?' I ask myself, slipping into that same black-and-white mosaic of questions without answers, events without explanations, the same circular pattern rotating like clockwork through the hours, through all the days and nights ...

Slowly I start to realize that everyone, including Mrs. Kelly, is staring at me. I can feel their eyes combing the back of my head as I focus on their reflection in the window.

"Welcome back to seventh period algebra, Mary Jane," says Mrs. Kelly after I snap my head around.

I feel my face turning holly berry red as the class erupts in an uproar of laughter and jeers.

"That'll be enough now, class," Mrs. Kelly admonishes, tapping her plastic pointer against the blackboard. "Mary Jane," she goes on, "we were discussing the equation, $a^2 + b^3 = c$, whereas ..."

But the bell rings, announcing the end of class. Everyone around me gathers up their books and notepads and scrambles toward the back of the classroom to grab their coats and school bags from their lockers.

It's the crack of the pointer again against the blackboard. "Your assignment for the weekend," says Mrs. Kelly in a loud voice, "can be found on page one hundred and twelve of your algebra text – exercise number nineteen. Did everyone get that?"

But only about half of everyone reply: "Yes, Mrs. Kelly," the remaining half scooting toward the doorway.

After I go to my locker and get my stuff, I decide to walk home because I don't feel like taking the school bus. I guess I'm in one of my "moods" again, as mom sometimes says, referring to those occasions when I like to be by myself, trying to figure things out.

On the front steps of the school, I zipper my coat and pull my hood up. I put on my gloves and pick up my school bag, slinging it over my shoulders. And then I just stand there, watching the handiwork of the wind as it sweeps down East Juniper, reeling the limbs of trees, swinging the electric wires like wild jump ropes, animating the wooden arms of the snowpersons as if they were alive.

Instead of heading towards home, I walk the other way, towards the intersection of Juniper, Elm and Mulberry. In the distance I hear the trucks and tractors, the cranes and steamrollers on Beech Boulevard as they move plastic girders and trestles into place, building the bridge that will never be finished, that will never span the frozen marshes near Wakefield Lake, that nobody will ever be able to use.

'So why do they do it then?' I ask, hopscotching to another question without an answer.

At the corner, I choose Mulberry instead of Elm, passing the houses of Tommy Burks and Doris Hunter and Brett Tolliver. At the curve, Billy Carson waves from the gas station across the street before yanking the gas nozzle from the pump and jamming it into Mr. Caterson's bright blue Pontiac. I wave back and continue on, moving past Hartmann's Apartment House.

It's three o'clock. On the corner ahead, the bells of St. Nick's peal three times, announcing to everyone in hearing distance that it's three o'clock on a dreary Friday afternoon. The wind whips around the bell tower, the whoooosh of it racing to catch the tolls of the bells.

I should be happy instead of glum. I should be skating on the lake or sledding in the snow with Emily instead of walking to nowhere in particular. I mean, after all, it is Friday – the end of the school week and the beginning of the weekend. This morning, in home economics, I finished the woolen hat and scarf for mom and tonight is the Christmas pageant at school, which is something that I always look forward to because Roger and Todd – twin devils garbed in angel's costumes – will make utter fools of themselves again. On stage, in front of everyone, they'll get nervous and stammer and turn bright red because it's not that they forgot their lines so much as the fact that they never learned them right in the first place. It's the same way every year. They'll stand there, looking at each other, watching each other's face turn into a sort of ugly, twisted mask before they both burst into a big tears-and-crybaby scene that doesn't end until one of the teachers rushes out on stage, tries to console them but, failing, leads them by the wire supports of their false halos out of view. The whole thing is so ridiculously funny that I won't be able to contain myself any longer, letting out a big, belly laugh that shreds the curtain of silence that has fallen over the audience since the crying episode began. Mom will scowl at me with bulging eyes, squeezing my wrist until I stop. When we get home, she'll send me to my room with a – "No ice cream sundae for you, young lady!" – the special treat intended to celebrate the twin's performance but which really commemorates their stellar, unforgettable moment of embarrassment. I guess I should feel guilty and I do, but not all that much because they deserve what they get – the little brats.

At the end of Mulberry Street, it's the dilemma of which way to go. I can either turn right on West Juniper and head towards home, stopping at the Christmasville Inn to get a free cup of hot apple cider to warm myself up. Or I could go left, past the radio station, and either continue along West Juniper, or veer down Oak Street toward MacGregor's Tree Farm, the Consolidated Factory Works and the Oak Street Train Station. I suppose as well that I could just go straight, through the spruce grove on the other side of Juniper and under the trestles of the Overland Freight Express until I reached the elevated coaling station that straddles the railroad tracks of the passenger train. And then what?

'It's forbidden to cross the train tracks,' I remind myself.

For as long as I can remember, parents and teachers drummed the stern warning into the heads of every kid in Christmasville.

'No one is permitted to cross the train tracks.'

They said it because of the passenger train, of course, which charged along the steel rails at breakneck speeds. But it was because of the cliffs as well – towering, mountainous cliffs that pretty much encircled all of Christmasville. That's what everyone said. And in certain parts of town – on Jenkins' Hill, for example, behind the buildings on Maple Street – you could look beyond the plastic fencing and see the massive walls of rock and ice, rising into the sky like ink-stained sheets suspended on a giant clothesline. Or, from the platform of Union Station, you could look across the train tracks and see the very edge of the cliffs as they plunged toward the bottom of the abyss far below.

Everyone said ... No – everyone knew – that the only way out of Christmasville was by passenger train. Nobody really said it because, as far back as I can remember, nobody ever expressed any interest, any desire, any reason whatsoever for leaving Christmasville. And why would they want to leave? – They don't know what I know. And as for the passenger train – well, I already tried that once but I didn't get very far, did I? I suppose I could try it again, sneaking on board like a stowaway when no one was looking. I could hide beneath one of the tables in the club car or climb into a food cabinet in the kitchen area. Maybe things would be different somehow if Mr. Lionel and Mr. Bachmann didn't know that I was on board. Or, another possibility – after the train had departed from Union Station, I could follow the train tracks through the tunnel on foot, using dad's flashlight to guide me. It would be dangerous, of course, in the dark, in the cold, maybe getting lost or tripping on the tracks – you always have to take risks when the stakes are high. Of course, that all sounds good and well when you read it in a book but the fact of the matter is ... well, it would really be dangerous. And hitching a ride on the freight train doesn't sound too safe either. It never stops and I don't know how I would climb the huge plastic trestles that support it even if it did.

'So,' I say to myself, my teeth chattering as I stand on the street corner and watch the cars go by, 'what are your options, Mary Jane?'

Maybe if I explored every square inch along the town limits, I could find a tiny breach in the mountains and squeeze myself through. Maybe if I found a part of the cliffs that weren't so steep. I could take my sled along and ... – I must remember to write "camping equipment" and "canteen" and "compass" on my Christmas list. What if I found a country road that somebody forgot to put on the map and ...

A blast of frigid wind dashes from the spruce grove and smacks against me. It makes my face turn numb and tingly.

Through the stained glass windows of St. Nick's, I see a tall shadow, moving from the back of the church toward the front. It must be Father Conover because it's coming up to three-thirty on a Friday afternoon, the time that confessions start.

Maybe if I ...

Forgive me, Father, for I have sinned ... etcetera, etcetera ... Do you know about questions without answers, Father? Do you know about a snowman that was made in China? Do you know of any roads that maybe somebody forgot to put on the map, Father? Do you know about games of checkers or about algebra problems that can't be solved?

I never liked checkers and algebra – algebra stinks!

Shivering, I go up the winding walkway and climb the steps. Inside the church, it's warm and cozy and smells like Christmas because of the fresh evergreen wreaths that hang between each of the stained glass windows, and the tall fir tree, standing to the left of the altar. Seated in its plastic stand and secured by guy lines, the tree looks stately and majestic. They must have just brought it in because it isn't decorated yet. I notice too that nobody's tied the red ribbon bows on the wreaths between the windows. And no sooner have I said that than Mrs. White, the church secretary, followed by Mr. Gabriel, the custodian, exits the sacristy from the left of the altar. She's more than six feet tall and carries a white bow with gold trim that she tacks to the front of the pulpit where Father Conover gives his sermons. Mr. Gabriel is short and carries in his outstretched arms three large boxes that rise well above his head. The box on top doesn't have a lid. Plastic garland and strings of lights dangle down the side of the box, swinging back and forth as the custodian moves forward. At the very top is a fake white dove that sways slightly in the motion, as if it were making a nest of the decorations. It's an ornament for the tree that I remember from last year.

A really weird thought occurs to me: if they named trees after the people who decorated them, then the fir tree would be called "Lucy-Fir" because that's Mrs. White's first name.

I don't know where that came from, I think to myself as I sit at the end of the second pew, near the stained glass window of St. Jude, the patron saint of impossible tasks. 'Sorry,' I say mentally, motivated by sudden guilt, realizing that I really shouldn't be thinking things like that, especially when I'm inside *His* House.

In the pew in front of me, eight people wait their turn for confession. On my left, starting with old Mrs. Phelps, are six more, so, if I really want to talk to Father Conover, it looks like I'm going to be camped out for a while. Some of them are sitting while others are kneeling. I know that I shouldn't but ... I start to wonder, like I always do, just exactly what kinds of sins did each of them commit? What grave transgression did our next-door neighbor, Mrs. Morrison, perpetrate? – Kneeling directly in front of me, she shifts the weight of her ample body from one knee to the other, her face buried in her hands in prayer.

'Gluttony,' for one,' I decide, after remembering seeing her in Aunt Sarah's Confectionery Shop, "sampling" what must have been a half pound of chocolates, courtesy of Aunt Sarah, before deciding which quarter pound to buy.

'And for Mr. Grubbs,' who is next in line, 'it would be *greed*,' I imagine, because he charges too much for the stuff that he sells in his hardware store. That's what dad says anyway.

'Mr. Evans? – I think it's called *sloth*,' which is just a fancy word for laziness because he never really kneels in church. Oh, sure, he assumes a kneeling position when everybody else does, but he cheats by resting most of his butt on the pew behind him. 'And stinginess, too,' I add, having watched him once as he dropped nickels and pennies in the collection basket while everyone else put dollar bills in.

For Mr. & Mrs. Rausch, the owners of Jack's Toy Store, it's difficult to imagine any kind of sin. They've always been kind and generous, wrapping gifts from their toy store and donating them every Christmas to families who are less fortunate. Once, I remember listening to dad and mom in the kitchen and they were talking about how the Rausch's had supported the Robinson family for a whole month because Mr. Robinson had lost his job at the Consolidated Factory Works. That's where they make all the plastic for Christmasville. It was only temporary because Mr. Robinson got his job back. But it sure must have cost a lot of money because there's nine kids in the Robinson Family. Anyway, I think that Mr. and Mrs. Rausch are going to confession only because they did something by accident – a technicality – like doing something that seemed normal at the time, but then discovering afterwards that it was a sin.

'Mrs. Clark? – *Compulsive gossiping*.' She should really be seeing Doctor Sperry instead of Father Conover because I don't think it's so much a spiritual problem as it is a psychological one. Even now, every few minutes or so, Mrs. Clark leans toward Mrs. Watts and whispers something into her ear. And you just know that it's some juicy bit of gossip because of the way Mrs. Watts suddenly widens her eyes and drops her mouth open, as if she's mortified by what she's just heard – but can't wait to hear more. And now that I think about it, maybe Mrs. Watts is far guiltier than Mrs. Clark because she encourages her. I mean, if nobody listened to Mrs. Clark, then she wouldn't be gossiping, would she.

And another thing: maybe Doctor Sperry should operate like Father Conover does. If he set up his office like a confessional so that he wasn't able to tell who was pouring his heart and soul out on the other side of the screen, then maybe he would get more customers.

Mrs. Jenkins is seated at the far end of the first pew, dressed in her fake fur coat that she likes to show off to everybody. Being the mother of Lisa Jenkins, who, as everyone knows, is the biggest spoiled brat in Christmasville, she would be guilty of ... intemperance, which, I'm sure is very bad, though I really don't know what it means. She's a snob as well, and self-indulgent, but her most serious sin would be pride – the deadliest of the seven deadly sins.

'*Repent! Oh ye wicked sinners! For the Lord God sees all your ... your wicked perp ... perpetuations and your evil abdominal ... your evil abominations. Repent! I say unto you!*'

Someday, maybe I'll try out for a part in the school play. Not a big part but one that's important and forceful and powerful like an archangel who delivers to the masses the stern warnings of the Almighty.

'*Repent! Oh ye wicked sinners!*'

But unlike the twins, I would memorize my lines before I got on stage.

From the doorway of the sacristy, I see the beginning of a long stepladder. Carefully, Mr. Gabriel, who is midway down the ladder and holding it in the center, squeezes himself through the doorway without banging things around with the end of the ladder that is still inside the sacristy. You would think that Mrs. White would help him but, no, she's busy tearing through things in the boxes, sorting them into piles. Setting the ladder up near the tree, Mr. Gabriel pulls the hinged supports down, locking them into place before he disappears in the sacristy again.

Poor Mr. Gabriel – sometimes he has such sad eyes. Who wouldn't? – After what he's been through, losing his wife and daughter in the blizzard like that. They were in the deep woods, beyond the trailer park where they lived on the edge of Wakefield Lake. It was about a week before Christmas and they were looking for a tree to cut down because they couldn't afford to buy one. Mr. Gabriel didn't own a truck then, like he does now, and his only job was shoveling snow for some of the stores and businesses throughout Christmasville. Anyway, they were in the deep woods and it had begun to snow, lightly at first, as Mr. Gabriel went one way, looking for the right tree, and Mrs. Gabriel, and their daughter, Caroline, went another. I'm sure that they didn't think anything about it because, I mean, it snows all the time so how were they to know that suddenly, before they had time to turn back, it would surge up into a fierce, blinding white-out. How would anyone know? When Mr. Gabriel realized what was happening, he began to look for Mrs. Gabriel and Caroline. But, in the wind and the heavy snow, he couldn't see anything. When he shouted out for them, it didn't make any difference – he knew that it didn't make any difference – not only because of the howl of the wind, but because Mrs. Gabriel and Caroline were both deaf and couldn't hear anything. Two days later, they found Mr. Gabriel near the frozen edge of the lake. Dazed and muttering incoherently, he was pushing his way through the two and a half foot snows that had fallen. They never found Mrs. Gabriel and Caroline. But for every waking hour since then, aside from working and eating, that's where you'll find Mr. Gabriel – making his way through the deep woods, scouring the rocky ledges of ridges and hillsides and, every now and then, calling out their names as if by some minor miracle they might hear him.

'Poor Mr. Gabriel – life isn't fair sometimes,' I think to myself as I lower my head and say a prayer.

When Mrs. Morrison comes out of the right-hand confessional – there are two of them, of course, a right one and a left one, which enables Father Conover to maximize his time by spinning back and forth in his swivel chair, sliding the panel shut on the screened window on the one side – the side of the person whose confession he's just heard and is leaving – and sliding the panel open on the side of the person who has been waiting to give his confession ... Sometimes when I'm inside the confessional, waiting for the person on the other side of Father Conover to finish, and I know that I'm supposed to be patient and humble and putting together the list of sins that I want to confess, I listen to the mumblings on the other side, trying to hear what sins the other person in the opposite confessional is confessing. I know that's probably a sin by itself but ... but I do it anyway. I mean, there's nothing else to do, kneeling in the dark and waiting, after your list of sins is done.

But anyway, when Mrs. Morrison comes out of the right-hand confessional, Mr. Evans gets up from the pew and goes inside to wait for Father Conover to finish up with Mr. Grubbs. And then it will be the Rausch's turn. As each person in the front pew gets up and goes into the confessional, everyone else slides down the pew toward the number one spot at the far right. At the same time, everyone in my pew slides to the left as the person at the end stands up and moves to the first pew, filling in the empty spot.

In the meantime, Mr. Wright – not Otis, but his brother, Willy – comes into church and sits beside me in the pew.

From the sacristy, Mr. Gabriel carries more boxes that he lays across the floor for Mrs. White to rip through. Helping him is Brett Tolliver, who serves as an altar boy on Sundays. He's a nice boy – shy and quiet – but every time that I see him on the altar, I want to break out in laughter because I always picture in my mind the first time that he served Mass with Father Conover. He was nervous and clumsy and when he picked up the Bible to move it to the other side of the altar, like you're supposed to do before Holy Communion, he tripped on the hem of his cassock. It wasn't his fault because the cassock was much too long for him. But anyway, the Bible and the stand that it rests on went one way, and Brett Tolliver went the other, which happened to be where the second altar boy was. He was holding the special bells that are rung during the more solemn moments of Mass. Between the Bible and its stand crashing on the carpet, the two boys tumbling to the floor, and the bells, tossed high up into the air, only to land smack on the back of Brett's head ... well, yes, it was sort of tragic because it was Brett's first Mass, and you felt genuine sympathy for him because it was all so embarrassing, especially when they lifted him up and sat him in a chair at the center of the altar where he had fallen. Dozens of people had gathered around him, gawking at him and saying things like, *'Are you OK, Brett?' 'Somebody get a damp washcloth for Brett!' 'Would you like a glass of water, Brett?'* It was all so terribly embarrassing. But it sure was funny.

As Mrs. Clark leaves the confessional, Mrs. Jenkins gets up from the pew and goes inside to wait for Father Conover to finish up with Mrs. Watts, whose giving her confession from the other side. I haven't any doubt that Mrs. Jenkins presses her ear firmly against the closed screen, listening intently as she tries to make out what the other woman is confessing.

When Mrs. Watts exits, she goes toward the padded step by the altar rail. Kneeling, she bows her head and closes her eyes as she says her penance. She must have had quite a lot to confess to the good Father because she stays there for a long time.

Having slid all the way down the second pew toward the center aisle, I gather up my hat and scarf, my backpack and gloves and, genuflecting, move to the first pew. Old Mrs. Phelps smiles as I sit down next to her again. She's always kind and sweet and it's difficult for me to imagine what kind of sins that she's committed. Even if I didn't see her face, I would recognize Mrs. Phelps by her perfume, which is thick and musty and fills the air with the smell of overripe fruit. It makes me want to sneeze.

On the other side of Mrs. Phelps are Mrs. Marshfield and Mrs. Sperry, the wives of the stuffy school principal and the silly school psychiatrist. They're going to confession to ask forgiveness (again!) for harboring what amounts to ... *envy* – an uncontrollable jealousy that expresses itself in the fabrication of stories, rumors, false accusations. It's all about Miss Perkins, of course, the biology teacher, whose "sinful ways" are nothing more than being unmarried, pretty and the constant apple of their husband's eyes.

At the beginning of the pew are Mrs. Mason, the milkman's wife, and her daughter, Rebecca. Mr. Mason is in the confessional, having replaced Mrs. Watts. Rebecca is only eight years old and the most beautiful child that I have ever seen. She looks like a porcelain doll-cherub that you might see in Jack's Toy Store. She's quiet and respectful and so perfect in every way that I can't imagine ... I don't know – maybe her idea of committing a sin is getting her hands dirty or crying over spilt milk.

Mrs. Jenkins finally opens the door to the confessional and steps out. She looks so pretentiously pious and wholesomely holy that you would think that Father Conover ordained her a saint.

' "*To commemorate your sainthood*," says Father to Mrs. Jenkins, "*we'll order the stained glass immediately.*" '

'Or maybe the glass should be unstained – you know, because she's so pure and all.'

But anyway, she doesn't kneel on the padded step by the altar like everyone else does. No, the Saint Mrs. Jenkins goes to the center aisle and kneels on the floor, stretching her arms out as if she were offering up her whole being while she says what is the shortest penance. But it can't be penance, can it? – I mean, after all, Mrs. Jenkins is as pure as a saint.

As I look around the church, sliding down the pew periodically, I can tell by the stained glass windows that it's getting dark outside. It's funny how the saints and the angels become gloomy and stern when it's darkness that spills through the glass rather than the bright sunshine of a Sunday morning. St. Jude appears mean and angry now, as if he would lean down from the window frame and bite my head off if I did something wrong. In the window next to him, St. Bernard looks like a mad dog. And on the other side of the church, the expression on St. Veronica's face – it's like she's got an upset stomach and is about to upchuck whatever it was that she had for lunch. She could really use a Pepto-Bismol because if she does puke all over the place, I don't think it would smell so heavenly.

At the top of the ladder, Mr. Gabriel begins the task of stringing the lights around the Christmas tree. Brett helps by holding the strand of lights out and feeding them to Mr. Gabriel. They're white lights and they're plugged in so Mrs. White can tell the custodian to move a strand from this branch to that, or to push the wire further back into the tree. Sometimes he peers down from his position on the ladder, waiting for Mrs. White to give her stamp of approval, before he clambers down to rotate the ladder to the next spot.

In my opinion, Mr. Gabriel is the one who Father Conover should order the stained glass for. He has such sad eyes.

When Mrs. Sperry exits the left-hand confessional, old Mrs. Phelps gets up from the pew. She smiles again and then moves forward, using her plastic cane to help her along. I slide down into the number one position. Mrs. Sperry doesn't go to the altar rail to say her penance but, instead, joins Mrs. Marshfield at the statue of the Virgin Mary. Like her "partner in crime", she drops coins into the metal box and lights a candle in a tall, red glass before kneeling. I bet Father Conover really laid the penance prayers on the two of them.

Outside, I hear the wind as it rushes through trees and slams into the church. It makes the window frames creak, the saints to shudder, draughts of cold air to run through the aisles and between the pews like pagan faeries.

And now it's my turn: I go into the confessional and kneel on the velvet-padded ... the kneeler, I guess you call it. I'm sure it has a special name – just like the bells that fell on Brett's head – but I don't know what it's called. And you haven't any choice either – you have to kneel because there isn't any place to sit. I hear Father Conover and old Mrs. Phelps mumbling on the other side of the screen. I don't want to listen because ... well, because I really like old Mrs. Phelps and I don't want to know what's she's confessing. So I wait in the dark, thinking about how I'm going to bring up the topic of checkers and algebra because I already have my list of sins ready – and they're real sins – not like the ones that I used to make up when mom made me go to confession and I couldn't think of any to report.

' "Well, well, Mary Jane, I had no idea that I raised such a perfect little daughter," mom would say sarcastically. "I wonder what your father will say when he finds out that our Mary Jane is as free from sin as the other Mary is – you know, Mary, the Mother of God." '

So I made them up. Sins like "parsimony" and "lassitude" and "bigamy" – words that I heard from other people but didn't have the slightest notion as to what they meant.

The screen on the other side slides closed. I hear old Mrs. Phelps as she struggles to get up, the taps of her cane before she plants it on the floor and rises. The screen in front of me slides open and I can see the silhouette of Father Conover through the meshing.

'How come you get a chair and old Mrs. Phelps doesn't,' I feel like asking, but say instead:

"Forgive me, Father, for I have sinned. It's been three weeks since my last confession."

As usual, I disguise my voice so that Father Conover doesn't know who I am.

"Good evening, child. What sins do you have to confess?"

' "Child?" – I should have made my voice deeper,' I think, though realizing that it's too late now.

"Let me see, um, I guess I've been a little bit disrespectful to certain school administrators – the Principal, Mr. Marshfield, and Doctor Sperry, the school psychiatrist."

"And how have you been disrespectful, my child?"

"By not showing them any proper respect because ... because I don't have any respect for them because I think that they're narrow-minded and self-righteous and stupid."

"I see," Father Conover replies. "But everyone, regardless of our opinion concerning their aptitude and capabilities, is entitled to our respect. Wouldn't you agree?"

"Yes, Father," I answer, agreeing with him in principle though knowing in advance that I'll be as guilty as sin once I see them again (I almost let out a little chuckle because I suddenly realize the pun that I had made with 'principal' and 'principle').

"What other sins would you like to confess?"

"Once in a while I use bad words – curse words, I guess, when I get mad at something."

"And do you take the name of the Lord in vain when you become angry?"

"No, Father, I never do that. It's other words – words like ..."

But I don't say them because I don't think it's right to repeat those words in church.

"It's good that you don't take the name of the Lord in vain, my child. But you should try and refrain from the use of curse words. They belittle you in the eyes of others. They invite their disrespect. Don't you think?"

"Yes, Father."

"Is there anything else?"

"Sometimes ... sometimes I tell fibs. Most of the time they're tiny, snowy white fibs that don't harm anybody. In fact, almost all the time, they protect people from telling them the truth. Like when somebody asks: 'Isn't my dress pretty?' – And you say, 'yes', even though the dress is about as pretty as dog ... as dog excrement."

Father Conover coughs once, clearing his throat.

"Are there times when you fib and they're not so snowy white? Are their times when you cross over that line and a fib becomes a lie?"

I was afraid he was going to ask me that.

"I suppose that once or twice you could say ... well, that they weren't so snowy white, that they became sort of dark gray fibs. I guess it's a matter of interpretation, Father."

"Then perhaps you'll allow me to interpret," Father Conover says. "What were the circumstances that caused them to become 'dark gray fibs', as you put it?"

"Well," I reply, resigning myself to the fact that I would have to tell him. "Tommy Burks accused me of putting rotten eggs in his locker and I told him he was as nutty as a fruitcake."

"You put the rotten eggs in Tommy's locker – but then denied it when he confronted you?"

"Yes, Father."

"I would say that's a fairly substantial fib. Wouldn't you?"

"Yes, Father."

I hear the person in the other confessional sneeze and then blow his nose. It's Willy Wright, waiting his turn. I wonder if he can hear any of this.

"And were there other occasions in which you didn't tell the truth, my child?"

I thought that maybe he was going to move on so I could get started with the other topic.

"I took two packs of bubble gum and chewed them up into a big glob. Then I dumped the gum into a napkin and smeared the gooey glob in the pockets of Tommy Burks' new ski jacket while he was playing basketball in the school gym."

"And you denied it when Tommy accused you?"

"Yes, Father."

"This isn't good, my child. Not only did you not tell the truth – you lied, in fact, re-gardless of what shade you might choose to make it – but you also damaged someone else's personal property."

"Yes, Father," I say, feeling guilty about it now.

"What seems to be the problem between you and this boy, Tommy Burks?"

I explain to Father Conover what Tommy Burks did with the spray paint. I thought that maybe he would be a little sympathetic to my cause if I provided him with the extenu-ating circumstances that led up to my ... my transgressions. Maybe he would go easy on the number of prayers that I would have to say for my penance.

"Now please correct me if I'm wrong, but it's my understanding that not only did you lie, and not only did you engage in an activity that damaged someone else's personal property, but you also perpetrated the above as an act of revenge? Am I understanding this correctly?"

'Sometimes you really put your big, fat foot in your big, fat mouth, Mary Jane!'

As Father Conover delivers his lecture on my evil-doings, I decide to take the remain-der of sins on my list and save them for the next time around. Enough is enough.

"Now," Father continues, "do you have any other sins that you want to confess?"

"No, Father," I reply, and not fibbing because I don't want to confess any more.

"As I beseech our Lord, Jesus Christ, for the forgiveness of your sins, please say a perfect Act of Contrition, my child."

"Father?"

"Yes?"

"Father, before I do that, can I ask your advice about something?"

"But of course you can. What can I help you with?"

This is the hard part – trying to find the right place to begin without sounding like a lunatic.

'I don't remember exactly when I started remembering, Father. Or when it was that everyone else forgot.'

I can't say that. It has to be something more general, especially since I suddenly realize that, somewhere along the way, my voice had slipped out of its disguise. I was speaking like I normally do, which means that there's probably a good chance – a better than fifty-fifty chance – that Father Conover knows who I am. And even though priests are forbidden to reveal what somebody confesses – they could get in serious trouble with the Big Guy for that – who knows? Father Conover could drop an innocent hint to a certain school principal or psychiatrist, a perfectly innocent hint that's well-meaning because it would end up by leading the little lost lamb back to its flock – the Good Shepherd thing.

"Father?"

"Yes, my child?"

"Father, were you ever in a situation ... a situation where you believed – where you knew – that something was true but everyone else thought that it wasn't?"

"Not that I recall," he replies, after pausing a moment to consider.

"Did you ever think that there was more to it than what you could see and hear and smell? Something beyond the boundaries, the day-to-day routines, of Christmasville?"

"But of course there's 'more to it' than what we perceive, child. There's a whole other universe out there, waiting to receive us."

'Really?' I think with encouragement.

"Places like Easterville and St. Valentine's?" I ask, blurting it out. "Do you know where China is, Father?"

"China?" he says, pondering. "No, I've never heard of China before. But then that's not what I meant, either. When I speak about the 'other universe', I am referring to the Kingdom of God where one day the Heavenly Host will receive us with open arms, rewarding the faithful for their good deeds."

"Oh," I reply with disappointment.

I shift my weight from one knee to the other.

"But could you tell me a little bit more about this place called 'China'?" asks Father Conover. "Is it a town or village? How did you hear about it?"

It sounds like he's preparing his case for Doctor Sperry.

"I don't know anything about it, Father. That's why I was asking. I saw it written down on a scrap of paper that a schoolmate had. I thought it sounded like the name of a place but ... but I guess it was just doodling – you know, like kids sometimes do when they're bored."

It was a fib – a *lie*, but I didn't have any choice, did I? I couldn't tell Father Conover the truth about the snowman. No, I couldn't do that, I think to myself, tossing the fib – the lie – onto the pile of sins, but *tiny* pile, that I would have to confess the next time around.

"You know, it just occurred to me," Father says thoughtfully. "What you were saying before – about believing that something was true when everyone else thought it false?"

"What about it, Father?"

"Well," he begins, "I'm thinking now of someone who was in the same predicament, someone who believed that something was true and, in spite of public ridicule and persecution, persisted in his attempts to convince everyone else of what indeed was the truth. I think you might know whom that is."

I try to think of the answer but my knees are really starting to ache.

"Who, Father?"

"His name is Jesus," Father Conover says. "And what Jesus teaches us is that we always have to be true to ourselves. We have to do – we have to act – in a way that always reflects what our hearts believe to be true."

A long burst of wind crashes into the side of the church, making the plastic supports creak and groan in the onslaught.

"Of the many gifts that Jesus gave us – that He continues to give us – there's a very special gift that helps us to find light in the midst of our darkness, to find peace and solace in the storm of our confusion. He gives us – again and again does He give us – the gift of faith."

Usually, when I come out of the confessional and go to the altar rail to say my penance, I have my head bowed, staring at the floor. It's not that I think that I'm holy or anything like that. It's because I don't want to look at anyone. I don't want to look at them because they're probably thinking that I'm really, really bad because I spent so much time in the confessional, making them wait. But this time, I glance at each of them as I pass in front of the pew, quickly looking into their eyes, almost daring them ... to judge.

Surprisingly, I only have to say three prayers for penance – and short ones, at that. When I'm finished, I stay at the altar for a minute, thinking about what Father Conover said, looking at the pictures of angels that hang from the walls around the front of the church. I hear the wind again, especially when it slams against the side of the church and presses against the stained-glass saints, making them moan.

I don't see anyone on the altar. I guess they're finished decorating for the day because the Christmas tree lights are turned off and the door to the sacristy is closed shut.

'Poor Mr. Gabriel,' I think, saying another little prayer before I get up to leave.

Genuflecting, I walk down the center aisle to the back of the church. It's completely dark outside and it occurs to me that mom and dad are probably wondering where I might be. When I go to push the heavy door open so I can leave, the wind wins. It slams the door shut before I can scoot outside, the snow swirling through the brief opening and dancing across the floor toward the altar.

"Geez," I say aloud, pushing the door harder the second time, slipping outside before the wind calls for reinforcements.

It's a blizzard and now I know that mom and dad are really worrying.

I make my way down the steps, trying to find the sidewalk that takes me to the corner, where I'll turn north on West Juniper and head for home. But I can hardly see in the blinding snow, the wind driving it like pellets that sting when they strike the parts of my face that aren't covered over by my scarf. With my eyes shielded by my hands and my body turned away from the wind, I trudge through the snow along what I believe is the sidewalk. Behind me I hear the sound of a horn. Stopping – and turning just far enough into the wind to see where the sound's coming from – I make out the headlights of a pickup truck. All I can see inside is a hand, waving me toward the truck.

It takes me a moment to make my way to the door, swinging it open once my hand finds the handle.

"Jump in, Mary Jane. I'll drive you home."

Climbing inside, I slam the door shut and brush the snow away from my face. Unwrapping my scarf, I pull the string of my hood so I can swing it back over my shoulders.

I should have known.

"Thank you so much, Mr. Gabriel."

It's funny because ... well, because I know what's he thinking. And I think he knows what I'm thinking but neither of us say anything because ... because we both know.

When he drives his truck up to the stop sign, he turns right onto West Juniper. He spins the knob of his windshield wipers to make them go faster and when he does that, I see the little plastic statue that's glued to the top of the dashboard. It's a statue of Jesus and stamped into the base is a single word that says, "*FAITH*".

I look at Mr. Gabriel and smile and he smiles back at me with his sad eyes because we both know.

The Constant Nuance of Trees

It's no secret to anyone. The best day of the week is Saturday. It has a flavor all of it's own, like butterscotch pudding or tollhouse cookies or the malted milk balls from Aunt Sarah's Confectionery Shop. But unlike pudding or cookies or candy, the taste of it lasts all day long. It has a certain smell too – the smell of roasted chestnuts or the scent of a Christmas tree when dad and I first bring it into our house, its pungent fragrance pricking your nose like pine needles as it fills up the air and spills from the living room into the kitchen, the study, my bedroom.

Sunday has the heavy smell of spices because we go to church in the morning. I suppose it's all the reverence and the holiness that builds up inside the church until it leaks through the stained-glass angels or floods through the thick, white doors of St. Mary's, fastened open once the service is over, peppering the rest of the day with seriousness. Sunday is like baked ham with too much clove or the time that mom slipped up and put curry, instead of cinnamon, in with the apple pie. If I had to pick out a cookie that reminds me of Sunday, then it would be gingerbread cookies, which are fun to make but only so-so to eat.

I guess the biggest problem with Sunday though, is Monday. It waits at the gates of midnight, impatiently, pacing back and forth as if to say: "Let's goooo-ooooh! Let's get on with it so we can rise and shine for school tomorrow!"

With the exception of Friday, Monday and the other weekdays are asparagus and lima beans, pickled beets and sauerkraut. But I don't want to think about that now because it's Saturday, the very best day of the week.

The twins, as usual, are misbehaving. Twice, dad threatens to strap them to the top of the station wagon like Christmas trees, cut and bundled for the ride home. But, being the brats that they are, their good behavior lasts for about thirty seconds and then it starts up all over again. They never take dad seriously until it's too late, until they push him a little bit too far. Not that he would actually tie them to the top of the car, but he would punish them. He would make them tag along as we went through the snowy fields of MacGregor's Farm to find our tree. Or, what's worse, he would make them sit in the car and wait. To avoid that, mom intercedes, which makes my stomach turn sour because she uses bribery to try to control the little brats.

"If you don't behave yourselves, boys, then we won't be able to get ice cream sodas on the way home!"

I can see dad's face in the rearview mirror as he rolls his eyes, glancing at mom just long enough to convey his disapproval with her "solution" to the problem. The problems, I mean, since, after all, there are two of them.

I have the misfortune of sitting between Roger and Todd in the back seat. And I want to help them – I really do. I want to help them get their ice cream sodas that they so richly deserve. So I slide my hands beneath each of their thighs and gather up a mound of soft flesh between my finger and thumb. I use just enough pressure to snap their heads around, their eyes widened in fear. They look at me and they know. They know that I'll pinch not both of them, but one of them – the one who opens his mouth first – and so hard that I'll leave my signature on the back of a leg well beyond that point in time when Santa arrives, less than two weeks from now, to leave his beneath the Christmas tree.

As the twins settle back in their seats, miraculously quiet, I wonder if mom and dad will ever learn.

Last year, MacGregor's Tree Farm used to be on the outskirts of Christmasville, in the fields behind the gas station. But this year it's planted – trees and all – at the end of a little road, off of Oak Street.

When dad swings our car into the path that leads to the barn, I look out the window and try to find the blue spruce that we tagged two weeks ago. But the heavy snowfall has all but covered the yellow, plastic flag that we wrote our name on, that we tied to the tippy-top of our beautiful tree.

"Good Morning, Tom, Evelyn," Mr. MacGregor says to dad and mom, tipping his hat.

Mr. MacGregor is a stocky man with a brown beard that springs from his face like a wild bird's nest. The sound of his voice is warm and pleasing.

"Good morning, Bob," dad replies.

"Hi Bob," adds mom.

"I see you're prepared for the big dig," he says, after leaning down and seeing the shovel and pick, the ropes and gloves that dad had put in the back of the station wagon.

"We're always ready, Bob," dad says, sticking his arm out the window to shake Mr. MacGregor's hand.

"Maybe the saplings will pitch in this year," says the tree farmer, looking at each of the twins in the back seat, "and give you and Mary Jane some extra sets of hands."

"Of course they'll be pitching in. Won't you, boys?" mom says, though dad and I know better.

Roger and Todd look at each other, making screwed-up faces before giggling. They know better too.

"I must say, Evelyn," adds Mr. MacGregor before we get out of the car to look for our tree, "Mary Jane is getting prettier than a snow bunny".

I guess that's a good thing even though I don't know exactly what a snow bunny looks like, or how pretty it is, because I've never seen one. But just the same, I can feel my face turning bright red, which makes the twins giggle again.

Roger looks at me and boldly moves his mouth without speaking: "Pretty as a fruit-cake."

Holding up my hand in front of his face and snapping my index finger against my thumb, like the pincers of a spider, makes him jump from the car in a panic.

Unlike most everyone else in Christmasville, dad doesn't cut our Christmas tree down. He digs it up. Shoveling the snow away, dad swings his pick, breaking the bare earth into frozen chunks until a circle is formed around the base of the tree. Then he digs down, making neat piles of dirt that are pushed back into the hole once the tree is removed. The hardest part is finding the taproot – that's my job – getting down on a plastic tablecloth that we spread beneath the branches and pulling the softer soil out with a tin can until I can find it. Dad takes over again then, digging deeper so when he cuts the taproot with his shovel, it's as long as possible.

"That's the trick, princess," dad always told me when we carted the tree out of the house after Christmas to plant it. "A long taproot, good soil and a spot in the yard where it gets plenty of water and sunshine."

When we're finished, dad and I drag our tree to the side road so we can bring the car down and lift it up onto the tailgate of the station wagon, wrapping its roots in an old tablecloth. Mom sits in the car, listening to Christmas carols on the radio. Or sometimes she acts like our supervisor, telling us – "suggesting" – she says between carols, that we do this or that when it's already done or we were just about to do it anyway. The twins are off in the snow someplace, taking turns riding Mr. MacGregor's German Shepherd, throwing snowballs at passing cars, perpetrating their peculiar brand of terror.

For a moment, I wonder: what makes Mr. MacGregor's dog a *German* Shepherd anyway?

When our tree is secured in the back of the car, we wish Mr. MacGregor a "Merry Christmas", pick up the twins and head back toward town. Mom turns the radio up so we can all join in, singing "Jingle Bells" and "Deck the Halls" and "Joy to the World". It's fun, but more importantly, it keeps Roger and Todd pre-occupied until dad finds a spot to park near the pharmacy.

All the stools at the service counter are taken. We have to wait a couple of minutes until Amy Jurgenson, the waitress at Link's Pharmacy and Luncheonette, clears one of the booths. It's really busy because it's Saturday and a lot of people are eating their lunches or getting hot cocoas or fountain sodas because they've been Christmas shopping. Almost everyone in Link's has packages or shopping bags on the floor by their stools or squeezed between them on the benches of their booths.

When we slide into our booth, dad sits on one side with mom and I sit on the other. The twins are at the metal racks that display the comic books, spinning them around until either Roger or Todd becomes fascinated by a superhero or an arch villain, boldly depicted on a cover in some sort of weird, ridiculous adventure. Because of the way that they behave, I don't have any doubt that it's a villain that attracts their attention first.

"Oh – I forgot to tell you," dad says, remembering something that must be funny because he starts to laugh. "Otis Wright came into the lumberyard yesterday."

"Oh, no," mom replies. "What is it this time?"

For what seems like a long time, I wait for dad to explain, wondering if Mr. Wright had said something about our conversation in the diner.

"Don't bite your nails, honey," mom says, reaching across the table and tapping my arm. "You'll make a mess of them."

"Well," dad starts, "apparently there was a big maple tree that was growing against the hothouse where he cultivates fruits and vegetables for his produce stand. So Otis cut it down. He cut the branches off and started to chop the trunk of the tree into logs for firewood. And I guess that's when it hit him."

"Another invention," mom says, familiar with the long history of gadgets and contraptions that didn't work, were too expensive to make or too impractical to use. "Honestly, Tom, if Otis Wright devoted as much time to his fruit and vegetable stand as he did to his inventions, then he'd probably be a millionaire by now."

"I know," dad agrees, laughing again. "But anyway, this one really takes the cake," he continues, shaking his head incredulously. "He cut part of the maple into sections and then he and his brother, Willy, carried them into their workshop. He knew what he wanted to do but he wasn't sure about how to go about it. Anyway, to make a long story short, he ended up by milling some of the wood into thin sheets. Then he cut them into different shapes and pieced them together, gluing them into all sorts of models."

"He made them from the wood?" mom asks.

"Yes – from the maple wood. And do you know what he made models of?"

"I don't know," mom says, looking at me from the other side of the table. "What do you think, Mary Jane?"

I shrug my shoulders. "Doll houses? Toy furniture?"

Mom laughs until she sees dad looking at me with a sort of puzzled look on his face.

"What made you say that, Mary Jane?" he asks.

"I don't know. I just thought that it would be something that Mr. Wright might make."

"Well," dad says, "that's pretty close to hitting the nail on the head."

"You're kidding," mom says.

"No, I'm not. Otis got it into his head that instead of building houses and furniture out of plastic sheathing – just like all the houses and furniture in Christmasville are made – that they could be built out of trees, cut into planks and panels of wood that were glued or somehow fastened together."

"That's crazy," mom remarks. "Why would he want to do that? – Everyone knows that houses and furniture are made from plastic. Wood? What would Otis have us do? – Cut down all the trees in Christmasville? And what would you call the lumberyard, then, Tom, if you sold *wood* sheathing instead of *plastic?*"

When Amy brings our order to our booth, Roger and Todd magically appear. Each of them has a half dozen comic books rolled up in their hands, pleading with mom for the money to pay for them. Dad drinks his hot cocoa, looking at me every now and then with the same kind of expression that he had before.

I guess I'm a little puzzled too because I remember ... I remember sitting in the club car of the train. The table of the booth where I sat wasn't made of plastic. It was made of wood.

When we get home, the twins run up to their rooms with their stash of comic books, eager to discover what new ways of villainy might be added to their repertoire. After more than two hours of enduring their giggling and nagging and whining, it's a real treat to see them disappear, to experience the genuine pleasure of their absence.

I help dad take our blue spruce out of the car and carry it into the garage. We plop it down in a plastic tub, packing topsoil around the roots until the tree can stand by itself. Then we pour a half of bucket of water in. It's important to go easy on the water and to put only enough soil into the tub to cover the roots because otherwise it might be too heavy when dad wheels it up the steps and into the house on his hand-truck a couple of days from now, before it needs water again.

"Why don't we bring it into the house right away, dad, instead of letting it sit in the garage by itself?"

"So we don't shock it, princess. So it gradually becomes accustomed to the change in temperature and the climate inside the house."

By the time that we're done, it's almost three-thirty in the afternoon. Saturday afternoon. I grab my sled from the garage and go out onto Pine Street, dragging it by the rope behind me. There's a lot of traffic so I have to watch for cars, stepping up on the banks of plowed snow along the side of the street to let them pass, and then down again. I pass by the lumberyard where dad works, moving toward Jenkins' Hill. In the back lot, plastic sheets are stacked on plastic racks to keep them off the ground and out of the snow. In front, by the entrance of the small office building, a cedar tree towers high up into the air. Alongside of the office building is a group of white pines, two hemlocks and then further back, near the far corner of the lumberyard, a single oak. Its barren branches sway slightly in the wind, moving against the graying sky, its limbs like a web that dances when a spider dashes across it.

Trees. The constant nuance of trees. Some of them have needles and cones and hold armfuls of snow in their full branches while others – the oak behind the lumberyard and the maple that Mr. Wright cut down – have bare limbs, arms without hands. Why are some trees full and feathery while others look like dead poles stuck into the ground? Why are some trees evergreen while others are never green?

Dad loves trees. That's why he digs them up and plants them in the yard after Christmas has come and gone. He doesn't have the heart to cut them down, to kill them. This year, we have eleven trees from Christmases past, planted throughout the yard around our house. Six are in the backyard against the fence; two are out front by the sidewalk and three of them are in the side yard next to the Morrison's. I don't know how we managed to pick up three extra trees because last year, counting the Douglas fir that we planted in our yard on Maple Street, there were only eight. Where the two Norwegian firs in the front yard came from, and the blue spruce on the side, next to the Morrison's, is a mystery that maybe I'll never figure out. When I asked dad about them, he stood in the front yard and took off his cap, scratching the top of his head. He narrowed his eyes and started biting his lower lip like he always does when he's thinking about something serious. "You know what, princess," he said, staring at the trees as if they themselves would be able to give him a hint, "I'm not really sure when we planted those trees."

But who knows anyway? – Maybe tomorrow all of our trees will disappear and end up in some other place. Just like the snowman from China.

When I get to the foot of Jenkins' Hill, I have to carry my sled up the fifty million steps of the staircase contraption. Stopping to rest on the last landing, I decide that I really need to talk to Mr. Wright about this stupid thing. There's got to be a better way to get yourself up a hill, doesn't there? – Something like a big box or a closet that you step into and that rises up alongside the staircase when you push a button because there's a motor and a pulley and a cable that's attached to the top of the closet. He could call it … 'the Wright Way Lift Box', or 'the Otis Elevator Closet', or something like that. But of course there's other things that are more important that I need to talk to Mr. Wright about.

Crossing Maple Street, I slip through the alley between Jack's Toy Store and Clauson's. Behind the department store, a group of younger kids arrange empty boxes into an elaborate fortress. Some of the boxes are so big that it looks like refrigerators or stoves came inside them. It looks like a lot of fun and if I wasn't fourteen, or if the kids were older, then I would probably stay and play with them. It's funny but, sometimes when you get things for Christmas, the boxes are more fun than the toys are that were once inside them.

The sledding hill: it's one of the best places in all of Christmasville. There's the obvious reason, of course – the reason why more than a hundred kids bundled themselves up and braved the cold and the snow and the wind to make their way here from all parts of Christmasville – to slide merrily down as many as fifteen sledding trails etched into the hillside like a word ... like the word, "excitement", written quickly across a sheet of white paper. Some of the trails dropped down straight and fast and you had so little time to enjoy the rush of speed before your sled plowed into the deeper snows of the tiny valley that was cradled between the hillside and the ridge on the other side. Other trails swung into a wide arc across the hillside, slipping between trees or skirting around huge boulders that stuck out of the ground like massive noses from a giant face, covered over in snow. And there were still other trails that criss-crossed one another halfway down the slope. These were the favorites of the older boys, who played "broadside" on their long three-man sleds. Two teams would launch themselves from different points on top of the hill at the same time, racing down the hillside to meet each other halfway down the slope. Sometimes the two sleds would collide, causing each team to topple over and to tumble haphazardly down the slope through the snow. At other times, they would swing next to each other – to "broadside" – the boys on one sled wrestling with their opponents on the other until one team was upturned while the other – the boys on the winning team – glided successfully toward the bottom of the hill, shouting victoriously all the way down.

But there was another word, beside "excitement", which described the view – the feeling that you got from the top of the sledding hill. It was scribbled into the ridge on the other side and you saw it – you *felt* it – when you were alone and you took your time to look for it carefully. In the evening, it was written by the stillness that settles in the leafless trees along the ridge, the barren branches of oak and elm spelling the word in a snowfall that had borrowed some of its blueness from the sky. Or it would be that time just before dawn, the word whispered by an amber silence that rose after the bark of a faraway dog, the word echoed in the lazy smoke that drifted from chimneys; in the tracks of a single fox that had pranced, maybe moments ago, in the snows along the bottom of the ridge; in the measured movement of Stark, the Iceman, as he led his horses and hauling-sleigh out of the distant woods and onto the frozen lake to cut broad chunks of ice that he would bring to market, leaving behind holes, gaps, spaces in the surface of the lake which, if you looked carefully, resembled the very same word that had been scribbled and written, whispered and echoed across the hillside. It was the word, "enchantment".

When I arrive at the edge of the sledding hill, I see Emily as she climbs to the top, pulling herself up with the long knotted rope that stretches from the trunk of a tree down the side of the slope.

"What took you so long?" she says with a sour face.

She catches her breath, pulls her arms from the rope handles that holds her plastic saucer against her back.

"The Christmas tree," I reply. "It always takes time to dig it up and to pot it. And we stopped for sodas at Link's Pharmacy, too."

"Why don't you just cut your tree down like everyone else does?"

I guess Emily is mad at me because I'm nearly an hour late.

"Because we dig it up – that's why," I answer, irritated because it's not like she had nothing to do while she waited for me, or because there wasn't anyone else around to sled with.

"Well I think it's stupid," she remarks with a nasty expression, turning her back to me and smacking her saucer down on the icy ledge.

She sits on top of it and crosses her legs, her body duplicating the contour of the saucer – like a circle inside another. She reaches down, her hands fumbling for the rope handles.

"Let me help you, Emily."

Instead of guiding her hands toward the handles, I put my foot on the edge of the saucer and give her a nice push.

"Mary Jane!" she shouts as the saucer glides to the edge and tilts downward.

I watch her spin and bounce as the saucer races down the slope, her hands groping frantically for the handles. But by the time she manages to grab on with both hands and to lean her body this way or that – to control the direction of her descent – it's too late. The one half of her saucer catches the launching ramp that's embedded in the snow about three-quarters of the way down. The boys buried it there at the beginning of December, packing it with snow and ice so you could fly high into the air, just when you thought your ride was coming to an end. Anyway, when Emily slides across the ramp, half on and half off, the saucer bends and buckles, dumping Emily one way and then, snapping back, shooting off in the other direction.

"*It is not stupid*," I say to myself, turning around and leaving because I suddenly realize that I didn't want to go sledding after all.

Darkness, with its train of stars, is pulled across the sky and tucked along the edges of Christmasville as if by invisible angels. The yellow lights of houses and stores, the white lights of electric candles perched in windows, the colored lights draped around doorways and roofs and snow-covered trees – all seem to become illuminated at the same time, as if by the flick of a single switch, as if by magic.

I can't use my sled on the hill from Maple Street down to Juniper because there's traffic. I have to use the stairway again. On Pine Street, I go beneath the trestles of the freight train, past the lumberyard and then the houses of our neighbors – the Mason's and the Bonner's, the Rausch's and the Watts'. Along the way, I glance through the front windows as they move through their homes – setting the table for supper, carrying boxes of decorations, getting ready for the holidays.

When I get to my house, I dump my sled in the front yard and walk out into the middle of the street. There isn't any traffic here. About a hundred yards down the block, it looks like Pine Street ends but it doesn't. It bends north sharply before turning west again and continuing toward the power station on the right, to the parking lot behind the Union Train Station on the left. Where Pine Street starts its bend, Linden Lane stretches down to meet Poplar Street. That's where Wright's Produce Stand is – on the corner of Poplar and

Linden Lane. Behind it are the hothouse and the workshop where dad said that Mr. Wright made his wooden models of houses and furniture.

From where I'm standing, I can look straight down Pine Street and see the doorway of the workshop, the overhead light glimmering through the grove of cedar trees.

Cedar trees: they always look so stately and majestic, their bushy limbs all pointing towards heaven. They remind me of priests and ministers and rabbis.

Moving past the Morrison's and the Caterson's, the Kelly's and the Franklin's, I arrive at the corner of Linden Lane. But I go straight through the cedar trees, making a beeline toward Mr. Wright's workshop.

The panes of clear plastic in the lower windows are glazed over in a patchwork of icy crystals that are slowly melting. It makes everything look blurred and distorted inside. I take my glove off so I can scrape some of the ice away with my fingernail but that doesn't work because the ice is on the inside. Looking around, I can't find anything to stand on, to raise me up so I can peek through the upper panes. I guess I'll have to make do as it is.

Against the far wall, a long workbench is scattered with tools and what looks like chunks of wood. On a long shelf over the workbench is some sort of sign. But because the ice and the water on the windows blur things, it's difficult to decipher what it says exactly. The letters are big and red and printed on a white plank. They look wrinkled through the plastic panes – as if a strong wind was rushing by, stretching the letters out of shape, trying to pull them from the sign.

... 'rench' ... 'renchla' ... 'renchla Bus' ...

I kind of rock back and forth without moving my feet, bringing each letter into focus so I can read it.

'Frenchland or Bust!' the sign says.

But I don't know what that means.

At the end of the workshop, a coal stove is going full blast, the flames licking the roof of its mouth or slipping through the iron teeth of its front grate. In one of the corners is a square table that's covered over with a piece of cloth. There must be things underneath it because lumps – of different shapes and sizes – prevent the cloth from laying flat against the top of the table.

"Hello there."

Startled, I snap my head around, trying to find the face in the shadows.

"Are you looking for something in particular? Or are you just plain snooping?"

He steps toward the door and now I can see by the overhead light that it's Mr. Wright – not Otis – but his brother, Willy.

"I wanted to see the models ... the models that you and Otis made."

"I see," he replies, grabbing the doorknob and swinging the door to the workshop open. "Then why don't you come in and get out of the cold, Mary Jane."

As I approach the doorway, I hear Willy call out to his brother who I guess is in another part of the workshop.

The smell: it's pungent, but pleasant, and rises from the chips and flakes and shavings that lay across the floor like a strange snowfall that's spongy when I walk on it. And though it's not all that cold inside, I can feel the dampness seeping through my coat and leggings, chilling me to the bone.

Mr. Wright – Willy – goes through a doorway into a much larger section of the workshop. It must be where Mr. Wright – Otis, that is – works on his more ambitious projects because along the windows on the other side is a huge framework of ... It must be wood ... wooden ribs that are curved and fastened to wooden planks that run along the whole top and bottom of the thing to make ... I don't know – some kind of intricate cage that's maybe fifteen feet long and four feet wide, the longer side of it rounded at the edge and thicker – about twelve inches high while the opposite side is flat and ... But it can't be a cage because part of it is wrapped tightly with a fabric that looks waterproofed like my coat. And what kind of animal would you keep for a pet in a cage like that anyway? A hamster or gerbil? A family of mice?

When I go up to it, I run my fingers along one of the wooden planks. I never imagined that wood could be so soft and warm and smooth, its exposed ... its flesh, having long sweeping veins like you sometimes see in a rock but more graceful and flowing like the water that moves in a stream around the surfaces of rocks. And it's like it sweats, too, because there's an oily stuff that comes from the wood, but it doesn't smell like some people do when they sweat. It smells nice, like a forest perfume – but peppery and spicy – like gingerbread cookies, only better.

"What do you think, Mary Jane?"

Mr. Wright – Otis – comes up beside me while his brother, Willy, goes toward the door and leaves, toting his toolbox.

"I think it might be a float for the Christmas Parade," I say on a whim. "But I've never seen one that was made from wood."

"And I don't know if you ever will," he says, laughing. "No, it's not a float, Mary Jane. It's something quite different."

"Is it a cage?" I say, blurting it out.

"No, it's not a cage either. And, to be honest with you, I don't know what to call it because I'm not even sure how it's going to work when it's done. I'm not even sure if it'll work at all," he adds, laughing again.

"What do you mean: 'if it'll work'?"

"When it's finished, Mary Jane, you'll be one of the first to know about it – OK? Besides", he goes on, "like you, I'm a little reluctant to talk about things that are unusual, unorthodox, out of the ordinary. People might say that I was ..."

"Emotionally challenged?" I suggest.

"Yes," he says with a big belly laugh. "That's it – 'emotionally challenged', as Doctor Sperry is fond of saying, particularly about those of us who dream, who see things that others may not – those of us who are cut from a different grain. But anyway, Mary Jane, that's not why you came to my workshop, is it? – To look at contraptions that don't have a name, that might not work and that aren't finished yet. You came to see something else, didn't you?"

"You made models? – Models of houses and furniture?"

"Yes. I did indeed," he replies, moving toward the room where I first came in. "Step right this way, young lady, and I'll show you a sight to behold!"

He leads me to the square table in the corner of the other room and carefully removes the cloth, tossing it onto the workbench.

"Oh my God!" I say with sudden surprise. "It's beautiful!"

It looks like a little toy village – with houses and stores, cars and streets that are all finely detailed and made in different colors.

"I can only take some of the credit," says Mr. Wright. "I might be the one who comes up with the ideas, but it's Willy who does most of the work. He's the one with the talent, who actually transforms the ideas into the reality."

"Can I?" I ask, reaching toward a blue Pontiac that is an exact replica of Mr. Caterson's.

"Sure you can, but you have to be careful if you try to handle any of the buildings and furniture – they're more delicate than the cars. OK?"

"How does Willy make them so real?"

I hold up the car so I can study it in the light, noting the license plate and the flap that covers the gas cap, the radio antenna and even the word, "Pontiac", written across the trunk.

"For the cars, he carves them out of a single block of wood – except for the antenna. He cuts out a splinter and uses the tiniest dollop of glue to fasten it in the hole that he's drilled. The buildings and roadways are assembled from thin sheets of wood that I cut from my power saw."

"This is incredible," I remark, genuinely amazed by the talent and patience it must take to make a single car. "But how do you get the wood in different colors?"

"Oh, that's easy. I mix up different ingredients – berry juices and fruit extracts, inks, vinegar, even milk, glues for thickening agents – I use all sorts of stuff. I guess you could call it, a 'homemade paint'," he adds. "But for the furniture and most of the buildings, I use oils and the saps from trees mostly – tinted with coal dust or talcum powder – things like that. I call them, 'stains', because they become absorbed by the wood, highlighting its grain, rather than just covering it over like the paint does."

"You can't do that with plastic. Can you?" I ask, not entirely sure.

"Nope. What's great about wood – aside from the way that it feels and smells – is that you can stain it or paint it or change the color of it any time you please. Plastic won't hold a stain and if you try to paint it, it peels right off when it gets wet. With wood, you can cut it and shape it just about any way you like. Try doing that with plastic! And wood feels so warm and alive. Plastic feels cold and unnatural."

I put the car back on the table, looking from one building to the next. "Do you think we'll ever have houses in Christmasville that are made of wood, Mr. Wright?"

"I don't think so, Mary Jane," he replies, covering the table with the cloth. "But you know what? – I just thought of something else that you might like to see. That is, if you're interested?"

"Sure I am," I reply with excitement.

From the hook on the door, Mr. Wright takes his coat and swings it around his shoulders to climb into it.

"Let's go over to the hothouse," he says, opening the door from the workshop.

It's a long rectangle of a building on the other side of the backyard and where Mr. Wright and his brother, Willy, grow fruits and vegetables for the stand in front of their house. Except for the thick, green slabs of plastic that rise up as high as my waist, the whole building is constructed of windows – clear, plastic panels that are stacked in rows along the two longer walls and then arched over on an upward slant to become the roof. The panels are clear so that the plants inside always get enough sunlight to grow. But because of all the heat and the moisture inside the hothouse, the windows are always fogged over so you could never peek in to see what kinds of plants the Wrights are growing, or how the plants are making out inside when it's so freezing cold outside. I know because Emily and I snuck into the backyard once and tried to find out.

As Mr. Wright and I move through the snow, along a path illuminated by strands of lights that wind through the branches of trees that are both evergreen and never green, I see a pond. The pond is frozen over but the snow has been swept away to reveal its crystal clear veneer. A brown footbridge straddles the pond.

"Why did you do that?" I ask, pointing to the pond.

"Why did I do what?" he says, turning around to look.

"Clear the snow from the pond."

"Oh," Mr. Wright replies. "That's one of Willy's pet projects. He likes to keep an eye on his fish."

"Fish? – There's fish in the pond?"

"Let's go and have a look," he says, turning back and leading me toward the footbridge. "But you really won't be able to see the fish because it's dark and they always stay as close to the bottom as they can without touching. And they almost never move, which makes it difficult enough to see them even in the daylight."

The plastic planks of the bridge creak as we walk toward the top of the arch.

"Why? – Why don't they ever move?" I ask, leaning over the railing and staring as hard as I can through the ice.

"That's what Willy's trying to find out," answers Mr. Wright. "But we both agree on the same theory: we think that they're sleeping – as far away from the surface as possible – waiting for the ice to melt."

"They're waiting for spring."

"Spring?" he asks, turning to look at me.

"That's when the ice melts," I reply.

When we go inside the hothouse, it's hard to say what sensation strikes you first. There's the heat and the humidity that pushes against your face and seeps inside your clothes to make you hot and sweaty. It's like going into the locker room after gym when everyone's taking their showers. And then there's the smells – the heavy mixture of fruit and vegetable fragrances that swarm into your nose as soon as you take your first breath. For your eyes, it's the colors – dozens of different shades of green, curled up into heads of lettuces or crinkled into leafs of spinach or stretched tight and smooth into stalks of broccoli. Between the many greens are bright splotches of color: yellow squashes and red peppers, purple kale and cream-colored cauliflowers, blueberries and raspberries and strawberries.

The hothouse is much larger and far more complex than I had ever imagined, divided up into sections by long sheets of soft, clear plastic that hang from hooks in the ceiling all the way down to the floor. To get from one section to the next, the plastic is cut into broad strips so when you step through them, they swing back into place, closing the way from the section that you just left.

"It's not as easy to grow fruits and vegetables as you might think," Mr. Wright explains. "For each one of them, you have to discover the correct temperature, the best level of humidity and the proper amount of sunshine for them to thrive. You have to figure out how often to water them – some need a lot while others require very little. And then, of course, there's the composition of the soil. Some do better in loose, sandy soil with good drainage; others prefer rich, compacted loam that's high in nutrients."

When we get to the last section, a motley assortment of plants spring from all the plastic containers that are lined up along the tables. Some grow like wild fire, shooting long, thin stalks high into the air, with balls of feather-dust at the end of them. Others are scraggly and haggard – like old Mrs. Phelps – and look exhausted by the their plight to survive.

"This is our experimental section," Mr. Wright explains, "and it all began as an accident."

"An accident?"

I pull my hat and coat off, tucking them under my arm.

"Willy and I often go out in our truck in the fields around Wakefield Lake, or beyond MacGregor's Tree Farm to find new sources of soil for our plantings or to replenish soil that's lost its nutrients. We have to shovel the snows aside and then break up the soil with our picks into frozen chunks that we load into our truck and bring back to the hothouse. It's really quite the chore – one that I never look forward to. But anyway, once we arrive back at the hothouse, we lay the frozen soil across the plant tables, spreading it out and turning it so it melts. And that's when it happens."

"When what happens?" I ask, eager to find out.

"Well, there was a time when Willy and I would use the new soil as soon as it was ready, which is when the ice inside it melted. But one time, we were so busy with this project or another that we couldn't begin to use the new soil for several weeks – well after it had thawed. I'll never forget the expression of wonder on Willy's face when we came back to this very section to start using the new soil. All kinds of strange plants had taken root, spreading themselves according to their nature across the piles of soil. Some were flourishing; some were struggling to survive. You see, Mary Jane, what Willy and I discovered was that there were seeds – all kinds of seeds – mixed in with the new soil that we had brought in. The seeds were only sleeping, waiting, like the fish in the pond, for the ice to melt."

"They were waiting for spring."

"Yes," Mr. Wright agrees with a smile. "They were waiting for spring."

When I go up to one of the plants and lift my hand as if to touch it, Mr. Wright grabs my arm.

"Be careful not to touch them, Mary Jane," he cautions, "because some of them can be quite harmful."

I guess he sees the expression of disbelief, mixed with bafflement, that's on my face.

"No, they won't bite you. But some of them, however, can prick your fingers with their thorns or give you such a terribly nasty rash – like the ivy that got Willy – that you'll have to bandage your arms up so you don't itch it or pick at the scabs."

I pull my arms back quickly, scratching them as if I were suddenly infected with the horrible rash.

"How can a plant do that?"

"Because some of them, though only a few that we've discovered, are poisonous," he replies. "And that's not the only way that they can get you either – with their thorns or the terrible rash that they can give you. Sometimes Willy and I take different parts of plants – the stalk, the flower, the fruit, or even the root – and taste them to see if it might be a new food that we could put in our stand for everyone to buy and enjoy. And I guess I'm the lucky one because I only got sick once, and just a little bit. But Willy – Willy's been sick three times now. Once he was so bad with the fever and the sweats and the stomach cramps that I had to take him to the hospital. But they couldn't do anything because they didn't understand what was ailing him. The poison just had to run its course through Willy's body until it was done with its mischief."

Mr. Wright leads me to a row of plants on the tables by the windows.

"I know it sounds like we're taking a lot of silly chances, Mary Jane, but sometimes it does pay off. This plant here," he says, folding back a leafy branch to reveal its bright red fruit, "is shaping up very nicely. The way it looks reminds me of Tom Atkinson's considerable nose, especially after he's been out in the bitter cold for a spell. So we call it the 'tomato', for short."

"Can I taste it?" I ask.

"Not until Willy and I try it out first. You don't want to find yourself in the hospital, do you? – Sick with the sweats and the cramps because there was something in it that didn't agree with your tummy."

As Mr. Wright leads me through the rows of tables that make up the experimental section, I become more and more fascinated – so much so that I'm not sure if I want to be a reporter for *The Courier* after all. When I grow up – of course, *if* I grow up – I'd like to work right here, in Mr. Wright's hothouse.

"Most of the plants that we find don't have any purpose. None that we're able to discover anyway. Then we have to pull them up and cart them off to the far end of the backyard so we can make room for the new batch of soil that we're bringing in. I don't like doing it because there's always a chance that they might be useful in a way that we've overlooked. But the hothouse is only so big, Mary Jane. And there's the labor and the cost of it all, especially when you figure that the coal stoves and the fans have to be constantly going to keep up the heat and to circulate it. We really can't afford to make it any bigger than what it is now."

When we turn the corner into the last row of plants, the colors of the plants are so stunning that I'm mesmerized.

"We don't know what to do with this group. We can't find any reason to keep them except for the fact that they're so darn pretty."

Attracted by the color, the shape, the beautiful convolutions that wind through its blooms, I lift my hand up without thinking. I want to cup one of them and breathe in the lovely fragrance that ...

"Ouch!" I shout, pulling my hand away from a thorn.

"I did warn you, Mary Jane," says Mr. Wright sympathetically, taking my hand and inspecting it.

"I know you did, Mr. Wright. But for a minute, I didn't think."

"It looks all right though," he says. "I don't see any blood."

Nevertheless, I press my hand against my mouth and lick it, which makes it feel better.

"What do you call these plants?" I ask.

"Well, we name them by their color," he replies. "We call this one with the thorns, a 'rose'. The little ones next to it are 'violets' and then 'lavenders'. This one here," he says, moving down the aisle and pointing, "is a 'lily-white'."

The last one on the table is the most beautiful – but also the strangest of all, having two leaves that are green and shiny and plastic in appearance. The leaves are at the very bottom of the plant, hanging just above the thick tangle of roots that have pushed themselves up and out of the soil. A long barren stalk shoots upward. It's tied with yellow string to a plastic stick that helps support the four identical blooms, which sprout from the wiry branches at the very top of the stalk.

"We call it, an 'orchid'," says Mr. Wright.

It is so beautiful that it doesn't look real at all. It looks like something spawned from a fairie's dream, left behind well after the fairie had awoken and slipped away to do her magic or her mischief, whichever so inclined her.

"Otis?"

Stepping through the plastic curtains, Willy stops to look for his brother through the green jungle of plants that sprawl, spill, shoot from the tables of the experimental section.

"Otis? – You in here?"

"We're over here, Willy."

"We should be getting along soon," he says. "It's getting late."

"I'll be right with you, Willy", he calls out.

"We're going over to the Atkinson's house for dinner," Mr. Wright explains.

"I should be going home as well," I say, realizing that it's nearly suppertime.

"But just another minute, Mary Jane," he says, leading me toward the other side of the experimental section. "We got so caught up with these plants here that I forgot to show you why I brought you into the hothouse in the first place."

"But I thought ..."

"Well, yes – there's all this, of course. But there's something in particular that I want you to see."

It's in a large, plastic pot near one of the coal stoves. It's about four feet high and has tiny green leaves that look like the webbed feet of baby ducks.

"When I had to cut the big maple tree down because it was growing against the panels of the hothouse, I found this behind it. It's a sapling – a maple – so I dug it up and brought it in here."

"It has leaves!"

"How about that? – A maple tree with leaves," Mr. Wright laughs. "I guess we tricked it into thinking ... well, that it's spring."

I nod my head, grinning from ear-to-ear. It's not only because I've found ... *leaves* – living, growing *maple* leaves – which, in a crazy, sort of mixed-up way proves that there's more than just the Decembers and the Januarys of winter, that there's more to Christmasville than just Christmasville. It's also because I've found in Mr. Wright what dad calls, 'a kindred spirit' – somebody who faces the same kinds of challenges, 'emotional' or otherwise, that I do.

"Mary Jane," says Mr. Wright, "how would you like to bring the maple tree home and take care of it?"

A Game of Checkers

Before I let them into my room, I make them stand at the door and close their eyes. "And no peeking – or else Santa Claus won't leave you any presents," I say, warning mom and dad of the dire consequences.

I grab the knob and swing the door open. First, I lead dad by the hand over by my dresser.

"Can I look now, princess?" he says teasingly. "It's so dark in here that I'm afraid I might fall asleep at any moment."

"Don't peek, dad," I say sternly.

"I really should get back to the kitchen, Mary Jane, and check on the boys," mom says as I steer her into my room and position her by the desk. Her arms grope in the empty air in front of her because I guess she thinks that I'm going to lead her into the bed or a piece of furniture.

The twins are supposed to be helping mom make tollhouse cookies in the kitchen. But they're only doing it so they can stuff gobs of dough into their greedy, little mouths when she's not looking.

"Just another second," I reply, going over to the light cord and plugging it into the outlet. "OK – Now! You can open your eyes now!"

It's standing in front of the window where my old toy box was before I dragged it into my closet, pushing it toward the back. I never used the toy box much anyway, except for storing toys that I never played with, or Christmas presents that I made or bought for my family and friends.

When dad opens his eyes, he doesn't know what to say as he scrutinizes it from top to bottom, looking at the lights, the old ornaments that we don't use any more, the bows that I made from strips of green and red ribbon.

"My, isn't that ... isn't that different," mom says. "You've got your very own Christmas tree, Mary Jane."

"It's not just any Christmas tree, mom. It's a maple tree – and it's alive. See the leaves that are growing from its branches."

"Well, imagine that," she says, turning her head to listen to the twins in the kitchen. "A maple tree with leaves."

"Well, I'll be damned," dad says, stepping toward the tree.

"What did you say, Tom?" mom asks, arching her eyebrow like she always does when she's slightly perturbed.

"Well, I'll be darned," dad says, going up to the maple and inspecting it. "It is growing, Mary Jane. And it does have leaves."

"Mr. Wright gave it to me," I explain, telling them how he had transplanted the sapling from the back of his hothouse.

"But where will you put it when it gets too big for the window?" mom asks. "And when all the leaves come out and grow larger, they'll block the sunlight that's coming in from the window. I don't know if this is such a good idea, Tom," she remarks, turning toward dad.

It really irks me when mom asks me a question, says something that prevents me from disagreeing with whatever she's decided the answer will be, and then turns to dad to support what she's decided. It's like I'm not even there, like I don't have any say in the matter at all.

"When the time comes, we'll figure something out, Evelyn," dad replies.

"What about watering it?" mom continues. "I don't want water stains all over the carpet."

There she goes again – the question, followed by the comment that makes it impossible to answer. What she's really saying is: *'You have to water it, Mary Jane, but you can't water it because of the carpet – so you might as well get rid of it.'*

The buzzer on the oven goes off.

"I have to get back to the kitchen and pull the first batch of cookies out. Nobody likes to eat tollhouse cookies that are scorched – do they, dear," she says to me, reaching out and pushing my hair back before leaving.

"I guess mom's not too happy with the maple – huh, dad?" I ask.

"She'll be fine with it, Mary Jane. If you know your mother, then you know she doesn't like dealing with anything out of the ordinary. It's how she is. But anyway, I wonder how big the leaves get?" he asks, leaning down and laying one carefully against the palm of his hand. "They're so unusual – like the webbed feet of ducklings. Do you think it can be trimmed back when it starts to get bigger? – Sometimes I trim the trees in the yard after they go through that spurt of growth in early December. It doesn't seem to bother them. In fact, I think that they get fuller and bushier the following year because of my trimming them back. What does Otis say, Mary Jane? I know that trees aren't his specialty, but did he have any suggestions about how to take care of the maple?"

It makes me feel better that dad's excited about my maple tree. But it doesn't surprise me because dad, of course, loves trees. That's why he goes through all the trouble of digging up our Christmas trees and planting them after the holidays.

"Mr. Wright said that it had to be kept in a place where it gets plenty of sunshine and to give it lots of water, but only after the soil gets pretty dry – like you always say about our Christmas trees when we take them outside to plant them. And he's going to make up a batch of fertilizer that I have to put into the soil every month so that the maple gets enough nutrients."

"Had he ever seen one before, Mary Jane – a maple tree with leaves sprouting from it?"

"Nope," I say, nodding my head. "That's what makes it so special, dad."

"It sure does, princess," dad agrees. "And it's going to be interesting to watch it grow."

The thought crosses my mind to tell dad about the pretty plants that Mr. Wright had grown from seed in his hothouse. But I can't because I already asked Mr. Wright if I could buy the rose as a Christmas present for dad and mom and I didn't want to ruin the surprise of it. He said he would only charge me a quarter for it – and that was only to cover the cost of delivering it on Christmas Eve, he said.

"Why do you think it happened, dad? Why do you think the maple tree suddenly started growing leaves when Mr. Wright brought it into the hothouse?"

"I'm not really sure, Mary Jane," he says, sitting down on the edge of my bed. "But it must have something to do with the heat that's generated in the hothouse. I guess it's like a spark that triggers the growing process."

"Or an alarm clock that wakes it up," I suggest. "But it doesn't make any sense, does it, dad? – I mean, if you look around Christmasville, there's plenty of maples and oaks, elm trees and sycamores, but there isn't any alarm clock to wake them up. And why should there be? – Pine trees and spruces don't need alarm clocks. They're always awake because they always have leaves, even though the leaves are more like needles. Anyway, I guess what I'm getting at is – why are there maples and oaks at all, if there isn't any alarm clock to wake them up?"

"I don't have an answer for you, Mary Jane," dad says as he scratches the back of his head. "It's not always easy, trying to figure out what Mother Nature is doing. Like when certain trees get 'the blight'."

I pull out the chair from my desk and sit. "What does that mean, dad? – 'The blight'?"

"I can't say that I know all that much about it," he says. "It's a disease that attacks certain kinds of trees. Not all trees, just a certain kind. Let me ask you something – have you ever seen a chestnut tree?"

"No," I reply. "I haven't."

"And unfortunately, you probably never will, Mary Jane. Did you know that there used to be a large grove of chestnut trees in the valley at the bottom of the sledding hill?"

I turn my head from left to right.

"And that there was a grove of chestnuts, with maybe twenty or so trees in it, where the parking lot is behind city hall? – That's what old Mr. Phelps told me. He said that every single one of them was destroyed by what he called, 'the blight'. And the strange thing about it was, it only destroyed the chestnuts – not pines or maples or any other kind of tree. It was only the chestnuts."

"How did the chestnut trees get it, dad?"

"Nobody seems to know for sure," he replies. "But you may want to ask Otis or Willy Wright. They thought it was some kind of fungus that was airborne – a tiny, microscopic germ carried by the wind. Geez," he adds, staring at the floor, "that seems like such a long, long time ago when old Mr. Phelps told me about the chestnut trees ... almost as if it was something from a dream."

From the living room, I hear Roger and Todd. They're marching through the house in a clamorous parade, banging pots with metal spoons as mom yells at them from the kitchen.

'The twins', I think to myself. 'Fungus? Funguses? – A pair of nasty germs that if only the wind would carry someplace else.'

"And come to think of it," dad says, his hand poised reflectively up to his chin, "I remember my father telling me about another kind of blight. But it didn't affect trees. It had something to do with ... – Mary Jane, have you ever heard of a *chardonnay* grape?"

"I know about grapes – they grow on vines in Mr. Wright's hothouse."

"Yes, but like trees, there's different kinds of grapes. There's the Concord grape. And the Niagara grape. They're both used to make grape juice – but then you know that already. But there used to be another grape – the chardonnay – and it was used to make what they called, 'wine', which was aged in oak casks and then drunk during holidays or on special occasions. The chardonnay grape no longer exists because it was destroyed by 'the blight'. But," he adds, "it was a different kind of blight than the one that got the chestnuts."

I bite my thumbnail, thinking about this strange and scary phenomenon – 'the blight'.

"Is that what you think happened to the maples and the oaks, dad? Do you think they got 'the blight'?"

"I don't know, princess. It's possible, I suppose. But if they did, how do we explain the existence of the little maple tree that you have here? If it got 'the blight', how could it be sprouting leaves?"

In the living room, mom is having a difficult time of it with Roger and Todd, who continue to bang their makeshift drums unabatedly.

"Tom?" mom calls out.

'Mommy's little angels,' I say to myself, secretly smiling because the little devils have gone too far now.

Dad gets up from my bed and marches down the hallway toward the living room. "What's all the ruckus out here?" he says, raising his voice but lowering the tone of it just like he always does when he's become irritated by the twins' behavior.

The banging suddenly stops.

"Tom, they ate half the bag of chocolate morsels," mom says in a whiney voice. "How am I to finish the tollhouse cookies now?"

"Todd ate them all," Roger says, taking advantage of the tiny window of opportunity between mom's accusation and dad's response.

"No I didn't," Todd reciprocates with a sneering tone. "Roger ..."

"Enough!" dad shouts. "The two of you – into your room! Now!"

I can hear the metal clanking of pots and spoons tossed upon the couch and then the scramble of the twins as they dash toward their room.

"And don't come out until I say so!"

One of them slams the bedroom door behind but then, realizing the impropriety, wisely cracks it open. "Sorry", Roger says, "the door slipped out of my hand."

I wish I were a fly on the wall of the twins' room, watching the little animals as they cope with what must be an incredible, cookie-dough-and-chocolate-morsel sugar-rush in the confines of their cage.

Dad goes out to the garage to finish the platform for the new train set. He bought it at Jack's and it looks something like the one Emily and I saw in the display window. But it's different because it doesn't have any Santa Claus or toy soldiers.

Dressed in snow boots and winter coat, mom heads for Cauldwell's Supermarket to replenish what the twins ate. As she's going out the door, mumbling things that can't be heard – things that probably shouldn't be heard – Emily arrives.

"Hullo, Mary Jane " she says, coming into my room.

"Hullo, Emily," I reply.

Because of the incident on the sledding hill, it' been a week since we talked to each other. I suppose that she's finally – and graciously, too, I could add, knowing Emily as I do – I suppose that's she's finally decided to forgive me.

"What's that?" she asks, pointing at the maple that is illuminated with Christmas lights and bedecked in bows and ornaments.

From the twins' room, I hear them wrestling with each other, knocking furniture about, thoroughly destroying their lair.

After I furnish Emily with all the details of Mr. Wright's hothouse – the maple, the rose and the 'tomato' plant – it seems like things are getting back to normal between us. But not quite because even though Emily may have decided to forgive me, I still need a little more time to forgive her for what she said about dad digging up our Christmas tree.

"And Otis' brother, Willy – he's got fish that he keeps for pets in the pond behind the workshop."

"Fish?" Emily says. "Where'd he get the fish from?"

"From Stark, the Iceman," I reply. "He puts fishin' lines down through the holes that he makes after he cuts out the blocks of ice. And some of the fish are so big that they won't even fit in Willy's pond!" I remark, stretching the truth out as far as the fish that doesn't exist.

"Holy cow!" she replies in astonishment.

"Willy said that too."

"Said what?" Emily replies, confused.

"That some of the fish are big enough to eat a whole cow."

Watching Emily picture in her mind the terrible monster from the deep, its giant jaws snapping up a grown cow in two or three bites – "Moo! Moa! Moan!" cries the cow, "Moo! Mor! More!" says the fish – ... Well, this is really too much fun paying Emily back for her nasty comment. It's just that she's so naive and immature and gullible sometimes that it's easy to trick her into believing just about anything.

"It really makes you stop and think about ice skating on the lake, doesn't it, Emily?"

"What do you mean?" she asks, snapping her head around.

"Think about it," I say, trying to stay serious. "If you're skating on the lake and there's a fish that's big enough and powerful enough to eat a grown cow, and he's swimming around underneath the ice, following you along, and he's really hungry, and he finds a spot where the ice isn't so thick ... Well, you can just imagine the horrible consequences, can't you?"

Emily stares into space that's suddenly animated by the terrible tableau that I had drawn out for her. The expression on her face changes to one of sheer dread.

"I'm not going ice skating any more," she announces with a monotone voice.

"Oh, but wait a minute," I say, realizing that maybe I had gone too far in paying Emily back for her comment. "That's right – I forgot – Stark said to Willy that the fish was a vegetarian and only ate plants at the bottom of the lake. He doesn't eat meat so that could never happen, Emily."

She makes a sour face, realizing that I had been stringing her along – like the fish that doesn't exist.

"That wasn't very nice, Mary Jane," she says, preparing to leave.

"OK. I'm sorry, Emily. It wasn't very nice. But it wasn't very nice saying that my dad was stupid for digging up our Christmas trees either."

While Emily solves word puzzles in the book that she ... in the book that I bought for her in the Five & Dime because she never did pay me back, I finish up my project for Mrs. Franklin's civics class. The map that I got from Mr. Carson's gas station fit into it very nicely because the theme of my project was to illustrate how the town of Christmasville – its streets and buildings and geographical formations – could be re-developed into a much better community. I named the project, *The Plan – Making Christmasville A Better Place To Live.*

The first thing that I did was to add two more sledding hills. For the first one, I had all the dump trucks that were working on Beech Boulevard transport dirt and rock to the ledge at the far end of Maple Street, across from the diner and the bank. Then they covered it with snow. The hill was much bigger and steeper than the sledding hill that we have now and it gave you a much longer ride. And I made it into a circle so when your ride was over, all you had to do was to take the 'Otis Electric Elevator Box' from the bottom of the hill to the top to do it all over again. If you wanted some hot cocoa to warm yourself up, you only had to cross Maple Street to the diner at the top of the hill. The only downside was, I had to put the power station underground – beneath the sledding hill – and move Union Station about a hundred yards south and borrow some of Otis and Willy Wright's land to make the hill circular. To compensate, I moved the Atkinson's house next door to the Wright's because Mr. Atkinson is their best friend. But to do that, I had to move some of their existing neighbors someplace else. I hope that they didn't mind. Oh, and I made the hothouse three times bigger and created a special "Hothouse Tax" so that everybody in Christmasville paid for all the coal and the electricity and the water that was needed to operate it. Emily's father, the mayor, wouldn't like the tax but ... well, you can't make everybody happy, can you?

The second sledding hill was built by MacGregor's Tree Farm so the kids in south Christmasville didn't have to drag their sleds all the way up to the one by the diner. The only thing is, they couldn't get any hot cocoa unless the diner started some sort of delivery service.

I squashed the whole project of Beech Boulevard. It was a stupid idea anyway, building a highway that didn't go anywhere, that never got finished. In its place, I put a huge indoor playground and gymnasium. And I expanded Wakefield Lake, making streams that went underneath the train trestles and beneath little bridges that I built for some of the streets. One of the streams came right into our backyard so I didn't have to walk all the way to the lake to go ice-skating any more. I just went out the back door of my house.

"Brett Tolliver has a crush on you, Mary Jane."

I turn around from my desk and look at Emily on the floor, circling a word with a pencil.

"What did you say, Emily?"

"On Monday I was getting my books from my locker and I heard Debbie Lister talking to Susan Wilson. She said that Brett Tolliver has a crush on you."

"I don't believe it," I reply. "She only said it because you were nearby and she knew you were listening."

"No. It's true," insists Emily. "Did you ever see Brett when he sees you? – He gets all goofy and clumsy."

"Brett's always that way."

"No, he's not. It's only when you're nearby that he gets that way."

When I look up from my project, Emily is erasing a mistake that she made in her puzzle book. She's mistaken about Brett Tolliver, too.

Except for a couple of minor changes on Maple Street, I pretty much left it alone. I liked the fact that in this year's "plan" of Christmasville – the real "plan", that is – it made up the bustling shopping district. But I did put the park back in front of the bank, like it was before, when we used to drink hot cocoa on Friday nights and watch the fire drill. It also gave you a place to stop and rest when you wanted to take a break from sledding on the new hill that I made across the street from the diner.

To make room for Aunt Sarah's Confectionery Shop between the bank and the diner, I did away with the parking lot. I didn't drive anyway and probably never will because they'll never issue a driving license to a fourteen year old. In order to expand the size of Jack's Toy Store – tripling it – I had to shrink Grubbs' Hardware Store and Cauldwell's Food Market, sliding them west along Maple Street to make room. I hope dad wouldn't mind because he likes tools and hardware and, hopefully, mom wouldn't lose her job because the supermarket was downsized.

The last change on Maple Street – and I guess what you could call the most aggressive – was using dynamite to blast a road through the rock wall at the end of the alley between the police station and the firehouse. The road took you to St. Valentine's and then on to Easterville.

For the rest of Christmasville, I only made some minor changes. I made the library bigger and the bell tower of city hall, taller. For the hospital, I put stores on the first floor: a clothing store but for girls only, an ice cream and pudding parlor, a jewelry store and another hardware store – not only to compensate for making the original one smaller, but also to give dad a place where he could buy all his tools really cheap. I mean, the hospital is one of the largest buildings in Christmasville but hardly anybody ever used it. Sure, Willy Wright had to go there when he got the poison from the ivy, but the doctors didn't do anything for him anyway. And Wally, the postman, had to stay there for three days while they tried to figure out why he couldn't tell the difference between purple and violet or burgundy and maroon.

"Color-blindness," they said eventually, but without really telling him why or how he had got it in the first place.

But I guess the most important reason we had to have a hospital at all was the time that they rushed Mr. Mason, the milkman, to the emergency room in the ambulance. He was having what somebody called "a conniption". To calm him down, doctors gave him sedatives and tranquilizers, followed by a bunch of medical tests that nobody ever heard of. But what I remember most about the incident was the terrible sadness of Mrs. Mason and Rebecca, their daughter, when mom and I ran into them when they were coming out of the hospital nearly a week later. They had just heard the results of all the medical tests: "Mr. Mason is experiencing the initial symptom of what is both an irreversible and incurable condition," the doctor had told them. "He's suffering from a chronic case of baldness."

But if you didn't know that Mr. Mason was getting the baldness, then you would never be able to tell because he does a good job covering over the bare spot by brushing his hair back over the top of it.

The only other change that I made to the "Plan" of Christmasville was to move Tommy Burks' house to the far side of the Consolidated Plastic Works in the far corner of town. I didn't do it because it made any sense. I only did it because ... well, because I decided to do it.

"I bought daddy a new hammer for Christmas," Emily announces.

"That's nice," I reply, trying to recall if I ever saw Mayor Thompson so much as use any instrument, besides a pen or a pencil, that could be loosely construed as a "tool".

"That's why I couldn't pay you back the money I owe you."

"That's OK," I reply to Emily. "You can pay me back when you get it."

"I lost his old hammer in the snow so I thought I should get him a new one."

"That's nice," I say. "I bought dad a radio for the garage."

"Really?"

"Yep," I answer. "Want to see it?"

"Sure," she says, dropping her pencil on her book and sitting up.

From the toy box in the closet, I take out a rectangular box that shows a man in a suit and tie with thick black hair and a blonde woman with a black and yellow polka-dot dress. They're dancing the cha-cha or something on the cover. Musical notes float from the radio like they're dancing as well. The notes curl around the couple, getting bigger and bigger as they swing up and into the air. It looks stupid because it's like the man and the woman are having a party all by themselves. And the box is pink.

"The box is pretty," Emily says. "She looks like Veronica – one of my dolls," she adds, pointing at the blonde woman on the cover.

"And doesn't the man look like Mr. Mason, the milkman?" I say – kind of sarcastically, I guess, because the man is tall and thin and ... well, his hair is *really* thick.

"Yes," Emily agrees. "He does."

She's so gullible.

I put the box on my bed and open the flap at the end, sliding the radio out. But before I can remove the clear plastic bag that's wrapped around the radio, there's a knock on my door.

"Mary Jane?" dad says, knocking again.

"One second, dad," I reply in a frenzy, scrambling to jam the radio and the box beneath my bed.

"Mary Jane – I need you to help me carry the train platform in from the garage," he says from the other side of the door.

"I'll be right out, dad. We'll meet you in the garage."

The platform is a white, four by eight, section of plastic paneling that dad bought from the lumberyard for the new train set. In the garage he drilled a series of holes so he could mount the railroad track before bringing it into the study – mom didn't want him making a mess of it in the house.

With dad on one side and me on the other, we turn the panel sideways and carry it up the steps from the garage, through the laundry room and into the kitchen. Emily opens and closes doors as we move from one room to the next.

"Can we put it down for a minute, dad?"

I need to rest a minute because my arms are tired.

"Sure, princess. We can probably slide it along the floor anyway from this point."

To make the turn from the kitchen into the hallway that leads to the study, dad has to bend the paneling a bit. But then it's home free as we push the platform along the carpet and into the study.

"Hold it a minute right here," dad says, letting go and arranging the four plastic horses that will support the platform. "OK," he says. "That's better."

We swing the platform up and over, setting it down on the horses so that it's about two feet above the floor.

"Why don't you and Emily bring the train set in from the garage, Mary Jane," says dad as he begins to screw the platform to the horses.

When we get back from the garage, mom is removing her coat and hat. "I don't know, Tom," she says, "maybe we should try it in the living room like you said, with the Christmas tree situated in the middle of it. I didn't realize that it would take up so much room. You can hardly get to your bookshelf the way it is now."

"It's too late now, Evelyn," dad says, removing the transformer and the wires from the box of trains. "I'd have to make a different set of supports because of the weight and the height of the tree. And with the tree already potted, watered and decorated, it would be difficult moving it around without tipping it or preventing the ornaments from falling."

"Yes, I suppose," mom says with a dose of disappointment. "But did you have to make the platform so large? – A smaller one would have done nicely."

Hanging her coat in the hall closet, she goes toward the kitchen, picking up the bag of chocolate morsels from the couch on her way.

The locomotive is black and silver and is supposed to make smoke after the engine heats up and you put these special drops from a plastic tube down its smokestack. I know because I read it on the side of the box. On each side of the locomotive are three metal wheels that are linked together with a metal strip that's fastened to the center of each wheel with a metal peg – I guess that makes it so the wheels all run together at the same time. The wheels are ridged so that they fit snugly against the track, preventing the locomotive from tipping over when it cruises around a curve at high speed. There are two sets of smaller wheels – one at the front of the engine and one at the back – and they swing back and forth like a hinge, allowing it to turn because the engine is so long that it would not be able to otherwise. To turn, that is. At first, I try setting the engine down on a piece of curved track but it's just impossible to line up all the wheels. So I move it to a straight section and it's much easier, locking the big wheels into the track and then looping my finger around each set of smaller wheels to bring them in line.

"Did you get it, Mary Jane?" dad asks.

He was watching me as I figured it out.

"I think I got it, dad."

"Then let's give it a try before we hook all the other cars up, OK?"

Dad flicks the switch on the transformer and then slowly swings the plastic thumb of the speed control upward. The single headlight of the locomotive comes on, but dimly at first. At the same time, a light at the back of the engine begins to glow through a piece of translucent red plastic. It looks like the fire of a coal stove. And then it's the sound of the wheels as they grab the track and propel the engine forward.

"I guess I wired it up all right," dad says, cranking the engine up faster.

Smiling, I clap my hands. "Good job, dad."

Emily removes the coal tender from the box and I help her connect it to the engine. Aside from its sets of metal wheels at each end, it has a much larger plastic wheel in the very center of the car. While half of the wheel is embedded in the car itself, the other half curves down to meet the center strip of the railroad track. I don't really know what it's for because it's hollow and, when you shake it, it sounds like there's pebbles or granules of something inside.

Next, it's a blue boxcar, followed by a green ... a green ...

"A gondola," dad says, after I ask him.

The red flatcar has a black fence that you snap into holes around the edge. It prevents the plastic pipes and girders, the stacks of plastic panels, the barrels and crates from falling off when the train moves.

"What kind of stuff do you think's inside this one?" Emily asks, pulling the tanker car from the cardboard flaps that secure it in the box.

"It's white so maybe it carries milk from farmlands to the place where they pour it into plastic containers."

"Maybe," Emily says. "But I always thought that milk came out of cows already in the container."

Dad chuckles at Emily's little joke.

The last car is the caboose. It's black and silver like the locomotive.

"How come you didn't wait for us?" Todd says behind me.

Dad snaps his head around as the twins rush into the study, followed by mom.

"Because you were in your room being punished," I reply, hooking up the caboose with the rest of the train.

"It's Christmas, Tom," mom says, knowing that dad isn't happy that she let the twins out of their cage before their time was up. "I didn't want them to miss out on all the fun."

"Make it run, daddy!" Roger exclaims.

It's too late, of course, for dad to say or to do anything about the twins.

"Here, Mary Jane – you take the controls," dad says, waving me over. "This controls the direction of the train," he says, pointing at the red switch. "Up for forward and down for reverse. But you always want to stop the train before you change it's direction."

"What's this button?"

"Go ahead and push it."

Except for dad, I guess everybody's startled when the horn goes off really loud because I pushed the button down so hard.

"Make the train go, Janey!" Roger says.

"Make the horn sound!" says Todd.

Swinging the speed control upward, the train starts. Instead of punching the horn button the way I did before, I pump it with my finger so that it sounds like a real train. As the coal tender moves behind the locomotive, I discover the purpose of its plastic wheel: the granules that slide around inside go "shooooo, shooooo, shoooo, shooo, shoo", imitating the sound of a real steam engine as it picks up speed.

"Look!" Todd says to Roger, pointing toward the back of the locomotive. "There's a fire inside that's burning coal!"

"Make it go faster, Janey!" Todd says.

"Yeah! Make it go as fast as it can!" Roger chimes in.

I push the lever up to the halfway point.

"It's adorable, Tom," mom says. "But the platform looks so bare. Didn't it come with anything else? Toy houses? Buildings? A little farm would be nice – something to make it look more real."

It's like a light switch goes off in my head.

"I've got an idea! Come on, Emily – You can help me."

Dashing to my room, I open the closet door and pull my coat from the hanger.

"Where we goin'?" Emily says, swinging her arms into her coat.

"You'll see."

When we return home with the boxes about twenty minutes later, dad is surprised to see Otis Wright with us.

"I didn't want the girls to carry the boxes all the way home," Otis explains, dropping one on the couch. "So we loaded them up in the pickup."

"Boxes of what, Otis?"

"These are the models that Mr. Wright made, dad," I say, pulling one out. "Aren't they beautiful?"

"Let me see!" Roger says, leaving Todd to clean up the carnage – an army of toy soldiers, a zooful of exotic animals, troop and tribe of cowboys and Indians who all met their Maker in the path of the locomotive when Emily and I were at Mr. Wright's.

"Geez," dad says, holding the model of a painted red barn as Emily pulls out a stained church. "These are made really, really well, Otis."

"Willy made 'em," Otis says. "They were laying around in the workshop, collecting dust, so you might as well make good use of them, Tom."

"That's real neighborly of you, Otis. I really appreciate it."

After removing the remaining bodies and carcasses from the platform – 'May they all rest in peace' – we start laying out the streets and neighborhoods that will make up our town. Most of the houses and buildings are either painted red or stained a sort of dark charcoal color. But that's OK because they're all so finely made.

"What's this?" mom says, coming in from the kitchen with a platter of cookies.

The unmistakable smell of tollhouse weaves into the room.

" 'Houses and farms'?" dad says. "Why, it's just what you ordered, Evelyn. Mary Jane thought of it and Otis was kind enough to accommodate."

"Oh, how nice of you, Otis. And they're sooooo cute!"

"Look, mommy!" Roger says, pointing to a red house that he's set on the platform. "Look inside the window!"

"What, honey?" she says, leaning down to peek inside. "I don't see anything."

"It's Mary Jane," says Roger. "She's goin' pee-pee on the potty."

Everyone laughs except me. I don't think it's very funny at all.

After at least a half dozen cookies and two tall glasses of milk, Mr. Wright gets up from the couch to leave.

"Now Otis," mom says, handing him a plate of cookies that's covered with plastic wrap, "please be careful not to get too many crumbs on the seat of your truck. OK? And do be sure that at least a couple of cookies make it as far as Willy's mouth."

"I can't make any promises, Evelyn, but I'll do what I can."

I sit on the stuffed chair by the platform, watching the twins play with the train and the wooden cars that Willy made. Emily's gone home for supper and mom's switched from cookie making to decorating mode, stringing plastic garland and clusters of holly around the pictures and candles on the mantel. Dad's departed for the garage, gathering his tools, determined to drill holes beneath each of the buildings on the platform so he can bring light, like an unseemly god, to the tiny town, dubbed "Mini-Christmasville".

"I want this one over here," Roger says to Todd as he switches places, a red rancher and a charcoal supermarket.

"I want the gas station over here," Todd responds, exchanging it with a crimson colonial.

"If you do that," says Roger, grabbing the stained church, "then"...

I sit on the chair, watching the twins move buildings across the platform – a painted red one, a darkly stained one; a red one, a black one ...

A game of checkers! A game of checkers, just like the one that's played year after year in the town of Christmasville! – Houses and buildings switched from one place to another, all according to the new "plan" of things'...

It strikes me all of a sudden, the notion spreading like 'the blight' throughout my arms and legs, sinking like a stone to the pit of my stomach. My mouth is dry. I feel hot all over, a patch of cold sweat bubbling up on my forehead near my hairline ...

' *"Chestnut brown"*,' someone once said, referring to the color of my hair. I think it was old Mr. Phelps who said it.

I've never fainted before but the sensation begins to blossom – a dark rose unfolding itself inside me. It makes me feel weak and limp and wobbly as the room around me, the twins in front of me, the platform across from me kind of floats and flutters as if the reality of my surroundings are slipping away, evaporating, becoming a wisp of smoke that drifts up into the dry air ... or a memory – a memory that isn't remembered any more ...

Roger lifts the red house that he made a joke about. "Whoops! There goes Janey – she's fallen off the potty again!"

Todd giggles. Roger laughs.

I feel like I really am falling, sinking into a dark, bottomless hole.

Are there whole worlds that are bigger than us? Smaller than us? If I look very carefully inside the red house in Roger's hands, will I discover a dad and mom, another set of twins, a fourteen year old girl as "emotionally challenged" as myself? Will I see another train platform? – A "Mini-Mini-Christmasville" with tiny houses and buildings, streets and cars, another game of checkers?'...

' *"How big is an angel?"* ' Todd asked mom once as we were leaving church.

' *"Some are so big that all of Christmasville could fit in the palm of a single angel's hand,"* she said. *"But others – why, they're so small that a thousand angels could dance on the head of a pin."* '

I look at the twins, at the shuffling of things as they move them across the platform.

'Christmasville – our Christmasville – maybe it sits on a four by eight section of plastic paneling ...'

The house slips from Roger's hands, falling to the platform.

"Roger!" mom shouts angrily. "What have you done now?"

The sharpness of her voice punctures the strange bubble that's enveloped me.

"It's OK," Roger replies. "It didn't break."

"Well, stop moving everything around, for crying out loud. Do you want me to get your father again?"

I look toward mom as she finishes decorating the mantle over the fireplace. Plastic garland and clusters of holly, red berries and green candles in brass sconces, sprigs of greenery with leaves like the webbed feet ...

"What's that?" I ask, focusing on the familiar leaves.

"What's what?" mom says.

"The leaves in front of the candlesticks?" I ask, pointing towards them.

I get up from the couch and approach the mantel for a closer look.

"Oh," mom says, "I used a couple of the smaller branches from your maple tree for highlights. They make a nice contrast to the darker leaves of the holly and garland, don't you think?"

"You cut branches from my maple tree? – You shouldn't have done that!" I say, raising my voice.

"I don't think I like your tone of voice, young lady."

"You shouldn't have cut the branches! You shouldn't have cut the branches without asking me first!"

"That's enough, Mary Jane!" she says, turning her back to me and arranging the sprigs of maple. "It's a tree, isn't it? – Before you know it, it'll have more leaves than you'll know what to do with."

Ignoring her, I reach around her, trying to remove the sprigs from the mantel.

"You just leave them alone, Mary Jane!" she says, smacking me on the back of the hand. "How can you be so selfish?"

"Selfish!" I shout, becoming really angry. "Selfish!" I repeat.

"Yes – selfish!" she replies, turning about and putting her hands on her hips. "And since we're discussing the topic, I don't think you've been setting a very good example for the twins – you could learn to share your things much better than you have been lately."

"Sharing? – It's not about sharing!"

"It most certainly is!" she says, raising her voice. "Who do you think you are anyway – setting up your very own Christmas tree in your room? – Like you really are a little 'princess' or something. I suppose you were going to charge Roger and Todd just for the luxury of going into your room to see it."

"What Christmas tree?" Roger says.

Up to that point, the twins have been silent and standing absolutely still. Although Roger and Todd are accustomed to the harsh tones of reprimand, they're inexperienced when it's directed at someone other than themselves. They seem almost embarrassed by the imposition.

"It's not about sharing! It's not about your precious brats!" I shout. "It's all about you and you're trying to kill my maple tree!"

She's furious now because her eyes are bulging and her face is as red as the berries on the mantel behind her.

"Go to your room this instant!" she shouts.

"What's going on in here?" dad says, coming into the study with his toolbox and electric drill. "I could hear the shouting all the way out in the garage."

"It's Mary Jane!" mom says to dad. "She's been disrespectful, selfish and ... and challenging – the way she talks to her mother! Honestly, Tom, I don't know what we're going to do with her."

"Stay away from my maple tree, mom!" I shout at her, turning to head for my room.

"Don't you dare talk to your mother like that, young lady!" she says, starting after me.

"Evelyn!" dad shouts.

When I go into my room, I slam the door behind me and lock it. There's a brief silence at first but then I can hear dad raising his voice like he does when he's irritated by the twins. Only I don't think it's Roger and Todd that he's aggravated with.

From the top drawer of my desk, I take out the Christmas tag that I had made up for the rose. "To dad and mom – love, Mary Jane," it says. I rip it in half and toss it into the wastepaper basket. On the new tag, I eliminate mom because she would probably rip the roses from their stems, sticking them in places that they don't belong. I'll only give her the woolen hat and the scarf that I made in home economics because she can't kill those.

The door to the garage slams shut and I feel like crying but I don't.

There's a knock on my door.

"Janey?" says Roger from the other side.

"What do you want?"

"Janey, can we see your Christmas tree?"

"Go away," I reply. "You can see it later."

I look at my damaged maple tree and I feel like crying again but I don't.

Sticking out from the bottom of my bed, I see the corner of the pink box. I lean down and lift it up to my bed. Pulling the flap down, I slide the radio out and remove it from the plastic bag. The radio is black and shiny and has two chrome knobs. The first one turns it on and off and controls the volume. The second one spins the little pointer across the numbers, which correspond to different radio stations. It's kind of silly though because, in Christmasville, there's only one radio station – WHYY of Christmasville. You can't get St. Valentine's or Easterville because of all the mountains.

Setting the radio on top of my desk, I unplug my reading lamp – it's either that or the plug to the Christmas lights that I have draped throughout the branches of my maple tree.

With the plug to the radio in place, I turn the first knob, but keep the volume down as low as possible. Because it's a Christmas present, I don't want anyone else to hear it. The antenna, which is on top of the radio, snaps away from the plastic clip. It telescopes outward and swivels around so you can adjust it for the best reception.

There's a lot of static and sputtering, a sort of humming sound, voices and music that overlap each another, compete with each another. I play around with the antenna for a minute or so and then decide to try the second knob, slowly turning it back and forth.

"... *Rockin' around ... Christmas tree, what ... happy holi...*"

It's a catchy holiday tune, but it's difficult to home in on.

"*... Double your pleasure ... double ... chewing gum ...*"

It must be a commercial now.

"*... A unilateral concern ... throughout ... world ... what's being called, 'sputnik' ...*"

It must be the news but ... What the heck's a 'sputnik' anyway?

"*...ingle bell, jingle bell, jingle ... rock ...*"

"Damn it," I say to myself, losing my patience because of the poor reception.

I can't imagine why it's so difficult to zoom in on Station **WHYY** of Christmasville. Why is there so much static when the radio station is only a couple of blocks away? It's not like there's a storm or something. And why do they keep switching between songs and commercials and the news?

I turn the volume up a bit and move the metal rod of the antenna.

"*... It's Christmas time in ... city ...*"

I reach for the other knob, turning it ever so slowly.

"*... Brisk and cold ... snow flurries ... as Jacqueline ... children ...*"

"There! – That's better," I say, listening to the radio announcer, his voice becoming clearer, with less interference.

"*...resident Elect, John F. Kenn ... arrived in New York City today ... while gathered along Fifth Ave ...*"

'New York City???'

My mouth drops open in astonishment. I can't believe what I'm hearing.

'New York City???'

I picture the menu in the diner, the items listed in the menu – '*New York cheesecake*' and '*Boston cream pie*' and '*Philadelphia cream cheese*' – I say to myself, the names of the items, becoming larger and bolder, as if they were names ... the names of places that you might find across the pages of an unfamiliar map.

The Eve of St. Nick

Every year, the Department of Public Works erects a raised platform where public officials would take their turns in front of the podium on Christmas Eve, offering speeches that were about as meaningful as the scraps of paper that they were written on, once the speeches were over.

"Nothing's for free," dad says to mom. "It's one of the prices that you have to pay if you want to see the parade."

I haven't spoken to mom since she wounded my maple tree two days ago.

This year the platform is located directly across from the police station, in the middle of the long promenade that runs from one end of Maple Street to the other. The platform's wider than years' past, but not as deep because otherwise the back end of it would be dangerously close to the steep edge of Jenkins' Hill.

And wouldn't that be funny! – If the supports beneath the platform suddenly collapsed, turning it into a giant toboggan that's sliding and bouncing its way down the slope, the city officials bobbing about, holding on for dear life.

But no – I suppose not.

On the right side of the platform, standing on a three-tiered grandstand, is the school chorus. Dressed in flowing red and white robes, members of the chorus carefully watch the beautiful, bachelorette biology teacher, Miss Perkins, who leads the ensemble in Christmas songs. It's a bit awkward though with the band, which is directed by Principal Marshfield, situated on plastic chairs on the left-hand side of the platform. Because of all the commotion, on and around the platform, Mr. Marshfield and Miss Perkins have to communicate with sign language before the start of each song. But that, too, sometimes gets lost in translation as public officials – eager to shake hands or to kiss the cheeks of babies in front of the platform before they deliver their speeches – interrupt the line-of-view between band director and choral leader. Sometimes the chorus begins singing before the band is ready to play, or vice-versa. Sometimes both band and chorus start at the same time but, after a moment, realize that what's being played isn't the same thing as what's being sung. Then they have to stop, as Mr. Marshfield and Miss Perkins desperately try to re-establish a line of communication, before they can start again.

Standing at the curb in front of the Five & Dime, dad and mom exchange holiday greetings with passing friends and neighbors as they listen to the musical fiasco, waiting for the speeches to begin. Emily and I are behind them, looking at the animated display in the window.

A fat Santa Claus swings his head up and down as he ponders the names on the list in front of him. When his head is up, he's deciding who's naughty or nice. When his head is down, his right hand moves across the list as if he's recording his decision. Beside him,

Mrs. Claus – with rosy cheeks and wire-rimmed glasses – slowly raises then lowers a cup of cocoa from her mouth. Between 'mouthfuls', she moves her head to the side as an elf, with oversized hat and slippers, leans down to whisper something into her ear.

"Uh-oh, Emily."

"What?" she says, turning away from the window and looking at me.

"Did you see what Santa wrote by your name?"

She spins her head back, squinting her eyes as she tries to read the script.

I help her out. "It says: 'Emily Thompson – black coal for losing her father's hammer in the snow'."

"No, it doesn't," she replies with a droll face. "If it says anything at all, it says: 'Emily's been a good girl. But Mary Jane? – She tells fibs'!"

At the conclusion of the pitiful performance by band and chorus, Mayor Thompson dispatches them to the parking lot of the bank and diner at the far end of Maple Street so they can take up their positions in the parade. They really don't perform that poorly – in fact, the band is pretty good and the chorus has several people in it with voices that sound like a cross between opera singers and ... well, maybe not angels. Anyway, it's just the circumstances of their surroundings that made them sound so pitiful.

"Friends and neighbors," Mayor Thompson starts.

The microphone screeches.

"Friends and neighbors," he repeats.

It screeches again – only louder this time – prompting the commissioner of public works to get up from his chair behind the mayor and to inspect the equipment.

Looking into the audience, the mayor shrugs his shoulders, offering his broad, toothy smile as a consolation for the technical difficulty.

"Try it now, Fred," the commissioner advises the mayor.

"Testing – one, two, three, four," the mayor says into the microphone.

No screeching, but then ...

"And it's one, two, three, four," the mayor sort of sings as he dances a little two-step.

"What 'cha all waitin' for?"

"Why don't 'cha just ask for more?"

He kicks his legs up into the air, spins, leans into the microphone again.

"And maybe I'll sing a song or two –

"Do a little dance for you."

I guess – in a sad, pathetic sort of way – the mayor's attempting to bring a little levity into the incident with the microphone. And now that I think about it, I remember Emily telling me that her father had always wanted to be an entertainer on the radio, singing songs and telling jokes.

'The radio', I think for a moment, remembering the strange broadcast that I had heard in my room. *'Who is John F. Kenn, anyway? And where in the world is New York City?'*

Beside me, Emily's cringing, her face contorted like she has to go the bathroom or something.

"Daddy drank an awful lot of eggnog this afternoon," she says dryly.

As the commissioner returns to his seat, a couple of people in the crowd applaud. The mayor tips his top hat in appreciation, though I suspect that the applause is really meant for the commissioner of public works who fixed the problem with the microphone. It was either that or for the mayor's wise decision to end his song-and-dance routine and to move on with the speeches.

"Friends and neighbors, colleagues and co-workers, faithful members of my constituency ..."

He always uses that word – 'constit ... constit-u-en-cy' – and I'm never a hundred percent sure of what he means by it. Maybe Mayor Thompson read it in a book somewhere and he doesn't know what it means either. It just sounds good when he says it.

"As First Citizen of the Town of Christmasville, it is my esteemed honor and privilege to accept the duties and responsibilities that you have once again bestowed upon your mayor. It is with great pleasure and dignity, but with a profound sense of humility, that, as Grand Marshall of the Annual Christmasville Parade ..."

Throughout Mayor Thompson's speech, there are brief eruptions of applause from the same pockets of people in the large crowd that's gathered along street and sidewalk.

'The constit-u-en-cy,' I think.

When all the speeches are over and done with, the mayor gives the signal for the start of the parade. Beyond the platform – on the tower of city hall – the clock reads five fifty-four, which sets a new record: the start of the parade is nearly an hour late this year.

The band, waiting in the bank parking lot for their turn to march, begins playing "Jingle Bells". At the same time, the first float, which is sponsored by the Greater Christmasville Chamber of Commerce, starts down Maple Street. It makes me stop and think: 'I wonder why we never see the Lesser Christmasville Chamber of Commerce. And if we did, would they all be pixies and elves? But if they were, wouldn't everyone in the *Greater* one be giants?'

For a moment, the notion of *'Greater'* and *'Lesser'* makes me think about the twins as they moved houses and buildings around on the train platform.

'Are there whole worlds that are bigger than us? Smaller than us?'

' *"Whoops! – There goes Janey again!"* said Roger.'

But I can't think about this stuff right now. I don't want to think about it because it's Christmas Eve, the very best night of the year.

The first float is always the same. Santa Claus, surrounded by his elves, waves to the spectators, shouts "Ho! Ho! Ho!" and tosses candy canes to the kids who are following along. I can see the twins, who have been off with their friends, scramble toward the float, gathering up as many candy canes as hands and pockets will hold. Such little piglets!

When the float arrives in front of the platform, it stops. The mayor waits until the band finishes its rendition of "Jingle Bells" and then gets up from his seat.

"Welcome to Christmasville – jolly, old St. Nick!" the mayor says.

Santa Claus gets up from his chair and bows. His nose is as big as Mr. Atkinson's, as red as one of Mr. Wrights's tomatoes.

A single band member plays a drum roll as an elf from the float jumps down and scampers toward the platform.

"On behalf of all citizens of Christmasville," the mayor announces at the end of the drum roll, "it is my special honor to present you, St. Nick, with the key to our fair city. May you find us all worthy and be well-rewarded in the dispensation of your generous gifts and goodly favors."

Holding the huge, plastic "key to the city" up over his head, the mayor turns right, then left, before passing it to the elf. Running back the same way he came, you can hear the bells on his slippers and hat jingle as he returns to the float, presenting the key to Santa Claus.

"Ho! Ho! Ho!" says Santa Claus, holding it, like the mayor had, high above his head. "Shank you all show very much," he says, swaying a bit to the right and then to the left. "Ho! Ho! Ho!"

I turn toward Emily. "I think Shanta Claush had shum of the shame eggnog ash your daddy did."

Spectators applaud. The band starts playing, "Rudolph, the Red Nosed Reindeer". The float begins moving again, causing Santa to fall backwards into the ample embrace of his chair.

It's the two fire engines next. With sirens blaring every few minutes or so, the bright red and silver trucks are decorated with garland and strings of light that make the chrome and steel gleam and sparkle. On top of the first truck, the fire chief waves to the crowd as Tucker, with a red elf's hat tied to his head, barks until the chief gives him a treat.

For the hospital float, it's as if doctors and nurses are performing a serious operation. They're wearing their white smocks but have red furry boots and floppy hats with white pompons on them. You can't see who it is on the operating table because the patient is covered with a white sheet that has a hole in it – that's where two of the doctors are doing the surgery.

"Sponge," the one doctor calls out.

A nurse passes him the sponge.

"Forceps," shouts the other doctor.

Another nurse passes him the forceps.

"Nose," cries the first doctor.

The nurse looks horrified.

"Nose???" she shrieks, holding her hands up to her face in a panic.

Suddenly all of the doctors and nurses scramble across the float, looking for the lost nose.

"Ah-ha!" says the nurse, pulling a red something or other out of a plastic barrel that's labeled, "Sour Pickles".

Running as fast as she can, she hands the "nose" to the doctor, who carefully inserts it into the hole in the sheet. They all step back from the patient. Nothing happens. They look at each other with silly, stupid, dumb expressions on their faces before the first doctor scratches his head and then taps the patient with his hand. Nothing happens. The second doctor scratches his head, taps the patient with a bit more force than the first doctor had. Again, nothing happens. The two doctors look at each other and then, simultaneously, begin shaking the living daylights out of the patient, trying to wake him. And now there's movement beneath the sheet as the patient stretches before slowly rising up, the sheet slipping from his body.

It's two people in a costume of "Rudolph", of course. But, still, something is not quite right. It's not until the nurse – the one who had found Rudolph's nose in the pickle barrel – reaches up and gives the reindeer's red nose a firm twist, causing it to glow brightly, that the operation can be deemed successful.

Everyone laughs and applauds. The doctors and nurses and "Rudolph" bow to the crowd before scrambling back to their original positions so they can perform the same operation all over again.

The next float, sponsored by the Department of Education, is no big deal. A couple of teachers – Mrs. Kelly and Mrs. Franklin – sit at desks, reading Christmas books. Behind them, leaning against a bookshelf, are three giant books: *The North Pole Adventures, An Elf's Tale* and *The Legend of Kris Kringle – An Unauthorized Autobiography.* The books are about seven feet high and four feet wide. On top of them is a sign that says: "Read! – It's Larger Than Life!"

It's the kind of float that's supposed to make you stop and think for a minute about the wisdom of the message. It's supposed to make you arrive at the same conclusion, causing you say to yourself: "By golly, I should 'Read!' because it's ... it's ... why 'It's Larger Than Life!' "

I don't know – I think teachers could be a little more creative than that.

The float for the First Bank of Christmasville is a big, moving advertisement that Joe Matthieson tows behind his pickup truck. Some of the placards read: "THE BANK THAT SANTA BANKS ON" and, "Interested in earning higher interest?" and, "The Christmas Club at the Bank of Christmasville – Preferred by Elves Everywhere!" Near the front of the float, Mr. Jenkins, the bank president, speaks with a thin, sickly-looking Santa Claus about ... I guess it's about taking out a loan for a new sleigh because Mr. Jenkins keeps showing Santa drawings of different models. Maybe Mr. Jenkins should show him pictures of fudge brownies and lemon meringue pie so he might think about eating stuff that would fatten him up like a real Santa Claus. Behind them, about a dozen elves wait their turn at the bank teller's window, exchanging wads of fake money for Christmas Club deposit books that are green and red and so big that the elves have difficulty maneuvering them across the float.

It's pretty disgusting if you ask me – and presumptuous – because how do they know what bank Santa "banks on"? And how do they know that it's the bank "preferred by elves everywhere"? I think Santa and his elves should talk to a lawyer and give the bank a nice lawsuit for Christmas, taking every dime in its vault.

Emily tugs on my coat sleeve.

"I'm thirsty," she says.

"Emily, you're always thirsty – thirsty or hungry."

"I know," she whines. "But I want an ice cream soda."

"We'll miss the parade."

"No we won't," she says, moving toward Link's Pharmacy next to the Five & Dime. "It'll just take a minute."

Luckily, there's no one at the fountain service so Emily doesn't have to wait. "I'll have a large black cow," she says to Amy, the waitress.

"I'll have one, too," I say on impulse, "but a small one."

The combination of chocolate ice cream and root beer soda cannot be resisted.

Through the display window of the pharmacy, I can see the float for the post office passing by. At the front of the float, Wally, the postman, pulls snowballs from a plastic barrel ands hands them to Frosty the Snowman. He spins his arm around a half dozen times, winds up and then launches the snowball toward the bank float, which is moving down the street in front of him.

Smack! – The snowball smashes into the back wall of the float, its remnants sliding down and dropping to the street.

On top of the post office float, it says: "From Ice Boxes to Snowballs, We Always Deliver – On Time and Every Time!"

"Hello Mary Jane."

He's seated at a booth, behind the comic books rack.

"Oh – Hello ... Hello, Mr. Gabriel," I reply. "I didn't see you back there."

Sitting opposite him, with his back toward me, is another man.

"You're staying out of blizzards, I hope," says Mr. Gabriel.

"Yes, I am – and thank you so much for driving me home that night."

"And midnight trains to grandma's house?" says the other man. "Are we staying away from those as well?"

I don't know what to say as the other man turns around in the booth and faces me. It's Mr. Bachmann, the stationmaster.

"Yes," I reply, finding my tongue. "Those too."

Emily follows me as I quickly exit the pharmacy.

In the parade, the two cars that make up the Police Department are moving down the street. With sirens wailing, they inch forward, one behind the other.

"What was that all about?" Emily asks.

My heart is still fluttering because ... because I didn't expect to run into Mr. Bachmann like that. I hadn't seen him since last ... since Emily and I had trudged in the snow and darkness to the Union Train Station.

"What? What did you say?" It's difficult hearing Emily over the sirens.

"Mr. Gabriel and Mr. Bachmann? – What did they say to you?"

"Nothing," I reply, trying to calm myself down. "It doesn't make any difference."

But it does because ...

'How did he know? How did Mr. Bachmann remember what no one but me remembers? Was it he and Mr. Lionel who had carried Emily and I back to our homes, to our beds, before the night of the 31st rolled over in its sleep? Was it the stationmaster and the train conductor who had taken our tickets, exchanging them for our money? And what else do they know? What else do they remember about Christmasville's past?'

"What are we going to do this year?" Emily asks, a smear of chocolate ice cream on her chin.

"What do you mean?" I reply, wiping her face with my paper napkin.

"What are we going to do when it's January 31st?"

"I don't know, Emily. I really don't know."

And that's the God-honest truth – I really don't know what I'm going to do this year.

Behind the police cruisers, the chorus flows down the street in rank and file, their robes swaying as they walk. Miss Perkins, in response to the band's rendition of "Deck the Halls," removes her robe, exposing a radiant blue and red uniform, with silver spangles quivering all around it. It's pretty skimpy actually, revealing the full length of her legs, her shoulders and arms. Running off toward the street curb, she exchanges her robe for a baton and a majorette hat. And now she's prancing down the street, twirling her baton or tossing it high up into the air and catching it – just as surely as she's caught the undivided attention of just about everyone watching the parade.

But I suspect that the interest of the crowd is split right down the middle because half the population is smiling broadly and applauding loudly while the other half – the female half – expresses itself in faces that range from mild annoyance to downright outrage.

"Look over there," I say to Emily, pointing.

Standing across the street, near the base of the platform with the city officials on it, are Mrs. Marshfield and Mrs. Sperry. Dressed in their fancy, fake fur coats and matching hats, their mouths move without stopping, their faces – twisted into searing scowls.

You would not think that any float, sponsored by the public library, would stimulate such a humorous impact as the one moving down Maple Street now. At first sight, it looks simple enough and boring enough with the two librarians seated at the front of the float, with reading tables and bookshelves behind them. There isn't any comedy or cleverness in the tinsel and the strings of light and the usual decorations that, year after year, adorn the same float, with very minor changes ever affecting it. But nonetheless, everyone laughs as the float passes in front of them, the two librarians looking across at each other, slightly embarrassed, reddish, non-plussed, which adds to the amusement because neither one of them ever thinks to look at the sign, in big baby-block letters, on top of the bookshelves behind them. Somehow the first "L" block in "PUBLIC LIBRARY" had fallen off the back of the float and was being pushed by the truck pulling "The Christmasville Courier" behind it until …

"Uh-oh. There it goes," I note, watching the "L" block suddenly get stuck beneath the tire, the weight of the truck flattening it.

"Read all about it! Read all about it! – Santa Claus is coming to town!"

Two newspaper delivery boys stand on each side of the float, swinging the papers above their heads as they shout the headlines from the special evening edition of *The Courier*. One of the boys is Tommy Burks.

Without even thinking about it, I cup my hands around my mouth and shout: "Read all about it! Read all about it! – Tommy Burks is going to hell!"

Everyone around me turns to look. I think for sure that mom and dad are going to come over and say something. But mom turns back to watch the parade while dad shakes his head, as if he can't believe what I shouted, before he, too, swings around the other way.

Emily takes a couple of steps away as if she doesn't know me.

"You shouldn't of said that," she says after a moment.

"Why not?" I reply. "Tommy Burks is a jerk."

"Because," she says, cupping her left hand so she can point in secret with her right.

Nearby is Father Conover – and, what's worse, he's talking with Doctor Sperry, the school psychiatrist.

It's my turn to cringe now. 'They'll be prices to pay for that little outburst', I think to myself, wondering which one will be the most expensive – dad and mom's? Father Conover's? Or Doctor Sperry's?'

It's the float for Clauson's Department Store next. Because it's the largest store in town, I suppose, it always has one of the biggest floats. But it's kind of stupid because all they did was to take a bunch of stuff that you would see in the department store anyway and plop it on the platform that makes up the float. They added some lights and decorations, put up a fake, plastic Christmas tree in the center, which you could barely see anyway because of all the stuff around it. At mock counters throughout the float, employees of the department store act like cheerful salespeople and gleeful customers. The sign at the front of the float reads: "At Clauson's, the Best Customer is a Happy Customer". Another, raised up at the back of it, says, "Merry Christmas to All, and to All a Good Bargain! – Sale Starts at Clauson's on December 26th!"

I bet the Clauson clan is a pack of pickled pagans.

Girl Scouts, Boy Scouts, the Christmasville School Cheerleaders, led by their captain and paragon of spoiled brats, Lisa Jenkins, march down the street, behind the department store.

"She wears too much make-up," Emily comments.

"It's so she can cover up all her pimples," I add.

When the float for Jack's Toy Store appears, all the kids clap and cheer, running round and round the float. It's because Mr. Rausch – "Jack" – and Mrs. Rausch, dressed in their everyday clothes, reach into huge red sacks in front of them to grab clear plastic bags that are filled with tiny toys and little games, rubber balls and pretty plastic barrettes, and loads of penny candy, tossing them to the kids on the street. Because there are "boy bags" and "girl bags", they take extra care to make sure that each one lands in the right set of hands.

The theme for "Jack's" float is really different. It's not green and red and brightly lit. It doesn't have a single decoration. It's made up of two scenes in which the Robinson family – Mr. and Mrs. and all nine children – have volunteered their services to act out different parts, like in a play. In one scene, Mrs. Robinson hands out soup and slices of bread to the hungry, who are really her six daughters. In another, Mr. Robinson passes clothes to the needy, which is the part played by his three sons.

At the top of the float, the sign doesn't say "Jack's Toy Store" or advertise sales or make claims about Santa Claus and his elves that just aren't true. It only says a single word: "GIVE".

There are some people who don't want Jack's Toy Store in the parade at all. I've heard them say things like, "It's depressing" or, "It doesn't contribute to the joy of the season". But then, what do they know anyway? And besides, if they did force the Toy Store out of the parade, how would they handle the rebellion by just about every kid in Christmasville, deprived of the precious loot that the Rausch's always handed out?

As chance would have it, the twins appear with their bags.

"Didn't you get your goodies, Janey?" Todd says in a snide way, dangling his plastic bag in front of my face.

Roger laughs, pulling out a stick of red licorice from his bag and stuffing it into his mouth.

"Before you sleep tonight," I reply to Todd in dead seriousness, snapping my finger and thumb together, "the terrible spider will strike again."

His eyes widen. "Mommy," Todd says, moving toward her. "Janey's scaring me again."

"Come on, Emily. Let's go someplace else."

We move up the street a bit to the police station. Climbing the steps, we do a one-eighty onto the platforms – one on each side of the steps – that jut back toward the street and that support the two lampposts in front of the station. With Emily on one side and myself on the other, we can see much better over the heads of people on the sidewalk in front of us.

The float for the diner passes by. Doris Caterson and Clyde Bonner, alternate between waving to the spectators and warming themselves at the coal stove at the back of the "diner".

"They must get tired of waving all the time," Emily says, holding on to the lamppost on the other side of the steps.

"And of always smiling," I add. "When the parade's over, I bet they're faces are so sore that they don't smile for a week."

Next, it's the floats for Cauldwell's Supermarket, the Five & Dime, Link's Pharmacy and Luncheonette and Grubbs' Hardware Store. Then, it's the band, who have begun to play, "Silver Bells".

"There's Brett!" says Emily.

Swinging his head back and forth, his red cheeks swell like balloons as he sucks up air and blows it through his clarinet.

"Brett Tolliver!" Emily shouts, waving one arm while holding onto the lamppost with the other. "Brett! – Over Here!"

"Emily! – You'll mess him up."

Sure enough, Brett turns his head to the left, scanning the crowd. At the same time, Mr. Marshfield directs the band to slow up it's pace because, marching faster than the floats are moving in front of them, they've begun to bunch up against the back of the "Grubbs' Hardware" float. Distracted, Brett pulls the mouthpiece of his clarinet away from his mouth, zeroes in on Emily, who continues to shout and to wave her arm. I wave as well because ... well, I don't want to be rude.

Brett's foot catches the heel of the trombone player in front of him, who kind of arches backward for a second, but just long enough for Brett to walk smack into him.

"Didn't I tell you?" Emily says.

"Tell me what?" I ask.

"That Brett always gets clumsy and goofy whenever he sees you."

"Emily! – We messed him up. Anybody would've ..."

"I told you, Mary Jane," she insists. "Brett Tolliver has a crush on you."

Luckily, the only thing that fell was the hat of the trombone player in front of Brett. Scooping it up from the street, he sets it back on top of his head, swings the strap beneath his chin. As he hurries back into place, he gives Brett a nasty look as if to say, "Thanks a lot!"

The float for the Christmasville Inn looks warm and cozy as Mrs. Clark and her family snuggle up on couches and chairs that are arranged around a fireplace, the logs crackling and spitting live embers against the screen. For the "United Houses of Worship" float, Father Donnelly and Reverend Mitchell and Rabbi Reubens wave from the balcony of a makeshift steeple. Then it's the float for Aunt Sarah's Confectionery Shop, followed by the hospital ambulance, its sirens blaring like the fire trucks and the police cars that preceded it.

It's so piercing that I have to hold my ears until it passes.

From our elevated position in front of the police station, we can see the end of the parade as it approaches. There's the float for city hall, which is nothing more than a reproduction of the clock tower, except that the clock isn't real and doesn't work. Gathered around it, waving to the crowd and drinking stuff from plastic cups, are about twenty city employees. The whole point of the float is to give them – the employees, that is – the opportunity to be in the parade.

Next, it's the float for the Consolidated Factory Works of Christmasville. It's the biggest float in the parade and it's kind of interesting because there's all types of machines that are puffing smoke and shooting out jets of steam. It's like a factory on wheels and it's supposed to show you all the different processes that are involved in the production of plastic parts and plastic furniture, plastic panels and plastic buildings. It's one of those floats that are educational, but entertaining too.

Between the "Factory" float and the last float in the parade is a giant truck that's pulling a flatbed trailer behind it. On the flatbed is a colossal yellow crane and a huge bulldozer. They belong to the construction company that never finishes Beech Boulevard.

The last float is "Wright's Produce Stand". Except for the single sign that announces its sponsor, you'd never think that it had anything to do with fresh fruits and vegetables.

"What the heck is that?" Emily says, holding her mouth open long after she had spoken, studying the odd contraption that's moving down the street.

I guess a lot of people are thinking the same thing because they're all milling around, scratching their heads and talking to one another, trying to figure out what it is.

In his pickup truck, Willy tows the float behind. Perched at the front of it, Otis stands tall and firm, braced against the wind, the night, the onslaught of public conjecture. Wearing a long leather coat and boots that nearly come up to his knees, his arms are folded across his chest, making him look ... *defiant*. Yes, that's it – defiant – as if he were deliberately inviting the ridicule of the spectators. But the impression is kind of offset by the tight cap that encircles most of his head, it's chin straps dangling loose, and by the plastic goggles that are pulled down over his eyes. They make him look bug-eyed and funny.

"What 'cha got there, Otis?" a man in the crowd shouts. "Another one of those farflung inventions that don't work and never will?"

"It looks like a billboard that fell down!" somebody yells out. "I hate to tell you, Otis, but somebody already invented the billboard!"

Laughing and snickering, they scrutinize the large, wooden object behind him. It's the same contraption ... something like the contraption that I had seen in his workshop – that I had asked him about – "Is it a float for the parade?"

I guess Otis changed his mind – not only about using the contraption as a float – but about ... well, about what's it's supposed to be in the first place. And that's because it's entirely different now than when I had first seen it. Instead of looking like a long, narrow cage for something or other, there's a platform that's about as big as Willy's truck. Running along each side of the platform, but extending at least five or six feet beyond the ends of it, is a long tube. The tubes are about a foot and a half thick and look like they're completely wrapped in canvas. Giant timbers run crosswise along the bottom of the platform and are bolted to each tube at opposite ends of the timbers. And he's added a number of skis to it – a larger set of plastic skis that are attached with struts to the front of each tube, and a smaller set at the back.

"It's a skiboggan!" somebody suggests.

"A what?" asks another.

"A skiboggan – that's what you use when you can't make up your mind if you're goin' down the hill on skis or a toboggan."

"Hey!" a third man laughs. "My wife might like one of those – she can't never make up her mind neither!"

As the parade spectators fill in the vacuum that's left behind by the "Produce" float, I see the sign that's attached to the back of it. Nobody else seems to notice it but me. It's the one that I had seen in his workshop: *"Frenchland or Bust!"*

I wonder what made Mr. Wright change his mind and put his strange contraption in the parade. But more importantly: I wonder what its real purpose is?

To announce the official conclusion of the Christmas parade, a flurry of fireworks and rockets are shot from the bank parking lot. Exploding in mid-air, the bursts shower light and grace and good cheer upon all in Chrismasville.

City officials disperse from the platform, joining their families. A blast of wind shoots down Maple Street, catching a few people off-guard as their hats spring from their heads, tumble in the snow before stopping. In the steeple of St. Mary's, the bells toll seven times.

Christmas Eve.

Christmas Eve in Christmasville.

What you always remember about the best night of the year are the different parts of it. It's like a Christmas present that's wrapped a dozen times, each layer of paper prettier than the one before it. And it's only after you've peeled all the layers away that you arrive at the present itself, which is Christmas morning. Or it's like a parade – a long, joyous parade of special moments – only with Santa Claus at the end of it, leaving you things that you wrote on your list and, sometimes, if you're lucky, things that you wanted but forgot to write down. But of all the things that you remember, the very best is the feeling you get on Christmas Eve when you snuggle into your bed, all warm and cozy. It's a feeling that spreads through your body like hot chicken soup after you're cold and hungry from sledding, or when you go to church on Christmas morning and everyone sings from their hymn books and you don't feel different any more. You feel ... you get that feeling of ... *togetherness* – like everyone in the whole world is your family because you belong, because you all belong together, and because – as tiny and small as you are – you're part of all the "plans" of Christmasville, year after year, just like everyone is, and that no matter what happens, you'll always be part of it.

But I don't know if I'll get that feeling this year because I haven't spoken to mom for two days.

"I'm tired," Emily says, sitting down and closing her eyes as she leans back against the lamppost. "I want to go home and go to bed so Santa can come to my house. Can you carry me home, Mary Jane?"

"I can pull you home, Emily – if you don't mind running over to my house and getting my sled."

"Very funny," she says, making a screwed-up face.

I jump from the platform down to the sidewalk, nearly falling over on my face.

"Come on, Emily. Let's go home."

When I turn around, I almost walk right into dad. He's by himself so I think maybe mom already started for home with the twins.

"I thought we might have a little talk, Mary Jane," dad says.

"I better find mommy and daddy," Emily says, sensing the serious topic of the 'little talk'.

She raises herself up on the platform, scampers down the steps. "Merry Christmas, Mr. Higgins! See ya tomorrow, Mary Jane!"

I know what the topic's about too. It's about Tommy Burks. Geez! – That Tommy Burks always gets me into trouble!

When we get home, dad and mom quickly complete the final preparations for our house party. The twins, fueled by all the candy canes and lumps of fudge and penny candies that they had jammed into their mouths at the parade, race through the house like wind-up toys. Dad and mom let them run, knowing that they'll fall asleep much sooner once all their energy is used up. Not that they'll have any trouble sleeping – they won't even argue about going to bed later – because Christmas Eve is the only night of the year when Roger and Todd can't wait to jump into their 'jammies, dive into bed and plunge into the dark void of their sleep.

From the kitchen mom brings out the last bowls of appetizers and dips, arranging them near the punch bowl on the dining room table.

"Oh, how lovely!" says Mrs. Mason, interrupting Mrs. Lister to compliment mom's handiwork.

"Your table looks just beautiful," adds Mrs. Lister, though anxious to continue her story about Mrs. Carson and the problem with her pet poodle, "Scruffy", who has a certain penchant for raising his leg and discharging on just about anything that remotely resembles a shoe.

Throughout the evening, mom's friends – mostly from the Sewing Club – will come and go, gathering in the dining room to visit, to chat, to nibble, to gossip, each according to her inclination.

Dad's retreated to the study with some of his friends from the lumberyard – the "menfolk", he calls them. They run the toy train, stoke the fire in the fireplace, pour "nips" of stuff from metal flasks into their glasses of punch.

"Miss Perkins," says one of the men as I pass the study toward the living room, "was in particular good form this evening."

Regardless of what dad says, the "menfolk" are far more relentless, more blunt, more insensitive than "womenfolk" in the offering of their peculiar brand of gossip. I know because I've heard both men and women in their separate camps, caught up in their different wildfires of gossiping, and, as far as I'm concerned, women can't hold a candle to men when it comes to roasting somebody alive.

In the living room, Debbie Lister is showing her cousin, Sally Horton, something that she wrote in her diary. But as soon as she sees me, she closes it up and locks it with the key that's on her necklace. It's real, top-secret stuff, I'm sure, like, "Today I finished my homework all by myself", or, "Today I read a *whole* book – It was called, *Santa's Big Coloring*

Book".

"Hello, Mary Jane," says Debbie. "Where's your little friend? What's her name? – Millie?"

They both start giggling. I guess it's because they find it funny that my best friend is nearly a year younger than me, and in the eighth grade rather than the ninth. She couldn't come to our house because the Thompson's always hold an open house for city officials on Christmas Eve. It's a tradition of theirs and has been ever since Emily's father became mayor, which ... well, for as long as I can remember – Mayor Thompson has always been mayor of Christmasville.

"What a pretty dress," I reply to Debbie. "I never realized that the Salvation Army had such pretty things to give away to the needy."

"It's not from the Salvation Army!" she snaps back. "My mom bought it for me from Clauson's and it was the most expensive dress in the whole store. Come on Sally," she says, turning to her cousin, "let's go get something to eat."

When they leave, I pull the curtain back from the living room window, looking for Mr. Wright's pickup truck. I don't want dad, or mom either, to see the rose when he delivers it. Coming up the front walk, I see someone carrying something in a large plastic bag that the supermarket uses for groceries. But it's only Mr. Cauldwell – mom's boss – and he's making his rounds like he always does on Christmas Eve, delivering turkeys and fruitcakes to his employees. I let him in, point him in the direction of the dining room and return to my station.

Across the street, Mr. and Mrs. Caterson exit their front door and start down the steps. They just make it because a little avalanche of snow slides from the roof and lands on the porch behind them. They both turn to look, glance at each other and continue down the sidewalk toward our house as if nothing happened. In her hands, Mrs. Caterson holds her mincemeat pie, which she always brings. It's one of those things that you either really like or you really don't. Personally, I prefer desserts with chocolate in them.

When they arrive, I open the door and let them in, pointing them in their respective directions: Mrs. Caterson to the dining room, Mr. Caterson to the study.

Billy Carson speeds by in his red Chevy. Mr. and Mrs. Tolliver arrive but Brett isn't with them.

"He says he's catching a cold," Mrs. Tolliver explains. "But he seems fine to me."

After the Tollivers, it's the MacGregors, who own the Christmas tree farm. As I let them in, Mr. Cauldwell leaves, moving on to his next delivery.

I look at the cuckoo clock on the wall over the radio. 'It's eight twenty-two. He couldn't have forgotten, could he?'

Roger and Todd run into the living room. They each have a toy car with a loop of ribbon attached to them.

"We made 'em for your Christmas tree, Janey," says Roger.

"Can we hang 'em on your tree?" Todd asks.

I'm surprised that they asked. Usually the little brats do what they want first and then ask if it was all right to do it later.

"What exactly are they?" I ask, stalling, I guess, because, even though one car is red and the other is green, they're really not the kinds of things that I want for decorations on my tree.

Todd rolls his eyes as if the whole notion of explaining what they are is totally ludicrous. "They're Christmas ornaments, Janey. Can't ya tell? Look – Mine has a sticker with Santa Claus on it. See?"

"And my car has Rudolph on it. Right here," he says, pointing. "So? – Can we hang 'em on your tree?"

"OK," I reply, giving in. "But only because you're so nice about it and asked first."

The two of them charge from the living room toward my bedroom at the end of the hall.

"Be careful with the branches!" I shout after them. "Don't break any of them."

When I turn back to the window, there he is – Mr. Wright – he's making his way up the walk toward the porch. I run to the door, checking to make sure that dad and mom aren't nearby.

"Sorry I'm late, Mary Jane" he says, stomping his feet on the porch to get the snow off the bottom of his boots. "I got my truck stuck in the snow coming out of the driveway."

In his hands is a large pot, the rose bush hidden by the Christmas wrapping that loosely encircles it, that protects it from the cold.

"Let's take it to my room," I whisper, which is kind of silly – whispering – because of all the noise that's circulating throughout the house, most of it emanating from the dining room.

Sometimes I wonder if I'm getting old and senile because, that fast – in less than two minutes – I'd forgotten about the twins. In my bedroom, the two of them are standing by the maple, their hands at their sides, watching the toy cars sway back and forth from the branches of the tree.

But it's too late now because we're already in the room. I guess I could make a deal with them, which is something that I usually learn to regret. Or I could bribe them or ...

"Let's put it down right here," says Mr. Wright, placing the pot on the floor at the foot of my bed.

It's a big pot and it must really be heavy because Mr. Wright is out of breath.

"What is it?" Roger asks.

"Yeah. What is it, Janey?" echoes Todd.

They're both staring at the pot, their eyes as round and wide as the rose blooms that are perched at the top of the bush, pushing against the paper wrapping.

"You can keep a secret, right?"

They look at each other, their faces expressing the same response: 'No, we cannot keep a secret. We can never keep a secret. It is against our very nature to even attempt to keep a secret.'

"Let me put it another way," I say, changing my tactic. "You both like surprises, don't you?"

"Sure. We like surprises," Todd says.

"Well, dad likes surprises too. And I got this beautiful plant from Mr. Wright so I could surprise dad on Christmas morning. You wouldn't want to ruin the surprise for daddy, would you?"

They think about it for a minute and then shake their heads.

But I'm not convinced. "If you say anything at all to daddy – or to mommy – then you'll be taking away all the fun that he'll get when he's surprised. You wouldn't want to take away dad's fun, would you? And besides, if you did say anything, then the *dark* Santa Claus might find out."

I turn toward my desk and open a drawer, fidgeting around inside as if I'm looking for something. I want to give them a moment to think about what I said.

"The *dark* Santa Claus?" Todd says. "Who the heck is that? – The *dark* Santa Claus?"

"Oh, come on – you know about the dark Santa Claus, don't you? Everybody who's heard of Santa Claus knows about his evil twin – the dark Santa Claus, who has a black beard and wears a green and gray suit instead of a red and white one. He follows the real Santa Claus around on Christmas Eve in a black sleigh that's pulled by nine ferocious wolves."

The twins look at each other, expressing their horror in their eyes, bulging, and their mouths, stretched out into a grotesque grimace.

"You didn't see any of his ugly, dark elves hanging about, did you, Mr. Wright?"

"No, I can't say that I did," he replies, playing along.

Mr. Wright has sat himself on the edge of my bed, catching his breath while I deal with the twins.

"That's good – because we all know what happens when the evil elves report back to the dark Santa Claus."

"No. We don't," Roger says. "What happens?"

"Well, that's how he finds out which houses to visit when he follows the real Santa Claus around on Christmas Eve. That's how he knows which kids have been bad throughout the year so he can steal their presents after the good Santa leaves."

"Uh-uh – you're making it up, Janey," says Todd. "They're ain't no dark Santa Claus."

"Then how do you explain it when bad little boys get black coal for Christmas? Because that's what happens – the dark Santa Claus steals all their presents, leaving them chunks of coal as black as his beard."

There is that long silence as they swallow the terrible logic that I laid out for them.

Todd turns toward Roger. "We don't want to take any chances."

"No," Roger agrees. "OK. We won't say anything, Janey. Can we look at the plant now?"

"Sure," I reply, stepping aside so they can peek inside the wrapping. "But don't touch it because it's real delicate."

Tight-lipped but smiling, I can tell that Mr. Wright has appreciated the tall tale that I've spun for the twins.

"The maple looks like it's grown a bit," he says, "but it doesn't seem to have as many leaves."

"Mommy took some off to decorate," Roger blurts out.

"Janey and mommy got in a big fight about it," Todd volunteers.

Embarrassed by the bluntness of the twins, I explain to Mr. Wright what happened.

"It probably wasn't a good thing – removing some of its leaves," he says, getting up from the bed for a closer look. "But, since the damage is done, you'll want to keep a close eye on it over the next couple of weeks, Mary Jane. OK? You'll want to let me know if there's any change in the color of the leaves, especially if you see any brownness around the edges. Or if you see any leaves falling off, then by all means get in touch with me right away."

"When will I know if it'll be all right?" I ask.

"If it's OK, then you should see some new growth – first buds and then the new leaves as they unfold. If it's not all right ... well – we'll just wait and see, OK?"

"Mom should never have touched my maple tree," I say sternly.

"I wouldn't blame mom too much, Mary Jane," Mr. Wright advises. "She didn't know. And besides, at least she appreciates the beauty of its leaves. I can't say that about some of the other people I know."

"Ouch!" Roger exclaims, suddenly putting his finger up to his mouth. "The plant bit me!"

But there isn't any blood. Except for a tiny, reddish mark, his finger looks fine to me. "I did warn you not to touch it, Roger," I say.

"I guess it runs in the family. Huh, Mary Jane?" says Mr. Wright, who had said the very same thing to me in his hothouse.

Bored by the novelty of the rose plant, the twins finally leave. I pull out the chair to my desk and sit.

"So, Mr. Wright, what made you change your mind about your invention? What made you turn it into a float?"

"I knew you were going to ask me that," he replies with a big grin. "Especially since it was your idea in the first place – turning the contraption into a float."

"Well – kind of," I timidly agree.

"No, Mary Jane – not 'kind of' – it was your idea. And a darn good one, too. That's why Willy and I made the modifications to it. But anyway," he explains, "we decided to use it in the parade because ... well, to be honest with you, we ran out of time. Willy and I have been so busy with the hothouse lately that we plumb forgot about building the float. So, at the last minute, we decided to use the contraption, moving it to the trailer and dressing it up a bit. We wanted to make it look like Santa's sleigh – a wooden, Santa's sleigh but – oh well. We did the best that we could," he says. "And I guess the only other reason for using the contraption was because of what happened the other day, when I was in the hardware store, picking up parts and materials. I heard them talking in the next aisle over. They were talking about Willy and me."

"Who was talking?"

"It doesn't make any difference, Mary Jane. And I'm not going to repeat what they said because ... well, because it wasn't very nice at all. But anyway, it got me thinking. And when I told Willy, it got him thinking too. And you know what?"

"What?"

"It doesn't make any difference what people say. It doesn't make any difference if they think that Willy and I are a couple of nut cases, dreaming our lives away with silly inventions. What's important is that we're doing what we have to do, which also happens to be what we want to do. How many people can say that? – Not many, I think," Mr. Wright says, answering his own question. "What's important is that Willy and I believe in ourselves. We believe that what we're doing is important and that some day, some day soon ... – Well, we'll just see what happens."

For a second, I picture the plastic statue that's glued to the dashboard of Mr. Gabriel's truck. "You gotta have faith," I suggest.

"That's what it all boils down to, doesn't it, Mary Jane? You gotta have faith," he says, reaching down to tie a bootlace that had come undone. "That's why Willy and I said to each other, 'What the heck? – We'll use the invention for the float and come what may'."

"Can you tell me what it is yet? – The invention?"

He smiles again, moving toward the bedroom door. "I need a couple more weeks to see if it's going to work or not. And if it does? – Well, it'll be a big surprise for all of us."

He grabs the doorknob and opens the door. The sound of music and laughter and merriment floods into the room.

"I should be getting back now," he says.

"Oh, wait a minute, Mr. Wright. I didn't pay you yet for delivering the rose plant."

I jump up from the chair, looking for my little red purse.

"Don't be silly, Mary Jane. I was just kidding about the quarter. You don't owe me anything."

"But ..."

"Merry Christmas, Mary Jane," he says, moving down the hallway toward the front door. "I gotta get back and dig that truck of mine out of the snow before the cold sets in."

"Merry Christmas, Mr. Wright!" I say, watching him as goes out the front door and down the walk. "And thank you!"

It suddenly occurs to me: that's why Mr. Wright was out of breath when he brought the rose plant in – he had carried it all the way from his driveway, where his truck was still stuck in the snow.

The bells of St. Mary's toll eleven times, slicing the chocolate custard silence into equal segments – like the pie cutter that Doris Caterson uses at the diner, sliding the desserts into display cases on the counter when she's done.

The last of dad and mom's friends have left for their homes. The twins have been put to their beds. Restless and excited, I can hear them mumbling through the wall of their bedroom as they talk to each other in the darkness, seeking their separate paths toward sleep.

I water my maple tree; slide the rose bush into my closet. I brush my hair a hundred strokes, change into my flannel pajamas with the Christmas trees on them. When I pull my blanket and sheet down, making ready for bed, I discover a package and note by my pillow.

"*To Mary Jane*", it says on the envelope. I recognize the handwriting.

When I open the present, I discover one of my favorites: a box of malted milk balls from Aunt Sarah's. Putting the chocolates down, I pick up the note, take a deep breath, and read:

"Dear Mary Jane,

I'm never really good at this. And I know that I shouldn't write it in a note but should be saying it to you instead. But if I did, I know that I would start crying and never get it out.

I'm so sorry! I'm so sorry that I took the sprigs from your maple tree! It was wrong of me to be so thoughtless and inconsiderate, taking something that belongs to you, something that's so important to you. And without even asking!

I hope I didn't hurt your maple tree. I hope that it will be all right.

I'm sorry for everything I said!

Please find it in your heart to forgive the shortcomings of an insensitive mother.

All my love,

Mom."

It takes me a minute or so to re-compose myself, tossing the tissues in the wastepaper basket when I think that I'm finished.

Dad's out in the garage doing something or other, though I can't imagine what's so important that it has to be done in the dwindling hours of Christmas Eve. Mom's in the kitchen. I can hear her washing the dishes and glasses from the party and stacking them in the plastic rack to dry. She's humming to herself very softly – it's almost sad – the tune that she hums as she looks up every now and then to stare through the window over the sink, as if she's remembering something from long ago, something that made her happy, that continues to make her happy, but also sad because it happened so long ago.

"I'm sorry too, mom," I say, stepping into the kitchen. "I'm sorry that I yelled at you."

When she turns toward me, she has that strange mixture of opposite expressions in her face. Her eyes are watery and sad but her mouth is creased into a warm and generous smile. And it's only for a second that I'm uncertain, that I'm not sure exactly if it's the sadness of her eyes or the smile of her mouth that's going to win out before I realize the outcome – her face, her *whole* face, changing into a single and unmistakable expression because it was her mouth, after all, that was able to convince her eyes, in that fleeting moment of time, that it was the joy of whatever it was that she was imagining that far outweighed its sadness.

Christmas Eve.

Christmas Eve in Christmasville.

The bells of St. Mary's toll twelve times. In the coziness of my bed, I wrap the blankets tightly around me, the warmth spreading through my body like hot chicken soup.

"Merry Christmas to all! And to all, a good night!" I whisper, turning in my bed toward the gentle embrace of sleep, closing my eyes and reminding myself that I must remember to change the tag on the rose plant in the morning.

First Night

At the far end of the dinner table, Mayor Thompson cuts his beef tenderloin into square chunks, his knife scraping the plate as he pushes the cubes into a neat pile away from his peas.

"You know, Tom," he says, "I was talking with Joe Carson down at the gas station the other day and he said the oddest thing."

At our end of the table, by Emily and I, dad swallows a forkful of mashed potatoes. "What was that, Fred?" he asks.

The mayor spears a piece of beef, dips it into the puddle of sauce on the side of his plate and inserts it into his mouth.

"Well," he starts, chewing the meat a couple of times before pushing it off to the side to store it in his cheek like a chipmunk might do. "He said that there was talk among my constituency about my wanting to re-zone different precincts of town. He said it was because of all the problems that we're experiencing."

"Problems?" dad asks. "What problems?"

I stare down at my plate, the brown gravy pooled in the hollow of my potatoes. It reminds me of the pond by Mr. Wright's workshop, its dark surface encircled by a white ridge of fluffy, peaked snow.

Beside me, mom pauses in her conversation with Mrs. Thompson, who is sitting opposite her. "Yes. What problems, Fred?" she repeats, though turning back immediately to discuss items of far greater significance – the group project at the Thursday Night Sewing Club.

"That's just what I asked Joe Carson – 'What problems'?" the mayor replies. "And who among my constituency had voiced such nonsense?"

A spike of anxiety rises up from the pit of my stomach. I glance at Emily across the table but she's humming a little song to herself, making her peas dance to the melody with her fork. She probably doesn't remember the stupid comments that I had made to Mr. Carson when we picked up the maps. How could she? – She was in her own little world then, too.

"He said," the mayor continues, chewing his beef and swallowing, "that he couldn't remember exactly who had said it to him. It was either that or else he didn't want to remember, the old codger."

"I wouldn't put too much stock in what Joe Carson says, anyway, Fred," dad suggests. "I think he's just aggravated because you're the mayor and he's not. You know how he always talks about throwing his hat into the political arena but never manages to find the time – or the energy – to toss it."

The mayor lets out a laugh. "If Joe put only half the effort that he puts into reading his newspaper and sticking his nose into everybody else's business, then maybe he'd have half a chance in getting his name on the ballot. But you know what, Tom? – I just don't see Joe getting off his stool long enough to run for any kind of office."

"Wait a minute, Fred – did you say 'run' for office?" dad asks with deadpan seriousness. "I'm sure Joe would be the first to admit: why would you want to 'run' for anything when it's a heck of a lot easier to just take your time and walk?"

Another laugh rolls from the Mayor, his jowls jiggling like a bowl of pink Jell-O. Lifting his napkin up, he covers his open mouth to prevent any food from falling out.

"Whether he runs – or walks – old Joe Carson better think long and hard about tangling with Mayor Fred Thompson."

Scooping up a mound of mashed potatoes causes the dam around the pool to break, the gravy flooding into the remainder of my peas. I take a deep breath and thank my lucky stars for Mr. Carson's lapse in memory.

"The nerve!" mom replies, reacting to something Mrs. Thompson said about Mrs. Jenkins. "Roger! – Stop playing with your peas and eat! Or else no dessert for you, young man."

Seated next to her, Roger screws up his face, making Todd giggle across the table.

"Speaking of which, would anyone like coffee with their dessert?" Mrs. Thompson asks, getting up from the table to start clearing some of the dishes away. "We'd better get moving if we want to see all the festivities."

"Let me help you with those, Betty," says mom, getting up as well.

The twins, seeing that it was now or never, dig into their peas, cramming them into their mouths and swallowing as fast as they can.

What I always like about eating at Emily's house are the desserts. Even if sometimes you had to tolerate the asparagus or the lima beans, the pickled beets or the sauerkraut, it was well worth the unpleasantness because, at the end of it all, were the best desserts that you could imagine. And you always had a choice too! That's because Mrs. Thompson is the pastry chef at Cauldwell's Supermarket, her reputation celebrated far and wide throughout all the households of Christmasville.

And now that I think about it, maybe that's why Emily's parents decided to marry each other. If Mr. Thompson was the apple of Mrs. Thompson's eye, then she was certainly the chocolate mousse and strawberry shortcake, the pie a la mode and apple brown betty of his. While Mrs. Thompson prided herself on her abilities to create spectacular desserts, Mr. Thompson showed a remarkable aptitude for demolishing each and every one of them.

"OK everyone," says Mrs. Thompson, standing between kitchen and dining room in her 'I am NOT the cook, I am the CHEF!' apron. "The dessert bar is now open. Please help yourselves at the kitchen table."

Mr. Thompson is first in line but, after a stern look from Mrs. Thompson, defers to his dinner guests.

Black forest cake and chocolate custard, lemon meringue pie and mixed berries jubilee.

For me, it's easy to decide since I take a little sampling of everything.

"So," mom says after everyone's seated at the dining room table again, digging into their respective desserts, "did everyone put their list together?"

"List? – What list?" Mr. Thompson asks. "In case no one's told you, Evelyn, Santa's already arrived. That is, of course, unless you weren't a very good girl throughout the year and Santa didn't bring you anything that you asked for."

Grinning, Mr. Thompson spoons a lump of custard into his mouth. Like me, he has taken samples of each dessert, though his portions are substantially larger.

"Oh, I must have been plenty good, Fred. Tom bought me my electric mixmaster with all the attachments – and my new coat and gloves. Mary Jane gave me a beautiful hat and scarf set that she made all by herself. And then there's the rose, of course," she says, turning toward me and putting her arm around my shoulder, "which Mary Jane gave Tom and I. It's the best present that anyone could receive."

"It certainly is," says Mrs. Thompson, having seen it the day after Christmas. "After the holidays, I'm going to drag Fred over to that hothouse of Otis Wright's to see if he can't buy me something that's a little more ... well, that's a little more feminine and less practical than a vacuum cleaner and bathroom towels."

Mr. Thompson pauses in his demolition of desserts, his spoon hovering between mouth and plate. "You don't like your new vacuum cleaner, Betty?"

"I love my new vacuum cleaner, but that's not what I meant, Fred."

"Mommy?" says Todd. "You didn't say anything about the socks that we gave you."

"And the box of jellybeans," Roger adds.

"Oh, and what beautiful woolen socks they are! – Red and yellow striped ones, blue and green checkered ones. And I couldn't forget about the jellybeans, could I boys? – But it would have been so nice to actually taste just one of them had the two of you not eaten the whole box before I had the opportunity."

Everyone laughs as the twins turn as red as the raspberry jellybeans that no longer existed.

"But anyway, Fred," mom continues, "I wasn't referring to our Christmas lists but to our New Year's lists – our list of resolutions."

"Fred's giving up desserts for the year," Mrs. Thompson declares, causing Mr. Thompson to nearly choke.

"Fat chance of that," he says. "I'd sooner give up politics than give up any of your delectable desserts, Betty."

"Well, we'll see about that," Mrs. Thompson replies. "It wouldn't hurt to lose a couple of pounds, you know."

Mr. Thompson swallows a hunk of black forest cake. "But it's what keeps me jolly, Betty. You wouldn't want me to lose any of my jolliness, would you?"

"If you ask me, I think it's more about folly than jolly," Mrs. Thompson retorts. "Besides, if I start cutting back on preparing desserts, then you won't have any choice but to cut back on devouring them, Fred – which incidentally, Evelyn, is on my list of resolutions – to develop better nutritional habits."

"That's on my list, too, mommy – to eat things that are better for me," Emily says, speaking up.

"I know it is, sweetie, because your dentist says that you have to."

"How about you, Evelyn?" dad asks. "What's on your list of resolutions?"

Mom puts her elbows up on the table, folding her hands beneath her chin. "I think I want to spend more time ..."

' " *... helping others who are less fortunate than us* ",' I say to myself.

" ... helping others who are less fortunate than us," mom says.

It's the exact words that she said last year, and the year before that, saying it in the same way, sitting in the same chair at the Thompson dinner table with her hands folded beneath her chin. But she doesn't remember any of it, which makes it so difficult and so confusing for me to understand what's happened to everyone around me – or what it is that's happened to me. The whole notion of remembering – of *memory* – is something that is almost too much to bear. Like when dad talked about 'the blight' and the chestnut trees – old Mr. Phelps could have told him that twenty, fifty, a hundred years ago. And yet he still remembers it. But if I point out the Christmas tree in the backyard that both dad and I planted last year, he'll scratch his head, stare at it for a few minutes and say, "You know, I don't remember exactly where that tree came from, Mary Jane." And next year, it'll be the same thing all over again. They'll be a new "plan" of Christmasville; houses and buildings will be re-situated; we'll live in a new neighborhood; dad will have forgotten all about the Christmas tree that we planted in the yard of our house this year – and nobody but me will remember the way it was. And if I say to mom – "Geez, isn't that a beautiful rose plant that I gave you last year, mom?" – she'll look at me like I'm crazy because she won't remember that I gave it to her. She won't remember any of it. And yet, sometimes, it's better that no-body remembers. Nobody remembers that last January I had to go to the school psychiatrist every week during home economics class because I was "emotionally challenged". Doctor Sperry doesn't remember it. Even Tommy Burks doesn't remember writing, "Mary Jane is a fat fruitcake", across buildings and walls with green spray paint or of doing community service after he got caught. He doesn't even know why I dislike him so much because he doesn't remember. He doesn't remember the way it was. But the thing is, it couldn't have always been this way because ... well, because dad and mom, for example – they remember things that happened long ago, things that happened before I became fourteen years old. They remember their childhood and the classes that they took when they were back in school. They remember their wedding day and the day that I was born. They remember *my* childhood – at least everything that happened to me in the thirteen years before I became fourteen. I remember nothing about it. I don't remember being five or seven or ten years old. I don't remember being thirteen. So what happened then? And why? Why did Father Time suddenly decide to take a nap without anyone but me knowing about it? And when will he ever wake up? Why do the years repeat themselves again and again between the beginning of December and the end of January, like a record on a phonograph? And this issue of ... *memory?* – This enormous burden, this strange enigma of remembering what everyone else forgot, and of having forgotten what everyone else remembers. Maybe .... maybe what everyone else remembers is only a fantasy, a dream, or the memory of a dream that is so real that you confuse the reality with the fantasy. And it's me, *only me* – Mary Jane Higgins – who doesn't remember the dream.

'But if all this is true,' I think, suddenly remembering the incident in Link's Pharmacy on Christmas Eve and the comment that Mr. Bachmann made about staying away from midnight trains to grandma's house ... – *'How could he have remembered that? How could he re-member what happened last January?'*

"... the rose and the maple tree," dad says, as I fade back into reality. "And maybe Otis and Willy can give me some other ideas about what to put inside."

"I think that's a marvelous idea, Tom," says Mrs. Thompson. "If I can get Fred away from the desserts and the politics long enough, then maybe he can build us a little hothouse off of our garage as well."

Everyone looks toward Mr. Thompson at the end of the table.

"Your chocolate custard really takes the cake, Betty," he says, deliberately avoiding the topic.

Mrs. Thompson is not amused. "Well then, Fred," she says, watching him as he scrapes the remainder of his desserts from his plate, "if you won't even consider the hothouse, then maybe you should think about the doghouse."

"What doghouse? – We don't have a doghouse."

"We do now," she remarks. "It's the one that you just put yourself into, Fred Thompson."

After we help clear the dessert dishes, stacking them in the kitchen sink, everyone gathers up their coats and gloves, climbing into them for the ride downtown. For the festivities of First Night, you aren't allowed to drive your car into town because Maple Street is closed to all automobile traffic. You have to take the shuttle bus, which runs every fifteen minutes or so, picking up passengers and dropping them off at designated spots throughout town. The closest pick-up point for us is just three houses down, on the corner of Juniper and Poplar.

Walking toward the corner, the twins are ahead of everyone while Emily and I lag behind.

"You didn't tell anyone what your New Year's resolutions are," Emily says.

"No, I didn't," I reply.

"How come? – Don't you have any, Mary Jane?"

"I've got some resolutions," I answer, "but I didn't want to say them because dad and mom wouldn't approve."

"Why wouldn't they? They're only resolutions – nobody really sticks to them anyway. It's not like they're promises and you cross your heart and hope to die if you break them. If they were ... well, everybody would run out of resolutions for the next New Year's. You know what I mean?"

It isn't snowing, or windy, but it's so bitterly cold that I can already feel it working into my boots and gloves, wrapping around my toes and fingers.

"I don't care about next year, Emily. I don't care if I run out of resolutions. I'm only concerned about this year – and what I have to do about January 31st."

As we walk toward the corner, Emily kicks a clump of frozen snow along the sidewalk in front of her.

"Can you tell me just one of your resolutions?" she asks.

"I guess – but you know that it has to stay a secret. Right, Emily?"

"I can keep a secret."

Behind us, I hear the shuttle bus approaching, the loudspeakers on its roof announcing its arrival with holiday music.

"The most important resolution," I say, turning toward Emily and lowering my voice, "is probably the most ... the most *dangerous*."

Emily snaps her head around.

"I have to cross the train tracks, Emily."

She doesn't have to say anything because I can read it in her eyes: *It's forbidden to cross the train tracks. No one is permitted.*

On the bus, we all decide to break up into groups so that everyone can do what they want. Dad and Mr. Thompson want to see the antique tool collection and then, afterwards, the tractor parade. Mom and Mrs. Thompson want to see the quilt and needlepoint display at city hall and to listen to the swing band in the school auditorium. Since the twins haven't the slightest interest in either tools – antique or otherwise – or in quilts and needlepoint, Emily and I have the misfortune of watching them during the first shift.

"So what should we do first?" I ask them, after resigning myself to the chore.

"I want to ride the fire truck," Todd says.

"I want to see the jail," says Roger.

"The puppet show!" clamors Todd.

"Let's see the magic show first!" Roger cries.

The shuttle bus swings left onto Elm Street and stops in front of city hall.

"We'll meet you in front of the Five & Dime at eight o'clock," mom says to dad as she gets up with Mrs. Thompson to depart. "Then we'll take the twins with us. OK?"

"Eight o'clock," dad repeats. "You girls have a good time of it."

"Bye girls," mom and Mrs. Thompson say, moving to the front of the bus. "And you boys better behave yourselves for Mary Jane and Emily," mom adds. "I don't want any bad reports. Do you hear me?"

Roger and Todd look at each other and giggle.

"Quilts and needlepoint," Mr. Thompson says to dad. "Why would anyone waste their time with anything as boring as that?"

"They're probably saying the same thing about us, Fred – tools and tractors – how boring!"

The shuttle bus moves down Elm, turns left onto East Juniper Street. As it comes up to Maple Street and swings right to ease up the hill, I glance at the public library. Although the entry steps and the central hallway are illuminated, the rest of the building looks dark and gloomy. Maybe it's too early yet and the fortuneteller hasn't arrived. I hope that's all it is because, of all the activities of First Night, that's the only one that I'm really interested in. I want to have my fortune read.

At the top of the hill, across the street from Jack's Toy Store and where the promenade begins on Maple Street, three clowns toss bowling pins back and forth to each other. I don't know how they can do it, each clown keeping track of the pins coming in from the other two while tossing out pins, alternately, to their partners. All three of them look kind of funny – not because they're dressed as clowns – but because over their costumes they're wearing gloves, scarves, earmuffs and – instead of the big, floppy feet that you always see them wearing when they perform – snow boots. In fact, they look like weird creatures that you might see in one of the twin's comic books. Maybe that's why nobody's around to watch them – because they look so weird – or because it's so cold outside that everyone's indoors, keeping themselves warm and cozy.

When we arrive at the parking lot at the end of Maple Street, you can tell how cold it is by how much frost has accumulated on the plastic windows of the diner. It must be near zero because the thick layer of frost makes the people inside look like shadows ... or ghosts, getting a hot cocoa or a bite to eat before the bus arrives – not the shuttle but the other bus – the one which takes them to a place where they won't have to worry about hunger or thirst ever again.

"My God it's cold!" dad says, exiting the shuttle first and wrapping his arms about him.

"Colder than a witch's ... toes," says Mr. Thompson.

"What does that mean, daddy?" Emily asks, stepping down from the bus.

"What does what mean, sweetie?"

"What you said," she replies. "What's a witch?"

"Oh. It's just an expression – something that you say to express how cold it is."

"I know, but ..."

"Brrrrr," Mr. Thompson says, shivering. "Let's get out of this ungodly cold."

The antique tool display is in the lobby of the bank so dad and Mr. Thompson only have to cross the parking lot to get inside.

"Mary Jane?" dad says. "We'll meet you at Clauson's at seven o'clock for the magic show. Then I'll take Roger and Todd with me. OK?"

"OK, dad," I reply.

"And don't stay outside too long," he cautions, moving with Mr. Thompson toward the bank. "Even though there isn't much of a wind, it's cold enough to get frostbite if you're not careful."

As dad and Mr. Thompson hurry away, I inspect the twins. Roger's coat is wide open so I have to remove my gloves and play around with the stupid zipper until I finally get it lined up, pulling it up as far as it will go. Then I pull up his hood, drawing the strings taut and tying them into a bow. Todd has his scarf stuffed into a coat pocket rather that wrapped about his neck. By the time that I secure it about him, my fingers are so cold that they ache.

"OK. Let's go see the fire trucks," I say, pulling my gloves on before my fingers snap off. "Are you ready, Emily?"

But she isn't here.

"Emily?" I repeat, looking around.

It takes me a moment to find her in the darkness, her coat and hat blending in with the thick fabric of the night sky behind her.

"Emily!" I shout.

She's crossed the street, wandered to the rocky ledge of Jenkins' Hill.

"You guys run up ahead to the firehouse. I'll get Emily and meet you there."

"What's she doin' anyway?" Roger asks.

"Come on. Let's go," Todd says, heading for the firehouse nearby. "Emily's a dodo head."

"Emily?" I call, moving toward her.

When I arrive, I see what it is that's drawn Emily to the ledge.

"I could hear them from the parking lot," she says, mesmerized by the giant transformers below, humming loudly in the quiet of the night. "Do you remember, Mary Jane? Do you remember the sparks and fireworks that lit up the sky like lightning?"

"I remember," I reply, surprised because – twice now – Emily's recalled what she shouldn't have.

"I wish that I didn't," she says, closing her eyes as if that simple gesture could erase the terrible fear that she had once experienced, the biting memory of fear and the gnawing suspicion that something – something dreadful and inexplicable – was utterly wrong with Christmasville.

"I wish that I didn't remember anything," she says, starting to cry.

"It's all right," I say, putting my arm around her shoulder and trying to calm her down. "Everything will be all right."

"No it won't!" she says, shaking my hand off and opening her eyes. "It won't be all right! Why do you have to cross the train tracks, Mary Jane? Why can't you just let it go? Why can't you just be like everyone else?"

I don't know what to say to her.

"Can't you just try?" Emily continues, wiping her eyes with her gloves. "Can't you just let yourself ... forget, and try to be like everyone else?"

If only it were that simple – forgetting, allowing myself to forget about snowmen from China, about games of checkers and algebra problems that have no solutions, about maple trees and radio stations in New York City. Wouldn't it all be so easy then? – If only there weren't such constant reminders, repeating the same thing over and over again, telling me ... No, not telling me but hinting, suggesting that there's other seasons and other places, that there's so much more beyond the ends of Christmasville. Forgetting – trying to forget – would be like trying to forget that the sun rises in the morning and that night descends in the evening. Or like trying to forget that you're awake instead of asleep, that you're not hungry when you're stomach knows otherwise.

"I can't, Emily. I can't forget and I can't be someone that I'm not."

"Fine then!" she says angrily. "Be that way! – Go and kill yourself like Mrs. Gabriel and her daughter did when they went too far!"

"They didn't ..."

She brushes past me, marching across Maple Street, the vaporous plumes of her breath rising in the air like blooms of roses.

When I arrive at the firehouse, I discover that the twins have all but taken over. Two firemen, garbed in their heavy jackets and metal helmets, are down on all fours like a pair of horses. Beneath them, padding their knees as they charge one another with Todd and Roger on their backs, are fire mattresses, strewn across the floor.

"Faster, horse-y!" shouts Todd, directing the charge toward his brother.

The twins have fire helmets on as well, loosely strapped beneath their chins, and clear plastic masks that protect their faces when the two firemen broadside and the twins pelt each other with pillowcases, stuffed with towels. Behind them, at the edge of the jousting field, Tucker barks at the assault because he doesn't understand what's going on.

"We're not running the fire trucks tonight," explains the fire chief, "because of the cold. So it's a good way for the boys to burn off some steam."

"Which boys?" I ask bluntly. "The ones on top or the ones on the bottom?"

You can hear the chief's laugh echo through the firehouse.

"For both," he says, continuing to laugh.

Dismayed by the ineffectiveness of his weapon, I suppose, causes Todd to toss his pillowcase to the floor and to lunge from his 'horse-y' toward Roger. There is the clash of helmets and masks as the two of them tumble to the fire mattress, the knightly joust degenerating into a simple wrestling match. Each 'horse-y' moves off to the side, panting for breath.

"OK, boys," the fire chief says, seeing the match escalate into something beyond a playful contest.

After the chief pulls them apart, Todd rises to his feet first.

"I won!" he shouts, removing his hat and mask and dropping them to the mattress. "I won!" he repeats, raising his arms up in victory.

"No, you didn't, Todd," says Roger's loyal 'horse-y', getting up to his feet and removing his helmet and jacket. "Roger won because you cheated."

"No I didn't! – You fat old horse-y!" Todd says with a nasty look, sticking his tongue out.

"You did too!" Roger exclaims, pushing his brother.

"OK, baby brothers," I say, turning toward the exit. "I'm going to get dad now and you can tell him about your bad behavior. See ya!"

"No!" Roger says, scrambling for his coat.

"Wait up, Janey!" says Todd, following suit to his brother.

I go outside and, leaning against the firehouse, watch the second hand on my watch. "One, two, three ..."

In eleven seconds the twins are standing in front of me, out of breath, pleading with me not to get dad.

Since the police station is next and the twins are practically begging me to continue, I – being as patient and considerate as I am – decide to grant them their wish. Besides, I have a better idea for dealing with Roger and Todd.

At the dispatch desk, Sergeant Myers explains to Mr. Carson how police calls are forwarded to "officers in the field". Neither one of them sees us as we sneak around the sergeant's desk and hurry toward the back of the station. I particularly want to avoid Mr. Carson because then he might remember who it was, among the mayor's constit ... constit-u-en-cy, that said that there were "problems".

In the back, there are three jail cells. The barred doors are swung wide open because there aren't any prisoners. Of course, there's never any prisoners – none that I ever heard about anyway.

"That's where they kept Pinky Pigface," I say to the twins, pointing to the last cell, after closing the soundproof door between the front of the station and the jail.

Pinky Pigface is one of their favorite comic book villains.

"No, it's not," Todd says, his face expressing his disbelief.

"Pinky's never been caught," Roger adds. "He's too smart for the cops to catch him."

"Well," I say, fabricating as I go, "I've been reading the comics a lot longer than you guys and that's where they kept Pinky Pigface after they caught him. But it wasn't even a day before he busted out."

The twins look at each other, becoming ensnared in my web of deception.

"How'd they catch him then?" Todd asks.

"It was when Pinky and his gang were robbing the city garbage center and Hogbreath double-crossed him."

"Hogbreath? I never heard of any Hogbreath," Roger says.

"Yeah," Todd chimes in. "There ain't no Hogbreath."

"Hogbreath used to be in Pinky's first gang, the Mad Muckers. He was Pinky's right-hand pig before he double-crossed him. But he's not around any more because Pinky busted out and ... well, he paid him back good. He'll never mess with Pinky Pigface again."

Todd steps into the cell and looks around for some small trace of the gangster's brief detention.

"Can't you smell him, Todd?" I suggest. "They tried everything to get rid of the horrible stench that he left behind. They used bleach, ammonia – but no matter what they used, they were never able to get rid of the smell entirely."

I can see Todd sniffing about.

"It does smell kind of funny," he says. "Like somethin' rotten."

Roger steps into the cell next to his brother. "Yeah," he says, "I can smell it too."

Slamming the door shut, I turn the key and pull it from the door.

"Does it smell foul – like in 'foul play'?" I ask, tossing the key on the floor away from the cell and walking quickly toward the soundproof door.

"Hey!" Todd says.

"Janey!" Roger calls out. "Let us out!"

"I hope you little brats enjoy your First Night – your First Night in jail, that is!" I add, laughing quietly as I make my escape, shutting the soundproof door behind me.

Sergeant Myers and Mr. Carson are at the cabinet with all the billy clubs stored inside.

"Do you think I could try one out?" asks Mr. Carson.

"Sure you can, Joe," the sergeant says, grabbing his key chain that's attached to his belt. "As soon as I can figure out which one of these babies unlocks the cabinet."

Dashing toward the exit, I glance toward them. There must be at least fifty keys on that key chain.

Outside, I take a deep breath, breathing in the fresh air of freedom.

When I get to Link's Pharmacy on the other side of the Five & Dime, I have to wait because there's a line. But it's only a couple of minutes because Amy, the waitress, has reinforcements to help her out. I order a large hot cocoa.

The plastic cup is really hot so I put my gloves back on to hold it. When I turn away from the counter, I see the Tolliver family seated in a booth. Brett's staring down into his cup in front of him – like he's daydreaming.

"Hello Mr. and Mrs. Tolliver," I say, approaching the booth. "Hi Brett."

"Oh, hello, Mary Jane," Mrs. Tolliver replies.

Mr. Tolliver smiles at me but Brett continues to stare downward.

"Brett? – Say hello to Mary Jane," his mother says, nudging his elbow.

"Hello Mary Jane," he says without looking up.

I can see his ears turning red as he picks up a spoon and fidgets.

"Where's your mom and dad?" Mrs. Tolliver asks. "I don't see them."

I explain the arrangement.

"You know, Bud," says Mrs. Tolliver to her husband, "I think we'll visit city hall after we're finished here. I'd like to see the quilts and needlepoint too."

Mr. Tolliver smiles politely but I can tell that he's not too thrilled about the prospect.

"Oh, but the twins – where are the twins, Mary Jane?" asks Mrs. Tolliver. "Where are my cute little darlings?" she adds, looking around for them, ready to dote all over them.

"Um ... the twins," I reply. "I should be getting back to them now. I left them in the police station where they're getting a first-hand look at the evils ... the evils of the criminal element. So I'd better go and get them now," I say, back-stepping toward the doorway. "Bye Mr. and Mrs. Tolliver. Bye Brett."

"Give my best to mom and dad," Mrs. Tolliver says.

Brett glances up, watching me as I turn to leave. "Bye, Mary Jane," he says.

I stop at the doorway, sipping hot cocoa from my cup. And it's a good thing that I stop because, passing the pharmacy without seeing me, are dad and Mr. Thompson.

'Where are the twins?' dad would say, wondering why I had left them, insisting on going to get them.

After they disappear down the street, I head back toward the police station. Standing in front of the Five & Dime, staring at stuff in the display window, is Emily.

"We're going to see the magic show, Emily – if you want to come," I say, walking behind her without stopping.

I figure – if she wants to come along, then fine, she can come. But if she wants to stay mad at me for the rest of First Night, then that's fine, too – she can be that way. It's her decision if she wants to mope around all night.

"Why ya goin' in the police station?" she asks when I'm at the top of the steps, ready to sneak myself in. "The magic show's at Clauson's."

"I have to break the twins out of jail," I reply. "Want to help?"

"They got arrested???" she says, running over and scampering up the steps. "What'd they get arrested for?"

"For being spoiled rotten brats," I reply.

Sergeant Myers is sitting at his desk. It looks like he's erasing something with a pencil so I guess he's doing the crossword puzzle. Mr. Carson must have left because he's nowhere to be seen.

"OK, Emily, this is what we'll do."

After I explain the plan, we open the door and approach the sergeant at his desk.

"Hello Sergeant Myers," we say in unison.

"Hello girls," he says, looking up. "What brings you to the police station on this bitterly cold First Night?"

"We want to see where you fingerprint criminals," Emily blurts out.

"No we don't!" I butt in, glaring at Emily because she must have gotten the plan all wrong.

The place where they did the fingerprints is in the back, near the jail cells.

"We want to see the dispatch station – where you call police cars up and send them out to the scene of the crime. We want to see the dispatch station – right, Emily?"

"Oh ... yeah ... We want to see the dispatch station," Emily agrees, getting things straight. "Is that what the dispatch station's for?" she asks, turning toward me. "Calling up police cars on the radio?"

"Yep – that's what's it for," the sergeant says, getting up from his chair and coming round the desk. "But I can show you the fingerprint station first, if you like, and then we can look at dispatch."

Sergeant Myers moves toward the soundproof door that leads to the back.

"No!" I say, raising my voice in alarm. "No – we'd really like to see the dispatch station first, sergeant. I *really* want to see how you use the radio to call up police cars. We *really* want to see that *first*, don't we, Emily?"

Emily nods her head as Sergeant Myers tucks his pencil behind his ear.

"Well, sure – we can do that first," he says, leading the way to the dispatch station.

When we arrive, the sergeant turns a knob on what I guess is the transmitter. He makes an adjustment on another knob and then picks up the big, metal microphone.

"There's not too much to it, really," he says. "We only have one car out in the field – Officer Horton – and ..."

"Oh, geez," I say, interrupting. "You know what? – I have to go to the ladies room real bad. But you two just go on with what you're doing and I'll be back in a flash."

Giving Emily a little wink, I hand her my cup of hot cocoa and head off, determined to complete my mission.

"OK, then," Sergeant Myers continues, "as I was saying, Officer Horton ..."

On the other side of the sergeant's desk, I make my dash for the door to the jail cells. The twins jump up from the bed simultaneously. It's red around Roger's eyes, which makes me think that he was crying.

"When mommy and daddy find out ...," Todd starts.

"Fine," I say, doing an about-face and heading back toward the door that I just came through. "Then you can just stay here and rot if you're going to squeal."

"Janey!" Roger says. "We won't say anything!"

"No! – We won't squeal on you," says Todd.

"You promise?"

"Cross my heart and hope to die," Roger says.

"Todd?"

He makes a screwed-up face. "OK – I promise."

Quickly, I pick up the keys that I had thrown on the floor and insert one into the lock. But it's the wrong one.

"Besides," I say, slipping the next key into the slot, "I only wanted to show you how Pinky Pigface broke out of jail."

"What do you mean?" Roger asks.

"Emily's creating a diversion," I explain, turning the key and swinging the heavy, barred door open. "She's keeping Sergeant Myers busy – just like Sylvia Satin did when one of Pinky's henchman snuck into jail and busted him out."

"Really?" Roger says, buying my story.

He's as gullible as Emily can be, but I don't think Todd is convinced.

"Sure," I reply. "You remember Sylvia, don't you? Pinky's old girl friend?"

"Sort of," Roger says.

"I don't remember any Sylvia Satin," says Todd. "How come you don't read about her any more?"

"Because she got fed up with Pinky. Because he wouldn't marry her," I continue. "So she ran off with Pork Chop – but that didn't last either."

"How come?" Todd asks.

"Because Pinky caught up with the two of them," I reply, grabbing the knob on the soundproof door and twisting it. "And now they're *both* pork chops."

I must say: Emily's done a really good job of it. She's sitting on the dispatch desk, facing Sergeant Myers, who's seated in the dispatcher's chair. He's got his hands folded behind his head and his feet are propped up on a desk drawer that's pulled out. He looks as if he's about to fall asleep at any minute – not because he's tired but because he's so incredibly bored by Emily's long recitation. She's describing for him, in minute detail, each of the more than hundred dolls in her collection.

"And then there's Harry," she says, finishing up the rest of my hot cocoa. "He's not really a doll but a teddy bear. He's got golden fur and ... Are you asleep, Sergeant Myers?" she says, tapping him on the leg with her foot. "It's not very nice falling asleep when someone's talking to you."

Jolted, the sergeant sits up in his chair and wipes his eyes. "Oh, no ... No – I was just closing my eyes so I could picture in my mind what Harry looks like."

"Are you ready, Emily?" I ask, glancing at the clock on the wall as I move toward the front door of the station with the twins. "The magic show starts in ten minutes."

"I guess so," she says, sliding down from the desk. "I wouldn't want to keep the sergeant from sleeping on the job."

"I wasn't sleeping," he says, getting up from the chair and yawning. "I was only resting my eyes. Hey," he adds. "Where'd the twins come from? – Hello boys!"

They wave to the sergeant, remembering to keep their traps shut.

"Oh, they were just hanging around," I reply.

"Don't you want to see how we do the fingerprints?" the sergeant asks, seeing that we're leaving.

"Maybe later," I answer. "We have to be on our way now. But thank you, Sergeant Myers. Thank you so much."

On the first floor of Clauson's Department Store, they set up a stage where you would usually find the shoes and the pocketbooks. I guess they moved them all to the back of the store, lining into rows the chairs that you would normally sit in to try the new shoes on. There's a lot of people so we're lucky when we find seats in the last row. I don't see dad or Mr. Thompson yet but I'm sure they'll be along shortly.

"Ladies and gentlemen," announces Mr. Clauson, after stepping out from behind the stage curtain. "We at Clauson's Department Store are once again proud to sponsor this year's magic show for the amusement and entertainment of our loyal customers. With great effort on our part and sparing no expense whatsoever, we searched high and low for what we considered the best magic show that money could buy!"

It sounds like a lousy advertisement for the department store.

"And I'm absolutely certain that once you've witnessed the spectacular feats of magic on this very stage tonight, you'll agree: just as Clauson's provides you the best shopping value for your hard-earned dollar, we provide you with the best in entertainment experiences as well. So, without further ado," says Mr. Clauson, wrapping up his crummy commercial, "it gives me great pleasure to present for your enjoyment tonight – again, compliments of Clauson's Department Store – the incomparable and inimitable, Marco, the Magician!"

There's a poof of smoke and then suddenly, appearing from nowhere, it's Marco in his top hat and tuxedo, his cape and cane.

The crowd applauds because Marco is pretty good when he appears out of thin air like that. But I don't know if he's the best magician that money can buy because I've seen other acts that I thought were better. What I do know, however, is that Marco, the Magician, is Mr. Clauson's nephew.

"Thank you, ladies and gentlemen," says Marco, bowing graciously to the audience. "Thank you very much. And now – allow me to introduce my beautiful assistant and stunning protégé, who also happens to be my lovely wife, Muriel! – The Magician's Assistant!"

Her entrance is less spectacular: she pulls the curtains back and steps on stage, offering a curtsy to the audience while Mr. Clauson's takes his leave.

The crowd applauds again – with equal enthusiasm – which, I think, kind of irks Marco because, after all, he's the magician. It's his show. Muriel only helps him out.

Anyway, the show starts with card tricks, like it always does, and then it's the 'watch-me-as-I-saw-Muriel-my-lovely-wife-in-half' routine. It's a good trick – one that Muriel acts out really well, especially when she twists her face up in horror as the blade of the saw approaches her belly.

By the time it's the 'rabbit-out-of-the-hat' trick, I still don't see dad or Mr. Thompson. It occurs to me that maybe if I gave Marco, the Magician, twenty bucks at the end of the show – that is, if dad doesn't show up – then he could make the twins disappear, sending them off to the same remote vicinity as the snowman from China, wherever the heck that might be. Geez, wouldn't that be a cheap price to pay! – Twenty bucks and then, Poof! – No more twins!

"Mommy says she might buy me a rabbit like that for a pet," Emily whispers. "A white one with big floppy ears," she adds.

"That's nice," I reply, glancing on the other side of her to make sure that the twins are behaving.

"But she won't buy it until daddy builds a cage for it first," says Emily.

'In that case,' I think to myself, 'you'll never get your rabbit, Emily, because your daddy couldn't build a cage for a dead duck let alone a live rabbit.'

There's a tap on my shoulder. When I spin around, I see dad standing behind me.

"Sorry I'm late, princess," he whispers in my ear. "We waited for the start of the tractor parade but they ended up canceling it anyway. It's the weather – it's too cold."

"Oh – sorry you missed it, dad."

"It's OK – they'll be other ones," he says.

"Where's Mr. Thompson?"

"He met up with some of his political cronies," dad says. "He'll be along shortly."

The audience starts clapping again as Marco makes doves appear from an orange scarf. The birds flutter their wings a couple of times and then fly off to another section of the department store. I wonder how Marco will catch them again. I wonder if the doves ever have accidents as they fly over the audience below them.

"Emily?" I say, nudging her. "I'm going to leave now. I want to have my fortune read. Are you coming with me? Or are you staying?"

She glances at me but quickly looks back toward a wall sconce where one of the doves is perched.

"Ohhhhh – such a pretty white one," she remarks. "Maybe I'll get mommy to buy me a dove instead of a rabbit."

"Emily?"

She scrunches her face up, swaying in the dilemma of magic acts and fortunetelling. "I don't want to miss the rest of the show, Mary Jane," she whines. "You go and I'll see you later."

I turn about in my seat. "You can sit here, dad. I want to go over to the library and see something else."

Instead of going to the end of the aisle, interrupting everyone as they watch the show, I slide my chair back, toward dad, and step out.

"If you want, Mary Jane, you can meet us at Jack's when you're done. We'll be watching the puppet show."

"OK, dad – if I get done in time. Otherwise, I'll catch the shuttle bus and meet you at home."

It's even colder outside than it was before. And the wind's whipped up, racing down Maple Street and slamming into storefronts or dashing through the alleyways between them. I don't see the clowns any more. I guess they had enough of it, especially since the only audience that they could attract were the ones passing by in the shuttle bus. And even then – it's not like the people on the bus had a choice in the matter – it was the only route that the bus driver could take to get where he was going. But I do feel kind of sorry for the clowns. All that work and practice and freezing themselves to the bone for nothing. I guess that's where show business gets you.

When I arrive at the top of the hill – where Maple Street drops down to meet Juniper in front of the library – it's an easy decision. There isn't any traffic, except for the shuttle bus, of course, which passes every fifteen minutes, and that's nowhere in sight. So, in the middle of the street I lay myself flat and push off, body-sledding down the hill until my feet drive into the ridge of snow at the bottom.

Brushing myself off, I approach the library. It looks the same way as it did before. The lights over the front steps and in the main hallway are turned on, but I don't see anyone around. Maybe the fortuneteller looked into her crystal ball and saw that no one was coming – so she never showed up either. You'd think she'd be able to do that since, after all, it's her business, peeking into the future. But I wonder: can fortunetellers see their own futures in the palms of their hands or in their crystal balls? Can they spread their decks of tarot cards on the tables before them and determine what's going to happen to them? Or do they need another fortuneteller to read their fortunes for them? I don't know. Maybe I'll ask the fortuneteller – if I ever find her, that is.

The front reading rooms in the library look so strange with the lights turned off. Sometimes, when I'm sitting in the library and I take a break from my reading, I look at all the books on the shelves around me and picture them in the darkness when no one's around, just like they are now. I know it sounds crazy but I imagine the characters in the books – whispering to each other at first – but then suddenly coming to life, stepping from their books into the ones next to them and kind of interacting with the other characters to create entirely different stories, with completely different conclusions, like a fiction within a fiction that nobody could ever read about because ... well, because it all happens at night and nobody can read in the darkness. But it would have been different entirely if a character from another book stepped into the book that I finished reading last week. It would have been different if a character from another book saw the little girl, Madeleine, as she approached the top of the steps with the basket of clothes held out in front of her and, at the last moment, grabbed her by the arm, preventing her from falling and tumbling down, from bumping her head and breaking her wrist, from screaming so loud that I could almost hear my ears ring. But nobody heard her because her dad was at work. And though her mom was in the kitchen, she couldn't hear her either. But if only a character from another book had reached out at the last moment and grabbed Madeleine by the arm ...

Anyway – and this sounds even crazier – maybe it would be different, too, if someone from one of the books on the shelves, stepped from a page right at this moment and said, "I'll help you, Mary Jane. I'll help you find your way beyond the train tracks and through the mountains ..."

"Can I help you?"

I'm so startled by the sound of the voice behind me that I think my heart's going to burst from pounding so hard. Slowly I turn around in the darkness, not knowing what to expect.

"Did you come to have your fortune read?"

I take a deep breath and let it out

"I'm sorry. I didn't mean to frighten you," the girl says, apparently realizing that she had scared the living daylights out of me. "Are you all right?"

"Just give me a moment," I reply, coaxing my heart to settle down.

As she approaches me, I recognize her from school. Her name is Esmeralda and she's a couple of years older than me. She lives in the trailer park out by the lake.

"Are you here to see the fortuneteller too?" I ask.

"Well – no," she replies, adding, "I am the fortuneteller."

"But I didn't expect you ..."

"You didn't expect me to be so young," she interjects.

"How did you know I was going to say that?" I ask.

"Because everyone always says that. Because everyone expects me to be an old gypsy woman with a gold tooth and an evil eye," she explains. "But – you didn't think that I knew *beforehand* that you were going to ask me that, did you?"

"Oh no! No – I was just surprised because ... because you're so young. That's all."

With Esmeralda leading the way, we go into one of the smaller reading rooms. Draped around the room are sheets – curtains, I guess, but they look more like sheets. They're midnight blue and have stars and crescent moons that glow in the dimness of a black light. On the table are two candles and a deck of cards.

"I don't see your crystal ball," I say with disappointment.

"I didn't bring it with me," she replies, seating herself at the table. "Unfortunately, I left it in the trunk of the car yesterday morning and ... well, if I were to look into it now, the only determination that I could make about the future is that it's cold and unchanging, as if it were frozen in time."

" *'Frozen in time'?"* I repeat, sitting opposite her. "You mean that the future is like it is now? – Frozen? – With very little ever changing from year to year, with no one remembering ... What do you mean? – *'Frozen in time'?"*

"I mean that the fluid inside the crystal ball is frozen solid," she replies, looking at me with a puzzled expression. "I left it on the mantle over the fireplace so it could gradually thaw. But what did you think I meant?"

"Oh – I see. It froze ... it froze because of the temperature ... because it's so cold out," I stammer, wanting to move forward. "Yes, that's what I thought you meant. I guess you'll be using the cards then."

"Yes. I'll be using the cards," she says. "Have you ever had your fortune read before, Mary Jane, with tarot cards?"

"No," I reply. "I've never had my fortune read."

"OK, then let me explain a little bit about them," says Esmeralda. "But first, why don't you pick up these cards here and start shuffling them. It's important for you – and for you alone – to touch them as much as possible so that the energy, which is peculiar only to yourself, is transferred into the cards themselves. It's one of the crucial elements in a successful reading."

It's only part of the deck – what she calls "The Principals" – the remaining two-thirds of the deck left on the table by Esmeralda. I have this weird idea that if I turned the cards in my hands over, there would be pictures of Mr. Marshfield, the school principal, on the other side. 'Here's Mr. Marshfield picking his nose; here he is stuffing his face with his lunch; and – Look! – In this picture he's scratching his butt when he thinks no one's looking!'

"Now lay them face down on the table and swirl them about. As you mix them around," she advises, "close your eyes and think about events and experiences that have influenced your life, remembering in your mind's eye things that you've done, things that have yet to be done. Think about your hopes and aspirations, about your dreams. And most importantly, Mary Jane, think about things not only with your mind, but with your heart as well."

When I stop she tells me to choose one of the cards and to set it aside.

"Now," she says, "I want you to close your eyes again and mix in the rest of the cards with the ones in front of you."

I reach for the pile of remaining cards and start swirling them around, merging them in with the others.

"And remember, Mary Jane, think with your heart as well as your mind."

As I move the cards around, snapshots from the camera of memory develop in the darkroom of my mind. I see our Christmas tree on Christmas morning and all the presents, wrapped in their fancy ribbons and bows. I see my new backpack, my canteen and compass that everyone thought I was crazy to ask for. And there's the twins, ripping into their presents until dad and mom warn them to control themselves. There's dad with the new radio that I bought him and mom with the hat and scarf set that I made in home economics. She tries them on, kissing me on the cheek and then ... then it's the rose – carefully I carry the rose from the closet of my room ...

"OK," says Esmeralda. "Now push the cards back together again, into a deck."

When I finish, I open my eyes and slide the deck toward Esmeralda.

"Before we begin," she says, "is there anything in particular about the future – about your future – that you would like me to address in my reading? It can be something specific, like the answer to a question, or something more general, like how well you'll be doing in school this year."

"Do I have to say anything? Or can we just see what the cards have to say?" I ask, choosing to remain non-committal.

"You don't have to say anything, Mary Jane."

"OK – then that's the way that I want it. I don't want to say anything."

"As you wish," she says, sliding in front of her the single card that I had removed from the deck initially. "Now, let me explain briefly how the reading will proceed. I will draw ten cards and lay them into a pattern in front of me. The sequence in which each card is drawn represents the different sphere of influence, such as the present or the past, the environment or your emotions. The card itself reveals the nature of the influence – what it is, or who it is, that may have some impact in what happens to you in the future. For example, this first card that you drew," she says, pointing to it, "because it was the first card means that it represents yourself, Mary Jane, *The Questioner*. Whatever the card is will suggest the essence of your character and personality, the heart of your hopes and aspirations. Do you understand how it works?"

"I understand," I reply, nodding my head.

"Good," says Esmeralda. "Then let's begin."

She closes her eyes for a moment, concentrating on the task before her. Outside, I hear the wind charging through the trees, glancing from the windows of the library.

"Ah, *The High Priestess*," she says, after flipping over the first card – *The Questioner* – and what was supposed to represent my character and personality.

"I see someone who strives for knowledge and understanding, particularly in practical matters," says Esmeralda. "You are someone who enjoys learning, discovering, finding answers to difficult questions. It's because you are curious, because you have a deep-seated drive to understand how everything works around you. And from this – this thirst for knowledge – you derive great satisfaction when you succeed, but frustration and impatience when you do not."

This is true, of course. I remember once taking apart my alarm clock so I could figure out how it worked – how its components contributed to the precise movements of its hands as they repeated their circular journeys across the face of the clock. But I couldn't put it back together again so I got mad and threw it into my toy box, which ... – I wonder: *if I did put the clock back together again, then maybe Father Time would wake up. Maybe it's the clock ... because the clock stopped working that it made everything ...*

"This next card represents *The Present Influence* – that which affects you at the present moment, which occupies your current interests."

The card depicts *The World*. On top of the world is a woman, who is seated on a throne. Cupped in her right hand is a bunch of seeds; in her left, a basket of fruits. At her feet are a lion and a lamb – the lion looks sleepy and tame though I suspect, if the woman on the throne got up and left, the lion wouldn't think twice about having lamb chops for dinner. Perched at the top of the throne are three birds – they look like eagles or hawks because they have piercing eyes and sharp beaks and talons.

"This is a powerful card," says Esmeralda. "It represents the balance and order that we find in the world, but reminds us as well of how delicate and fragile that balance may be. The woman in the picture is often interpreted as Mother Nature – She who charges the world with the cycle of life, who oversees the order of its complex operations."

"Then it's a good card," I comment.

"Yes ... generally so," replies Esmeralda. "Unfortunately, Mary Jane, *The World* is inverted – it's upside down – suggesting that something in the world, either real or as you perceive it, is not quite right, in disarray. Something is out of balance, at least for the present moment, and we won't know if order is restored until we see what your future cards hold for you. But tell me, is there something that's troubling you now? Something about the world around you that's causing you distress?"

I don't like to fib – I really don't – but sometimes I don't have any choice in the matter either.

"No," I reply, though not looking directly at Esmeralda but down at *The World*. "Nothing's bothering me. What do the three birds mean?"

I don't think that she believes me because there's an uncomfortable silence before she replies.

"Each bird views the different temporal spheres that influence the world. The one on the left peers into the past, determining events that may explain variations in the order of the world as it becomes expressed in the present. The bird on the right examines the future as it unfolds from the present, measuring the impact of current events on what is to come. The middle bird has the most difficult task: viewing events as they occur in the present while listening to the advice of his brethren. He is the only bird that addresses the woman – Mother Nature – suggesting to her ways to avoid catastrophe."

As Esmeralda turns the next card over, she narrows her eyes, clenches her teeth ever so slightly. I don't think this is a good card at all.

"*The Moon*," she says, closing her eyes. "*The Moon* suggests great danger."

Even if Esmeralda didn't say anything, I'd know that *The Moon* isn't a very good card to draw. The upper portion of the card shows a young man playing a guitar – or a mandolin, I think it's called – for a girl up on a balcony. In the corner of the sky above them is a round face that's emerging from a full moon. The expression on the face is kind of neutral, not really expressing anything. If that was all there was to it, then it wouldn't be so bad. But it's the bottom portion of the card that paints a different picture. There's a close-up of a snake as he slithers up one of the supports on the railing of the balcony and you know that it's just a matter of time before he reaches the girl. She has her hand on the railing so the odds are – unless she removes her hand before the snake arrives, he's going to bite her with his poison.

"This card represents the *Immediate Obstacle* so the threat of danger is imminent, something that will materialize in the very near future."

"But ... but what kind of danger?" I ask. "How serious is it, Esmeralda?"

I don't like this at all. I thought fortunetellers were only supposed to tell you about good things.

She flips the next card over.

"*The Ten of Batons*," she says, closing her eyes again. "*The Ten of Batons* represents your *Specific Goal*. The card usually suggests a journey, a journey that ... Yes ... Yes, I see it now! – Not one journey but several and they're not the kind that are taken for pleasure, like a vacation, but journeys that are made for a specific purpose, to find answers to questions, to seek knowledge that you would not be able to obtain had you not embarked on your journeys.

"I see," she continues, her hands curling into fists that are clenched so tightly that her knuckles turn white. "I see ... I see at least three journeys in front of you," she goes on, the veins along the temples of her head swelling in her efforts. "Three journeys but for each ... Each journey offers its own challenges, its own peculiar brand of danger ... There is darkness! – A deep, dark blackness that swarms around you, that pushes against you ... in a place where you've never been before. But this darkness – it is so thick and sticky that you can almost smell it, and taste it, like ... like stale black licorice ...

"And now," she continues, "I see in this other place ... There is lightning! – Huge thunderous cracks that split the sky into jagged fragments. Its flash is blinding. The roar of it's thunder is deafening as it rolls over hills and valleys and ... Yes! – Yes, I see far below a ... a train, a train moving swiftly along, the smoke streaming from its stack like the breath of a wild animal in the cold ...

"And now ... in this third place there is ... there is ...

"Ohhhhhhhh ..." she says, jerking forward and gasping for breath as she slams her hand up to her breast.

I jump in my seat, jolted by her sudden movement.

"Are you all right?" I say, swallowing.

"For a moment ... for a moment I felt myself ... falling ... falling into a ...," she stammers, looking around the library as if she's trying to get her bearings again. "I felt myself falling into a bottomless void!"

"Would you like me to get you some water?" I ask, starting to get up from my chair.

"No ... No, I'll be fine," she says. "Just give me a moment."

While Esmeralda composes herself, I think about leaving. Maybe having my fortune read isn't such a good idea after all. Maybe the reading itself will influence what I choose to do in the future – like the journeys. When the time does arrive for me to decide if I must go somewhere, like crossing the train tracks, will it be because I've finally decided to do it? – To actually fulfill my New Year's resolution? Or will it be only because Esmeralda has foreseen it?

"What you must remember, Mary Jane, is that my visions – my predictions – represent only glimpses into possible futures. It's very important to understand that," advises Esmeralda. "Is that clear?"

"I understand," I reply, wondering if she possesses the additional gift of reading one's mind.

Pulling a handkerchief out, she dabs the beads of sweat that have bubbled up along the bridge of her forehead, along the ridge of her upper lip.

"Now," she says, closing her eyes again, "regarding your journeys ..."

Her hands tighten into fists. The veins along the temples of her head swell again in the grueling process of her visions.

"There is some other thing ... some other thing that drives you, attracts you, that may provide you with answers to your questions. I see," she continues, "I see ... figures ... giant figures in a strange place – a place that you've never seen before. But ... but it is a place of much joy and merriment – a place unlike the roads that take you here. The one figure ... the one is huge and muscular – and strong like iron – as he must be because he carries upon his straining shoulders an enormous weight. The other figure nearby – he glows like ... like gold, and floats in the air as if he were carried by the wind. In his hand ...," she adds, straining to see in her darkness, to interpret the strange shadows that animate her darkness. "In his one hand is ... is *fire*."

Esmeralda pauses to breathe deeply, to inspect other elements in the mindscape of her vision. Outside, a blast of wind swings through the trees and buffets the library, its windows and doors shaving splinters – drafts of frigid air that carom through the reading rooms, that make the curtain behind Esmeralda sway like a pendulum.

"There are many people here – laughing and shouting ... gliding ... – yes, gliding along as if they were floating on the same wind that carries the golden figure. Lively and spirited, they move about, swirling ... A figure eight! – They're skating! – Skating on a frozen lake as the golden figure hovers nearby!

"And ... and behind it all, there's a ... a tree – a single, colossal tree with gold and silver ornaments, with thousands upon thousands of lights that sparkle in the night, and ribbons ... broad bands of ribbons that are ... – yes, plaid – a sort of red and black plaid pattern in the ribbons that are draped across the huge tree.

"Does that mean anything to you?" she asks, startling me as she suddenly opens her eyes. "Is there a significance to 'red' and to 'black'?"

"Red and black remind me of checkers," I reply, though choosing not to say anything more.

"Checkers," she repeats, thinking of the possibilities. "Or the suits in a deck of cards," she adds. "They're red and black as well."

"*The Six of Cups*," says Esmeralda, flipping the next card over and closing her eyes. "This card concerns your *Past Foundation* – the building blocks upon which the present and the future are based. I see ... I see much happiness here – a home life steeped in warmth and love, one which has provided you with a sense of security and balance, though one certainly not without its typical measure of confrontation and disagreement. The journeys ... the journeys that I foresaw are not the result of any conflict in your home life – in fact, if anything, it is the warmth and comfort of your home that holds you in place, that detracts you from your journeys.

"No – It is that other image," she says, concentrating, "that image of the figures – one of iron and one of gold – the frozen lake and the giant tree, draped in ribbons ... It is that image that draws you away.

"*The Three of Batons*," she goes on, after turning the next card over. "This card reveals the impact of *Recent Events*, particularly as they influence your current state of mind. It suggests ... alienation ... polarization – a movement away from that which you hold dear. It may be in response to the *Ten of Batons* over here," she says, tapping with her finger the card that represents my *Specific Goal.* "It is because you require answers to difficult questions that you find yourself drawn away, becoming isolated as you attempt to deal with your task at hand. It is possible that this alienation from family and friends is a preparation for the journeys that, shortly, you will be compelled to undertake."

This is becoming kind of scary because, although Esmeralda is revealing my future – the *possibilities* of my future in a general sort of way – I really can't disagree with anything that she's said so far.

"*The Queen of Swords!*" Esmeralda exclaims, widening her eyes. "She is a powerful figure – one whom rivals *The Magician* in his capacity to manipulate, to change things, to accomplish through cleverness and cunning what others cannot. She is a very powerful influence, a skilled and resourceful ally, though one not easily placated should you find yourself in her disfavor."

'*The Queen of Swords,*' I think to myself, picturing one face after another, wondering who she could possibly be.

"I can't think of anyone," I point out to Esmeralda. "Anyone whom I might imagine ..."

"That's not surprising," she replies, "because ... – I don't know how to explain this, Mary Jane, but ... she is someone whom you know, someone whom you do not."

I guess she understands my perplexity by the expression of my face.

"*The Queen of Swords,*" Esmeralda continues, "represents *The Future Influence* – someone whom you will encounter beyond the horizon of tomorrow, someone who will shape, for better or worse, what path you choose to follow. But there is something else, something about her that is ... familiar. I have the impression that you've met her before – perhaps a long time ago – but there is something ... something that has transformed her, something that has caused her to be ... to be reborn, to be resurrected as *The Queen of Swords.*"

"When? When will I meet her? – Meet her again, that is. And how do I know if *The Queen* is going to help me? Or ... or if she isn't?"

"We've three cards left, Mary Jane," says Esmeralda. "Shall I continue?"

Three cards left. I really didn't think it would be like this. I really thought that it would be more like a parlor game – something playful and amusing, something that you didn't take too seriously and forgot about once it was over. But this ... this is so different from what I expected.

"The last three cards – can you tell me what they represent before you turn them over?"

"But of course," she replies. "This next one represents *Environmental Factors* – forces around you and which will invariably influence the final outcome. The one here," she says, pointing, "suggests the state of your *Inner Emotions* and what it is that motivates you toward the last card, which represents *The Final Result*, the culmination of what all the other cards suggest."

Only three cards left – three cards! It's impossible for me to ignore them.

"OK," I say. "Let's continue."

She flips the *Environmental Factors* card over.

Like *The Moon*, the card is divided into two scenes. The one at the top shows a prince in some kind of courtly setting. He has a jeweled crown but he's dressed in armor, as if he were going into battle. In his right hand is a scepter, which I guess proves to everybody around him that he's the prince. The picture at the bottom of the card depicts him in a chariot, drawn by four horses, racing across a bridge.

"It isn't good, is it, Esmeralda?"

"It's not as bad as it could be," she replies. "It's inverted so the impact of the environment is less pronounced. Unfortunately, however, it does suggest outside forces that are not conducive to your purposes. It suggests strife, tension, difficulties. I would venture to say that when the time does arrive, Mary Jane, for you to venture upon your journeys, you should be well-prepared to address the roads in front of you."

For a moment I picture again my new backpack, canteen and compass. Everyone thought I was crazy.

"What would you have said if the card wasn't inverted, but right side up?"

"I would have advised you to forget about your journeys."

The next card – the *Inner Emotions* – makes me a little nervous because I get the feeling that Esmeralda can peer straight into the heart of me, fingering through my thoughts and feelings until she realizes that maybe I am ... crazy, hopeless, "emotionally challenged".

"I'm not surprised," she says, turning over the card to reveal *The Five of Swords*. "It suggests stasis – a state of inactivity, of standing still. It represents the confusion and turmoil that are brought about by a failure to act, to take steps that address a situation at hand. It can be something as simple as ... as driving a car up to a stop sign and becoming so flustered because you don't know if you should turn right or left that you just sit there, unable to decide which way to go. Or, it can be as serious as ... as a deer, for example, suddenly freezing in its tracks as it crosses a road, mesmerized by the headlights of an approaching car."

This is all so true. It's already New Year's Eve and what have I done so far? – Oh sure, I've gotten some equipment that I'll need for my journeys. And I've managed to upset Emily by telling her that I have to cross the train tracks. But what have I really done? I don't even have what I can call a real plan yet.

"Before we turn the final card, Mary Jane, I want to summarize everything up to this point," says Esmeralda, folding her hands in her lap. "First, we discover in *The High Priestess* that you are someone who is curious about things around you, that you seek answers to questions, particularly those that explain the nature of things and how they work. We see in *The World* – in *The World* inverted – that there is something, either real or how you perceive it, which you do not understand. This is what occupies your current interest, what you strive to resolve – this issue about *The World* and whatever it is about it that unsettles you. It is *The Ten of Batons* that suggests at least three journeys, undertaken for the specific purpose of discovering knowledge, answers, explanations regarding your vision of *The World*, your sense that something is not quite right about it. We know by *The Moon* and by *The Chariot* that these journeys will not be easy ones. In fact, they will be far from easy because *The Moon* suggests great danger along the way. With *The Chariot*, although it is inverted, we discover that the form of this danger is to be shaped by the environment around you – as if nature itself were rising up against you, attempting to prevent you from finding answers to your questions.

"I would caution you again, Mary Jane: when the time does come for you to go, you must be well-prepared for your journeys and extremely careful.

"*The Six of Cups* reveals a happy home life – warm and loving. It is this bond between you and your family that holds you back, that anchors you, that impedes you from taking action, particularly in embarking on your journeys. It creates the tension between heart and mind, between remaining with your family and pursuing answers to your questions that has kept you indecisive, alienating you from others, contributing to a state of confusion and turmoil.

"What we do not know at this point is the significance of the figures – the one of iron, the other of gold. We do not know why the broad ribbons that adorn the huge Christmas tree are of a red and black, plaid pattern. Perhaps the tree," Esmeralda suggests, "is the Tree of Knowledge. Perhaps its ribbons – the unraveling of its ribbons – will provide you with answers to your questions. Perhaps they will reveal to you things that you want to know, things that you do not.

"In the shadows of *The Future* hovers a powerful figure – *The Queen of Swords*. Rivaling *The Magician* in cleverness and cunning, her influence – whether beneficial or malicious – will dictate the success, or failure, of the journeys before you. It is this last card," she says, touching it with her finger, "that indicates *The Final Result* – that which is yet to come, that which reveals what all the other cards suggest."

'*The Queen of Swords* – someone whom I know, someone whom I don't – I can't help but try to imagine the image of her face. Who could she possibly be? And what influence – for better or for worse – could she possibly have upon the outcome?'

"The last card," says Esmeralda, flipping it over.

The picture on *The Final Result* depicts a young woman pouring water from a pitcher into a river. In the sky over her head is a single star. This must be a good card to get because Esmeralda is smiling.

"The goddess," she says, keeping her eyes open this time, "replenishes the river with the water of life. She provides us with that which others cannot – a gift that is so simple yet so precious that, without it, we would be hard-pressed to continue on our way, helpless in arriving at our destination."

"She gives us hope," I offer, looking at the face of the goddess that is kind and benevolent, at the star in the sky above her.

"She gives us hope," Esmeralda repeats, pleased that I had figured out the meaning of the card all by myself. "She gives us the star to illuminate our path. She gives us the star to find illumination at the end of our path."

It is the door to the library opening and closing, followed by a draught of wind that announces the arrival of Esmeralda's next visitor.

"Do you have any questions, Mary Jane, about the reading? Is there anything that you don't understand? – That you would like me to clarify?"

I can't think of anything to ask Esmeralda. But what I do know is that it's time – it's time to do what I must and come what may.

'Hope,' I think to myself as I zipper my coat and head for the exit. 'Hope *and* faith,' I think, picturing in my mind not only the goddess, who pours from the pitcher the water of life, but the image – the plastic image of Jesus, glued to the dashboard of Mr. Gabriel's truck.

Maiden Journey

Instead of turning around and going back up the sledding hill, I grab the rope of my sled and pull it along the valley in a southerly course. The bad news is: the ridge opposite the sledding hill is too steep to climb straight up so I have to move at an angle, inching my way toward the top. It takes longer that way. And with my backpacks and equipment tied to my sled, I have to be careful that it doesn't topple over. But the good news is: it hasn't snowed for over a week – my sled glides easily across the frozen surface – with far less effort than if the snow were newly fallen. And my boots leave half-inch pockmarks rather than foot-deep craters behind me so I can save my strength for more difficult terrain in front of me. The crunching sound of each footstep reminds me of Roger and Todd when they sit at the kitchen table, eating Cheerios right out of the box.

When I arrive at the top of the ridge, I park my sled and climb a huge boulder near the edge. The wind has swept most of the snow away so it's easy finding footholds, enabling me to scale the smooth contour of the rocky surface without worrying about sliding off.

The view of Christmasville, slumbering in the cold shock of dawn, is so beautiful and peaceful that it seems almost holy – timeless and unworldly – as if it were a chunk of landscape, borrowed from heaven. Poking through the tops of the trees, I can see the bell tower of city hall and the steeples of all three churches – St. Mary's, St. Nick's and St. Ives'. Beyond the roofs of Clauson's and of Jack's Toy Store, the buildings and stores along Maple Street remind me of dominoes turned sideways, except the dots are dark, rectangular windows instead of bright, white circles. I see the top of my school, the second floor of the hospital and, in the distance, the upper part of the power station. At the intersection of Elm and West Juniper is a green car. It has its right blinker on but turns left, out of view. I bet the driver is delivering newspapers – still half-asleep as he folds them in three and slips them into their clear, plastic wrappers before chucking them out the window of his car.

At the far southern corner of town is the Consolidated Factory Works. It rises over the treetops as if it were a monument, its smokestack scribbling a gray scar against the creamy, porcelain dome of the sky – like a crack inside an old bowl. Even though it's early Saturday morning and mostly no one's working inside the plant now, I guess they have to keep a couple of people on so the furnaces don't go out.

Closer to where I'm standing, I see two kids on the sledding hill. They must be boys because they make a giant "X" as they slide down the slope, playing "broadside". But their timing is off because the boy in the red coat crosses well before the boy in the navy jacket has time to catch up with him. To the left, stretching southward and dotted randomly with yellow construction vehicles, is Beech Boulevard. And then it's the bare skeleton of Wakefield Bridge, swinging out over the frozen marshlands, the snow-covered lake, the trailer park where Esmeralda lives.

I wonder if her crystal ball is crystal again – if the future thawed itself out. I wonder too: if Esmeralda said that I was going to be rich, instead of making journeys, would I be home now, stuffing as many coins into my piggy bank as I could find?

Although the anxiety of encountering danger along the way made it difficult for me to prepare and to actually set out, it was the promise of at least three journeys that made it possible. I mean – if there really were going to be *at least three journeys*, then the first couldn't be so dangerous as to prevent me from embarking on the second, and the third ... could it? And what could be so frightening about the darkness, or a little thunder and lightning, or of falling down? It doesn't sound all that dangerous to me. Anyway, I'll just see how this first journey goes and then take it from there.

The boys on the sledding hill have climbed to the top and are on their way down again, missing their "broadside" again. A flock of black crows fly over the valley towards me and then, lifting higher, pass over my head toward the deep woods. From where the crows are – flying eastward over the treetops – they can probably see the distant plume of smoke, coiling like a rope from the passenger train as it races through the forest, as the long burst of its whistle threads a thousand paths through the trees. Judging by the sound of it, I figure the train tracks are about a mile away.

Retrieving my sled, I continue along my journey. It's pretty easy going, swinging around spruce trees with their snow-puff skirts, through a grove of majestic cedars, beneath the barren limbs of oak trees. I have my new compass out, checking it every hundred yards or so, to make sure that I'm moving due east.

After about forty-five minutes, I stop to rest on the edge of my sled beneath a tree. The bark of it is similar to an oak, having the same network of canals that snake around crusted, gray chunks that are raised up against the surface of the trunk. But it isn't until I unhook my canteen from my backpack and unscrew the cap, swinging my head back for a long drink that I realize the difference between this tree and an oak. Hanging from its bare branches are dozens of light-green balls that are about the same size as the ones that you hang on your Christmas tree. I don't know what they are and none of them are within reaching distance.

Sticking up from the snow nearby is the dead limb of a tree. I get up from my sled and, grabbing a branch with both hands while holding the limb in place with my foot, give it a good tug. The snap of it breaking startles me a bit because the silence of the woods around me amplifies the sound, making the snap of it louder than I expected. For a moment, I wait. I wait until the silence rushes back in, covering everything like the snow does. Although there's no one around, I have the feeling that someone's about to shout at any minute, "Hey! – What are you doin' over there? Why'd you break that branch?"

Of course, the notion of somebody saying anything is just plain silly because there isn't anyone around.

After about two or three attempts at whacking a ball on the tree and missing, I decide to aim for the branch above it. I wind my stick back over my shoulder, concentrate on the exact spot that I want to hit and then – "Smack!" – the branch in my hand shatters in half, but not without accomplishing its goal. The ball swings up and skyward but, tethered by the string of its stem, it spins once, twice, around the branch, the arc of its spin diminishing on each turn until the stem breaks.

When I dig the ball out of the snow near my feet, I break the little branch off that tethered it to the tree. Although the ball is slightly marred by the impact of the branch, it's perfectly round and looks like it's been dipped into a liquid, light-green, velvet fabric because there's no seam to it at all. And it has a strong, peculiar smell to it – vaguely familiar – like some of the nuts that Mrs. Thompson might put in her desserts.

I think about laying the ball on my sled and cracking it open but, as I'm standing there – analyzing it and trying to figure out what the thing is – something in the snow, in the background, comes into focus: *animal tracks*. They're big and pretty deep in the snow and there's at least three sets of them so they must have been heavier ... and larger ... than foxes or squirrels or ...

I drop the velvet ball in the snow. A shiver runs down my spine.

Wild dogs???

A pack of ferocious wolves??? – (*I think of the tale that I had told the twins about the 'dark Santa Claus' and his sleigh, drawn by ...*)

Deadly, carniverous snow bunnies???

Giant, killer rats on a rampage???

Marching in a beeline back to my sled, I look straight ahead. I have to concentrate on keeping my eyes from veering off to the right or the left or into the woods beyond the sled because I don't want to see those red, beady eyes, those razor-sharp teeth, of ... of predators – big, ugly, furry, stinky predators that are famished, wild, drooling, crazed by hunger as they bide their time, stalking me, waiting to pounce at any moment ...

I grab the rope to my sled and start running back the way that I came and ...

"Wait a minute!" I say out loud, stopping in my tracks because I suddenly realize that I've steered myself right into a panic. "Esmeralda didn't say anything about wild animals."

I look around. There's nothing there.

"Hellllllooooo!" I shout, cupping my hands around my mouth. "Anybody home!"

Nothing. No predators, no animals, not even a bird, perched on the branch of a tree, wondering why this crazy person has come into the woods to disturb him.

I do an about-face, approaching the spot where I had seen the animal tracks. They're not that big, and not that deep after all.

"You know what, Mary Jane?" I say out loud. "They're probably only deer tracks."

No sooner have I said it that it occurs to me that the woods around me was where Stark, the Iceman, went deer-hunting with his bow and arrow in early December. I'm not a huge fan when it comes to hunting – unless, of course, it puts food on the table that otherwise wouldn't be there if you didn't. If you didn't hunt, that is, which is why Stark went into the woods with his bow and arrow and his dog, Blink, in December – to hunt for enough food to get by. But anyway – What a relief! – Not only because of my sudden illumination regarding the deer tracks, but also because nobody had witnessed my stupid panic attack. God! – That would have been so embarrassing!

Twenty minutes later, deeper into the woods, I remember the green velvet ball that I forgot to pick up from the snow.

My arms are getting tired as I move up the rise in front of me. I switch between my right arm and my left, lugging my sled across the frozen snow, lacing a path through the trees around me. When I get to the crest, I'm hoping that I'll find the train tracks on the other side. But no – there's no sign of the tracks and, to make matters worse, the terrain looks much more difficult to traverse, rising and falling as if someone had taken the landscape and crumpled it up like a sheet of paper, unfolding it when they were done. But the biggest obstacle – and the most immediate – is the steep drop in front of me. It's only about eight or ten feet to the bottom but it's a straight drop and I don't see any breaks where I could climb myself down without the risk of falling.

'Falling' – for a moment, I think about Esmeralda, about the brief sensation that she experienced when she was reading, when she was envisioning the card that told her about the three journeys.

"Maybe I should turn back and find another way," I say to myself, though not wholly convinced as I drop the rope to my sled and move northward along the edge of the slope, surveying it.

After about twenty yards, I find my solution. A tall pine tree, situated at the rim of the slope, had toppled over the edge. While its tangle of roots dangle in the air like one of Mrs. Marshfield's bad wigs, its thick limbs form a kind of ladder which, with a little time and effort, could be used, not only to make my way down the slope, but to climb my way back up again when I return. As for my sled and equipment – well, I could just untie everything and, with the exception of my new backpack, which contained the thermos of hot cocoa, toss them into the snow at the bottom. When I come back, I can use my rope to hoist them back up again.

With my new backpack slung over my shoulders, it takes me about ten minutes to work my way down. It's important to take my time because the branches are iced over with snow and I certainly don't want to experience the sensation that Esmeralda did – that of falling – not unless I can avoid it.

At the bottom, I start the process of securing everything on my sled again. I swing the rope beneath the slats, wrapping it snugly about my equipment. Something in the woods nearby catches my eye. It's a cabin! – A tiny log cabin with windows and a chimney, with a little porch that's roofed over and with logs stacked by the doorway, ready for the fireplace. Except for the gnome, who isn't, of course, sitting on the porch as he smokes his briarwood pipe, the cabin reminds me of a fairytale that mom sometimes reads to Roger and Todd at bedtime.

Pulling my sled across the snow, I approach the cabin. It doesn't look like anyone's home because it's dark inside and I don't see any curls of smoke billowing from the chimney. On the porch, I cup my hands around my eyes and press my face against the plastic window to peek inside. It looks empty, and messy too, with tin plates and cups stacked haphazardly along the counter near the sink as if someone washed them up but was too lazy to dry them with the hand towel, to put them back in the cabinets where they belonged. Newspapers are strewn across the floor. A chair lies on its back. The plaid, gray-and-white tablecloth looks like it needs a good washing. A few logs are stacked by the fireplace. In the corner, a bow and a quiver of arrows lean against the wall.

A hunter's cabin! That's why no one's home – because it isn't hunting season! Could it belong to Stark, the Iceman? Or to somebody else?

Lifting the latch, I push the door open.

This could be my base – my base of operations, I think. I mean – Geez, I could live here if I had to, cleaning the place up when it was too cold to go outside, fixing it up like a dollhouse. I could even learn to shoot the bow and arrow so I could hunt if I ... No – I don't think so. I don't think that I could shoot a deer or a rabbit, even if I was hungry. Besides, it's not like I'm going to live here. I'm only stopping long enough to have my sandwich and some hot cocoa.

The first thing that I do is to look for matches. I don't see any on the mantel over the fireplace. There's none on the counter. In the drawers of the cabinets, there's all kinds of stuff – a screwdriver, nuts, bolts, a pair of hinges, scissors, parts of a sewing kit, a sock, pliers, bits of wire, a ball of twine, three batteries, a can opener, buttons, a glove with a hole in it, a transistor radio, a bottle that's half filled and has a label with a name on it – but I never heard of any Jack Daniels ...

"Ah ha! – A box of matches!"

With the newspapers from the floor, kindling and two of the smaller logs that were stacked near the fireplace, I have a nice little fire going. At least it's enough to warm the place up a bit and to take the dampness out of the air.

After folding the tablecloth back from the table – it's too dusty and stained to eat on – I take a sandwich and the thermos of hot cocoa from my backpack. I could eat a cow! – I'm so hungry. While I jam my peanut butter and jelly sandwich into my mouth, I take two of the batteries that I found in the drawer and snap them into the back of the transistor radio, replacing the cover. I turn the volume dial up all the way and slowly spin the second dial, trying to home in on WHYY of Christmasville ... or, if I'm lucky, on that other station ...

New York City: maybe it'll be the first town that I stumble upon when I cross the train tracks. I guess it's the primary reason for my traveling due east – to find New York City, though I don't know why exactly I've convinced myself that that's where I'll find it. Of course, it's impossible to go directly north – straight towards St. Valentine's and Easterville – because of the mountains that loom behind the buildings on Maple Street. In the west are the cliffs. You can see the edge of them on the other side of the train tracks by Union Station. So – the only options remaining are east, which is the way that I'm going now; south, past the farmlands beyond the gas station; and north ... northeast, I guess, having decided once and for all to go through the train tunnel that winds beneath Jenkins' Hill. Three options ... *"Three journeys,"* said Esmeralda.

And now that I think about it ... – well, it was three times that I snuck out into the garage, where dad played the radio that I gave him for Christmas. I moved the antenna around to every direction there is, tried every possible setting with that stupid second knob but I couldn't pick up anything more than WHYY of Christmasville – not St. Valentine's, not Easterville, not New York City.

Swallowing the last bit of my sandwich, I decide that the batteries are dead. It's either that or the transistor radio is broken. Besides, I have to get moving anyway. I'm already behind schedule and I haven't even crossed the train tracks yet. Finishing up my hot cocoa, I get up from the chair and yawn. It would be so nice to take a little nap on the bed in the corner of the cabin, snuggling up beneath the blankets, even though they're dirty and dusty and I might get sick or something because they smell sweaty and musty like old socks. No – I guess it's the condition of the blankets that helps me decide. At the moment, time is more important than napping.

"I wonder if Jack Daniels owns this cabin," I suddenly say aloud, thinking about the label on the bottle. "I wonder if he knows Stark, the Iceman? – Maybe they both share the cabin."

'Or – and what's more intriguing,' I think to myself, 'I wonder if Jack Daniels knows John F. Kenn? Maybe that's why I never heard of Jack Daniels – because when he goes to his hunting cabin – *this cabin* – he travels west from his home in New York City, crossing the train tracks before he gets here.'

Tucking my thermos into my backpack, I zip my coat up, eager to push on. I slide my gloves on and grab the pail by the fireplace. Outside, I scoop up a load of snow by the porch so I can douse the fire. Looking off to the east, I review the terrain. It appears even more difficult to manage than when I had viewed it from the top of the ridge behind me. Punctuated by rocks and boulders and fallen trees, by sharp rises and drops in the landscape, I don't know how I'll be able to drag my sled behind me. Certainly, it'll take far more time and effort than if I proceed without it, consolidating in my new backpack only those supplies that are essential to continue.

Turning about, I head back toward the cabin. I put the pail down on the step of the porch and grab my sled, leaning it up against the stack of logs. It'll be safe here until I return. Inside the cabin, I exchange things between each of my backpacks until I'm satisfied that I have everything that I absolutely need. Swinging my new backpack over my shoulders, I test it to see if it's too heavy and cumbersome. It should be fine. I pick up the other backpack and set it on the floor by the front door. It's when I swing back up, adjusting the weight of the backpack on my shoulders, that I catch a glimpse of something, of someone, moving outside.

Whatever – *whoever* it is – is about forty yards away, near the pine tree that I had climbed down to get to the cabin. It was only for an instant that I caught the flash of what looked like something red as it swung behind the trunk of a tree. That's why it must be someone – because it was bright red and you don't find anything like that in nature. Unless it's a cardinal or a robin or maybe a red fox, but no – it didn't look like an animal. It looked like cloth – some kind of material – like the tail of a coat.

Quickly, I douse the fire with the pail of snow and go out the door, latching it closed behind me. I step from the porch and walk around the cabin, moving eastward so whoever it is that's watching me thinks that I'm leaving. I walk about twenty yards in the snow, veering off in a slight arc toward the right. Another ten steps and then, if I've judged correctly, the cabin should be directly between my present position and whoever it is that's spying on me. Turning around, I run as fast as I can back toward the cabin. When I get there, I lean against its back wall, catching my breath, listening for footsteps in the snow.

The way I look at it is: if – whoever it is – is intent on following me, then I'll hear them coming, probably off to my left, which is the way that I went around the cabin. When they're nearby, I'll dash around the other way, grab my sled and the backpack that I left inside the door and backtrack toward the fallen pine tree. By the time they figure out what happened, I'll be long gone. But if that same somebody is satisfied that they've chased me away, and he or she or whoever it is decides to go inside the cabin and to forget about me, then I'll just continue on toward the train tracks. I'll have to figure out later how to get my sled and the backpack that I left inside the cabin.

Flattened against the back wall, I remain perfectly still, holding my breath to listen. It seems like forever. A gust of wind swings through the trees, rattling frozen branches. I exhale, draw another breath, listening. A crow glides down to the stump of a tree and squawks three times. I exhale, draw another breath and now ... Yes, now I can hear the crunching sound of footsteps (I see that same idiotic image of Roger and Todd, stuffing their faces with Cheerios). It's getting louder – the crunching sound. Is it from my right? No ... No – it's coming from my left like I thought.

'*You have to move now,*' I hear myself whisper inside my head.

I don't budge.

'*YOU HAVE TO MOVE NOW,*' I hear the same voice say, but shouting this time.

Prying myself from the wall, I tiptoe toward my right, moving with the silence of a cat on the prowl and, turning round the corner of the cabin ...

I walk smack into him, bumping my head into his, sending us both backwards, our butts plopping into the snow.

"Brett Tolliver!" I shout. "What are you doing? – You nearly scared me to death!"

He rubs his head with one hand, gropes around for his cap with the other. "What are *you* doing?" he says.

I get myself to my feet and brush the snow off. "Why are you following me?" I demand.

"What are you doing out here?" he counters.

"I asked you first," I point out. "Why are you following me?"

Standing, he pulls his knit cap over his head. "I saw you from the sledding hill," he replies, "when you were up on the rock on the ridge."

"So?"

"So I wondered what you were doing."

"Well, I don't think it's any of your business, Brett Tolliver. You shouldn't be following me."

"OK – I shouldn't be following you," he agrees. "But why are you going into the deep woods, Mary Jane? And why are you going alone?"

"I told you, Brett. It's none of your business."

"OK – be that way," he says, turning away and starting off in the other direction. "But you know what?" he says over his shoulder. "Maybe I'll just go back and tell everybody that you're out here getting yourself lost like Mrs. Gabriel and her daughter did."

"No! – Don't you say a word about this, Brett. I won't never, ever talk to you again if you do," I state in a threatening way. "Besides, I have my compass so I can't get lost."

He stops in his tracks and turns about. "What will you do when I tell everyone that you crossed the train tracks?"

At first, I don't know what to say. But then slowly, gradually, the notion of betrayal sinks in – *Emily.*

"The train tracks?" I reply, stalling for time. "What makes you think that I'm crossing the train tracks?"

He steps toward me, looks off into the woods on his right. "It's forbidden to cross the train tracks, Mary Jane."

When he looks back, he's staring right into my eyes as if he can read everything that

I'm thinking. He knows – and there's no way, as much time and effort that I might put into it – that I'll be able to fib my way out.

"What else did Emily say?" I ask curtly.

"Nothin' else," he says. "Only that you wanted to see what was beyond the train tracks."

"She shouldn't have told you," I say, looking down at the snow. "She shouldn't have told you anything."

"I think she was ... I think she was worried that she wouldn't see you again."

"She shouldn't have told anyone," I repeat. "She promised."

There's an uncomfortable silence because neither one of us know what to say or to do. As for me, I can't turn back now because Emily decided to break her promise – I wonder how many people, besides Brett, that she did tell? I wonder what kind of trouble I'll be in when I get back? Anyway, how can I turn back now after I've come so far? It's already January 8th – there's only a little more than three weeks left before the end of the month, before that long string of days and nights starts up all over again, only to end up in another puzzling knot of December 1st.

"Maybe I should go with you," Brett suggests, looking down at the snow.

No sooner has he said it than a flush of red spreads into his cheeks.

"Why would you want to do that?" I ask. "You'll only get yourself into trouble."

"Because," he says.

"Because why?" I insist.

"Because ... because I want to," he replies without really answering, looking up from the snow.

I never noticed how pretty Brett's eyes are. They're a sort of greenish blue that remind me of that dreamy state that you suddenly find yourself in after your sled's raced down the hillside for the hundredth time. It's when you roll over, off of your sled and into the snow, tired but exhilarated, your face tingling from the cold, your breath pluming upward, and you just lie there, looking up at the sky, its blueness tinted by the ring of evergreens that stretch towards it, and ...

The sound of the train whistle charges through the trees, shattering the silence of the woods around us.

We snap our heads around, the both of us looking in the direction of the approaching train. In the distance, we can hear the powerful locomotive as it races along the tracks.

"Come on," Brett says, moving past me. "The train tracks can't be that far away now."

"Wait a minute!" I say, grabbing his arm. "If you're going to string along, Brett, then you might as well make yourself useful."

After retrieving my second backpack from the cabin, Brett hoists it over his shoulders. I make him drag my empty sled behind because I don't want to take any chances. Besides, there's the possibility that we might not be coming back exactly this way. And even though I have my compass, I don't want to go traipsing through the woods trying to find the cabin because I made a bad decision about leaving my sled behind. And, of course, with Brett tagging along and helping out, I don't have to leave it behind, do I.

Winding along dips and rises in the terrain behind the cabin, zigzagging around trees and fallen branches and boulders that seem to pop up from nowhere, we make our way through the woods. It's slow going. Every few minutes or so, I check my bearings with the cabin or, when it disappears in the woods behind us, with my compass, insuring that we're going due east. Even though Brett doesn't say much, it's a comfort having him along because ... well, it's good to know that if you get yourself in trouble, then you have somebody to help you out, somebody you can rely on. I guess I feel safer with Brett – though I don't admit it to him because, after all, he's a boy and the next thing you know, he'll start acting like one, trying to take charge of the journey and making all the decisions. And that's something that I just won't tolerate because it's *my* journey and *I'll* make the decisions – not that I won't ask his opinion once in a while because I'm not like that.

"Who were you sledding with? – Back on the hill before you started following me."

I turn sideways to move through two holly trees, careful not to get stuck by their pointed leaves.

"Ricky Caterson," replies Brett.

"Did he see me on the rock too?"

"No. And I didn't tell him either."

"Well, what did he say when you started to follow me?" I ask, anxious to know how many people knew what I was doing. "He must of thought it weird when you left him, when you started up the ridge on the other side of the sledding hill."

"He left before I started off," Brett answers. "He had to get home for his music lesson."

"He's learning to play an instrument?"

"The clarinet. But he'll never be any good at it."

"Why's that?" I ask.

"Because he hates it. Because he never practices like he's supposed to."

I slip through a crevice between boulders, struggling up an incline.

"Mary Jane?" Brett says.

"What?"

"Emily didn't tell anyone but me about you're being out here, about you're wanting to cross the train tracks."

"How can I be sure of that? What's more, how can you be so sure, Brett? – I mean, after all, she broke her promise and told you, didn't she?"

"Yes," he agrees. "She told me."

I reach up and grab a niche in the rock so I can pull myself up to the top. "Why do you think she told you, Brett? – *Only* you, and no one else?"

I turn around to grab the rope of my sled, enabling Brett to use both of his hands to pull himself up beside me.

"I don't know. I guess you'll have to ask Emily that, won't you, Mary Jane."

The train tracks: they're nestled at the bottom of a long, U-shaped hollow that stretches north and south in a straight line. It's like they scooped out a broad section of earth and rock – about ten feet deep and fifty feet wide – before they laid the tracks down in the center. Maybe they had to do it like that because of all the boulders, and to make the tracks level. And because it *is* completed, finished, over and done with – I know that the construction company that's building Beech Boulevard didn't do it. They never finish anything.

Standing on the rim of the hollow, I can look straight across to the rim on the other side. Somehow it looks different – 'primitive', I guess is the word that I'm looking for, though I don't know why exactly. Most of the trees are pines. Old and towering, their thick, crusted limbs reach toward each other as if for support. But what is peculiar – and what I suppose makes the forest look 'primitive' – is the pewter band that winds through the branches and trunks of the trees, twisting and curling like a soft, delicate scarf. I've only seen this phenomenon twice before – and both times, it was in the marshlands by Wakefield Lake.

"Why is there smoke?" Brett asks with some degree of anxiety, pointing toward the pine forest.

"It isn't smoke," I reply. "It's fog."

We tilt the sled over the edge and let it go. It slides to the bottom of the hollow. Together, we get down on our bellies and push ourselves out and over the edge, plowing the snow with our feet as we drop to the bottom.

When we approach the train tracks, the notion that I'm about to do something *forbidden* sets in. I've never done anything that was so blatantly disobedient before, something that was so absolutely and positively contrary to what I was told. I think Brett feels the same way because he's eyeing up the tracks, waiting, I guess, for me to make the first move.

I look to my right and then off to my left. This is a good place to cross because you can look up and down the railroad tracks as far as the eye can see.

"So," Brett says, "what do we do now, Mary Jane?"

In three steps I'm over, looking back at him from the other side.

"Toss the sled over first, Brett, and then you come."

He's really surprised, staring at me with his mouth open. Maybe he thought that I wasn't serious, that I was going to change my mind at the last minute and head back to Christmasville without doing what I set out to do. Maybe he thought that I was going to disappear in a puff of smoke or change into a toad or become somehow different because I had done what was *forbidden*.

"Brett? – Toss the sled over."

For a moment, I'm not sure if he's coming or not. He looks up and down the railroad tracks, scratches his head, turns toward the sled behind him.

"OK," he says, lifting the sled up and holding it before hopping over the tracks to my side.

"That wasn't any big deal," he says, almost giggling. "It makes you feel *bad*, doesn't it, Mary Jane? – Like we're rebels. Like when you swipe a Clark Bar from the candy store without paying for it."

"You actually ... You *steal* things?" I ask with disbelief.

I turn from the tracks and grab the rope of my sled in the snow.

"Only once," he says, changing his tune. "Ricky Caterson made me do it. And, to be honest, I felt so guilty about it that I tossed the Clark Bar in the trash without even eating it."

While getting down the one side of the "U" was easy enough, climbing up the other is more problematic. We keep trying to find footholds in the side of the snowy slope but find ourselves sliding back down without even getting close to the top. It isn't until Brett comes up with the idea of hoisting me up first that we succeed. He finds a large rock that's embedded in the snow so he can get a good foothold. It's about three feet up the slope. He cradles his hands so I can step into them and lifts me upwards until I can step onto his shoulders. Then he raises his hands and grabs the soles of my boots, pushing me up just far enough to pull myself over the edge of the slope.

"I never thought ...," I start to say from the top.

"You never thought what, Mary Jane?"

"I never thought you were so strong, Brett Tolliver," I reply, making his face turn a bright, bashful red.

From my backpack I take the long rope that I borrowed from dad's garage. Brett fastens the end of it to my sled and I drag it up the slope. Next, I toss the one end of the rope back down to Brett and loop the other end around the trunk of a nearby tree, knotting it securely.

"OK, Brett, try climbing up now," I shout from the tree.

When he reaches the top, I help to pull him up, to brush off the snow that clings to his coat and hat.

What's curious about moving through the pine forest is the absolute silence – the stillness – which, except for the crunching sound of our boots in the snow, completely envelops us. There's no birds chirping; no squirrels scampering about; no wind combing the needles of the pine trees back. It's eerie, this stillness, arriving like an invisible blanket that smothers everything when we stop for a moment to check the compass or to adjust the weight of our backpacks on our shoulders. And then there's the fog, too, that lingers thick and damp and motionless in patches among the trees.

"Where does it come from – the fog?" Brett asks.

"It's when something warm meets something cold," I reply. "That's what Stark says. Like when a warm pocket of air brushes against ice or snow."

We slip down into a ravine. It's getting kind of ... kind of scary because, as we move further into the ravine, into what was deepening into a pass, the western slope of it rises higher and steeper until we start to see caves. Yes! – They're real, honest-to-goodness caves that are formed into the rocky wall of the slope. I've never seen caves before and some are so tiny that a chipmunk might live inside one, but others – others are so big that the largest of animals could easily fit inside, waiting for its prey to pass. And the fog's thicker and pastier as we trek downward, almost as if it were a syrup, poured over the landscape to wind its way into the nooks and crooks of the lower regions.

"I don't think this is the right way to go, Brett," I say, after checking my compass. "We're turning north and we should be going east."

"What difference does it make?" Brett asks. "I mean – we're only exploring so what difference does it make, Mary Jane, if we go north for a while instead of east?"

Of course, I can't reply without making up a fib. Brett didn't know. How could he? – As far as he was concerned, the whole purpose of crossing the train tracks was to see what we could discover on the other side. For him, the objective, more or less, had already been accomplished. He doesn't know that what I'm really looking for is a passage away from Christmasville, a passage toward New York City.

"Look!"

He's pointing toward the entrance of a cave.

"What? What is it?" I say with alarm, scrutinizing the darkness inside the cave. "Did you see something inside, Brett? Did something move?"

I take a few steps backward but Brett moves off to the left, approaching the mouth of the cave.

"It's all right," he says, seeing me retreat. "Look! – It's right there in front of the cave."

I stop, scanning the terrain, trying to see what it is that's attracted Brett's attention.

"I don't see anything. What is it?"

He stops, looking down into the snow.

"Somebody's been here before," he replies. "There's footprints."

They do indeed look like footprints in the snow. They lead from the cave and then north, down into the deepening pass in front of us.

"They've been here for some time," Brett notes, getting down on one knee to study them. "It looks like two sets of prints, one larger than the other. And over here," he adds, pointing. "These could be a third set. But they're different than the other two."

"How long do you think they've been here, Brett?" I ask, moving toward him now that I feel comfortable that there isn't a wild animal inside the cave, ready to gobble us up.

"It's hard to tell," he replies. "Maybe a week, maybe a month."

When Brett rises to his feet, he looks toward the cave. "I wonder," he says, swinging his backpack down and opening it up.

"You're not thinking what I think you are," I say apprehensively. "Are you?"

"You can wait out here if you want, Mary Jane," he says, pulling my dad's flashlight from the backpack. "I mean, this is an opportunity that we can't just walk away from. What if there's a clue inside about what happened to Mrs. Gabriel and Caroline? How would you feel when you get back home and you say to yourself – 'Geez, if only we had looked inside that cave'."

It's difficult for me to disagree with him because he's right, of course. I wouldn't feel very good about myself if I knew that there had been a possibility, as remote as it might be, of discovering something about the disappearance of Mrs. Gabriel and her daughter. How could I ever look Mr. Gabriel in the eye again if I chose to ignore this opportunity?

"Wait up, Brett," I say, hurrying to catch up with him.

Aside from the ... 'darkness,' Esmeralda had said, 'a deep, dark blackness that swarms around you, that pushes against you ... in a place where you've never been before', she had warned.

But anyway, aside from the darkness inside the cave, pierced now by the single beam of light as Brett snaps the flashlight on and pans the rock walls, there is a dampness so palpable that it seeps through my clothes and skin, settles in the very marrow of my bones.

"How could anyone stay here?" I remark with a shiver.

"You would if you had to," Brett says. "Look over there," he adds, pointing the light toward a mound of ash and partially burnt logs that are encircled by stones.

Scouring the floor and walls of the cave with the flashlight, we search for a trace, a telltale sign of who, exactly, had been so unfortunate – or fortunate, dependent upon the circumstances outside the cave at the time – to have found refuge in this bleak and dreary place. But aside from the evidence of the fire, we discover nothing to suggest the identities of the cave's former occupants.

"What do you think, Mary Jane?" asks Brett, shining the flashlight down on the ground between us. "Do you think it was Mrs. Gabriel? And Caroline?"

"It could have been hunters," I suggest, "finding shelter during a snowstorm."

"I don't think so," he counters. "If they were hunters, then they would've had to cross the train tracks to get here."

'Unless they were hunters from the other side – from New York City,' I think without saying.

We spend a few more minutes kicking up dirt with our feet and turning the rocks by the ashes over, looking for a clue. It's pretty weird, actually, moving about on ground that isn't snow-covered.

"We could follow the footprints in the snow," Brett says, moving toward the mouth of the cave.

I edge up next to him. "If the prints were fresh, then I'd agree with you, Brett. But you know what would happen – we would reach a point where the wind and the snow had all but erased them."

"So what should we do?"

To help us decide, we sit on a couple of rocks at the mouth of the cave, eating the remainder of the sandwiches and the cookies that I had brought along. I open the thermos up and pour hot cocoa into the plastic cup that we pass back and forth until I have to fill it up again. It's almost eleven o'clock now and, although I'm fairly satisfied by the progress we've made so far, the fact is we only have about another hour – maybe two – before we'll have to turn around and head back towards Christmasville.

"So what do you think we should do?" Brett repeats.

It's a dilemma that hangs in the air with the same stillness as the fog. On the one hand, we could continue on our present course, moving deeper into the pass and maybe picking up clues along the way as to the origin of the footprints, the identities of those who had left them behind. But, as I had said to Brett, we'd probably discover along the way that the footprints were no longer distinguishable, having been covered over by the wind and snow. And of course, once we committed to that course of action, our choices would be dictated entirely by geography – there would be no recourse other than to follow the natural lay of the land, regardless of which direction it went. There would also be the distinct possibility that Brett and I could find ourselves in a similar predicament as whomever it was that had left the footprints. We could be stuck out here, in the wilderness, because of the snow or the darkness, finding shelter in caves, unable to return home. Lastly, I suppose – and what was wholly selfish on my part – if we ventured further into the pass, we would jeopardize the essential purpose of our journey – of my journey – which is to search for a passage out of Christmasville so when January 31st does arrive, I'll know exactly which way I'll be going.

Anyway, to get all the way back to the other hand of the dilemma, we could return now the way that we came – back to that point where we had started into the ravine. From there, we could travel due east again, for at least the remaining hour or so.

As I sit on the rock, considering what might be called, 'the impasse of the pass', something very strange happens. Brett is looking down, re-lacing his boots, and I'm staring into the trees that rise along the top of the opposite slope of the pass. It's funny how your mind works sometimes, forming patterns or shapes of things in the darkness of shadows or, in this case, the fog – sculpting the contours of tree branches into what looks like some kind of big ... A cow? A horse? – There's the head and its ears and now the ... *The eyes!* ... It's eyes are looking straight into mine as I suddenly realize, sketching its shape and features in the dim background of the woods, that it's not an illusion at all but a very real ... It's ... It's a *donkey!* – I know it's a donkey because Mr. MacGregor has two of them on his tree farm and ... and I'm just about to turn and to say something to Brett, who's looking down, tying his left shoelace, when, just as suddenly, the donkey dashes into the woods behind him and disappears as if he never existed at all ...

"Did you say something?" Brett asks.

I snap my head towards him and then back toward the donkey that isn't there any more.

"No," I reply. "I didn't say anything."

For no apparent reason, I picture in my mind the snowman from China.

When we get back to the beginning of the ravine, I take my compass out. I don't want to take any more chances – the excursion down to the caves already cost us too much valuable time and I don't want to squander what little of it is left.

"This way," I say, taking the lead and moving off.

As we move deeper into the pine forest, I begin to notice the first signs of weariness. It's a deep tiredness that parks itself in the muscles and joints of my legs and shoulders, that shapes itself into a growing soreness. Pushing forward, I remind myself that I must conserve enough energy for the return journey.

Aside from a concern for my diminishing stamina, what's unsettling, too, is the subtle transformations in the environment around us. The landscape rises in a gentle slope but otherwise is perfectly flat, devoid of any impediments that we had encountered before – boulders or broken branches or fallen trees. Although it's easier going through the pine forest, it seems ... it seems somehow unnatural. While the fog appears to be thickening, and stirring about, the accumulation of snow on the ground is definitely decreasing. And it's lost that crunchiness to it – it's softer and wetter and more slippery in spots because the temperature here must be at least ten degrees warmer than it was back in the ravine.

"Mary Jane? – How much further do you want to go?" Brett says behind me.

He must be tiring as well because he's stopped to sit on the sled.

"Not much further," I reply. "Why don't we go to the top of the slope and see what's on the other side. Then we'll think about heading back. OK?"

He nods his head, loosens the scarf that's wrapped about his neck.

Trudging through the wet snow, I think again about what Esmeralda had said, about what she had envisioned from her reading of the cards: *falling, darkness, thunder and lightning.* I can't say that any of her predictions has really materialized – though, 'knock on wood', I whisper to myself, since my first journey is by no means over. But if *falling* were to have been the ... 'the theme', I guess you could say, of this first journey, then wouldn't it have already occurred? The steep drop before I arrived at the cabin – or the slopes on either side of the railroad tracks – they would have been ideal locations for ... for falling if, in fact, the act of falling was to be the chief danger associated with this, my maiden journey. As for *darkness* ... well, there was the darkness of the cave. It was certainly damp and uncomfortable and very dark when we first went inside. And, of course, I had imagined a danger that emanated from the darkness – a predator inside the cave, poised to pounce upon us at any given moment. But, like the darkness itself, it proved to be of no consequence. There was no predator – donkeys aren't carnivorous – and any other peril that may have been vested in darkness, was readily discharged with the click of the flashlight. *Thunder and lightning?* – To be honest, I don't even remember the last time that I had witnessed the loud clap and bright flash of what were surely the scariest of natural events. Except for earthquakes and tornadoes and volcanic eruptions – but things like that just never happen in Christmasville.

'And the part about the Queen of Swords – how do I know if any of that's true?' I ask myself.

I don't know. Maybe Esmeralda's predictions were only the ramblings of an overly imaginative girl. Maybe Esmeralda is someone like ... someone like *me* – influenced by vivid dreams and by an intuitive sense that there's far more to everything around us than what we see and hear and smell. 'But if that's the case', I think with a shudder, 'if what Esmeralda said isn't true, then maybe the tracks that I saw in the snow by that strange tree with the green balls on it ... maybe they were wolves, or deadly snow bunnies, or...'

"What do you really think happened to Mr. Gabriel's family?" Brett asks from behind me. "Do you think they're dead?"

"No!" I reply adamantly, stopping for a second to digest the bluntness of Brett's question. "I think they're someplace safe. Someplace where they can stay until they can find their way home again."

It makes me angry that Brett would even think such a terrible thing, let alone verbalize it.

"But most people," he starts...

"Most people don't have any faith," I interject, choosing to end this topic.

As we approach the crest of the slope – what I think is the crest – the fog is so thick that you could carve out a big chunk and make a mattress of it. And wouldn't that be nice? – Stopping for a moment to nap on a soft and fluffy slab of fog.

But aside from the sort of spongy, passive quality of the fog, it's a bit alarming because it is so thick that I can only see about twenty paces in front of me now. And it's starting to really swirl, spinning in funnels from the treetops, sweeping through the woods as if it were running from the wind. Maybe that's what's unsettling more than is the fog – the wind – I can hear the rush and the unbroken howl of it as we move toward the top of the crest.

"Mary Jane?" Brett calls from behind.

"Come on," I reply with vexation because I'm anxious to keep moving.

"No – Look!"

I stop and turn around, scanning the fog, finding his red coat in the gray fabric that swarms around him.

"What is it?" I ask, marching back.

"Look! Over there!" he says, though keeping his voice so low that I can barely hear him. He points at something off to his left. I squint my eyes, trying to find a pattern in the fog, in the first snowflakes that are beginning to fall – big, wet asterisks of snowflakes that immediately spark the same fear that Mrs. Gabriel and Caroline must have experienced when they realized ...

"Can you see it?" he says. "He's right there, looking at us. I thought it was a horse. But it's a donkey!"

As I come up to Brett, I see the body and then the head and the eyes of the animal, standing motionless ten yards away.

"Can you believe it?" he says, slowly pulling the straps of his backpack down, carefully putting it down in the snow. "We could use a good donkey," he says, stepping towards it.

"What are you ..."

Before I realize what's happening, Brett charges toward the donkey, chasing it through the woods.

"Brett!" I shout after him. "Brett! Come back!"

Trotting after him, I watch him scramble into a grove of trees before veering toward the crest of the ridge, toward the sound of the wind as it scurries over the crest.

"Brett!" I cry again. "Come back!"

I can't keep up with him, the flash of his coat disappearing in the fog and the flurry of snowfall. Slipping, and nearly falling, I decide to stand perfectly still so I can listen while I catch my breath. There's a strong burst of wind as it swings over the crest and shoots through the trees, making them sway and creak.

"Ah-Ha! I've got..." I hear him say ahead of me, the rest of his sentence lost in the wind or...

The sound of his scream is so loud and chilling that an icicle, shaped like a bolt of lightning, rockets down my spine.

"Brett!!!" I shout, running in the direction of his scream as fast as my legs can carry me.

When I arrive at the crest, I notice immediately the startling change in the topography of the landscape. The slope on the other side drops down sharply. There aren't any trees. And it's more like ice than snow, encasing the rocks and boulders that populate the strange terrain, spotting the ground like the patches of dirty white that you see on a roan cow. And the wind! I can hear it – maybe fifty feet down the slope – a fierce, continuous whoosh that rakes the side of the slope or splinters off to shoot up and over the crest.

"Brett! – Where are you?" I call.

It's as if the wind grabbed my words like slips of paper, crumbled them up into tightly compressed knots, and hurled them back at me.

I raise my hands up to cup them around my mouth. "Brett!!!" I shout as loud as I can.

Edging down the slope, I carefully choose each foothold because the ground is just as slippery as the ice, having been first blanketed by the moisture of the fog and then frozen by the wind as it scurried across it. It is so desolate here that you can actually feel the ... the desolation as it oozes through your skin, as it becomes a dark stone that lodges itself in the pit of your stomach, making you feel empty and useless.

Off to my left... – What was that sound? Was it the wind playing tricks? Or was it the trees behind me, creaking and groaning in the windy onslaught? *There! There it is again – that same sound!*

Rather than moving directly across the face of the slope, I decide to make my way back up to the crest and then cross over.

"Brett!" I call out.

"Help!" he answers. "Help me, Mary Jane!"

"I'm coming, Brett! I'm just trying to ..."

I hear him groan, utter words without meaning.

There! – I see a patch of red about twenty feet down the slope. It looks like he slid all the way down, over a group of small, pointed rocks before slamming into two boulders.

I get down on my backside and inch my way toward him.

"I'm almost there, Brett," I say, slowly making my way down. "Just a bit more ... almost there ... almost there ..."

He's covered in dirt and grime and breathing heavily.

"I can't move ... I can't move my leg," he says, trying to raise his head up to see it but shuddering in pain in the attempt.

"Don't move!" I exclaim, putting my hand on his chest to prevent him from trying. "Just try and relax for a minute and catch your breath. Which leg is it?"

"My ... My right ... My right one," he says between groans.

When I look down the length of his leg, I can't see his right foot because it's lodged at the ankle between the two boulders.

"It looks like it's stuck, Brett," I remark, jockeying myself around so I can get a better view. "If I can just ..."

He lets out a piercing scream because I had cradled my hands beneath his leg and lifted, trying to dislodge his foot.

"It's OK. It's OK," I repeat, feeling a deepening sense of helplessness.

My gloves are covered in blood. When I look back at his leg, I see an odd, white thing, jutting out from the side of it, just below his kneecap. I think that maybe he got jabbed with a stick but ...

"Oh my God!" I say, realizing, with an overwhelming sense of revulsion, that it's his ... it's his bone!

"What? What is it?" Brett says, trying to twist himself around so he can see.

He lets out another scream.

"No! – No, don't move, Brett!" I say, pressing him down. "You'll make it worse!"

His outburst is enough to distract me from the nausea that's churning around in my stomach.

"It'll make ... It'll make what worse?" he asks after settling down a bit.

"It's your leg," I reply, electing to tell him the truth because ... because what else could I possibly tell him? "Your leg's broken, Brett."

"Broken?" he says, biting his lip. "How am I going to get out of here with a broken leg?"

He turns his head away because he doesn't want me to see his face. He doesn't want me to see the tears brimming at the corners of his eyes and spilling down along the cheeks of his face.

"It's OK. It's OK," I offer sympathetically.

"How can it be OK???" he says angrily. "How can it be OK when my leg's all busted up, Mary Jane???"

"I'll figure something out," I reply. "I have to figure something out."

Honestly, I don't know how, I think to myself. Even if I could manage to dislodge Brett's foot from the boulders and to somehow drag him back up the slope, I don't know how I would get him all the way back to Christmasville. I could put him on the sled and pull him until every ounce of energy was exhausted from my body. But then how would I get him past the train tracks? How would I get him up the embankment on the other side of the cabin? But if I could get him to the cabin, I could start a fire and make him nice and comfortable while I went back for help. But then, there's the train tracks again unless ... unless I could manage to stop the train.

"You have to leave me here, Mary Jane," Brett suggests. "You have to leave me here so you can go for help."

"No! I won't leave you here all by yourself, Brett! It'll take too much time – besides, you wouldn't ..."

"I wouldn't what, Mary Jane?"

His teeth are chattering and his face is turning a horrible blue color.

"I wouldn't what, Mary Jane?" he repeats.

"I'm not going to leave you!" I say sternly. "There isn't enough time to go all the way back and get help!"

"Then what are we going to do?"

"Just give me a minute to think, Brett!"

For a moment I start to feel guilty because, after all, this is my fault. I'm the one in charge and I should have been more ... more cautious and ... and responsible. 'But you haven't the time,' I say to myself, 'to start feeling sorry for yourself, Mary Jane.'

"Listen," I say to Brett, "I'm going to climb back up to the top and get the rope from the backpack on the sled. Then I can wrap it around you and pull you up. OK?"

"You'll never be able to pull me up. You're not strong enough."

"I'm plenty strong, Brett Tolliver. If I can carry Christmas trees and train platforms with my dad, then I'll be able to pull you up. So don't tell me that I'm not strong enough. Besides, the ground is covered in ice so that'll help. And you're arms aren't broken, are they? – You'll be able to help too."

I turn to start for the top of the slope.

"Mary Jane?"

"What is it, Brett?" I reply.

He bites his lip, turns away. "Never mind," he says.

"I won't leave you, Brett," I say, moving off. "I'll never leave without you."

The ground is so icy and barren that I have to find half-buried rocks to grab with my hands or to push off with my feet as I crawl, like a slug, toward the top. I want to move as fast as I can because of the falling snow, which is beginning to blanket the slope, and because of Brett's condition, but I have to constantly remind myself, with each lurch forward, that caution is just as important as speed. So I test each rock with my hand or my foot before I swing my weight onto it, insuring that it's not going to give way because one false move – and that's all it would take – would send me plunging toward the bottom, wherever that is. I have to be careful with the wind too. Sometimes I feel as if it has fingers, pinching the tail of my coat to peel me away. Or hands that slip beneath me, prying me upwards. The cold breath of it freezes the sweat along my forehead, crystallizes the moisture that's discharged from my mouth and nose. Pieces of ice, pulled away from the rocks above me, get in my eyes or snuggle in between my clothes and skin to make me shiver.

When I look back towards Brett, I try to gauge the distance I've traveled. Fifteen ... maybe twenty feet – but nearly half of it was sideways, moving according to the availability of hand- and footholds. Brett isn't moving – he's lying back as if he's asleep. *Why did he have to go chasing after that donkey? Doesn't he realize the seriousness of ...*

Careful! – A loose rock tumbles from its pocket in the slope, nicking my shoulder on the way down. I can hear it dislodging other rocks and rubble beneath me, the whole mess of it sliding downward and ... *Why can't I hear anything hit bottom? Is it because the wind is so loud? Or it it because ...*

My left foot slips from the rock. I squeeze the rock beneath my right hand but the tighter I squeeze, the more I can feel my grasp slipping. Desperately, I search for the foothold with my left ... There! – There, I found it. It feels pretty secure so I can relax my right hand a bit while stretching toward that other rock with my left hand ...

"Ohhhhhh!" I scream, my left foot slipping again, the fingers of my right hand buckling under the sudden shift in weight ...

"Mary Jane!" Brett calls, the look in his face one of pain and anguish and dread as he watches me slide down the slope ...

Falling! – Now I realize the full impact of the horror and the helplessness that Esmeralda must have experienced as she ...

... fell ...

... bouncing and plummeting downward, I feel the fast, hard, furious protrusions of rock and ice jabbing into me, tearing my trousers and coat and ...

My God! Is this the end of it! Is this ...

I see it but I don't know what it is. I see it rushing toward me in the fog and the snow like it's something out of a dream, something that you recognize but because it's moving so fast – because *I'm* moving so fast – that I only have time to see it before the notion of recognition ...

I must have blinked out for a moment. Maybe it was longer. I'm not sure. I'm not sure if it was the steady stream of wind sweeping by or if it was the howl of somebody's voice, calling my name that brought me back. What I do know is that I'm on the edge of a terrible precipice because, below me, there is nothing ... nothing but the wind and the fog, flowing like a wild river.

What saved me, I realize, was a pine tree, gutted from the top of the slope and snared at the edge of the precipice by two wings of the rocky ledge. I landed in the wiry mass of its gnarled roots, in the frozen cushion of dirt that still clings to its roots.

"*Mary Jane!!!*"

There it is again – the wind calling my name.

One of the straps on my new backpack ripped at the seam. And there's a gash down the side of it that's big enough to have caused some of its contents to spill out, to tumble down the slope to the bottom. My thermos! – I can't find my thermos anywhere inside my backpack – my beautiful, red and white thermos with the blue kitty cats ... It's so sad that it makes me want to cry and cry ...

"*Mary Jane!!!*" the voice calls again. *Can you hear me, Mary Jane???*

'*How could the wind know my name?*' I think, snapping my head up.

"Hello!!!" I shout. "Hello!!! – Brett???"

I listen, skeptical that he's going to reply.

"Can you see the rope, Mary Jane?"

'Rope? What rope? – Brett left the rope and his backpack at the sled.'

"I don't see any rope!" I shout. "There isn't any rope!"

In the wiry mesh of the roots, I move my legs around, making sure that nothing's broken. Except for the stiffness and the soreness and the weariness that's saturating my whole body, everything seems to be working.

"Can you see it now?" Brett shouts.

When I look up I see the rope as it uncoils in the fog and the snowfall above me, the end of it landing in the roots beside me.

I guess I'm stupefied because ... because how could Brett ... *'How did he get the rope from the sled? How could he toss the rope with his leg all busted up?'*

"Can you see the rope, Mary Jane???"

"Yes," I call back. "I see the rope."

"Wrap it around your waist and knot it as tight as you can!"

I grab it and wrap it around me three times, tying it off with a half dozen square knots.

"OK," I shout. "Brett? – Brett, you won't be able to pull me up! Your leg ..."

Seeing the rope become taut, I get to my feet but remain stooped down to keep my balance by holding on to the thick roots around me. This is really terrifying because the side of the slope is at least three ... maybe four feet away from where I'm at and once Brett starts hoisting me up, they'll be a split second when he'll have to support the full weight of my body as I swing over from the clump of roots to the slope. Unless, of course, I move ... I move closer, stepping through the roots and leaning towards the slope ...

"Brett!" I call out. "You won't be able to ..."

The rope tightens around my waist and suddenly ... suddenly I have an overwhelming fear as I swing out and slam into the slope and stop ... slip down about a foot or so as I hold onto the rope and kick my feet into the rocky ledge, searching for some kind of foothold before I feel one yank after another around my waist and ... and I'm actually moving upward, scraping against one rock after another, but ... but – who cares? – because I'm moving upward ...

It's difficult to see in the fog and the snow but – there he is – his silhouette on the top of the slope as he reels me up, his arms moving, one after the other, like a machine and ... and from the corner of my eye, off to the right, I see a blotch of red against the rocks, the leg suspended in the air because it's lodged between the rocks and ...

"Gotcha," he says, pulling me to the top as I turn back and look up, immediately recognizing the sad, unmistakable eyes of Mr. Gabriel.

Thirty-Two Degrees of Illumination

On Sunday I don't have to look too far in *The Christmasville Courier* because it's on the front page, right beside the story about the Morrison's English bulldog, "Duchess", giving birth to six pups in a bedroom closet. Personally, I think that would have made a much better headline than,

"CHURCH CUSTODIAN SAVES YOUTHS FROM CERTAIN PERIL",

especially since the Morrisons didn't even know that "Duchess" was pregnant in the first place.

The article is pretty accurate, explaining how Mr. Gabriel, trudging through the snows of the deep forest, had stumbled upon our footprints and followed them. That's how he discovered our desperate predicament.

"Brett Tolliver, an altar boy at St. Nick's," the article reports, "took a terrible tumble down an icy slope, breaking his leg in two places. Bleeding profusely, he was on the verge of unconsciousness when Mr. Gabriel, the church custodian, arrived at the scene.

"The girl, Mary Jane Higgins, was battered and bruised and in jeopardy of developing a serious case of hypothermia. Nearly delirious..."

That part's a bunch of baloney! – I wasn't delirious! I was physically exhausted and in a mental stupor maybe, but who wouldn't be after an ordeal like that?

The article proceeds to tell how Mr. Gabriel rescued Brett and I from the steep slope, "at great risk to his own personal safety. He dressed Brett's leg most admirably with a makeshift splint and bandages and secured him to a sled, which he dragged all the way back to his pickup truck near the lake."

"Were they close to the train tracks when the accident occurred?" the reporter asked.

I was waiting for that one to come up in the newspaper article, but Mr. Gabriel replied: "No, they were some distance away."

And it's true, too. We were at least a mile away from the tracks when Brett chased that donkey along the top of the ridge and fell on the ice. But what I really appreciate about Mr. Gabriel's reply is the fact that he didn't volunteer any additional information. He could just have easily said: 'Oh, no, they were well beyond the train tracks when the accident happened.' I'm glad, too, that he omitted the whole episode with the donkey. I mean, if you close your eyes and just picture us – Brett and I – out in the wilderness, in the snow and the fog, him chasing the donkey and me chasing him ... well, it looks kind of funny, doesn't it? Not only 'funny', as in comical, but 'funny' as in foolish and crazy.

The thing is though, it wasn't all that crazy because I remember Mr. Gabriel saying that he had seen the donkey several times before.

"The first time was the day after Christmas," he said as he pulled Brett through the woods toward his truck. "But believe me when I say this, Mary Jane," he added, "the donkey isn't the strangest thing that I've seen in these here parts."

But he did not elaborate and, at the time, I was too exhausted to ask him what he had meant.

I remain in the hospital Saturday night and all day Sunday and Sunday night because the doctors say that they want to keep me "under observation". In truth, though, I think that the hospital staff kind of enjoys having patients around. They don't get all that many so, when they do, they have an opportunity to put into action what they learned in all their medical books. It's entertaining for me, too, watching them scramble around, looking for the manual to the X-ray machine because they can't remember exactly how to operate the thing. Or when the nurse wraps my arm with the apparatus for taking my blood pressure and sits there, staring at the gauge for at least a half minute before the doctor says: "I think you have to pump the rubber bubble, don't you? – To build pressure up around the arm?"

From one o'clock until four o'clock on Sunday afternoon, I'm allowed to have visitors. Brett can't because he's in what they call, the "intensive care unit", where they want him to rest quietly and without interruption. They won't even let Mr. and Mrs. Tolliver in to see him. So they come to visit me.

"What in the world were you and Brett doing out there, Mary Jane?" Mrs. Tolliver asks, after we had gotten through the exchange of pleasantries.

It's the identical question – word-for-word – that mom asked me an hour earlier.

"Exploring," I reply – on both occasions. "Would you like a malted milk ball, Mrs. Tolliver? Mr. Tolliver?" I ask, holding out the box of candy that mom and dad had brought earlier. "They're from Sarah's and they're really delicious."

"No. No, thank you," they both reply.

"But ... but exploring what?" Mrs. Tolliver continues, refusing to be re-directed from her stream of thought.

"Oh, you know, we just wanted to see what was out there. Maybe a bigger sledding hill or an abandoned house – stuff like that," I answer.

"I see," Mrs. Tolliver says rather sternly. "Well I do hope, Mary Jane, that you've learned your lesson and will never go out there – 'exploring', as you say – again."

"Oh no! I'm never going out there again," I reply animatedly. "Not me, Mrs. Tolliver. I learned my lesson!"

It's true. I haven't the slightest intention of re-tracing my journey east, of seeking a passage to New York City through the forests beyond the sledding hill because, when all is said and done, it isn't the way to go, is it. I mean – in spite of everything that happened – the fact is, I did accomplish what was the principal purpose of my maiden journey, didn't I? – To determine if traveling eastward would provide me a way out of Christmasville. Now I could safely say ... well, maybe 'safely' is a poor choice of words, but anyway – I could safely say that traveling east would not provide the solution to my problem. Although I still don't know which way to go, I certainly know which way to avoid unless ... unless I went back to that ravine – the ravine that led into the pass where we saw the caves and the footprints.

No sooner do Mr. and Mrs. Tolliver leave – with the comfort of knowing that I wouldn't lead Brett into harm's way again – than Emily and Mr. and Mrs. Thompson arrive. Emily runs into my hospital room with a little more enthusiasm than I think the situation warrants.

"Oh, Mary Jane!" she says, throwing her arms around me and hugging me. "Poor Mary Jane!" she adds with her mien of melodrama.

I prefer to remain cool and aloof. Of course, with Emily's parents nearby, I can't delve into the matter as to why she chose to betray me, to reveal to Brett what she promised not to.

"And poor Brett!" Emily adds, withdrawing to my bedside.

'That's what happens when you break promises, Emily,' I want to say to her. 'No good ever comes of it. If you didn't break your promise, then Brett wouldn't have broken his leg, would he, Emily?'

"I brought you some books and a couple of magazines," says Mrs. Thompson, putting them on the nightstand. "And this too," she adds, turning to take the white box from Mr. Thompson. "It's a special dessert that I made just for you, Mary Jane. It's a German chocolate cake."

"It's made with coconut flakes," Mr. Thompson says, licking his chops as he sees me open the lid of the box to peek inside. "It's real yummy, Mary Jane," he adds.

"Would you like a piece, Mr. Thompson? – I could ..."

"Oh, no. No, I couldn't," he replies, waving the suggestion off, conscious of the watchful eye of Mrs. Thompson at the foot of the bed.

After the Thompson's leave, there's a continuous stream of visitors. First, it's Wally, the mailman, followed by a bunch of schoolmates and then Mrs. Mason and her daughter, Rebecca.

"Mr. Mason's waiting outside in the car," says Mrs. Mason. "He sends his very best wishes for a speedy recovery and a sincere apology for his not being able to ... Well, it's his condition, Mary Jane, and the treatments he's had for his ... his condition. Unfortunately, the thought of entering the hospital resurrects the trauma all over again."

She moves to the window, peering into the street below as Rebecca sits in the chair and draws a picture in her notebook with black and silver crayons.

"That's OK, Mrs. Mason", I offer sympathetically. "I really appreciate your coming to see me. As for Mr. Mason – who knows? Maybe someday everything will be all right again. Maybe someday they'll come up with a cure for his condition."

"Maybe," she says, turning from the window to run her hand wistfully through her daughter's hair.

When Rebecca finishes her picture, she carefully removes it from her notebook and gives it to me. It's a rendering of Santa Claus in his sleigh – a strangely curious one because she had drawn *the dark Santa, pulled across the sky by nine wolves.*

'I wonder if Rebecca dreams like I do?' I think after she leaves with her mother.

"So how's my best girl doing?" asks Mr. Wright – Otis, that is – as he enters the hospital room with his brother, Willy. "Ready to bust outta' here yet? Because, ya know, Mary Jane, Willy and I can help ya out in that capacity – if that's your intent, I mean – to bust out."

"Hello Otis," I say, smiling. "Hi Willy."

"Hello, Mary Jane," says Willy, stepping up to the foot of the bed as Otis moves around to the side. "Don't take Otis too seriously – OK? You know how he likes to blow everything up into some sort of far-flung, highfalutin scheme or what not."

"Oh, I know," I say, agreeing with Willy. "Like the float in the Christmas parade – that was pretty far-flung, wasn't it? Nobody had any idea of what that was supposed to be."

"Darned if I know what I was pulling through the parade," Willy remarks, playing along. "When it comes to Otis' wild ideas, I just go along with the flow. I was only glad that nobody asked me what the thing was."

"Whoa! What's this? – A conspiracy?" Otis exclaims. "By my very own brother and my best girl! My, oh my, what is the world coming to? And, the irony of it all, especially since it was you, Mary Jane, who gave me the idea for the float in the first place."

A nurse comes into my room, eyes Otis and Willy with what amounts to a cool distrust and announces: "Visiting hours are over in fifteen minutes."

Willy makes a funny face – as if his mother had caught him with his hand in the cookie jar. "Geez, maybe we should bust her out, Otis," he says.

When I ask Otis about the construction of his new invention, he says that it's moving along fairly well. But he does not disclose any real details or discuss the essential purpose of what it's designed to do.

"Can't you tell me anything more?" I ask, prodding.

"After I conduct a few more tests," he says, refusing to budge on the issue, "and then we'll see."

As for the hothouse, everything seemed to be doing as well as could be expected, including the odd array of plants confined to the 'experimental section'. The "tomato", which the Wright's had named after their friend, Tom Atkinson, was at first deemed a terrible failure because Willy had elected to try the leaves first. He had liked the smell of them and, thinking that they would taste something like spinach, tried them out raw, in a salad. He got so sick to his stomach that he thought his eyes were going to pop out. Otis tried the bright red fruit, not knowing what to expect, given the wretched condition of his brother. He bit into one of the larger tomatoes, sprinkled it with a little salt, and tried it again before proclaiming to his unfortunate brother that it was the tastiest specimen he had eaten since their discovery of the cucumber.

"We're still experimentin' with different ways to use it," Otis points out.

"And making sure that there's no long-term effects," adds Willy. "You're still feeling OK – right, Otis?"

"Fit as a fiddle," his older brother replies. "Say, Mary Jane, how's your maple tree doing? And the rose that you gave mom and dad?"

They were both doing fine. Although the maple tree hadn't produced any new leaves, it had grown a full, three-quarters of an inch. I know because I measure it once a week. The rose continued to produce new buds and blooms but the batch of fertilizer that Otis made was running low because the twins had used a lot of it up for a school project. Of course, they hadn't bothered to ask either.

"I'll fix ya up another batch in no time," Otis volunteers.

"You know, that reminds me of something," I say, biting my lip. "When I was out in the woods, not far beyond the sledding hill, I saw a tree that I had never seen before."

"What kind of tree?" Otis asks with interest, sitting the large frame of his body down in the chair by my bed. "Can you describe it?"

"I thought it was an oak tree at first," I explain, picturing it in my mind, "because of its bark. But it had green balls hanging from its branches like Christmas ornaments. The balls felt like velvet and had a strong scent to them that smelled like ..."

"A walnut tree!" exclaims Willy. "It's a walnut tree, Otis!"

"I'll be darned," Otis replies. "It sure sounds like a walnut tree, don't it?" he asks, turning to address his brother.

"You've seen one?" I ask.

"No. We've never seen one – not a live one," Willy answers. "But I recognize your description of it from one of grandpa's drawings. Geez! – We're going to have to find that tree, Otis!"

Otis nods his head in agreement. "You see, Mary Jane," he explains, "grandpa was a horticulturalist like Willy and me. But, first and foremost, he was an artist, recording in his drawings an encyclopedia of every different tree and plant that he had encountered in the wilderness. He used pencils and colored chalks so all of his drawings depict the minutest details of each specimen that he had drawn. Willy and I look at them all the time – especially when we discover something that we haven't seen before. Sometimes the drawings help us to identify plants and trees, to give us a glimpse into their histories and origins."

"Do you remember where you saw the walnut tree, Mary Jane?" Willy asks with excitement. "Can you tell us how to find it?"

"Sure I can," I reply.

And so I do, drawing a little map for Otis and Willy on a sheet of paper.

"It's too late in the day to go out there now, Willy" says Otis, looking through the window, at the afternoon sky as it succumbs to evening.

"We'll start out first thing in the morning," says Willy.

"Gentlemen," announces the nurse from the threshold of the doorway, "visiting hours are now over. It's time to leave."

"Yes – yes, of course," Otis agrees as he and Willy gather up their coats and gloves, their hats and scarves. "Mary Jane," he says after the nurse departs, "there's something that Willy and I want to say to you before we leave – a bit of advice, if you don't mind us offering it, that is."

"Sure," I say, having a high regard for their wisdom.

Otis twists his mouth around as he looks from one thing to the next – as if he might discover the right words etched into the ceiling or the floor, on the wall or the window.

"You might as well just spit it out," suggests Willy.

Nodding his head in agreement, Otis looks me right in the eye.

"You can't never cross the train tracks again, Mary Jane," he advises somberly.

At first I don't know what to say.

"You spoke to Mr. Gabriel?" I ask, after quickly shuffling through the possibilities. "He told you?"

"Oh, he didn't have to tell us, Mary Jane," says Otis.

"When we saw George ... when we saw Mr. Gabriel this morning," Willy explains, "he was heading out to where you had seen the footprints by the cave. He wanted to do a little investigatin' – you know, to follow the prints, to see if they had anything to do with the disappearance of Mrs. Gabriel and Caroline, their daughter."

"You see, Mary Jane, Willy and me – we *know* where that place is. We used to be pretty wild boys in our younger days, gettin' ourselves into more trouble than I care to remember and ... well, the fact is, we've been out there before. Although it seems like such a long, long time ago, we've been out to the caves ... and out beyond the caves."

"You crossed the train tracks? But it's forbidden."

"Yes, it's forbidden," Otis agrees. "And with good reason – not only because of the danger of the train but because ... well, out there, nature seems to operate by a different set of rules."

"Like the fog and the ice and the constant stream of wind by that ridge," Willy adds, "the ridge that drops off into the bottomless abyss. And you do know where that is, don't you, Mary Jane?"

The nurse appears at the doorway again. Scowling, she sets her hands on her hips, resolved to stand firm until Otis and Willy abide by the rules and depart.

"Think about what we said, Mary Jane," Otis says, heading toward the exit with Willy. "Oh, and by the way, Mr. Gabriel sends his best. He was going to stop by – if he got back in time, but I guess ..."

The nurse, persistent in the fulfillment of her duties, promptly ushers them away.

I manage to get through the rest of Sunday afternoon without raising any suspicions about crossing the train tracks. Except for Otis and Willy, of course, but I know that they won't say anything to anybody. Neither will Mr. Gabriel. They can all be trusted. Unlike Emily, of course, who – even if Brett was the only one that she did tell – might be compelled to add her two cents worth if the opportunity presented itself. There's simply no guarantee that she won't blabber – what's supposed to be a secret – to anyone who would listen. I can picture her in school, maybe listening in to somebody else's conversation and, in trying to impress them, say: *'Oh yeah? – Well did you know that Mary Jane crossed the train tracks?'* Or, to a reporter from the newspaper, who might be interviewing a teacher or a classmate for a follow-up story: *'Oh yeah?'* Emily might say, interrupting, *'Well did you know that Mary Jane crossed the train tracks?'*

There's no doubt about it – I have to talk to Emily, alone, and as soon as possible. And to Brett, too, because it's important ... No! – It's absolutely imperative that Brett and I tell the same story about the accident, that we selectively ignore the same issues.

On Monday morning, I discover that they moved Brett into a private room at the end of the corridor. He's doing well – better than expected – but he still isn't allowed to have any visitors because he needs a lot of rest to recuperate. So, if I'm going to talk to him before mom and dad arrive at eleven o'clock to take me home, then I'm going to have to sneak into his room as soon as possible.

"Dressed already, are we?" the doctor says, arriving at quarter past ten for my final check-up.

"I'm kind of anxious to get going," I reply.

He does a couple of tests, inspects my bumps and bruises and scratches, asks me some questions, and that's the end of it.

"A clean bill of health – that's what we like to see," he says, scribbling his signature on the paper on his clipboard. "Do you have any questions, Mary Jane?"

"Nope. Everything's fine," I answer.

"Good. If anything does come up, you be sure and let us know. OK?"

"Sure," I say. "Can I go now?"

"As soon as your parents arrive and sign the release papers, then you're free as a bird."

When the doctor leaves to make his rounds, I wait a minute before going to the doorway. It isn't going to be easy getting to Brett's room without detection because the nurse's station is almost directly across the corridor from my room. There are two nurses though one of them scurries off, carrying a glass of water and a little plastic cup with pills in it. The remaining nurse is the same one who had adamantly insisted upon Otis' and Willy's timely departure yesterday, who had gone so far as to grab each of them by the sleeves of their coats to escort them away. You can tell by her impeccably professional appearance – the bleached, spotlessness of her starched white uniform; the sleek severity of her black hair, pulled back tightly into a knot beneath her nurse's cap; the sternness of her wire-rimmed glasses – that she is not inclined to any bending of the rules. No, there would be no compromising with her – no subtle shades of gray between the stark contrast of black and white.

No sooner have I turned back into my room and plopped on the edge of the bed than a loud crash echoes down the corridor. It sounded like a breakfast tray striking the floor – the crash of plastic plates and glasses, of forks and spoons scrambling across tile.

'There she goes,' I say to myself, espying the nurse as she dashes down the left wing of the corridor.

Standing up from the bed, I go to the doorway and, without stopping, turn right, proceeding all the way down to Brett's room.

'A piece of cake', I think ... – 'of *German chocolate* cake!' I add with a mischievous smirk.

When I get back to my room about twenty minutes later, dad peers through the window at the traffic below. Mom sits in the visitor's chair.

"There you are!" she says, getting up. "We've had the nurses looking high and low for you."

"I needed some exercise," I reply. "So I took a little walk."

"It seems to me that you've been taking a lot of 'little walks' lately," says mom.

On the way home from the hospital, we drop dad off at the lumberyard. Mom fixes me up soup and a sandwich before she, too, has to rush back to work because Mrs. Cauldwell is covering for her at the cashier station.

"You get some rest now, you hear me, Mary Jane?" mom says as she swings her arms into her coat. "You've had a trying experience and you need to give yourself an opportunity to get your strength back. OK? – Oh," she adds, kissing me on the cheek and putting her hand up to my forehead to see if I had developed a fever (though I don't know why she thinks that I have). "This morning I took chicken out of the freezer for dinner. When it thaws, put it in the fridge. I'll see ya tonight, honey."

After she leaves, I mope around a bit – watering my maple, leafing through the magazines that Mrs. Thompson had brought me at the hospital, checking the chicken. I don't want to rest. I'm tired of resting since I'd gotten plenty of it at the hospital. Besides, with mom and dad at work, and the twins in school, I have that rare luxury of having the house all to myself. So why squander it by napping?

Moving from room to room, I sink more and more into that special reverie that comes from being alone, from looking at things without interruption, inspecting their private, almost separate existence – a wedding photograph in mom and dad's room, a cameo brooch, the fragile folds of a rose blossom; the cover of a comic book in the twins' room, a toy soldier, a plastic dump truck; the network of veins in a maple leaf; the pattern of flecks in the linoleum floor of the bathroom; the charcoal church perched on the edge of the train platform in the study. Sitting in a chair, I look at the church, at the barn, at the crimson colonial, wondering if things take on a life of their own when no one's around – like the books in the library at night, the whispers from books as each character awakens in the absence of ... people. I think: if I'm very, very quiet and hold my breath and concentrate real hard, will I be able to hear the sermon of the preacher in the little church? The mooing of the cows in the barn? And the chatter of the mom and the dad, the girl and the twins who live in the colonial?

' "Whoops! – There goes Mary Jane again",' Roger had said.

' "...You've been taking a lot of 'little walks' lately",' noted mom.

Sometimes I wonder. Sometimes I wonder about myself, about why I'm different from everyone else. Although I'm glad most of the time – because I am different, because I see things differently than most people – there are other times when I feel myself sinking, *falling*, you could say, into a sort of deep, sad pit. It's because I'm alone, I guess. It's because I know what no one else does: *I know there's a New York City because I heard it on the radio.*

' "It's the price that you pay the pie man",' I think, repeating one of dad's favorite expressions.

Around three o'clock, the doorbell rings. I'm expecting it actually.

"Hello Emily," I say, swinging the door open.

"I brought you your schoolwork," she remarks, dragging herself across the threshold and into the living room, pulling the plastic bag of books and assignments behind her.

With her tongue dangling from her mouth – as if she's a dog dying of thirst – she collapses on the couch.

"They're not that heavy, Emily," I say, lifting the bag and carrying it into the kitchen so the snow on the bottom doesn't melt on the carpet.

"I had to carry them all the way from the bus stop!" she replies with exasperation. "Do you have any soda?"

Pouring her a glass of ginger ale, I return to the living room. "Maybe we should put you up in the hospital, Emily? – You know, to recover from your ordeal. I think there might be an extra bed in Brett's room."

"Very funny," she says, taking the glass and gulping.

"But it would make it convenient for you," I suggest.

"What do you mean?"

"Well, if you were laid up in the hospital with Brett, then it would make it much easier for you to tell him all of our secrets. Don't you think?"

She puts the glass on the coffee table, staring at the glass until she can think of what to say. "I didn't tell Brett ..."

That's when I let her have it – about her being my best friend, about her revealing the secret of my crossing the train tracks, about her betraying me to Brett.

"I didn't want anything to happen to you!" she says, finally admitting her betrayal. "I was afraid! I was afraid that you wouldn't come back!" she shouts, holding back tears.

"Who else did you tell?" I demand.

"I didn't tell anyone else! Only Brett – and only because I knew that he would follow you, that he would help you out if you got into trouble."

Maybe that's true. Maybe Emily told Brett only because she wanted to protect me. But even so, it would be a long time before I ever trusted her again.

I didn't have to go back to school until Wednesday. Brett won't get out of the hospital until Saturday although, for him, I'm sure he'll feel like a celebrity on his birthday when he is released. It's because of all the newspaper articles leading up to it. The reporter and the photographer from *The Courier* had stopped by the hospital every day, pressing Brett for another slant on the story so, by the time Friday comes round, you might have thought that Brett was the hero of our adventure while the role of Mr. Gabriel was reduced to ... I don't know – can there be an assistant hero?

In the newspaper articles, I saw my name mentioned every now and then – like a few flecks of black pepper sprinkled across a pot of boiled potatoes to give them a little added flavor. I suppose the newspaper staff decided to spotlight Brett because he had experienced the greatest hardship, with his leg broken in two places and the road to recovery at least ten weeks long. I guess I was a little jealous, too, because he got all the attention while I got squat. 'But that's a good thing,' I kept telling myself throughout the week, because I really didn't want to see myself in the limelight. I have more important things to do.

But anyway, to give you some idea of how our whole adventure evolved into something that it wasn't, all you had to do was to read the headlines of the newspapers, starting with Tuesday, the first day after the press was allowed to interview Brett:

"BRETT CITES TRAINING, WILL POWER AS SAVING GRACE!"

By no means was Brett impaired when it came to describing, when it came to embellishing his ordeal in the wilderness.

"If it wasn't for my experience – you know, as a band member and an altar boy – then I don't think I would have had the strength and the discipline to do what I had to do."

What the heck did that mean? – '... *to do what I had to do.*' The only thing that Brett did on his own was to chase the donkey around. And I'd have to say that the donkey got the best of that deal because, after all, he didn't slip on the ice and tumble down the slope and break his leg in two places, did he?

"BRETT SAYS: 'I WANT TO BE AN EXPLORER!'"

read the headline of Wednesday's paper, though the story really didn't divulge what it was exactly that Brett wanted to explore. I think that maybe Brett should examine – maybe he should explore his motives for thinking that he wants to be an explorer in the first place. Either that or he should have his head examined (Doctor Sperry? – No, he's only good for a stick of candy when you've got a sweet tooth!).

And I wonder, too, what Brett's mother thought about his becoming an explorer. I bet she hit the roof when she saw that in the newspaper!

Thursday's headline was by far the most imaginative, the most exaggerated, and the most outrageous. In fact, it was so ridiculous that I don't think I could ever stomach being a newspaper reporter if I had to stretch the truth as far as a rubber band before it snapped:

"BRETT REVEALS BOUT WITH WILD BEAST"

What was maddening is that I had specifically told Brett not to say anything about the donkey because the less said, the better. But all of a sudden, he spouts off to the reporter about something that nobody but him and me and Mr. Gabriel were supposed to know anything about. I guess it was because Brett wanted to keep himself in the spotlight, to read again and again about his exploits in the wilderness, regardless of whether they were true or not.

The donkey: as if by a mysterious magic spell, cast between its reality and its recollection, the donkey was sprung from its secret cage to instantly become – Poof! – No, not a fluffy, white rabbit but a wild, raving "beast" that Brett had the misfortune of accosting in the wilderness. In his vivid, wholly fictional account of the episode, he explained that "it was big and mean and it may have been snarling too so … I don't think it was a donkey after all. It couldn't have been because I wouldn't have had a problem catching a donkey. It must have been a wolf! – Yes, that's it, a wolf … or a mountain lion … or something far worse – and I had to protect Mary Jane, you know, her being a girl and all."

'Bull!' I said to myself in annoyance, smacking the newspaper down on the kitchen table.

He made me sound like a two-year old. I don't want to be nasty but, if it wasn't for me, Brett wouldn't have had a leg to stand on – Oh, but I forgot, he doesn't, does he? – Have a leg to stand on, that is.

At first, I thought the bit about the donkey – the donkey transformed into the "wild beast" – might pass unnoticed, wholly eclipsed by the next ludicrous headline rising above the horizon, but then at the dinner table on Thursday night:

"Mary Jane?" mom asked. "What's all this in the newspaper about you and Brett encountering a wolf in the wilderness?"

My mouth was agape because my hand, holding a forkful of mashed potatoes, suddenly froze in place, two inches away from its destination.

"There wasn't any wolf, mom," I replied. "Brett made it all up."

"I never realized that Brett had such an imagination," mom remarked, after swallowing a mouthful of meat loaf. "So you didn't run into any wild animals? – Is that what you're saying, Mary Jane?"

"Yes – I mean, no," I explained. "We saw birds and squirrels and a couple of chipmunks – they're wild animals. And I saw some deer tracks and … and a donkey, but it was tame. Aside from that – the only other thing that I could say was wild, is Brett's imagination."

"Did the wolfie have sharp, pointed teeth?" Roger asked.

"And big, burning red eyes?" followed Todd.

"Can I be excused?" I asked, getting up from the table because the twins, as usual, were dopes and only heard what they wanted to hear. "I have a lot of schoolwork that I have to catch up on."

I thought it best to mention the donkey because I had the suspicion that somehow the topic was going to crop up again, especially since it was in the newspapers. And I didn't fib about the schoolwork either – I did have a lot because I was still catching up from being absent earlier in the week.

"BRETT GETS NOD FOR RELEASE FROM HOSPITAL!"

appeared as Friday's headline and was probably a greater relief for me than it was for Brett because it would soon be the end of it all – the newspaper stories, that is. The article explained the conditions of Brett's release and the duration of his recuperation. It went on to say that there would be a special, "cast signing celebration" in the hospital lobby at ten o'clock on Saturday morning. Afterwards, the ambulance was to take Brett on the short ride back to his home on Mulberry Street where he would start his long road to recovery.

Anyway, that's what the newspapers had to say throughout the week about our adventure into the wilderness. And I guess I should feel lucky – and I do – because, aside from Otis and Willy and Mr. Gabriel, no one had discovered that we had crossed the train tracks.

When I arrive with mom and dad at the hospital lobby on Saturday morning, it's a three-ring circus. Well-wishers from all over Christmasville flock like sheep around Brett – "Our hero of the day!" – waiting their turns to pen their greetings and signatures on the thick cast that encases his leg, from foot to hip. He lies in a bed with wheels on it. It's like a lounge chair really because the mattress is cranked up so Brett can comfortably review all the comings and goings in the lobby, like he's a visiting prince or something. Colored streamers are strung through the bars on his bed. A long banner on the wall behind the reception desk reads: "Get Well, Brett! *Soon!!!*"

Behind him, Mr. Marshfield directs part of the band in the school Alma Mater. If I did my schoolwork as poorly as they played their instruments, I'd be the oldest kid in kindergarten. Off to the left, by the emergency room, are a half dozen cheerleaders, performing their routine in their red-and-green uniforms, swinging their matching pompons about.

"Look! – It's the girl that Brett saved!" says the reporter from *The Courier.* "Let's get a shot of Brett and the girl," he says to the photographer.

I can just picture the blurb beneath the photo in the newspaper: *"Superhero Brett Poses with No Name Somebody Girl That He Saved All By Himself from Certain Doom!"*

"My name's Mary Jane," I inform the reporter. "Mary Jane Higgins. And I'm allergic to cameras – if you take my photo, the flash will turn my face bright red and make all my hair fall out."

"Geez," the reporter remarks with alarm. "That's a story all by itself. Isn't it, Bob?" he says to the photographer.

"That's a story, all right," replies the photographer, unconvinced of my ailment. "But you know what, sweetie? – There's enough light in here so I don't have to use the flash."

Reluctantly, I let them steer me toward Brett. They stick a pen in my hand so it looks like I'm signing the cast of my fabulous fabled hero and rescuer.

"OK," the photographer directs. "Let's look up at the camera and give us a big smile.

Say 'Swiss cheese', please."

I didn't even get to the 'cheese' part before the flash goes off.

Winking at me, the photographer pulls me aside as he changes the lens on his camera. "When you start glowing like an electric strawberry and the hair's all gone, you be sure to let me know – OK, Mary Jane? I want to get a picture of that one."

I talk with Brett for a minute or so but it's kind of uncomfortable with all the people around, with them listening to every word that's said between us. And even though I'm not about to turn into what remotely resembles an "electric strawberry", Brett is about as red as one of the tomatoes in Otis and Willy's hothouse. I guess he's embarrassed by my being here, by the possibility that at any given moment I might spill the beans – rectifying any number of the imaginary stories that he's told the press throughout the week. *'Yeah, that was really a wild beast that you wrestled with out in the wilderness, wasn't it Brett?'* I could say, instantly transforming the hero of the moment into ... – But I couldn't do that, of course. I couldn't do that to Brett.

Moving away, the vacuum left behind is quickly filled by two cheerleaders, eager for the opportunity of having their pictures taken for the newspaper. Near the reception desk, I see mom and dad talking with Brett's parents.

"But where are the twins?" asks Mrs. Tolliver. "I haven't seen my little darlings since ... – Oh my! – I haven't seen the little darlings since Christmas Eve," she says, her hand pressed to her breast in a theatrical gesture.

"Hockey practice," mom says, robbing Mrs. Tolliver of any chance to dote.

"I'm kind of tired," I say to dad. "I think I'll go home for a nap."

"Do you want me to drive you, Mary Jane?"

"No – thanks, dad. I'll just walk."

Winding through the clusters of – of "Brett fans" – I guess you could call them, I make my way toward the double doors of the exit. I see Mrs. Franklin and Mrs. Kelly, talking with Mrs. Marshfield near the food table that's been set up. Or rather: Mrs. Marshfield is doing all the talking while my civics and algebra teachers help themselves to big chunks of coffee cake. At the far end of the table, by the punch bowl fountain, are Tommy Burks and Zack Foster. They're playing around as usual until a nurse intercedes. She's very tall – over six feet – so the troublemakers are reluctant to argue. In a far corner of the hospital lobby, in front of a big plastic tree in a big plastic pot, is Wally, the Postman. He's with Miss Perkins and I guess he's explaining all the details and intricacies of the postal system because his mouth moves without stopping while the beautiful biology teacher nods politely, seemingly digesting each and every useless tidbit of information as she peers through the crowd and covers a yawn, probably because she's had enough of it.

When I get to the exit, I wait until Mrs. Jenkins and Mrs. Watts, make their entrance. As I leave through the one door, Esmeralda – of all people – enters through the other.

"Leaving already, Mary Jane?" she asks.

I can tell by the look on her face that she means something else.

"Not right at this moment," I reply, letting the door swing closed behind me, and leaving.

January 15th – there are only sixteen days left until 'D-Day'. That's what I call it now – 'D-Day' – which is short for either 'Departure Day', or 'Destiny Day'. I haven't made up my mind which name is better so I just call it, 'D-Day', and leave it at that.

Sixteen days! That's all that's left before the change sets in, before the strange night of the 31st rolls in from the east and settles down, collecting remnants from the night before – shadows that have hidden themselves away throughout the day in closets and pockets, cabinets and drawers, car trunks and clockworks, between the pages of an unopened book – the night, gathering them up like blind orphans who have lost their way. It is the night that brings the long sleep to all of Christmasville, the night that extinguishes in darkness all the spotlights of memory, save *one*, leaving in its stead, candles that cast vague images of things-that-were on the walls of forgotten caverns.

And of course there's the more prominent change – the gathering up of all the houses and buildings in Christmasville to re-distribute them according to the new "plan" of things, to move them about like another game of checkers. I'm always wondering: does it happen all at once? – In a single night? Or is it something that takes much longer, occurring in stages over weeks, months, seasons that come and go without a trace? Two months of spring, two of summer ...

'... And two weeks left to find out,' I think to myself. 'And at least two more journeys – "*one in darkness and one in lightning*", said Esmeralda.'

It's nearly midnight when I sneak from the house and head down the middle of Pine Street. I guess the main reason that I've decided to travel lightly is so I can move quickly, without hindrance, returning from my journey well before dawn. Geez – if mom and dad found out that I was taking one of my "little walks" again ... well, I don't know what would happen, but it wouldn't be very good. The other reason for traveling lightly is because I lost my new backpack and half of my equipment. Maybe 'lost' isn't exactly the right word because I know exactly where they are – in the clump of roots of that pine tree, suspended on the edge of the bottomless abyss. At any rate, I'll never see them again so they might as well be lost. And the compass too – I dropped it when Mr. Gabriel was pulling me up the slope so God knows where that ended up.

The neighbor's houses are tucked away in thick blankets of darkness. It's funny how sometimes night seems more ... nightly? night-li-er? ... than at other times – as if it's darker and more dense, making the streetlights and the strands of colored lights, fastened to all the houses, strain in the fulfillment of their purposes. The sky doesn't help either: fat with clouds, it casts a shadow that stretches clear across Christmasville, smothering it with the lingering promise of snow.

When I get to the intersection of Linden Lane, I continue along the curve of Pine Street – behind the Wrights' workshop and hothouse – until I arrive at the power station. No fireworks this time! The giant transformers hum gently like they're dozing, saving their energy for their more heated battles with the cold and the elements.

Moving along the alley between the north wall of the power station and the rocky slope at the base of Jenkins' Hill, I stop short at the end of the building. In front of me, I see the powerful locomotive of the passenger train, puffing and heaving, emitting short jets of steam as it waits – with little patience it seems – at the mouth of the tunnel. It should have left over half an hour ago.

Stepping back into the shadow of the alley, I lean against the plastic brick wall of the power station and peek around the corner. Down track, outside the train station, I see Mr.

Bachmann pass a clipboard to Mr. Lionel. 'The passenger list', I say to myself, though immediately realizing the pointlessness of the gesture because, 'Why would there be any passengers? – There are never any passengers.'

After a few exchanges between stationmaster and train conductor – although I can't hear them, I see their heads bob, their hands gesticulate as each man speaks to the other – Mr. Bachmann turns toward the station. With the clipboard in one hand and his brass lantern in the other, Mr. Lionel starts toward the locomotive, pausing twice to inspect the metal wheels of one car, the ice-encrusted undercarriage of another.

He looks sinister as he walks along the train. You could easily mistake him for a robber, a spy or a villain from one of the twin's comic books. It's the contrast between the lights from the poles on the other side of the tracks, illuminating him momentarily in the gaps between train cars, and then the long shadows of the cars themselves as the light from his lantern dimly delineates the features of his face.

Pulling back into the darkness, I wait for him to pass.

"All aboard!" shouts Mr. Lionel, before clambering up the steps of the locomotive.

First, it's the sound of the engine lurching forward, a discharge of steam, then two short bursts of the train whistle, followed by the click-clack of all the cars behind the locomotive as they pick up speed and enter the tunnel, one by one. For a moment I think about dashing out and hitching a ride but decide otherwise because ... well, because of the danger – I could fall and tumble beneath one of the wheels or, if I did manage to jump on board ...

'No! – I'll stick with the plan and leave it at that,' I say to myself, watching the black-and-silver caboose swing into the tunnel and disappear.

I look back toward the station to make sure that Mr. Bachmann isn't watching. I look at my watch – 'twelve twenty-two', it reads in the light of the street lamp. Adjusting the weight of my backpack, I step from the shadows and approach the tunnel.

My plan: even though I was indecisive about it at first, it's too simple to dismiss. I'll follow the train tracks through the tunnel until it opens up on the other side of the mountain. I mean, how dangerous can it be? – The last train for the day has already departed so there's no danger there. It's just a matter of walking the tracks in darkness, using dad's flashlight to illuminate the way. And how long can it be? – Maybe an hour's walking distance? Two, at most. And, with any luck, I should be able to see the lights of St. Valentine's or Easterville when I exit the tunnel. Even though it's not New York City, it's a big step closer, isn't it? It's a huge step. A giant step! And when I see the lights of the city, I can decide then and there if I want to continue on – if the town's close enough and I have enough time – or return home and prepare for my final journey on the 31st of January.

Entering the tunnel, I pull the flashlight out and snap it on. I can still hear the rumble of the train as it presses forward in the darkness, the ground beneath me vibrating ever so slightly. And that's a good sign, of course – the train moving away – because the last thing that I want to see is what happened to me when I was on the train – a power outage. Geez! – What would I do then if I'm walking along and find myself bumping into the caboose because the power died?

Anyway, moving off, I discover that it's best to walk on the railroad ties between the tracks. I have to adjust my pace a bit, taking quicker, smaller steps, and aim the flashlight down so I don't miss a tie and trip on the loose jumble of rocks that are spread beneath the ties and tracks, that extend on either side, right up to the walls of the tunnel. The rocks are so hard and pointed that they dig into the bottom of my boots – I wouldn't last a hundred yards if I had to walk on them.

Every few minutes, I stop and shine the flashlight along the tracks ahead or along the walls. I guess one of the reasons is because, tucked away in the back of my mind, is the notion that I'll suddenly find myself on the edge of a bottomless abyss. I know it's silly but it's easier to stop and to shine the light ahead – you know, just to make sure – rather than to argue with myself and to let the notion, as silly as it might be, get the better of me. Another reason is equally absurd: sometimes I feel as if someone is off to the side, watching, waiting to shout, "BOO!" because they might find it funny to scare the living daylights out of me.

It's really weird how your mind works sometimes but anyway, it's during one of those moments, when I stop to pan the rocky walls of the tunnel that I discover something odd. Something's *written* across the surface of the rock. It's hard to read because it's covered over with layers of smoke and soot from the train but ...

"That Tommy Burks," I say with disgust as I decipher the inscription on the rock: *"Mary Jane is a fat fruitcake"*.

He must have snuck in here to scribble his nasty handiwork before Mr. Bachmann caught him. Of course, since no one knew that he had written it inside the train tunnel, he wasn't about to volunteer the information when it came to his eradicating it with wire brush and mineral spirits. And why would he? He would have gotten in twice the trouble – once for the graffiti and twice for being where he wasn't allowed.

Or maybe he did it *after* he got caught, I think, which is just another reason to pay him back, to keep paying him back, in spite of the fact that he doesn't even remember it, regardless of what Father Conover had said about the evils of revenge.

After about a half hour of walking the railroad ties, I notice that the rocks to the right and left of the tracks have all but disappeared, revealing a flat, smooth surface to walk on. This is so much better because, on the ties, I had slowed my pace considerably – concentrating on each tie as it became illuminated by flashlight, as it became the target for my next step. You would never imagine that forcing yourself to take such carefully measured baby steps could be so tiring! And my neck was getting a kink in it from constantly looking down.

It's like a breath of fresh air – walking normal – and the surface isn't real hard like the concrete in a sidewalk, or the asphalt of a road, or the ice that covers both sidewalks and roadways. It's a softer material – spongy – something like ... like the *wood* shavings on the floor of Otis' and Willy's workshop.

It's so quiet in the tunnel that when you do hear something, you can't be sure if it's right next to you or a hundred feet away. Not that there's a lot to hear – the soft whistle of the slight wind as it runs across rocky crevices, an occasional dripping sound, a creak or a groan as if the giant rocks that jut from the walls and roof of the tunnel are adjusting themselves, trying to make themselves comfortable in the sleepy passage of night. Sometimes I start talking to myself, rambling on about stupid stuff, spoken just for the sake of hearing my voice, *any* voice. I know it's silly but I kind of wish that Brett was here, to have somebody to talk to – even though Brett really doesn't talk that much. Except, of course, to newspaper reporters – he had plenty to say them.

What I discover along the way is that the railroad tracks don't run in a straight line. I don't know why I thought that they would. But anyway, sometimes they curve left or right; sometimes the curve is hardly noticeable while, at other times, it is so sharp that the train must slow to a snail's pace so it doesn't tip over. What's frustrating about the curves is that I can't keep track of which direction I'm heading. Without my compass, I don't know if I'm going north or east – not that it makes any difference because I have to follow the train tracks, regardless of which way they take me. It's just that ... it would be nice to know. It would be nice to know, too, how long the tunnel is, and how long it will take me to get to the end of it. But, of course, I won't know that until I get there, will I.

As I'm moving along, pondering about the tunnel and about what I'll find at the end of it, another thought crosses my mind. I hadn't thought of it before, but ... what if I come to a point where the tunnel splits into two, each tunnel heading off into a different direction? But then again, there's really no sense in dealing with things that may never happen. I mean, it's good to be prepared for the unexpected, but kind of foolish, I suppose, to bother about the unlikely.

About twenty steps ahead, I see something shiny along the train tracks. It's flat and metal and has the same color as our copper teakettle. When I come up to it, my first thought is that it's a manhole cover – like the ones you see embedded in all the streets of Christmasville – except that it's bigger and shinier and doesn't seem to be fitted into the surface below it but, rather, resting on top of it. And it doesn't have the image of city hall engraved into the surface of it, or the 'Department of Public Works' etched into the metal below it. Instead, the copper disc has the profile of a man – he has a beard and it looks like he's wearing his best suit of clothes. I don't know who he might be. In a half-circle over his head are the words, '*In God We Trust*'. To the left of the man's neck is the word, '*Liberty*', and to the right, but lower on the disc near his chest, is the number, '*1951*'.

I don't know what it could be. It's too heavy to move – and there's no place where you can put your hand to get a good grip on it. Maybe the number on it means that it was the one thousand, nine hundred and fifty-first disc that was produced. But why would it be numbered? And where did they put all the other ones that were made before it? What could they all be used for?

I have to move on. It would have been wise if I had brought my camera – to take a picture of the copper disc with the bearded man engraved in the top of it. I could have ... I could of what? – Taken it to somebody and said: 'Look at this copper disc that I found while walking the train tracks in the tunnel in the middle of the night!'

Yeah – That would go over real good. I'd be grounded for the rest of my life! And it'd be well deserved too – not for exploring or doing things that were strictly forbidden, but for being so stupid as to actually provide the evidence of my wrongdoings.

'*Liberty*,' I think, picturing the image of the disc, 'that's gotta be a good sign because liberty means freedom.'

It's curious but the structure and the ... the composition of the tunnel around me seems to have changed. I hadn't noticed it until now. Panning the flashlight around, I see that the tunnel has become more square-shaped – it looks like the inside of a long box. And the material – I take my glove off and approach one of the walls to run my hand across its smooth surface – it isn't rock. It's made of ... *it's made of wood*. It feels the same way as the miniature, wooden buildings that Otis and Willy made, the same as the wooden ribs of the contraption that's in their workshop. This is all so strange! Why would they use wood in the construction of this part of the tunnel? Why wasn't it rock? Or, at the very least, why didn't they use plastic paneling just like everything else that's made in Christmasville?

Shining the flashlight along the tunnel walls and ceiling, inspecting its fabrication, I see ahead markings that are stamped into the wood. I move forward, crossing the train tracks to the other side so I can get a better view. The markings are along the top of the wall that I had run my hand against, near the ceiling.

I can see now that they're letters but some of them are so crusted by the soot of the train smoke that I can't make them out. Slowly, I read each one aloud:

"...?-e-a-n ... – No, it's not an 'n', it's an 'r' ... -s & ?-o-e-b-u-c-?, C-o."

What could it mean? – "_ears & _oebuc_, Co?"

"Bears & Doebuck, Company? Dears & Soebuck, Company? Fears & ..."

I never heard of this company. It isn't from ...

That's it!!! – It isn't from Christmasville! It must be a company from whatever town is on the other side of the tunnel! It's the only explanation! When they built the tunnel, it must have been a joint effort – workers from Christmasville burrowed through Jenkins' Hill on the one side while workers from St. Valentine's and Easterville (and maybe New York City too!) started on the other end so they could meet in the middle. That must be where I'm at right now – in the middle of the tunnel, where Christmasville meets St. Valentine's and Easterville and the rest of the world!

This is so exciting! I'm actually walking – nearly running as I hurry along – on real estate that isn't part of Christmasville but that belongs to someplace else! It must be so different there, too, because ... well, because they use wood – I wonder if all the buildings there are made from wood like Otis ... like he speculated about, him and Willy going so far as to construct models of buildings, proving – at least on a small scale – that it was indeed possible to make houses from a material other than plastic. And I wonder what other differences I'll discover there too! Maybe ...

I have to slow myself down. I'm so excited about the prospect of what I'll find at the end of the tunnel that I have to stop to catch my breath. I have to remind myself to conserve my energy as well because ... Geez! – I wish it were the night of the 31st so I wouldn't have to return to Christmasville! I wish I could keep on going – into St. Valentine's and Easterville and then beyond, to New York City.

Stopping only long enough to get a drink from the bottle of water in my backpack, I start up again. Too energized to walk, but concerned as well about tiring myself out if I run, I decide on a comfortable trot. I have to be careful though because, up ahead, I see rocks, scattered randomly along both sides of the train tracks.

I'm moving along at a nice clip, the tracks extending through a long, straight section of the tunnel before winding into a series of sharp turns. For the most part, I keep the flashlight aimed at the path directly in front of me though, at times, I swing it's beam to the left or the right, or to the ceiling above so I don't miss any signs or clues that might reveal the nature of the place that I'm going to. What I begin to notice is that the tunnel is becoming more like it was, the wooden walls and ceiling gradually yielding to rock again, the square shape of it transforming back into the jagged semi-circle that it was before. I don't know if this is a good thing or a bad thing. It could be good because it might mean that I'm approaching the end of the tunnel. It could be bad because ...

The instant my foot catches the edge of the rock I know that I'm going down, that I'm going to fall flat on my face without having any opportunity to break my fall with my hands. I feel the jagged protrusions of smaller rocks dig into my right knee and then it's my hands and a larger, pointed rock that jabs me between the ribs on the left side of my body. It doesn't hurt too bad – it certainly could have been far worse – but what is most alarming is the *sound*, the sort of clinking, clanking sound of the flashlight as it shot from my hand and struck a rock a couple of feet ahead, the sound of it giving rise to, birthing, a darkness so thick and dense and seamless that when I hold my hands up only inches from my face, the only image I can see is the one that I imagine.

After groping about for the flashlight and finding it, I click the switch back and forth. I give it a couple of good shakes, smack it into the palm of my hand until I realize that it's broken and can't be repaired.

' "... *Darkness!*" said Esmeralda. "*A deep, dark blackness that swarms around you, that pushes against you ... in a place where you've never been before ... this darkness – it is so thick and sticky that you can almost smell it, and taste it ... like stale black licorice.*" '

It is the same darkness of a blind person who, awakening, realizes that he is required to function, to move about, to perform tasks in an environment that is wholly deprived of light. And it must be the same fear – the same palpable fear that strikes me like lightning, that makes me shake and shudder and curl myself up into a ball – the same fear that a blind person must experience when he realizes that he is absolutely alone, in a foreign and unforgiving place, with little or no chance of finding his way.

My gloves are wet with tears. I can't cry anymore. There aren't any tears left. I sit myself up and wrap my arms around me, rocking back and forth, trying to shake this terrible shudder, this horrible fear. Without my flashlight, I don't know what I'm going to do now.

"*Faith,*" I hear myself whisper, my lips trembling as I say it. "*Faith and hope.*"

I wipe my nose with the sleeve of my coat.

"As long as you have faith, then you always have hope."

I guess the first step is to get myself up to my feet.

"And the second? What would that be, Mary Jane?"

For some reason, it seems better if I talk out loud. Maybe it's because, in this absolute darkness, the sound of my voice provides me with some sense of familiarity. At least that's something – some single thing that I can latch on to, that I can recognize even though I can't see it, of course, but hear it instead.

I get myself up to my feet.

"The second step is to find the train tracks," I say out loud. "But move slowly and carefully – stupid girl! So you don't find yourself laid flat again!"

I inch forward, trying to feel the steel rail with my foot.

"There it is!" I say aloud, finding an iota of comfort in my capacity to do things without the aid of sight.

"Now squat down and find a tie with your hand – you remember what the ties look like. You remember the baby steps that you took when you were walking the ties."

I find the rough, flat surface of a tie.

"OK – good. Now's the difficult part: which way do you go, Mary Jane?"

I stand in the center of a tie, peering into the darkness.

"Which way do you go, Mary Jane?"

Of course, there's three choices. I can do an about-face and return the way I came, carefully measuring each step until I arrive at the mouth of the tunnel in Christmasville. That's the safe way. Or, I could take my chances and go forward and ... and come what may. The final choice is to stay put and wait ...

"OK – there's only two choices then because no one is going to come along and help you out. You have to figure this out all by yourself. So," I repeat with resolve, "which way, Mary Jane? Forward? Or back?"

What's curious about being in an environment that can't be seen is how your other senses kind of pick up the slack and function better. Maybe it's because your ears and your nose, your tongue and your fingertips aren't distracted by what your eyes see. It enables you to concentrate more on what can be heard or smelled, tasted or touched – it kind of reminds me of the spigots of water in the science lab at school. If you run water from all of them at once, then the water only trickles out. But if you shut some of the spigots down, the water gushes into the basins so hard that you have to turn the spigots back. It must be the same – almost the same with your senses – if one of the spigots is shut down, like your eyes, then you end up getting more information because you channel your attention into what's flowing through your remaining senses. You perceive things that maybe you wouldn't detect if all five of your senses were working at the same time.

I guess the point that I'm trying to make is this: I can hear the wind – faintly – ahead of me; I can *feel* the slightest breeze of it as it brushes my cheeks. And the darkness – it tastes and smells like ... *'like stale black licorice'*. If I were using my eyes, I don't think that I would notice what my other senses have to say about what's around me.

I take a step forward – and then another – slowly until my legs memorize the precise distance that they must stride to find the center of each tie before me. Before I know it, I have my legs trained so well that I don't even have to think about them.

The wind feels stronger, fresher, against my cheeks. Water drips into a puddle, somewhere ahead. In the air that streams through my mouth and nose, I begin to detect another smell ... the seed of a smell that's deeply embedded in the slight breeze. It's the smell of trees.

It starts as a tiny, gray spot on the horizon in front of me. At first, I think it's only my eyes playing tricks on me – my eyes like a spoiled, jealous child who has been deprived of attention. But as I move forward, the spot grows larger and lighter until I realize, almost by surprise, that it's the other end of the tunnel!

Tucked away in the back of my mind, I thought that maybe – just maybe – that when I exited the tunnel on the other side, the landscape would be magically different: fields of grass swaying in a balmy breeze; fat tomato plants and wild orchids; green, velvet-coated walnuts, dangling amid thick plumes of leaves. But, of course, what I find when I arrive at the mouth of the tunnel is more snow – a broad field of snow that is broken only by the twin stripes of the railroad tracks, extending into the dark distance. From the sky – from that gray but wonderful sky – a light snow is falling.

Cupping my hands around my eyes, I scan the skyline, looking for the lights of a city.

"I wish I had my compass," I say, moving from the tunnel.

"I wish I knew what time it is," I add, stopping to hold my watch up close to my face.

But it's so dark that I can't be sure. It looks like the tiny hands ... three-twenty? Quarter after four? Geez! – In either case, I haven't much time before I have to start back.

I cup my hands around my eyes again, panning the sky from left to right until ...

"There!" I say with sudden jubilation. "The lights of a city!"

Off to the right is a yellowish glow, smeared against the bruised underbellies of snow clouds.

For a moment, I close my eyes and take a deep breath, slowly digesting the enormous significance of my achievement: all by myself, I've managed to do what no one else from Christmasville has ever done, has ever dreamed of doing – except for Mr. Lionel, the train conductor – which is to travel to a place outside of Christmasville.

'But I'm not there yet,' I caution myself.

It's a bit of a dilemma because the train tracks shoot from the tunnel and into the darkness on the other side of the snowfield. They don't lead directly toward the city lights but rather ... well, they must wind through woods and flatlands, approaching the city in a roundabout way.

So, the dilemma is: without knowing how far the train tracks meander about, or how much time it may take me, should I continue to follow them until I arrive at the city? Or, should I just head straight for the yellow glow in the clouds – through the snow and over a couple of hills along the way?

Stepping across the steel railroad track, I test the snow to see how deep it is. I sink about four inches before settling on a frozen layer beneath. I take a couple more steps to be sure.

'OK,' I say to myself, eager to get moving, 'then it's this way.'

I set out toward the lights of the city, traveling along the edge of the snowfield, by the steep, ice-encrusted hillside that swings away from the train tunnel. I figure it'll take me a good half hour to reach a point where I can get a birds' eye view of the town before me, of what I believe to be, is St. Valentine's.

Except for the sound of my feet slogging through the snow, and the rattle of what few things I have in my backpack, it's quiet and peaceful as I move along at a brisk pace. The wind – there isn't any wind at all – it's wholly absent, the field and rock and hillside around me embraced in an absolute stillness. This is so strange that I stop in my tracks, just for a moment, to close my eyes and to listen.

Nothing. Nothing but the silence and the light snow falling across my face.

"*...Out there, nature seems to operate by a different set of rules*",' Otis said in my hospital room.

I should have asked him what he meant.

Did '*out there*' mean only that terrible ridge that skirted the bottomless abyss? Or did it mean all the landscapes on the other side of the train tracks? – All the mountains and cliffs that circumvented Christmasville? Did it refer to all the towns and cities beyond Christmasville? Does 'nature operate by a different set of rules' here as well, wherever I might be?

I should have asked him what he meant.

The path in front of me rises in a gentle slope. I pass a grove of leafless trees on my left. In the darkness, I can't make out what kind of trees they are. They look different though – the way their leafless branches shoot crooked and twisted away from their trunks. I don't know what kind of trees they are. But I have the feeling, the sense, that they're not asleep, like maples and oaks. I think that they might be dead.

"Chestnut trees," I say aloud. "Maybe they're chestnut trees, dead from 'the blight'."

At the top of the rise, the yellow glow against the bottom of the clouds appears brighter. But I still can't see anything of the city yet. I have to move closer.

Ahead of me, the terrain opens up into a valley. It's formed, in part, by the rocky hillside on my right, which winds off into a crooked horseshoe, its steep and jagged wall gradually diminishing in height as it comes around to become the one ridge of the valley. From what I can make out of the opposite ridge, it looks like sheer rock, rising from the valley floor in a long, vertical line. Luckily, I don't have to climb that side because, if I did, I don't think that I would make it.

Pressing forward, I feel my legs and shoulders grow tired. The side of my stomach, between my ribs, aches more now than it did when I fell on the rock in the tunnel. I wonder if something is wrong with me – something physical. I wonder if I'll have to go to the hospital again once I get back. I probably should come up with some sort of explanation as to how I got hurt ...

I know! – Tommy Burks! He pushed me off the top of the sledding hill and I tumbled all the way down. Geez! – I guess I'm lucky because I didn't break my leg like Brett did! – That Tommy Burks!

No, that won't work. They'll want to talk to witnesses.

I slipped on the ice! – I was running ... No, I was walking down the front steps of school. If Principal Marshfield weren't so cheap, he would have had somebody buy salts for those steps because they're so slippery and icy.

The twins! Maybe I'll blame it on the twins ... If only they hadn't left their toys on the steps, then I wouldn't have fallen – like the girl in the book, Madeleine, tumbling down the stairs with the basket of clothes.

I don't know. I'll come up with some kind of explanation. I wonder if I'll have to get an X-ray like Brett did?

In the valley, the snow is deeper and I have to use more energy to push myself forward. I know that I'm using energy that I was saving for the trip back, but what else can I do? – After coming this far, I have to get to the top of this ridge. I have to see something of St. Valentine's or the whole purpose of my journey is pointless.

I guess it's a combination of things that's caused my mood to change. The sensation of triumph and jubilation that I felt when I exited the tunnel and spotted the lights in the clouds has kind of deflated, giving way to fatigue and lack of focus. I know that it's only temporary though because once I see the city... well, then I'll get my second wind.

Near the top, it's difficult going because, once my foot settles onto the icy layer beneath the new snow, I have to dig my boot in so I don't slip. The last thing that I need to happen is to have myself slide down to the bottom of the ridge, only to gather up what little energy is left and to push myself up again. I don't know if I could do that, not without resting for a while.

Wouldn't it be wonderful if I discovered a hunter's cabin at the top? – Empty, of course, and with a clean bed and a fireplace with logs and kindling to make myself cozy just long enough to get my strength back. If I could just take a little nap ... and rest ... and maybe the pain in my side would go away, too.

'OK – almost there. Almost there. Another step and then another ...'

Dotted with tall pine trees, the top of the ridge looks like it extends about twenty yards before it drops down into the next valley. I notice, too, that it's suddenly much lighter now, enabling me to see with better clarity and at greater distances.

"Oh my God!" I say, stopping in my tracks to make sure that I'm reading the correct time on my watch. "It's ten minutes of six! – How will I ever get back on time? How will I get back through the tunnel before the train starts up again?"

There's a moment of sheer panic as possible solutions race through my thoughts, each one encountering it's own peculiar obstacle until I realize that I don't know how I'm going to get back.

'Maybe my watch is broken. Maybe it's running really, really fast because I fell and ...'

"Then why is it getting light out?" I reply, looking up and seeing through the trees ahead of me the spire of a church, a clock tower, the roof of a building.

At the other edge of the ridge, instead of descending into the next valley, I decide to climb one of the pine trees to get a better look. It'll save me a heck of a lot of time and a lot of energy to boot. Then I can start back, figuring out how to return on the way.

Sliding the straps of my backpack off, I drop it to the ground and begin the ascent. I grab one branch, step onto another, scurrying up the tree because my second wind has arrived, shaped in equal parts by the panic of my predicament as by the curiosity of the town, emerging beyond the hill in the distance as I move further up the tree.

'One ... two ... yes – three ... three church steeples ... The clock tower of a public building ... A factory off in the distance, spuming smoke ... The upper level of a ... a roof ... The roof of a ... a hospital ... The sledding hill?'

'I don't under ... – How can this be? – I don't...'

"It's ... It's *Christmasville!!!*"

I sit near the top of the pine tree, mouth open, eyes wide, pondering this impossible conundrum, this chilling illumination.

'*How could this happen? How could I arrive in the same place that I started from?*'

I feel tired and cold, confused and befuddled. None of this makes any sense to me. For a minute, I scan the familiar features that make Christmasville, *Christmaville*, scrutinizing each detail to insure that I haven't made a mistake.

'Maybe I made a wrong turn in the tunnel, in the darkness – the one set of tracks leading me here while the other ... the other veered off into another section of the tunnel ...'

I take a deep sigh – "All for nothing!" – I say out loud, thoroughly discouraged by the bitter fruits of my efforts.

'Or rather – bittersweet,' I think – the bitterness, of course, arising from the realization that I haven't gone anywhere, except in a circle; the sweetness of my predicament, materializing in the resolution to the problem of getting myself home again. Instead of backtracking through the tunnel, all I need do is to cross the valley between here and the sledding hill. And then it's home free.

When I start back down the tree – physically exhausted and mentally ... emotionally numb, I guess you could say – the first indication that something's askew is the strong, pungent *aroma* that wafts in the air, that masks entirely the smell of sap and pine needles. It reminds me of the incense that's burned in church for special occasions.

Then it's the *sound* – a loud, *snorting* sound that ...

I think of the donkey. Remaining perfectly still in the tree, I think of the donkey that Brett and I had seen in the woods – the donkey that was later resurrected, altered, transformed into the wolf, into the mountain lion, into the "wild, raving beast".

'*There!* There is it again!' – It's off in the distance, in the valley behind me, the valley that I had crossed maybe a half hour ago. '*There – that loud snorting sound!*'

Turning slowly, carefully, I brace myself in the tree, squeezing a branch with one hand, hugging the trunk with the other.

'Can wolves climb trees? – No, I don't think so. Mountain lions? – Yes, maybe. They climb mountains, don't they? And what about ... "wild beasts"? I guess some of them can and some of them ...'

Movement! Through the branches of the trees, I see ... I see one ... two ... yes, three of them now, moving across the slope on the other side of the valley. Three riders ... three riders wearing long, flowing ... *robes* ... – Yes, they're robes! The first has a purple one ... The second – it looks green like maple leaves ... And the last ... the last is yellow ...

Three riders on horse- ...

But they're not riding horses – they don't look like horses. They look like animals that I've only seen in picture books ... *They look like camels* ...

I remember walking through the woods with Mr. Gabriel. I remember trying to keep my eyes open and my legs moving forward as Brett moaned from the sled beside me.

"*Believe me when I say this, Mary Jane,*" said Mr. Gabriel. "*The donkey isn't the strangest thing that I've seen in these here parts.*"

What The Iceman Said

If you were awake and you stood on the front porch and listened very carefully, you could hear him in the wee hours as he led his horses from stable. You would hear him swing the gates of the paddock closed and clasp them shut just as surely as Dawn rolled from her sleep at the edge of the world, moments afterward, rising to seal the night away. It would be the hooves of his horses clopping on the road; the long metal runners of his empty hauling-sleigh, gliding light as a feather across the white ice; the occasional bark of his dog, Blink, a spotted mongrel and smart as a whip.

Rising from my bed, I peel the curtain back and look through the window at the frozen stillness of Pine Street that is broken only by the passing of the Iceman.

Prince of the sleepy town, Stark is known by many things: his wide-brimmed hat, ragged at the edges and pulled down deep along the bridge of his forehead; his beard, curled like strands of fine silver wire; his wild woolly clothes that are patched at the elbows of his long overcoat and, more often than not, at the knees of his baggy trousers as well. But what strikes you most of all about Stark – and what you remember long after he's led his horses and dog away – is the sound of his voice in that pure and simple silence of the wee hours. It is deep and hoarse but always calm and tender as he speaks to his horses in the language that they know, prodding them along with the satin of his words rather than with the leather of his whip.

The larger horse, Courier, is pinecone brown and has a long golden mane that splashes down in front of his eyes when he moves. He got his name from the newspaper that Stark's grandfather started – *The Christmasville Courier.* The smaller horse, Ives, has the speckled complexion of eggnog after you sprinkle it with nutmeg. He's younger than Courier, and more rambunctious, and got his name because he was born on the Feast Day of St. Ives. When the two horses move together, pulling the hauling-sleigh across the road and down to the lake, Courier and Ives look so graceful that you would think that they stepped right off the page of a picture book.

Turning from the window, I change into my clothes and boots. I gather up my coat and hat, my woolen scarf and worn gloves, and head for the kitchen. Fixing a breakfast of cold cereal and toasted muffin, I sit at the table and eat.

It is the day of my next journey.

Through the window over the sink is the first sign of Dawn – the folds of her robe, a rosy bloom against the dwindling panoply of night as the goddess rises up and stretches, combing stars from her auburn hair, commencing the single chore accorded her.

It is a day offering the plumes of roses, a day promising the thorns of lightning.

' *"Falling"*,' said Esmeralda.

' *"Darkness"*,' she forewarned.

'And now ... now there was to be *"lightning".'*

It's difficult for me to get started, to motivate myself, to begin my next journey. I think it's because time is winding down – 'D-Day' is rapidly approaching – and, so far, I haven't managed to really come up with anything that I could say is definitive. In the journey east from the sledding hill, I discovered the bottomless abyss and the notion that "out there, nature seems to operate by a different set of rules". But if only I had followed those footprints through the ravine – maybe they did belong to Mrs. Gabriel and Caroline, who, in the snow and the wind, had stumbled accidentally upon a passage to New York City. Maybe that's were they were now – strolling along Fifth Avenue, having a lively conversation with Jacqueline and the children, and with Resident-Elect, John F. Kenn. All that I found out there was a donkey. Brett found himself with a broken leg. And Mr. Gabriel? – In his venture out to the caves where we had discovered the footprints, he found a sudden snow squall that whipped through the ravine, all but erasing them.

The journey through the train tunnel – the long, winding trek through the darkness and across the snowfield and up the hillside – what did I accomplish in that? Nothing. I found a grove of dead trees and maybe they were chestnuts. But that doesn't mean anything. And the three strange riders, traveling west across the valley – maybe they were riding ... – What bizarre creatures they were! Maybe they were riding ... camels ... – But where could they have come from? And where were they going? – They couldn't have been camels because camels only exist in myths and fairy tales, like unicorns and giraffes, dragons and elephants. Maybe if I wasn't so tired and I had followed them ...

Maybe if I hadn't stumbled on the rocks and broken the flashlight, then I would have seen the train tunnel divide into two, the first swinging north toward St. Valentine's and Easterville, the second looping me back, not far from where I had started.

It's like I've been moving in circles – my feet, the hands of the clock that march round and round, through the days and nights, moving without going anywhere.

Maybe I'm just a crazy girl, led by a damaged imagination, recovering from a twisted hallucination. Maybe my head's got 'the blight' and that's why mom is always checking to see if I have a fever.

One thing's for sure: there's far too many 'maybes' in everything that I do.

At the table, I dip my spoon into the bowl of cereal and lift a load of the tiny, milk-soaked doughnuts up to my mouth. I bite into the crumbly corn muffin, a few pieces of it falling into the cereal. Through the window, the western fringe of Dawn's robe glows orange while the eastern part rolls back into darkening shades of lavender.

Down the hallway, I hear the door to the bathroom open and close. I recognize its telltale creaks. Geez! – I hope it's not mom or dad because then I won't be able to get out of the house, not without another interrogation. It's because they suspect that something's wrong ... something's wrong with their crazy daughter.

Last Tuesday, after dinner, dad came into my room while I was doing my homework.

"Is everything all right, Mary Jane?" he said, sitting on the edge of my bed.

"Everything's fine, dad," I replied, without looking up from my desk.

"You don't seem to be yourself these days," he said. "You seem distracted, aloof, as if you're constantly trying to figure out the solution to a difficult problem. We can help, you know – your mom and I. That's what we're here for, princess."

"Everything's fine, dad," I replied.

The following Thursday, it was mom's turn. I sat at the dinner table, finishing up my green beans while mom filled up the sink to wash the dishes. She squirted the detergent in, frothed up the water with her hand like she always does, started to hum an unfamiliar song before stopping.

"The other day at the supermarket, I ran into one of your school administrators," she said, putting dishes and glasses in the sudsy water. "A very nice man – Dr. Sperry – though I've never had the occasion to really chat with him before."

She doesn't remember, of course, the stiff sentence that I had to endure last year – meeting with the "nice" Dr. Sperry twice a week because I had become "emotionally challenged".

"He seems like someone you could talk to," mom continued, thinking that she was being subtle, "someone who would listen to any problems that you might have, helping you to find answers. Do you know what I mean, Mary Jane?"

I was going to ask mom if the good doctor offered her a stick of candy. But I changed the subject instead.

The bathroom door swings open and closed, creaking.

There's two reasons why it must be one of the twins – no flush of the toilet, no splash of water in the bathroom basin because, after a pee, neither one of the little brats ever flushed or bothered to wash their stinky little hands.

'And he probably didn't lift the seat,' I think with disgust, getting up from the table and putting my dishes in the kitchen sink as quietly as I can.

On the front porch, I tighten the knot of my woolen scarf, slip my hands into my gloves. It is that first deep breath which startles you, which shocks your lungs with that first balloonful of frigid air. It makes you feel alive – the cold air – sending its wake-up call to parts of your body that are still kind of dozing. Or recovering. The only good thing about my excursion last week was that I didn't have to go to the hospital because of my tumble on the rocks. My bruised ribs turned out to be nothing more than just that – a bruise that hurt like hell last Sunday, but what got better and better as each school day throughout the week came and went.

Stark, the Iceman, has already led his horses and hauling-sleigh beneath the train trestles at the far end of Pine Street. In the distance, I hear Blink bark twice – probably because he saw a squirrel or a rabbit, scampering about for bits of food. Quick as he is, Blink'll never catch it though because he has big, floppy feet that help him run fast but prevent him from turning and dodging like the furry, little critters do.

Stepping down from the porch, I head into the backyard and cut across the Thompson's toward Juniper Street.

Emily. Things haven't been the same since she betrayed me. We're still friends, of course, but it's not the same. I know that I shouldn't hold grudges. I know that the only reason she told Brett about my crossing the train tracks was because she was worried about me. But a secret between friends should stay a secret, shouldn't it? – Regardless of the consequences. If she was so concerned about my safety, then she should have come to me first. How can I ever tell her a secret again if there's always the possibility that she'll reveal it? How can I ever trust her again? And then, too, she's so immature, Emily, with her dolls and teddy bear and books of puzzles. When will she ever grow up?

'Never,' I think, answering my own question. *'No one will ever grow up.'*

As I arrive on Juniper Street, a green car edges up the narrow driveway between the Church of St. Ives and *The Courier* building. He puts his right blinker on but turns left, swinging into the curve on Juniper. Although I don't recognize him at first – not without his cape and top hat, his tuxedo and cane – it's Marco, the Magician. I guess he needs a second job because making magic doesn't pay enough money. But you would think that a magician would come up with a better way to deliver newspapers than just driving around and chucking them out his car window like the other deliveryman does. You would think that he could make the whole bundle of newspapers disappear and then, after casting a magic spell, make them re-appear in their plastic wrappers on everyone's doorstep. But then again, I never thought that Marco was the best magician anyways.

On second thought – the heck with the newspapers – if Marco was so good at magic, why doesn't he just make a bundle of cash appear out of nowhere when he needs it?

Moving around the curve on Juniper Street, I see Mr. Mason, the milkman, as he pulls his white van into the parking lot of the Christmasville Inn. Hiding behind a tree at the corner of Willow Street, I wait until he's gathered up the inn's order in plastic crates and gone inside.

It would not be wise to run into Mr. Mason this early in the morning because ... well, because it'll turn into some sort of interrogation – 'Where you off to at this time of day, Mary Jane?' he'll ask. And then he'll mention it to Wally, the postman, who, in turn, will say something to Mr. Cauldwell, the owner of the supermarket, who will feel compelled to repeat it to mom and ... – Anyway, you know how that goes.

Instead of jumping from the side door of his van, Mr. Mason exits through the double panel doors at the back. In each hand is a crate of milk and cream, butter and cheeses. Walking along the side of the van toward the entrance of the inn, he stops. He puts the crates in the snow and then tilts the side mirror of the van outward so he can see himself. Shifting his head around – a bit to the right, a tad to the left, slightly downward – he inspects his appearance in the mirror until he's comfortable that the bald spot on the top of his head is sufficiently camouflaged by the thin wisps of hair that he's combed back over it. He tilts the mirror back into place, grabs the crates and goes inside the inn.

Stepping from the tree, I hurry along Juniper Street so I don't catch him when he exits. I wonder why Mr. Mason doesn't just wear a hat?

At the corner of Mulberry Street, across from St. Nick's, I veer off into the grove of spruce trees. Oh, the fragrance! – I'll never understand why they don't make perfume from spruce trees. I mean, if I used perfume, I'd be sure to always have a bottle of 'Spruce Juice' on my dresser, dabbing it behind my ears and on my wrists whenever I wanted to make myself smell good.

Moving in curly-cues, I make my way through the grove of spruce trees. I pass one of the towering, gray trestles that support the tracks of the freight train above, trudging through the snow until I see the coaling station ahead.

Of all the buildings in Christmasville, the coaling station is the most unusual. With tall, girder-like supports that straddle either side of the railroad tracks, the station is perched mid-air – almost as if it were floating in space, twenty feet above the tracks below. It's pretty remarkable actually because inside the brown, clapboard station are tons and tons of coal that slide down through a plastic chute into the coal tender of the passenger train, once its parked in place below. You would think that the floor of the station would collapse from all the weight. But I guess whoever built it, knew what he was doing.

To get up to the coaling station, there's a ladder that takes you up to a railed platform that's bolted to the side. At the end of the platform is a staircase of about six or seven steps. The staircase leads you up to a second platform, which stretches along the western side of the station. There's a door at the end of it. It leads into a section of the coaling station that's only about five feet wide and eight feet deep. From this section, a narrow shaft extends along the support girder all the way down to the ground. I don't know what this section's for. Or why there's a door that leads into it.

I never realized it before but the second platform ... if you went up the steps from the first platform and stood on the second, then, technically, you had broken the cardinal rule of Christmasville. Even though you were twenty feet or so above the ground, you would have crossed the train tracks to the other side without even being aware of it.

I always wanted to climb the ladder to the top but I was afraid because the ladder is narrow and wobbly when you start climbing. I never made it past the halfway point without stopping, looking down toward the ground and then, realizing how high I was and how flimsy the ladder was, closing my eyes and hugging the ladder for dear life until I could coax my hands and feet to start moving again – but the other way – down, not up. I guess the trick is to keep moving until you get to the top. And to never look down.

Arriving at the base of the ladder, I close my eyes for a second and take a deep breath, concentrating on the task before me. First it's one step and then the second, each arm raised to meet a rung of the ladder above me as each leg is lifted to meet one below. I move like a jittery machine, scaling the ladder in measured increments – hand over hand, foot over foot – one continuous, almost graceful, motion, unbroken by fear or indecision until I arrive at the top.

But it doesn't look very graceful when I sort of crawl from the ladder onto the platform and wiggle my way toward the wall of the station.

Rising to my feet, I press myself against the plastic clapboards and slowly turn about, remembering not to look over the edge of the platform to the ground directly below, but outward, toward the horizon.

Oh – It's so pretty! – The view reminding me of the time that I had climbed the boulder on the ridge, opposite the sledding hill. But this is prettier – postcard pretty – because I can see much more of Christmasville. The sleeping town is highlighted by the spruce grove in front of it – the V-shaped spaces between the trees framing city hall and the Church of St. Ives, the Christmasville Inn and the power station. And the treetops form peaked indentations along the elevated line of Maple Street which, if you squint your eyes, make them look like miniature trees, sprouting across the rocky slope of Jenkins' Hill.

If I were a photographer, this would be the picture that I would use, that I would put on the cover of ... of next year's map of Christmasville ...

'Next Year? – Where will I be next year? 'And the year after that?'

'Who knows?' I answer, as the image of the treetops, transformed by the squinting of my eyes into miniature trees along the slope of Jenkins' Hill ... the image, resurrecting a snap-

shot that I had locked away in a deep closet of memory, a snapshot that I've deliberately refused to acknowledge, to address ...

It's that snapshot from memory, yanked from its closet and fully illuminated in the closing of my eyes ...

' *"Whoops! – There goes Janey again!"* '

It's the snapshot of the train platform in the study, the mental picture of it suddenly brought into sharp focus, the tiny toy town becoming animated as the twins move houses and buildings from one place to another; propel cars along streets; make the train chug-chug from the station and race around the track while ... *People – suddenly I imagine real, live people that I know and love and ... This can't be Christmasville! This can't be Christmasville, year after year, assembled and dismantled on an eight by four plastic platform! This can't be the town where Mary Jane Higgins, never thirteen or fifteen but always – ALWAYS! – fourteen years old, the town where I, me, Mary Jane Higgins rise from my bed and go to school and church and sledding hill and do the same silly, stupid things, year after year, without purpose or meaning and ... And why can't anyone else see it??? Why??? – Why is it only me who sees it???*

It takes me a few minutes to recuperate, to compose myself from the sudden panic that sometimes overwhelms me, that gobbles me up like a wild animal devouring its prey. Taking a tissue from the pocket of my coat, I blow my nose and take a couple of deep breaths, breathing in the comforting scent of spruce trees and ...

'What is that other smell?' I think, bobbing my head about as I sniff.

It is a faint but familiar odor that is carried by the breeze, swinging down from the west.

Moving toward the end of the platform, I go up the steps that lead to the next level. I continue to brace myself against the wall of the station rather than to support myself with the railing along the edge. On the second platform, I turn the corner and slide along the wall until I'm about halfway down to the door at the end.

"It's the smell of ... of bacon," I say, sniffing again, suddenly recognizing the odor. "It's the smell of someone cooking bacon."

In the sky of the west is an opaque curtain. Deep blue at the very top – at a point in the sky directly above my head – the curtain swings out in a wide arc, becoming grayer and cloudier as it approaches the horizon, denser and foggier as it swings back toward the abyss just beneath me.

But I can only look down for a second because the steep drop of the cliffs makes me so dizzy that I slam back into the wall behind me and squeeze my eyes shut.

'But you have to look,' I remind myself. 'It's the whole purpose of coming up here, isn't it? – To be certain that there isn't a path or a trail, a road or a bridge that might lead me away from Christmasville.'

Prying my eyes open, I look toward the nebulous horizon of the west. I focus on the railing on the outside edge of the platform, lean forward, inching myself away from the security of the wall behind me. I slide my right foot forward, and then my left, stretching my arms toward the railing.

"There! – Got it!" I say aloud, grabbing the plastic railing with all my strength, proud of my bold accomplishment.

I take a couple of deep breaths and look down.

My stomach curls into a knot that rises like a hard bubble into my throat. I try to swallow but I can't.

Beneath me, the cliffs drop in a straight vertical line. It must be a quarter of a mile straight down before the jagged precipices sink into the dense, swirling nothingness of the fog. It's almost identical to the abyss in the east, the abyss which, had it not been for the fallen pine tree, for the clump of roots at the edge of the precipice ...

Panning the depths below, I realize the bleak truth: just as I thought, just as I had always thought, the west – like the east – would provide me with no avenue of escape.

'But I had to be sure,' I think, finding some minor sense of achievement in my venture up the ladder of the coaling station. 'I had to be ...'

"Hey! – Who's up there?"

I snap my head around, step from the railing back toward the wall of the station.

"I know somebody's up there," the voice continues, "because I see your footprints in the snow, leading up to the ladder."

'What'll I do now???' I think, scrambling for a way out of my predicament.

I hear the crunch of heavy boots in the snow as they approach the foot of the ladder.

'The door!' I reply, sliding along the ridged clapboards of the station towards it. 'I'll find a place to hide inside!'

The doorknob is frozen stiff. As hard as I squeeze, my gloves just slide around the stupid thing without accomplishing anything. Removing them, I jam them into the pockets of my coat and breathe warm air into my hands. First, I give the knob a couple of taps with my fist and then, grasping it with both hands, give it a good tug until the bolt slides from its latch.

Inside, the only light comes from the open door. There's the heavy odor of coal dust and oil – the kind of oil that you would smell around machines. I step inside, onto a small platform that's made of plastic two-by-fours, looking for a place to hide.

'A light switch!'

But there's nowhere to go! – Illuminated by the single light bulb in the fixture that's fastened to the side of the platform, I scan the scant surroundings for some place to hide. The platform is only about four feet wide and six feet long. To the right of it, is the long shaft that drops all the way to the ground. There's cables looped through two giant pulleys at the top of the shaft and, coupled with the oily smell that wafts up from below, I imagine there must be a machine or a motor or some kind of apparatus at the bottom of the shaft that's used for hoisting the coal up. I can't be a hundred percent sure though because I can only see glints of light that slip through cracks in the clapboards at the bottom of the shaft.

To the left of the platform, about four feet below the light fixture, is the huge mound of coal that's stored inside the station.

"OK, I've got an idea!" I say with resolve, swinging the door shut.

When he arrives, I don't know who he might be. He's big though, and heavy, because with each step across the platform, I hear a creak where the plastic two-by-fours are fastened to the support beams beneath the platform.

"Anybody here?" the man says in a deep voice.

I recognize him now. It's Mr. Burks – Tommy's dad and the stationmaster at the Oak Street Train Station. He's also responsible for operating the coal chute when Mr. Lionel needs fuel for the passenger train.

He flips the light switch once – and then several times, until he realizes that the light bulb will not cooperate.

"Geez!" he says with irritation, "I must have left the darn light switch on again. The bulb's burnt out!"

After he leaves – mumbling as he goes – I count to a hundred before clambering across the coal beneath the platform. I know I'm going to be a mess, the coal dust blackening my hands as I make my way across the mound, sticking to the sweat that's bubbled up along my forehead and upper lip. The stuff tastes horrible!

Reaching up to the edge of the platform, I slide my hand along until I find the light fixture. I twirl the bulb in its socket until light spills back into the station and I can pull myself up to the platform. Sure enough – I'm a grimy, cruddy mess.

When I open the door – the cold, fresh air greeting me as I'm about to leave – I step back, thinking that I should probably turn the light out. 'But no,' I decide, 'I'll leave it on just for the fun of it, just for the fun of vexing Mr. Burks when he returns with the light bulb that he doesn't need after all. It's the least I can do for someone who's made me such a mess.'

At the end of the upper platform, I peek around the corner of the station to make sure that Mr. Burks – or anyone else for that matter – isn't around. I start down the stairs toward the lower platform and, on the second step ...

'There's that smell again – the smell of someone cooking bacon.'

I look toward the gray nothingness of the west.

'Maybe there are others just beyond the thresholds of sight and sound – people rising and stirring, moving about the breakfast tables, greeting each other with sleepy voices ... "Good morning!" and "Sleep well?" and "How would you like your eggs cooked?" and "Toast? Or English muffin? Juice? Or a glass of milk?" ... like ... like in the book that I read last month, the book about Madeleine, when she tried to eat her bacon and eggs with one hand because she had fallen down the steps and broken her wrist and ... Maybe Madeleine and her mother and her father are out there right now, somewhere, someplace in the far regions of the west, their bodies and voices erased by the fog and the wind, and all but the bacon – the smell of the bacon – rising from the frying pan and through the kitchen, or out through the exhaust fan over the stove, swirling with the wind that swings down from the west ...'

When I get to the bottom of the ladder, I backtrack through the grove of spruce trees, stopping midway to wash my face and hands in the snow. On impulse, I fall forward and swing my arms up and down, slide my legs back and forth before flipping over and repeating the same movements until I'm satisfied that I've removed the black, powdery film from my clothes. When I get up to go, I see the results of my handiwork: embedded in the snow are a pair of snow-angels – *fallen* snow-angels, I guess you could say, because they're darkly stained with coal dust.

Back on Juniper Street, I continue south, passing the Church of St. Nick's and the radio station on the corners of Mulberry. When I arrive at the junction of Oak Street, I stay on Juniper as it swings east, squiggling its way around turkey farms and chicken ranches, cow pastures and woodlands. I've never been to the end of Juniper so I don't know where it goes exactly. On the map of Christmasville, it just stops near the southeastern tip of town with no explanation. Maybe it's because they ran out of room – on the map, that is, ending it there because otherwise they would've had to make the map larger than what it already is.

As for Oak Street – well, I've already been down Oak three times since December 1st. Twice we went to MacGregor's Tree Farm – to tag our Christmas tree, and then later, to dig it up. The third time was a couple of weeks ago. And that was because each year – *every year* – Principal Marshfield decides to bus everyone in school to the Consolidated Factory Works on Career Day. I guess he thinks that's what everyone wants to do when they grow up – to work in the plastic factory. And a lot of them do, but not everyone. Not me.

Anyway, there isn't much of anything down Oak Street – well, at least anything that might appeal to my sense of purpose. There's a lot of oak trees, of course, and houses along the beginning of it – the Foster's and the Horton's, the Matthieson's and the Bonner's. There's the train station at the north end of the crescent-shaped street. Midway down, sprawling along the bottom of the crescent, as it turns from a southerly to a northerly course, is the plastic factory. It's the largest building in Christmasville. On the far side of the factory are the parking lots and then a tall fence that runs parallel to the tracks of the passenger train as they curve east, right along the edge of the perilous cliffs. That's why it's pointless to think that I might discover anything of consequence beyond Oak Street. There's only the fence, the railroad tracks and then the cliffs of the abyss.

Moving at a brisk pace along Juniper, I hear sounds that are typical for this part – the rural part – of Christmasville. I hear the unmistakable cry – the "Cock-a-doodle-do!" – of a rooster and the squawking, fluttering sounds of chickens in a coop. There's a chirping of birds and the steady sound of a tractor, off in the distance. From a red barn is the mooing of cows, exchanging their milk for water and grain and a roof over their heads to protect them from the harsh weather. But they must be done with that now because, through the trees, I see the black-and-white cows sauntering from the barn, eager to get out in the snow pastures to play and exercise.

When I swing around a sharp bend in the road, I discover that I'm at the end of Juniper Street. It just stops in the middle of the woods, a pile of snow and ice chunks deposited by a snowplow at the end of it. It's just like the map says – there's no other road leading into it, nothing that leads away from it. It just stops. And now that I think about it, there isn't even a sign or an indication along the way to say, "Oh, in case you're interested, the street that you're driving on? (Or, in my case, walking on.) – But anyway, "The street that you're driving on? – You know, Juniper Street? – Well, it stops without really going anywhere so you might want to consider turning around right now."

Except for the little access roads that lead from Juniper Street to the farmhouses along the way, I'm not sure why they extended it as long as they did. Maybe somebody thought that the woodlands here could be turned into a housing development or some kind of commercial enterprise. Maybe they had too much asphalt when they were paving Juniper and just decided to keep going until they used it all up. Maybe the construction company that made Juniper Street is the same one that's constantly making Beech Boulevard – they don't know what the heck they're doing anyway so it certainly could have been one of their projects.

Anyway, regardless of the explanation, the fact is – I'm at the end of Juniper Street, so what do I do now?

I figure the best way to proceed is through the woods, in a southeast direction. I wish I had my compass with me – I really have to remember to buy a new one at the Five & Dime – and I kind of wish I had brought my backpack, too, but I wanted to travel lightly and quickly, exploring as much as possible before turning back. But I didn't buy a compass and I didn't bring my backpack, so I'll just have to make do. I can always use the shadows of the trees to get my bearings and there's certainly plenty of snow around so I won't find myself thirsty.

Walking in the snow through the woods, I think about the animal tracks that I had seen on my journey beyond the sledding hill. I wonder if there really are wolves and mountain lions, pushed by humankind into the remote corners of Christmasville. After all, I did see a donkey, and strange creatures that I thought were camels, so why couldn't there be wolves and mountain lions and wild beasts as well?

'That's what Brett Tolliver would have you believe, isn't it, Mary Jane?'

I reach down and grab a clump of snow, shaping it into a ball.

'Poor Brett,' I think. 'The excitement of his heroic escapades – as fictional as they were – faded faster than a snowball in a coal stove, once the newspaper articles had stopped.'

With that, I toss the snowball toward an oak off to the left. At the same moment that it strikes the tree dead center, crumbling into bits, I hear a sound that startles me, that leaves me with a vague, unsettled feeling. It's the sound of gunshot – maybe a mile away, near the lake.

'Target-practicing,' I suggest. 'With hunting season ended in December, somebody's probably target-practicing.'

Another gunshot echoes through the woods.

A couple of hundred yards into the woods, I see a clearing ahead me. Beyond the clearing, I can make out the broken outline of a large building. At the corner of the structure is a fat, round smokestack that rises up as high as the treetops. It looks like an abandoned factory, or an old power station.

When I get to the clearing, I can tell by the decrepit streetlamps that it must have been a parking lot at one time. As for the building, it's three stories high and made of plastic, rust-red bricks that are cracked and weather-stained. All of the windows are shattered, allowing the wind and the snow to scurry inside, accelerating the dereliction. Jutting away from the front of the building are double-doors that are boarded over with thick, plastic planks.

Making my way across the parking lot, between the snowdrifts, I approach the front of the building. Above, perched on a third floor windowsill, a snowy white owl watches me as I advance.

If the building didn't appear so ... so austere, and forbidding, it would be kind of fun to explore its contents. Although the doors are boarded over, I could easily climb through one of the window holes on the first floor.

I'm certainly tempted as I poke my head through, inspecting the vast disarray of dilapidated desks, chairs and filing cabinets that litter the first floor.

'All I need is something to stand on,' I think, looking in the snow around me.

By the front doors, I see lumps in the snow that are shaped like boxes. There's four or five of them. But when I brush the snow off the closest one and try to move it, the thin sheathing of the box falls apart in my hands, its contents spilling in the snow around it.

I'm not sure what they are. I'm not sure why the boxes are full either, having been left out in the snow for God knows how long unless ... unless the post office decided to deliver them, leaving them at the front door because no one was around to receive them.

But anyway, I reach down and grab a milk-white cylinder in each hand, inspecting the pair of them for a sign as to what they might be. They're made of ceramic, I discover, clapping them together and turning them about.

"They look like those things on the tops of..."

The sign on the front of the building suddenly comes into focus. It's a bronze plaque, with a greenish patina to it, and reads: *"Christmasville Electric"*. Etched into the metal background is a man with a helmet. In one of his hands is a light bulb, which also serves as the 'i' in *'Electric'*. His other hand is raised up high over his head and clutches an object that spans the whole sky over the company name. It's a *lightning bolt*.

I drop the ceramic cylinders in the snow and take a step backwards.

' *"Falling"*,' said Esmeralda.

' *"Darkness"*,' she forewarned.

'And now ... now there was to be *"lightning"*.'

Scanning the weathered, brick facade of *Christmasville Electric*, and the dark, scary holes that are punctured in rows along the front of it, I feel a nauseous knot churning in the pit of my stomach. It's not a good idea to be here, I decide, turning about and marching away as fast as my legs will take me. Over my shoulder, I see the white owl watching me as I depart.

It's strange how your mind works sometimes. It's so fickle! In one moment, you're as happy as a pig in ... You're as happy as a lark and then – That fast! – you see or discover something, which, by itself, is kind of neutral, being nothing more than what it is – like the sign on the electric building. I mean, it's only a sign but ... but the lightning bolt – the simple depiction of it on the metal plaque was enough to change my whole perspective, transforming the building from something that could be explored to something that should be avoided at all costs, charging each moment afterward with an acute sense of impending dread, as if something bad were about to happen at any moment.

It reminds me of my physics class actually – positive particles and negative particles ... – Can your mind do that? Can your mind change thoughts from a positive charge to a negative one simply because you see an object – a sign – which conveys more information, *different* information, than what the sign was intended to convey?

'Maybe it's only because the sign said that it was an *electric* building,' I think, suddenly realizing the irony of my speculations.

But even beyond the notion of positive and negative, there's that whole other matter of Esmeralda and her predictions. By turning away from the building and leaving, did I avoid the danger of lightning altogether? Does it mean that the danger no longer exists? Or does it mean that the threat of lightning was simply pushed off to another time in the future? What's more – by avoiding the lightning, did I turn away from something that may have provided me with an invaluable clue as to how to leave Christmasville?

It's all so confusing! It's so confusing that it gives me a headache just thinking about it. But, scooping up a clump of snow and biting into it, I do wonder: are there any ghosts in the electric building? And, if there are – are they negative ghosts? Or are they positive?

Moving deeper into the woods, I see another clearing up ahead. But it's different because, instead of one large building, a bunch of tiny, square ones are scattered throughout the clearing in no particular pattern. They're about the size of our garage. And they're not made of plastic brick but of some other material.

Removing a glove, I swipe the rough, light-gray surface of the first building with the palm of my hand. It feels like pebbles are glued into the top of it.

"It's the same stuff that they make sidewalks with!" I say with surprise, having never encountered such an oddly fabricated building. "It's cement!"

Encircling the structure, I determine that the building has a door but no windows. Set into the door is a clear sheet of plastic paneling that's protected by thick bars – like you see in the jail. Because the door is locked, I cup my hands around my eyes and lean against the bars to peek inside. But it's too dark to see anything.

When I step back to size up the building in its entirety, to try and figure out its purpose, I see what has to be the strangest thing that I've ever seen in my life. Over the door, deeply cut into the cement surface, is a word ... a *name* ...

" '*Higgins*'," it says.

I don't know what this means. I don't know what any of this means.

Moving through the cluster of cement structures, I note that each building is essentially the same. Some are a bit larger, a few smaller. Although there are slight variations in style and design, each has the single door – with the clear, plastic panel insert that's barred over – and an absence of any windows. The only notable distinction between each building is the word – the name – that's engraved above each of the doors.

" '*Caterson*' on this one. '*Phelps*' on that one over there."

Maybe each one is some kind of storage shed? – A place where each family puts stuff that they don't use any more but what's too valuable to be tossed away. But then why are the buildings so elaborate? And why are they made of cement instead of plastic?

What's just as curious as the buildings themselves is the clearing beyond. Situated in rows along the snowy field that rises up beyond the buildings, are what look like cement slabs, stuck in the ground and evenly spaced. Several of the slabs have statues beside them. Some are enclosed by a low-lying fence. It looks like something may be written on each of the slabs.

Off to my left, between two leafless oak trees, is a large panel. There's a road ... – No, it's too small for a road ... – There's a footpath in front of it and I think that maybe the panel might be a sign that explains what this eerie place might be.

'Another sign,' I think to myself.

When I arrive at the path, I discover that the writing on the panel is badly weather-worn. Although most of the letters in the first word have been erased or disfigured by the wind and the snow – it's pretty easy to figure out. It reads: "*Christmasville*". The second word, however, is more difficult to decipher:

"*Sem ... Sem-tant ... Sem-en-tant ... Cem-en-tant ... Cementary!*"

"Yes – that's it – '*Christmasville Cementary*'! It must be where they make cement!"

I look back at the '*Cementary*'. It doesn't make any sense though because ... *Where?* Where could they possibly make cement? In the little buildings? – I don't think so. Maybe at one time there was a larger building and ... – But why are there slabs of cement stuck in the snow like that?

While I'm pondering the mystery of the *'Cementary'*, I hear another set of gunshots in the distance. For some reason, I'm not convinced that it's target practicing. I suppose it's because the shots are sporadic, which isn't the way that hunters usually practice their aims. In target practicing, it's a series of shots, one after the other, until they stop to check the target to see how well they did. Or how poorly, depending upon who was doing the shooting. I know because I remember that dad bought a gun once, insisting that he was going to be a hunter. Sometimes he would take me with him when he went target-practicing in a field, off of Mulberry Street, where they had bales of hay – three of them – stacked one on top of the other. A paper bull's eye was fastened at the top of the center bale with a wire hanger. From fifty yards back, dad would raise his rifle up and concentrate on his aim before the long, steady squeeze of the trigger – firing off one shot after the other. ' "Deadeye Tom",' Mr. Tolliver would call him, after seeing all the holes in the bull's eye of dad's target, all tightly clustered around the center. But the thing is – when it came time for dad to buy his hunting license, he never bought one. ' "No, I don't think I'll be going hunting after all",' he said, after I asked him about it. ' "Maybe you won't understand, Mary Jane, but ... well, it occurred to me that hunting deer and rabbit would be like chopping down our Christmas trees instead of digging them up." '

It's funny how you remember things like that. It's funny, too, because I did understand and I guess it's one of the reasons that I always seemed to feel closer to dad than to mom.

' *"Kindred spirits"*,' dad would say.

I figure the lake is probably a half hour hike away. So – should I continue going southeast, like I intended, until I run into the tracks of the passenger train and survey the lay of the land beyond? Or, should I explore the woods that border the southern edge of the lake first, and then return? – After I've discovered what the heck is going on.

Three more shots ring out, contributing to my curiosity.

On top of the ridge that snakes the southern border of Wakefield Lake, I sit in the snow, resting against an old pine tree. The hike up the slope was a bit more than what I bargained for, sapping my strength, making my stomach growl for an early lunch. You would think that by eating snow, I could trick it into thinking it was food. But, no, that doesn't work very well.

Above, two squirrels bicker on a branch before dashing off, playing a game of tag.

From where I sit, Wakefield Lake looks like a giant, white egg. It stretches for maybe two miles from the marshlands on its western edge to the dense pine forests in the east. At its widest, it's about a mile across. The only shallow part of the lake is where it runs through the marshlands, through clumps of wiry bushes, frozen into tiny islands that barely break the icy surface. The islands, grouped together like fingers pointing east, remind me of the hairy knuckles of Mr. Rausch. This is where most of the kids in Christmasville ice skate – not only because it's shallow, but because it's the part of the lake that's closest to their homes.

Along the far eastern shore, trestles for the freight train are anchored into the rocky slope that girdles the shoreline. The freight train! – It scared the living daylights out of me as I made my way up the slope, only twenty minutes ago. Trudging through the snow beneath its elevated tracks, the train suddenly arrived from nowhere and screamed by, rumbling overhead and blasting its horn as it gathered momentum from its downward plunge, vanishing into the woods as quickly as it had come.

Another shot streaks across the frozen lake, echoing from the slopes around it.

When I get up from the snow to look, I see Stark, the Iceman, about a hundred yards from the edge of the lake below. I hadn't seen him before, his horses and hauling-sleigh concealed behind branches of trees. Beyond, nearly midway across the lake, are a group of about six or seven men, moving toward town. Several dogs tag along, scribbling their peculiar signatures in the snow on the lake as they chase each other, following the men in their wide, roundabout ways.

What's curious about the men is that it looks like all of them have rifles or shotguns, save one. He's the tallest among them and has his arms raised up as if he were carrying a sack up on his shoulders. Centered inside the group, it's as if the men around him are escorting back into town, almost as if he were a ... a prisoner.

Starting down the slope, I decide to approach Stark – to ask him about the group of men marching across the lake with their ... their prisoner, or captive, or whoever he is. But even this is curious because Stark ... well, he's not working like he normally would – he's scrunched down, studying something on the ice, touching it with a stick. His dog, Blink, is beside him, watching with the same fascination.

The process by which Stark extracts large blocks of ice from the surface of the lake is pretty ingenious actually. What he does first is to drive a long, metal chisel through the ice with a hand sledge. The chisel has a collar at the top of it so, once he punches through, it doesn't shoot into the water on the other side and sink to the bottom of the lake. Then he chips away at the hole until it's wide enough to slip his long, narrow razor-saw into the gap. I guess that's the easy part. The hard part is leaning over and sawing the ice, one stroke after the other, like the piston of a machine in the plastic factory. Even though the razor-saw is so sharp that it would probably cut an oak tree down, it takes Stark the better part of half an hour to finish sawing the rectangular shape in the ice.

The block is usually about four feet long but is always *exactly* twenty-two and half inches wide. How thick the ice block is depends, of course, on how forgiving – or unforgiving – the temperature happens to be. If it's been running close to zero, the block could be as much as twenty inches thick; if it's been hovering close to the freezing mark, it could be as little as fourteen.

Once the block is cut, the next step is to secure it with thick loops of rope, one on each end. To do this, the Iceman uses a special tool – a thin, metal rod that's 'U'-shaped at the bottom of it, and with a handle at the top that's perpendicular to the 'U' at the bottom. At the end of the 'U', he slips the one end of a rope into a notch. The rope is knotted, allowing the two teeth of the notch to get a good bite on the rope. With his left hand, he holds the rope taut against the notch; with his right hand, he slips the 'U' of the rod through the gash that's he cut on the closest side of the ice block. He lowers it and, using the handle at the top of the rod as a guide, turns the 'U' in the water beneath the block until the handle of the rod is lined up exactly with the gash in the ice below him. Then, dropping the rope from his left hand, he gives the rod a good upward thrust with both hands until the notch at the end of the 'U', with the rope attached, magically appears through the opposite gash of the ice block. That's why the block of ice is always exactly twenty-two and a half inches wide – because that's how wide the space between the two sides of the 'U' is – twenty-two and a half inches.

After Stark repeats the same process for the second rope at the other end of the ice block, he ties the ends of the ropes together, making two loops. Then he takes his hoisting contraption from the back of his sleigh, assembles it and slides it into place over the ice block. He anchors it with metal spikes. The contraption is a much larger, a much sturdier, version of the plastic "horse" that dad uses to support the train platform. At opposite ends of the thick crossbeam, which holds the "horse" together, are pulleys.

With the hoisting contraption secured, Stark unhitches his hauling-sleigh from his team of horses. He takes two long ropes, threads them through the pulleys and ties them to the loops of rope at opposite ends of the ice block. The far ends of the ropes are attached to the hitch of his horses.

"Easy now, fellas," says Stark with his familiar satin voice, grabbing the reins and prompting Courier and Ives to dig their shoes into the ice and to move forward.

But they only have to go a couple of feet because that's all that's needed to raise the ice block high enough for Stark to steer his hauling-sleigh beneath it. Then he backs the horses up, lowering the block into the sleigh and pushing it off. That's when he drops his fishing lines, too – usually two of them – tying them off to the legs of the hoisting contraption.

He'll cut several more blocks – as many as he needs for the milkman, the dairy farmers and the supermarket – from the hole that he's made from the first. They're easier to cut because after the first block ... well, because each block after the first already has one of its longer sides cut. With each new block that's freed from its icy prison, he pushes it with his 'U' rod along the widened hole to where he cut the first block. That way he doesn't have to keep moving his hoisting contraption every time he wants to raise a block from the frigid water. And now that I think about it, it's a good thing that ice floats because I don't know how Stark would manage otherwise.

When he's finished his work for the day, the Iceman pulls up his fishing lines to see what he's caught for his dinner. He dismantles his hoisting contraption and puts it back in his sleigh with the rest of his tools. He re-hitches his horses and off to market he goes, leaving behind heavy plastic cones that read: "Beware! Ice Hole!"

As I make my way across the frozen lake, Blink sees me. Barking and charging toward me, his floppy paws kick up big chunks of snow.

"Shut!" says Stark, after turning his head to see what all the commotion's about.

I don't know – maybe I startled him. Maybe Blink thinks that I'm a stray cat that wandered in from the woods, looking for a free fish dinner. At any rate, the moment the command is given by his master, Blink stops dead in his tracks and clamps his trap shut. He turns about and gallops off, back towards the Iceman.

"I ain't never seen no fish like this before," Stark says, without turning toward me.

He's still hunched down, looking into a pail of water.

"It's got whiskers," he adds, prodding the fish with his stick. "You ever see a fish with whiskers, Higgins girl?"

"Nope," I reply. "Can't say that I have."

The greenish, brownish, sort of black, mud-speckled fish is about a foot long. It's got bulgy eyes and its wide mouth makes the fish look like he's frowning. And sure enough, extending from its mouth, back along both sides of its stout muscular body is a pair of thick whiskers.

"You taking him home for dinner?"

"Already got my dinner with the other line. I was just pulling this one up to pack it away and ... – He fought like a bugger, he did! Didn't want to give an inch!"

Stark brushes the tail with his stick, forcing the whisker-fish to swim as best he can in the pail of water. The fish obliges, drawing in water and pushing it out with its wide mouth, breathing.

"But I wouldn't take him home anyways because he might be the last of his kind. And it's a dark sin if anybody was to end the last of a kind."

Having said that, Stark grabs the pail by the handle and heads for the ice hole.

"Stay away from fishin' lines," he advises the fish, leaning down to gently dump him and the water back into the lake.

We both stand at the hole, watching the whisker-fish as he looks up before diving into the deep.

"You know, Higgins girl," he says, moving toward his hoisting contraption to dismantle it. "It makes ya stop and think, don't it? – I mean, when ya look out over the frozen waste-land of the lake, who would ever think that there's a whole other world beneath it? Ya know? Geez! – Sometimes it makes me think: What would I find if I poked a hole in a fat cloud and slung a fishin' line through? Ya think I'd catch me a fish with wings? – A flyin' fish?"

"I think you might find yourself buried in a pile of snow," I reply.

"Yeah – maybe," he says, smiling. "But ya gotta admit – sometimes there's more than what always meets the eye. Just like that fish. I been droppin' lines in this here lake since I was old enough to walk. Granddaddy took me and I ain't never seen no fish like that. Ya just never know what lies beyond the surface of things."

It strikes me of a sudden. *"Like bacon ... like somebody cooking bacon,"* I say without real-izing it.

"What's that?" Stark asks, sliding the parts of his hoisting contraption into his hauling-sleigh. "What's that about 'cookin' bacon'?"

"Oh, nothing. I was just thinking about something."

He gives me a queer look – as if I had suddenly grown a pair of whiskers.

"What was all the commotion about before?" I ask, changing the subject. "The men shooting their rifles off."

"Oh – them," he says with a measure of contempt. "I'm surprised they didn't shoot each other – Tolliver and Caterson and the bunch. They shoot so bad the law oughta take their guns away."

"But what were they doing? Hunting season's over."

"Well, I guess they got themselves all riled up about the stories in the newspapers – the stories about the Tolliver boy and ... and you, Higgins girl – You was with him, weren't ya? You was with the boy when he busted his leg up, when he saw the 'wild beast', or whatever it was, in the deep woods."

"It was a donkey," I reply. "And it happened two weeks ago so why are they chasing it now – a donkey – and two weeks later?"

" 'Cause they been stewin' – the bunch of them sittin' around and stewin' because they done nothin' about what they imagine is a 'wild beast', waitin' out in the woods, lickin' its chops, waitin' for somebody else to come along. A bunch of fools! – The lot of 'em!"

Blink nuzzles up against Stark, trying to get to the fish that the Iceman's put in his box.

"Down!" says Stark, causing the mongrel to back off.

"But who was that with them? – The tall man with the sack up on his shoulders. Who was he?"

"It weren't no sack. It was a lamb – a baby lamb. And they think the man – he's really more of a boy than a man – but anyways, they think he's a shepherd who went after the stray lamb and was returnin' it to the flock."

"But what does the man – the boy – what does he have to say about it? Why are they treating him like a criminal?"

" 'Cause he don't speak. Tolliver said they tried talkin' to him but all he said was gibberish – sounds that didn't make any sense, that nobody understood ... like it was a ... a strange language that nobody heard before. Then he clammed up. I guess he realized that talkin' wasn't gettin' him nowhere because nobody understood him. And he didn't understand anybody else. And I'm sure he wasn't all that keen about being dragged into the police department for questionin' either."

With his equipment stowed, Stark moves to the front of the hauling-sleigh and re-hitches his team of horses.

"What 'cha you doin' out here on the lake anyways, Higgins girl?" he asks. "How come you're not off skatin' or sleddin' with all your friends?"

"Oh," I reply, unprepared to answer. "Well..."

"You out explorin' or somethin'?"

"How'd you know that?" I ask, mildly surprised because the Iceman had guessed.

"Aside from cuttin' ice block and hole fishin', there ain't much of nothin' else to do out here. Granddaddy and me used to go explorin' when I was a boy. We used to go ridin' round the countryside in this contraption right here," he says, running his hand fondly across the side of his sleigh. "It was a ridin' sleigh then – before I turned it into a haulin' one."

Stark reaches behind the seat and removes the two safety cones that read: "Beware! Ice Hole!"

"We used to ride everywhere – back behind Christmasville Electric when it was still operatin' and then over to ..."

" 'Christmasville Electric'?" I say, interrupting him.

"Yeah," Stark says, placing the cones at opposite ends of the hole and returning to the sleigh. "Behind the electric company – that was before it got struck by lightnin' and everythin' inside got pretty much burnt up. We used to ride the sleigh on the road behind it that's ... well – not so much of a road but a cow path that leads off to the rock bridge. It's where the trains meet – the freight train and the passenger train – one on top of the other – and with no more than a cow path beside it, the train tracks and the cow path sort of squeezed together as they shoot off across the rock bridge."

"But it's not on the map!" I say with excitement, pulling it from my pocket and fumbling to open it up.

"Maybe the road – the cow path – maybe it ain't on any map. But I remember it because granddaddy and me used to ride along the path until we came right up to the rock bridge," he says, stepping up onto his hauling-sleigh with Blink leaping up behind him. "You want a ride back to town, Higgins girl?"

The House at the End of the World

They house the shepherd boy in the city jail for three days, shipping in hot meals from the diner to feed him – him and the lamb, that is. The police chief doesn't know what to do with the lamb so he delegates the task to Sergeant Myers. I think the sergeant feels kind of sorry for the shepherd boy, who is no more than seventeen, maybe eighteen years old, and who is unusually calm and complacent – particularly in view of his circumstances. It's only when you try to separate the boy from his lamb that he gets himself all worked up.

What the lamb likes best from the diner is corn flakes and skim milk, with lumps of chunky peanut butter, strawberry jam and a dash of cinnamon mixed in. He can't get enough of the stuff, especially the peanut butter.

Anyway, what Sergeant Myers does for the lamb is to get bales of hay that he spreads across the floor of the jail cell. It works well enough because, even though the sergeant takes the boy and his lamb to the fenced-in yard behind the police station three times a day, you can't train a lamb like you can a dog, teaching him to do his business outside rather than in. So the hay works well enough, catching the lamb's business and allowing the sergeant to scoop it up and replace the hay without getting the floor all messy and stinky.

"What do you think this is? – A barn?" says the police chief, who isn't all that happy with the sergeant and his solution to the problem.

"OK then," Sergeant Myers counters, himself hot under the collar, "then *you* tell me how you want the problem solved."

The chief is none too happy with the newspaper either. It's because a reporter overheard the disagreement and writes all about it in *The Courier* the next day:

"SHEPHERD BOY CREATES RIFT IN RANKS OF POLICE DEPT!"

reads the headline in the paper.

Midway through the article is a photograph that depicts the sad, childlike face of the shepherd boy, framed by the thick bars of his jail cell.

"Do You Know This Boy?"

the caption beneath it says.

I don't know if it's the headline or the photograph that suddenly sparks the public's interest because on Tuesday night they schedule a special town meeting in city hall to deal with the issue. Dad and I sit in the last row of chairs. He brought me along because he wants me to get a firsthand look at "democracy in action". Mom would have come but she's busy, helping the twins with their homework. Or – it's probably the other way around

– mom's doing their homework for them while they help as little as possible.

At the meeting the police chief changes his tune entirely, publicly apologizing for his "inexcusable outburst" involving the sergeant. He also acknowledges the fact that he's at a loss as to what to do with the shepherd boy and his lamb. "We're crime fighters!" he proclaims with deep conviction, "not baby sitters and ... and lamb tenders!"

"And ya ain't no pork tenders or tenderloins of chicken either, Roy" someone shouts, causing the audience to burst out in a round of laughter.

"Here! Here!" exclaims Mayor Thompson, banging his gavel down and suppressing what might have exploded into a big belly laugh if the circumstances were different. "This is a serious issue and we will have order!"

The police chief – red-faced and huffy with indignation – scours the audience, scrutinizing each face for a sign as to who the troublemaker might be.

"Now," the mayor continues, after the ruckus subsides, "let's get back to the business at hand. First, is there anybody out there who knows this boy?"

He holds up the photograph from the newspaper.

People in the audience scratch their heads, shrug their shoulders or spin in their seats to see if anyone in the crowd raises their hand or steps forward in response to the mayor's inquiry.

Nobody knows the boy.

"OK then – has anyone ever seen the boy before? – Maybe near the lake or in a field or walking alongside a road. Anyone?"

But nobody's seen the boy before.

"All right," the mayor says, putting the photograph down. "No one knows the shepherd boy and no one has seen him before. So, my next question is: what's to be done about the shepherd boy and his lamb?"

Mr. Jurgenson, the commissioner of public health, speaks up first. He states that the boy and the lamb, living in the close proximity of the jail cell, pose a significant health hazard.

"Ya gotta separate them," he elaborates, "or the boy'll wind up sick and diseased and maybe infectious too. You wouldn't want disease runnin' rampant through the police department and into the civil population because we failed to take the proper precautions to prevent it, would ya?"

"What kinda disease ya talkin' about, Bing?" asks the police chief, suddenly becoming pale and sweaty, loosening his tie and moping his forehead with a handkerchief.

"Geez – There's all kinds of diseases out there, Roy. There's ones that give ya fever and cramps and knot your stomach up. There's ones that give ya the runs and make your skin all crusty and ..."

"OK," the mayor interjects, banging his gavel down. "We certainly get the picture, Bing. And that's what we're here for – to take up precautionary measures that not only insure the health and safety of the boy, the police department and the constit... – the population at large," he says, correcting himself, "but steps that also address the whole issue of the boy and the lamb and what's to be done with them."

Principal Marshfield suggests a physical examination and tests to determine the boy's aptitude and intelligence. "For all we know," he remarks, "the boy could be deaf and dumb.

Maybe that's why he doesn't respond to questions. Maybe that's why he only spoke gibberish when they found him in the woods."

"And we should conduct a thorough psychiatric examination as well," adds Doctor Sperry. "We need to understand the underlying causes of his abnormal behavior."

" 'Abnormal behavior'?" Mayor Thompson replies. "Except for his failure to carry on a conversation, the boy seems anything but 'abnormal' if you ask me."

You can tell by Doctor Sperry's smug expression that he doesn't appreciate being contradicted.

"With all do respect," the doctor says curtly, "the boy is sadly ill-equipped in demonstrating even the most basic of social skills. Why – he doesn't even speak, thereby eliminating the principal avenue in the engagement of communication and interaction. And, as Principal Marshfield suggests, it's possible that his capacity to hear is impaired as well. This could be attributable to either physical or psychological causes. Of course, we won't know until we thoroughly test the boy."

"Certainly I agree that the boy should be examined," the mayor responds. "As public officials, charged with the solemn duty of safeguarding the health and welfare of our citizenry, it rests squarely upon our shoulders to initiate any action which not only preserves the wholesome integrity of our community, but which insures the quality of life for each of our citizens as well. As such, the boy will be tested – I assure you, Doctor Sperry. He will be tested to insure that's he's properly nourished and in a healthful way. In addition, I would hasten to add that, should extenuating circumstances dictate, we will indeed subject the boy to extensive psychological evaluations – for his own sake as much as for the well-being of our citizens. But – and I want to be very clear on this point – I will not subscribe to Principal Marshfield's supposition that the boy is in any way 'dumb', or to your assertion, Doctor Sperry, that the boy exhibits behavioral patterns that might be deemed 'abnormal'. Without having submitted the boy to any such evaluations as of the moment, it remains pre-judgmental on our part, and a genuine disservice to the boy in question, to even formulate such hollow assumptions."

Doctor Sperry is on the brink of rebuttal but the audience intercedes, their applause thundering through the hall. Most of it, of course, comes from the mayor's constit ... constituency. And most of them support Mayor Thompson, not because they particularly agree with everything that he says, but because he says it so darn well. That's why Mayor Thompson is the mayor and why he'll he probably always be the mayor – at least until somebody else comes along, somebody who can speak in public as well as the mayor does.

"We still have yet ..." the mayor announces, pausing to allow the crowd to settle down. "We still have yet to address the principal issue at hand. What are we to do about the shepherd boy and his lamb? Aside from the health issue, arising from our housing of the boy and the lamb in the city jail, it would be criminal negligence, on our part, to detain the boy indefinitely. The fact is – he has committed no crime and, as such, no charges have been filed. We must either release him, or transfer him to a shelter where we can rest assured that he'll be properly looked after – that is, until such a point that somebody steps forward to claim him."

Mr. Mason stands up from his seat. "It seems to me," he starts, "that, on the one hand, a lot of testin' needs to be done – physical testin' and maybe psychological, too. On the other hand, the boy needs to be kept in a safe and warm environment, but one where he's free to move about. Well, it seems to me that the best place for that sort of thing is in the hospital. So why don't we move him there and ..."

"... And what would you have us do with the lamb?" interrupts Doctor Sperry in a snide way. "Wrap him up in a hospital smock and stick him in a bed by the boy? – So much for health and sanitation!"

"Well ... no. You didn't let me finish, doctor," replies Mr. Mason. "There's a large shed in the yard behind the hospital. I think they keep snow shovels and tools inside. But there's plenty of extra room because ... well, because I seen it when I was in the hospital, gettin' *my* testin' done. The yard's fenced in so the lamb could wander round if he had a mind to. He could go into the shed at night or when the temperature dipped to keep himself warm. That way, whenever the shepherd boy wanted to check up on his lamb, all he need do is look out the window."

It seems like a good idea. And except for Doctor Sperry, whose sourpuss face conveys his whole-hearted disapproval with the solution to the problem, the vote is unanimous: the following morning both the shepherd boy and his lamb are to be transferred to their respective accommodations in the hospital. Sergeant Myers is assigned as the boy's "guardian", instructed to keep a watchful eye on his charge, to overview tests conducted by the hospital staff and to report directly to the mayor's office of any changes or developments.

It seems like a good idea. And except for the fact that Sergeant Myers is only a single person, incapable of performing his assignment on continuous twenty-four hour shifts without catching a catnap or two, it would have been a great idea. However, by Friday morning, the shepherd boy and his lamb are nowhere to be found.

"POLICE CHIEF AND SERGEANT CLASH OVER LOSS OF SHEPHERD BOY!"

reports *The Courier*, causing the chief to cancel his subscription to the newspaper indefinitely, the sergeant to file a grievance with the mayor's office, citing "verbal abuse" and "severe tongue-lashing", directed at him by the police chief as the result of the boy's sudden disappearance.

Anyway, that's what happened throughout the week with the shepherd boy and his lamb, with the police chief and Sergeant Myers.

When Saturday morning comes round, dad and I drop mom off at Cauldwell's Supermarket for the early shift. We drive down the hill on Maple Street, turn left onto Juniper and then right onto Elm Street, heading toward the post office. Gathered near the tool shed behind the hospital is the same group that assembled the week before to hunt down the "wild beast" of Brett Tolliver's imagination but had found the shepherd boy and his lamb in its stead. Standing alone in front of the hospital, searching for something in the pockets of his hunting vest, is Mr. Tolliver.

"What's going on, Bud?" dad asks, after pulling the car over.

"Knuckleheads!" Mr. Tolliver says with exasperation, leaning down to speak to us through the open window of our station wagon. "Each and every one of 'em! – A bunch of knuckleheads!"

As he reaches up and pulls his orange hunting cap off, scratching his head in frustration, the men begin to appear in front of the hospital. They mill around, drinking coffee from their insulated mugs, discussing what to do. All of them have their shotguns because, as Mr. Tolliver explains, dependent upon the purpose of their mission into the wilderness – to find the shepherd boy and his docile lamb, or to stalk the "wild beast" – none of them can say with any degree of certainty. None of them is really sure if he's about to participate in a search party or a hunting one. What's more, the only thing that any of them can really agree upon is their lack of agreement in which direction to start off.

"Not a one of 'em has the slightest idea as to what he should do," says Mr. Tolliver.

"Why don't you just let it go, Bud?" dad advises Mr. Tolliver. "I'm sure that the shepherd boy made it back safe to wherever he came from. He's probably sleeping like a log in his bed right now while you're out in the cold, freezin' your bones, gettin' all riled up for nought."

"The shepherd boy? – I ain't spendin' my days off lookin' for no shepherd boy, Tom. That's what the others can do if it ever gets set in their minds. No, I'm goin' out to find that wild beast that attacked my boy!" he says, straightening up and slinging his shotgun across his back, marching down the street toward the lake with firm resolve.

Dad rolls his eyes and looks toward me. "Don't ever repeat this, Mary Jane, but ... I never thought I'd see the day when a donkey would make an ass out of a grown man."

While I'm still giggling, dad puts the car into gear and drives us home.

For the rest of the morning, I have to hang around the house and do chores. It's not that I mind – not like the twins, of course, who cry and whine about everything that's not remotely related to their having fun – it's just that ... well, it's the last Saturday before 'D-Day' and I'm anxious to find the rock bridge that Stark, the Iceman, told me about.

"Do we have to do it all by ourselves?" Roger complains, after dad tells the two of them to stack the wooden houses and cars from the train platform into the boxes that he's brought in from the garage.

"And don't damage anything of Mr. Wright's," dad warns, "or you'll be grounded for the rest of the weekend."

"Why can't Mary Jane do it?" Todd asks, slapping his hand up to his forehead in anguish.

"Because Mary Jane's helping me plant the Christmas tree – that's why," dad replies.

We're late this year – planting the Christmas tree, that is. It was because of the weather. Dad had intended to plant the tree two weeks ago but it was so cold that he wanted to give the tree extra time to adjust to the temperature outside. So he kept it in the garage by the window, rigging up two spotlights overhead to provide it with the extra light that it needed to survive.

"Your maple tree's doing well," dad remarks as he slides the garage door up and over. "Much better than I expected," he adds, slipping his hands into a pair of work gloves.

"I think it's because of the fertilizer that Mr. Wright makes up for it," I reply.

"It must be good stuff because pretty soon I'm gonna have to cut a hole in the ceiling of your room, Mary Jane – right up into the attic so it has enough room to grow."

I'm not sure if dad is serious or if he's kidding.

"On second thought," dad says, wheeling his hand truck up to the tree and sliding it beneath the bucket of roots and soil, "maybe I'll ask Mr. Wright to mix up a special batch of fertilizer for Roger and Todd. That way, by next year, the twins'll be big enough to plant the Christmas tree and you and I'll retire, Mary Jane."

The hole for our Christmas tree is already dug, covered over by a piece of panel – the same kind of plastic panel that dad used to make the train platform – and by an old, plastic shower curtain. Together, the panel and curtain keep the snow from filling in the hole. While dad wheels the tree across the yard, I hurry ahead to peel a corner of the curtain back. There's about a foot of snow on top but I manage to pull it back far enough for dad to position the tree where he wants it.

"That's good right there," he says, lowering the blue spruce to the ground and pulling the metal plate of the hand truck from beneath the bucket.

While dad grabs one corner of the shower curtain, I grab the other. We pull it back until the panel that covers the hole, and the pile of dirt beside it, are fully exposed. From the garage, I get the spade and the pail of water. Dad carries out the bags of topsoil that he bought from the hardware store.

I watch him as he works with the spade – breaking up the pile of dirt into frozen chunks, jabbing the sides and bottom of the hole until it's loosened up. He moves with the same mechanical motions, thrusting the spade in short, powerful, downward strokes as he steps around the circumference of the hole.

It's always kind of sad – planting our Christmas tree – like it's the end of one cycle, the beginning of another. But that's a good thing, I suppose – change, the whole process of change, of moving forward to new experiences so you can learn and grow. But it's sad, too, because there's so many things that you just don't want to let go of; so many things that you want to repeat, to keep doing over and over again because they give you so much joy and ... – I remember the expression on mom's face, the look on her face when I went into the kitchen on Christmas Eve and she was humming that song so softly, gazing through the window over the sink as if she were a million miles away. It was that expression – that rare and unusual expression when she turned from the window to look at me. It was the happiness of her smile and the sadness of her eyes sort of blending together, like oil and vinegar or flour and milk, a mixture of incompatible ingredients producing in the expression of her face – a soulful joy, a private celebration ...

And it's because you remember. It's because you remember what are special, personal, happy moments from your past, and you can reel those moments all the way across the years and into the present, and it is that memory – that sweet and delicious moment of remembering that gives you such joy and ... and even though I only remember moments, moments that are different than what everyone else remembers, still ...

"You're awful quiet over there, princess," dad says.

"What? What did you say, dad?" I reply, realizing that I was a million miles away.

"For a moment, you looked like your mother does when she drifts off into space."

He scoops a spadeful of dirt from the bottom of the hole and tosses it onto the pile. "I guess maybe I shouldn't say, 'princess' any more – huh, Mary Jane?" he suggests. "Maybe you're getting too old to be a princess."

When I smile, I know that it's similar to the smile that mom has when she's remembering something from long ago.

"You can always call me princess, dad."

After our Christmas tree is dropped in the hole, we pack the roots with the rich, dark topsoil and pour the pail of water around the base of the tree. While dad spreads the mound of dirt over the topsoil, I fetch an old woolen blanket from the garage. We wrap the blanket around the bottom of the tree to protect the roots from freezing, keeping the stained, yellowish cloth in place with a couple of rocks.

"Think the twins are done yet?" dad asks as we collect our tools and head for the garage.

"Bet 'cha a nickel they're not," I reply.

They haven't even started. Instead, Roger pushes a toy tractor along Main Street, bull-dozing cars and buildings. "Help me! Help me!" he says, emulating the screams of invisible people, caught up in the merciless progression of his tractor. Todd is on the couch, stuffing his face with Cheerios as he watches the decimation.

"What happened?" dad says with irritation. "Why aren't the houses packed up like I told you?"

Roger's hand freezes, causing the tractor to stop in its tracks, the sound of wholesale slaughter and destruction to terminate. Todd's mouth hangs open, revealing the pasty substance of crushed Cheerios.

"Oh, yeah," Roger says, grabbing a house and carrying it toward the box.

"Too late now," dad says. "Into your room – the both of you. I want it cleaned from top to bottom – dusted, vacuumed, sheets stripped from your beds and put in the laundry room. If I find you playing ..."

"Aw, dad," Roger starts, "We were just ..."

"Into your room now!" dad says, lowering his voice a notch because he doesn't appreciate being interrupted by Roger, especially when he's reprimanding him. "And Todd," he adds. "Close your mouth! I don't want to see what you're eating – It's disgusting, for crying out loud!"

After the twins drag themselves off to their room, whining and complaining, dad and I complete what was supposed to be the twin's chore. When we're finished, we carry the boxes out to the station wagon so we can return them to Otis and Willy Wright.

"If there's something else that you'd rather do, Mary Jane, I can drop these off myself," dad says, his car keys jingling as he removes them from the pocket of his coat.

I look at my watch. It's only nine-twenty.

"That's OK. I'll go with you, dad."

I haven't seen Otis and Willy since they stopped to visit me in the hospital.

When we arrive at the produce stand, Joe Matthieson is emptying crates of potatoes and onions into their respective bins on the table behind the cash register. Joe works for the Wright's part-time on weekends, which is the busiest time because that's when most people are out shopping, buying their groceries for the rest of the week.

"How ya doin' there, Joe?" dad says.

"I'm doin' fine," Joe replies, grabbing handfuls of onion and stacking them in their bin. "Something I can help you with, Tom?"

"I'm looking for Otis, or Willy. Either one of them around?"

"I think Otis might be in his workshop," Joe says, continuing to stack. "But Willy's at the other end of the stand, promotin' the new vegetable that he and Otis discovered."

It's difficult to see him – Willy, that is – because a number of people are clustered around his demo table, listening to him as he extols the versatile and prolific virtues of "the tomato". Almost everyone in the group holds plastic plates of macaroni, smothered in a red sauce, or French fries, with a little puddle of a thicker, though equally red, sauce beside them.

"Why it's – it's indescribably delicious!" Mrs. Morrison says to Mrs. Watts, stabbing a French fry with her plastic fork, dipping it into the red puddle and jamming it into her mouth.

"I never dreamed that macaroni could taste so good!" exclaims Mrs. Watts.

"I have to admit," Mr. Grubbs says from the far side of the table, "it's exceptionally tasty just like it is – sliced up raw, with a little salt sprinkled across the top."

"Isn't it though?" Willy agrees with an excitement that I've rarely seen him express before. "You can slice it up and eat it plain," he elaborates. "Or you can lay the slices on sandwiches – it tastes great with leafs of lettuce, bacon and a bit of mayonnaise spread across the bread. If you cut it into wedges and toss it up with your salad, well – it changes what would normally be a plain, ordinary, humdrum salad of mixed greens into a colorful, culinary sensation. Or you can cook your tomatoes up like I've done here, adding onion and peppers, sprigs of basil, dashes of salt and pepper and a bit of sugar until you've got yourself a nice red sauce for your macaroni. Or, if you modify the recipe – adding vinegar but subtracting the onion and peppers and basil – and chill it, then you've got yourself a great cold sauce for your French fries and hamburgers. Why – there must be a hundred ways to prepare it!"

When Mrs. Morrison steps away, I see Willy behind the table, a ladle in one hand, a spatula in the other. Draped across the front of him is a full white apron that's splattered with red polka dots. On his head is a floppy chef's hat that leans off to the side.

"What do you call it, Willy?" asks Mrs. Watts, spearing macaroni and depositing the forkful of comma-shaped tubules into her mouth.

She looks like she went haywire with her lipstick, the red sauce extending well beyond the perimeter of her lips and dripping, in fact, down the slope of her chin.

"Well, it's a tomato, of course," he replies.

"No, I mean the sauce on the macaroni. Does it have a special name?"

"Oh," Willy replies. "We just call it tomato sauce."

"And the stuff for the French fries? – What's that called, Willy?" asks Mrs. Morrison.

Willy furrows his brow and bites his lip, deep in thought. "Cold tomato sauce?" he says, shrugging his shoulders.

"You have to come up with something better than that, Willy," suggests Mrs. Morrison, who works in advertising at the radio station. "Something that's catchy and perky. You know what I mean?" she says, dipping another fry in the puddle of cold sauce and biting into it. "You have to think about sales and marketing if you want your tomato and your sauces to be successful in the marketplace. You have to catch up with the times, Willy, if you want your products to sell."

"Yes," Mrs. Watts chimes in, jamming the last bit of macaroni into her mouth. "Catch up, Willy!"

After dad and I try slices of tomato and a bit of the sauces, which really are as tasty as they're touted to be, we decide to look for Otis in his workshop around back.

"Do you know how Otis and Willy came up with their name for the tomato?" I ask dad.

"No, I don't," dad replies. "How did they name the tomato, Mary Jane?"

"Well, did you ever see Mr. Atkinson's – *Tom* Atkinson – did you ever see his nose when he's been out in the cold for a spell?"

I watch dad as he pictures the image in his mind. "No – they didn't!" he says, breaking out into a big grin. "Did they?"

"They sure did," I reply, wondering in the next instant whom it was, exactly, that they had in mind when they discovered – and duly named – the 'cucumber'.

Otis is banging away at something. As we approach the workshop, we hear the steady pounding of his hammer.

"Hello? Anybody home?" dad says, after knocking once on the door and then opening it wide enough to poke his head inside and to shout.

"Come on in," Otis replies. "I'm in the back."

The coal stoves – one in the front and another in the back – make the workshop warm and toasty.

"Hello there, Tom," Otis says, turning to greet us. "Mary Jane! – How are you?" he adds with a broad smile. "We haven't seen you in a while. Geez! – Not since they locked you up in the hospital. You and the Tolliver boy, that is. How's your maple tree doing? Need another batch of fertilizer?"

"The maple's fine, Otis. And I still have plenty of fertilizer left – thank you," I reply.

"Good," he says, switching the hammer from his right hand to his left as he walks towards us. "How's it goin', Tom?" he asks, extending his arm to shake dad's hand.

"Things are swell, Otis. And you?"

"Couldn't be better."

I can tell by dad's leaning off to the side that his attention is split right down the middle, half of it directed toward Otis, but the rest of it focused on the huge contraption behind him.

"That's a ... a curious project that you're working on there, Otis," dad says, stepping aside so he can get an unimpeded view. "Isn't that the, uh ... Isn't that the float that you had in the parade?"

"Same thing," Otis replies, turning around to view his contraption with dad. "The 'skiboggan', I think somebody called it – though, in fact, it's anything but."

It looks pretty much the same, except for the two sets of plastic skis that were fastened to the tubes in the parade. They've been removed. I guess they were only added for show, to make the float look more like a wooden version of Santa's sleigh. And it looks sturdier and more complete. The platform, which connects the two, long, wood-ribbed tubes, is much thicker, having additional timbers beneath it for support. And heavy, metal hardware's been added – a series of braces that run along both sides of the platform, bolting it firmly to the tops and sides of the tubes. But I suppose the most obvious change to the contraption is the introduction of Otis' pickup truck. With hood raised, it's seated on top of the platform and anchored in place with metal chains that drop down from the truck chassis, through the platform and across the bottom, shooting back up again into the bottom of the truck.

"Right now, I'm finishing up some modifications to the motor and the differential," Otis explains. "But aside from that, it's pretty much complete, except for the last component, the most important component, which Tom Atkinson is trying to make for me at the Consolidated Factory Works. Of course, if Tom finds that he can't make it – either because my design or formula is wrong – then all my work here is for nothing."

At the far end of the workshop, leaned up sideways against the wall, is the sign that Otis had painted: *'Frenchland or Bust!'*

Scratching his head, dad sort of blurts it out: "But what is it, Otis? What exactly is it designed to do?"

"We'll know shortly, Tom," replies Otis, refusing to budge on the issue of disclosing the nature of his invention. "Tom Atkinson assures me that, by Tuesday morning, he'll either have the final component finished – and in hand – or he won't."

"Well, whatever it is that you're working on," dad says, "I wish you the best. I hope it all works out for you."

"Why thank you, Tom," Otis says, moving toward his workbench and putting his hammer down. "Now – since you've got plenty of fertilizer for your maple, Mary Jane, what is that I can help you with?"

"Oh – yes," dad says, dragging himself away from the enigma of Otis' invention. "We've brought your models back – the wooden buildings and cars that you and Willy were kind enough to let us borrow for the train platform. Where would you like us to put them, Otis?"

"To be honest, I plumb forgot about 'em," Otis says. "But ... Where's your car, Tom? – Out front?"

"Yes, we're parked in front of the stand," dad answers.

"OK. Well, why don't you just bring your car up the driveway, Tom, and we can put them in here. That way, if you want to use them again next year, you'll know where to find them."

While dad brings the car up, I stay with Otis.

"Do you think it's going to work, Otis?" I ask, thinking that maybe he'll reveal more information if dad isn't here.

"What? – The invention?"

I nod my head.

"It's really up to Tom Atkinson. But I'll tell you what: if Tom does succeed with the final component – with what I call, 'elastic plastic' – and I've every confidence that he will, then you be sure and make it down to the lake after school on Thursday afternoon. Because that's when we'll see. We'll see if the invention is either a work of incredible promise, or if it's simply the folly of a foolhardy man."

"D-Day," I say aloud, suddenly realizing that Thursday is the last day of the month, the 31st of January.

"D-Day?" asks Otis.

"Destiny day," I reply.

"And so it will be," Otis remarks.

When dad arrives, we help him carry the boxes of wooden models into the workshop.

"You know, Tom, I should have told you to just keep 'em," Otis says, tucking a box beneath the workbench by the door. "Willy and I really don't have any use for them any more. So, next year – if you still want to use them – just take 'em home and keep 'em. They'll be right here. OK?"

"That's mighty generous of you, Otis. I appreciate it."

With our task complete, dad and I head back to the car. As I'm swinging the door open, Otis sticks his head from the doorway of his workshop.

"Mary Jane?" he calls.

"Yes?"

"I forgot to tell you – Willy and I found the walnut tree! You'll have to come over sometime and ... well, Willy'll tell you all about it."

It's eleven o'clock. It's eleven o'clock and all my chores are completed. I've had a hearty lunch that will last me 'til supper so now I have the rest of the day to do what I need to do.

Starting off the same way that I went last week, I feel a lot more confident about my journey. One of the reasons is because I bought a new compass – and a new canteen that I've filled with fruit juice. But it's mostly because this time around, I have a specific goal to my journey. I'm going to find the rock bridge that Stark, the Iceman, told me about. And, if his directions were right, I'm going to find it by way of the cow path, which starts on the far side of the old Christmasville Electric building.

It all seems simple and straightforward enough. But moving south along Juniper Street, I start to wonder about Esmeralda and her predictions again. 'Is this a journey at all?' I ask myself.

What raises the question, I suppose, is the sign that I had seen last week – the bronze plaque, depicting the figure of a man with the lightning bolt that was stretched out over 'Christmasville Electric'. If this is indeed a 'journey', does it mean that I can expect thunder and lightning along the way? I already did the 'falling' and the 'darkness' parts, but ... 'lightning'?

And I never did answer the questions that I had posed last week:

'By turning away from the electric building, had I averted the lightening altogether? Or was it simply deferred to the future? – The future, perhaps, being today. Or did the sign itself satisfy the requirement of the prediction? – By seeing the lightning bolt on the sign, was it over and done with, signifying that I was proceeding in the right direction? Or was it a warning, meaning that, if I continued beyond the sign, then I could expect ...

'Or maybe it's the fact that the building itself – Christmasville Electric – was struck by lightning ...'

'But it doesn't make any difference, does it, Mary Jane,' I answer myself. 'Because no matter what happens – lightning or no lightning – that's the way that I'm going!'

A few minutes later, another thought occurs to me: 'why didn't I ask Stark about that other place? – About the *Christmasville Cementary?'*

When I arrive at the end of Juniper Street, it's easy to find my way because my footprints are still in the snow from last week. I follow them along, pausing every now and then to make a snowball and to toss it toward an oak tree. And, of course, every time that I do, I expect to hear the same sound that I heard the week before – the sound of gunshot, ringing through the woods.

'Maybe I'll find the shepherd boy and his cute little lamb,' I think. 'Maybe the "wild beast" will find me.'

Trudging through the snow of the abandoned parking lot, the electric building looks more daunting, and spookier, than it did before. Through the holes where the windows were, it seems darker inside, and gloomier. I don't see the owl – the snowy, white owl that watched me last week as I approached, and then retreated, from his lightning-struck domain.

Stopping, I raise my hands up and cup them around my mouth. "Any ghosts here?" I say, but not too loudly because ... well – 'Do I really want to disturb them if they're occupied with something else?'

Nevertheless, after getting my nerve up, I call out again: "If there's any ghosts here, I command you to show yourself! Show yourself and speak! – Or forever hold your peace!"

As my eyes hopscotch from hole to hole, scrutinizing the darkness for any signs of movement or appa ... apparition, I hold my breath and count to ten.

"OK – nothing," I say, though not wholly convinced because, after all, I really didn't shout. It was more of a whisper – but a very loud whisper – one that certainly *any* ghost should have been able to hear. And, of course, I'm not sure if you can 'command' a ghost to show himself, or to do anything else for that matter, especially if he doesn't have a mind to do it. Or ears – Do ghosts even have ears?

Cautiously, I start off toward my left, the plan being to encircle the building as wide as possible until I find the cow path on the other side of it. There's just no sense at all in aggravating anyone, or anything, that might be inhabiting the old, dilapidated building.

But I should have gone the other way – circling the building from the right – because some of the snowdrifts are nearly waist-deep. The snow is soft and powdery in the shade of the pine trees, causing my feet to sink all the way to the bottom. Struggling, I press forward, every now and then peeking at the window-holes, insuring that no one – that no *thing* – is watching me.

When I get to the back of the building, I find a bunch of those big, plastic spools that they use to wrap electric wire around. They remind me of yo-yos. Geez! – I haven't played with a yo-yo since ...

But I can't remember. Sadly, I can't remember the last time that I played with a yo-yo because I'm fourteen, because *I'm always fourteen* and because I remember *how* to play with a yo-yo, making cat's cradles and walk-the-dogs, but I don't remember ... I don't remember *when*.

'*I absolutely refuse to go down this road again,*' I advise myself, clearing the snow off one of the spools and plopping down to rest my legs that are tired from the snowdrifts. Unsnapping my canteen from its strap around my waist, I take a long drink.

On this side of the building, you get a much better idea of the damages that were caused by the lightning strike, and by the fire that ensued. A large section of the brick wall by the shipping and receiving area fell apart, leaving mounds of snow-covered rubble. Part of the roof collapsed; part of it melted in the extreme heat of the fire, its long plastic planks bent down at varying angles to meet the floor of the first or second levels below. From a third floor office – its outer wall fallen away – a desk sits precariously at the very edge of the steep drop. I can actually see the typewriter on top of it because the far end of the desk is raised up sharply by the floor that is buckled and warped beneath it. It makes me wonder:

which will go first? – The desk or the typewriter?

After a final drink, I snap my canteen back on its strap and get to my feet. Behind me, there's a small outbuilding that's about the same size as the storage buildings – or whatever they were – that I discovered at *Christmasville Cementary*. The door's pushed open and, as I approach it, I see pipes and wires, an electrical panel and some sort of motor or generator that's bolted to the floor. It doesn't look like – or sound like – anything's working.

When I turn the corner of the outbuilding to look for the cow path ...

"Oh my God!" I exclaim, feeling the rush of adrenaline as it shoots through my body, making my heart pound so hard that I think it's going to jump from my chest and run away on little feet, made of veins and arteries.

"Oh my God!" I repeat.

My immediate impression – shot like the lightning bolt that struck Christmasville Electric – is that it's a ghost, a giant vengeful ghost, sent by his peers from the electric building, to scare the holy hell out of me. And it does. In that fraction of a second before my eyes convince my brain otherwise, it does indeed scare the holy hell out of me.

But it isn't a ghost ... *It's the snowman from China!*

He's got the same strange sparkle, the same sort of rainbow iridescence that he had when Emily and I discovered him in the side yard of the school. But just to make sure, I move – I coax my legs to move because my feet feel like they're glued to their footsteps – I move to the back of the snowman and brush the snow away from his base.

'*Made in China,*' it says.

"How did you get here, big boy?" I ask, half-expecting him to reply.

It's when I start to move around to the front of him again that I see something else. It's from the corner of my eye that I see movement – an orange something, moving in the shadows at the back of the building. And then it's a bright flash, immediately followed by a deafening explosion, the whistling sound of objects propelled through space and ...

Ducking down, I bring my hands up protectively to my head as I fall face forward into the snow. But I'm not quick enough because there's the burst and bang of another explosion right beside me, the sudden sting of something sharp and cold, shot through the fabric of my scarf, sticking me in the back of my neck.

I lay in the snow for a moment, rapidly digesting my predicament. When I peek up, I see someone moving from the shadows of the electric building, onto the rubble that litters the receiving dock behind it.

"Stop shooting at me!" I shout as loud as I can.

"Who is that?" a man shouts back. "Somebody out there?"

I get back to my feet and pull a glove off, reaching up to my neck. It stings like hell, especially when my hand brushes against the object that's stuck in the back of my neck.

"Stop shooting!" I scream back, grabbing the object and yanking it out. It's a piece of plastic, part of it reddened by blood – by *my* blood – part of it shimmering iridescently.

He's at the edge of the dock now, his shotgun aimed downward, his orange hat pulled down tight over his head. Turning, I look at the snowman from China beside me. He's only a hollow half of a snowman now, the upper part of him shattered into a thousand bits.

"Murderer!" I shout angrily. "You bloody red murderer!"

"Who ... Who is that?" calls Mr. Tolliver. "Higgins? – Is that you, Mary Jane Higgins?'"

I spin away and start running through the woods. Up ahead, I hear the freight train – the sound of its whistle and the rumble of its metal wheels as it rolls across elevated trestles.

It occurs to me – surprisingly, actually, in my frantic race away from the electric building – to scour the woods to my right and my left, searching for signs of the cow path. But there isn't any clearing, no broad break in the pine trees, suggesting anything that remotely resembles a path or a trail. There's only woods.

After about ten minutes, I stop to catch my breath. I can feel droplets running down my back, the patches of moisture making my thermal undershirt stick to my skin. Some of it, of course, is sweat. But I suspect that some of it, as well, is blood because the gash in my neck feels wet and runny and throbs like all hell.

'Geez! – How am I going to get the bloodstains out my thermal undershirt? Did Mr. Tolliver recognize me? Where the heck is the cow path anyway?'

"And why did that ... that donkey ass, Mr. Tolliver, have to shoot the snowman?" I ask, getting myself angry again.

In the woods ahead, I hear another train whistle. But it's different than the one before – two short bursts, followed by a long one. It's different because it's the sound of the passenger train.

'Wait a minute!' I think, biting my lip, scanning the woods. 'Stark said something else too: *"It's where the trains meet – the freight train and the passenger train – one on top of the other – and with no more than a cow path beside it, the train tracks and the cow path sort of squeezed together as they shoot across the rock bridge".'*

'I don't need to find the cow path! – It's probably all grown over anyway because that must have been twenty, or thirty, or a hundred years ago when Stark rode in his sleigh with his grandfather. All I need do is find the trestles of the freight train – or the tracks of the passenger train – and follow them through the woods to the rock bridge!'

After a few gulps of fruit juice, I check my compass and head into the deeper woods. I tighten the scarf around my neck as I walk, which makes me cringe and my eyes to water. Hopefully though, the scarf will stop the bleeding.

The woods thicken with pine trees. The plumes of their branches swing in the light breeze, scribbling shadows that dance across sheets of snow. Every now and then, I hear a bird squawking or a squirrel rattling the frozen branch of a tree as he scurries about. I constantly check the path behind me because I know that Mr. Tolliver is tracking me, following my footprints in the snow.

'But there's nothing I can do about it, is there.'

'But there is!' I think a moment afterward, because up ahead I see not only the trestles of the freight train, but beyond – along a snow-white strip of land that's raised up and cleared of pines – the tracks of the passenger train as well.

I guess you could say it's dangerous. You could say it's foolish and irresponsible and utterly careless. But it sure is brilliant if I can manage to pull it off.

What I decide to do is to walk in a straight line beneath the trestles and across the train tracks until I'm a single step away from the very edge of the precipice that drops down into the bottomless abyss. Then I stop dead in my tracks, carefully back-stepping until I get a foothold on the metal track of the passenger train.

'Old man Tolliver will think that I fell off the planet!' I think, a big smile spreading across my face.

It's a balancing act after that. I extend my arms away from my body as I tiptoe carefully along the steel track like a ballerina, one foot behind the other. Once I nearly slip up, stopping immediately to regain my balance, to take a deep breath and to press onward.

When I think that I'm far enough along, I run as fast as I can back into the woods, hiding beneath the trestles of the freight train. It occurs to me to wait a bit – to see if my plan to stump Mr. Tolliver actually works.

'But there isn't time,' I decide. 'Besides, I've more important things to do.'

Pushing forward, I notice that trestles and tracks are gradually moving closer to each other, as if they're converging. At the same time, they start veering southward – and slightly downward – which I interpret as a good sign. But the bad thing is ... fog!

It makes me freeze in place – the patch of fog up ahead, the patchy memory of fog, evoking the frightful sensations that I experienced with Brett when he chased the donkey toward the edge of the abyss and fell, screaming in agony. And then later, it was that horrible fear as I slid down the rocky slope, screaming and panic-struck until I slammed into the frozen clump of roots and dirt and ice.

The fog makes me choose my steps carefully as I proceed. The ragged fringe of the fog swarms around me, envelops me, pushes softly against me. What's encouraging, though, is that there isn't any wind here. And the slope is far less pronounced, and relatively flat. There are none of the rocky protuberances, which punctuated the other slope, which banged me and bruised me, which punctured and ripped long gashes in the back of my coat as I slid downward. Luckily, it isn't like that at all.

It isn't long before I encounter what Stark had revealed on the lake. With the ground leveling off, there's a series of trestles – three of them – that are bunched together, followed by a long space where there aren't any trestles at all. This is where the tracks of the passenger train slip directly below the metal plate that shoots away from the three trestles, that supports the tracks of the freight train in mid-air. In another fifty yards, I find a second set of trestles – again, three of them – but thicker than the first, and with supports that are set wider apart to allow the passenger train to pass between them unhindered. And that's where I see it! – Through the thinning fog, beyond the dwindling pine trees. It's the rock bridge!

The bridge looks like it's supported by fingers – long, stone-encrusted fingers, which taper as they stretch down, into the fog, to meet the bottom of the abyss far below. The tops of the fingers thicken into arches, connecting them in the same way that your fingers are joined to the end of your hand. But what's truly amazing – aside from the sheer size of it – is that the bridge really looks like it's composed of rock. It's not chunks of plastic, molded to imitate the shape and texture of rocks, like so many other structures throughout Christmasville are made. It looks like real, honest-to-goodness rock, as if the bridge were constructed in a distant age, modeled by an ancient race of stonemasons.

Moving along the tracks beneath the trestles, I approach the edge of the bridge. Along the way, I discover a pattern that's similar to the one behind me: two sets of trestles, separated by a long space, a metal plate that supports the freight train above. There's a switch attached to the tracks of the passenger train, enabling it to veer off toward the east, onto an entirely different set of tracks. Looking up, I see a similar configuration, duplicated for the freight train. I guess that allows the conductor of either train to choose which way he wants to go as he drives his locomotive across the bridge from the other side. He can go west, toward the train stations; or east, into the wilderness.

You could hardly call it a cow path. It's more of a chicken path – the little lane that runs parallel to the train tracks as they run in a beeline across the stone bridge to the other side. If I were a cow, I'd take my chances walking the tracks rather than to attempt the narrow strip beside it. Chances are ... well, in my opinion anyway, the chance of getting yourself flattened by a speeding locomotive is far less than slipping on the snow and falling into the abyss below.

So that's what I do. I walk along the track ties, just like I did when I made my journey through the train tunnel. Except that I move faster, glancing up, now and again, just to make sure that nothing's coming my way.

As I approach the opposite end of the bridge, I begin to make out the outline of the landscape on the other side. Through the fog, I see vast, vertical stretches of sheer rock-face, stippled with pockets of snow or with long, crusted braids of ice that form where hidden channels of water find their way to the surface. It's the side of a mountain – a huge, towering mountain that shoots straight up from the bottom of the abyss, lodging its invisible peak into the underbellies of clouds, which are nearly indistinguishable from the fog itself.

Moving along – in fact, quickening my pace – it's difficult to determine how or where the train tracks might go. I can't see a tunnel ahead. I can't see where ...

"... OK ... OK – There!" I say aloud, stopping for a second to cup my hands around my eyes.

It's actually the sides of two mountains, one sort of layered behind the other so that you can't see the narrow pass, which slips between them, which enables the train tracks to exit the bridge and to veer off at a sharp angle, out of view. But that's what it is – the tiny crease of a pass, nestled between two mountains, allowing the double-decker tracks of freight train and passenger train to proceed unabated.

Arriving at the end of the bridge, I stop again, tilting my head far back to view the incredible size of the mountains before me. There's the fog, of course, which limits my depth of view but still – the steep, vertical inclines look as if they might rise right up to the very gates of heaven.

As I'm about to start off again – through the mountains and up the rising slope of the pass – I hear the sound behind me. It's not so much that it startles me, as disturbs me – I guess it's because the notion of lightning, of experiencing the sudden jolt of lightening, remains lodged at the fringes of my thoughts. It's because initially, the sound behind me made me think that it was thunder – a double clap of thunder, ricocheting along the cliffs of the abyss and across the mountainsides. But it wasn't thunder at all. It was the double blast of a shotgun.

"It's that donkey's ass, Mr. Tolliver," I say. "Crazy Mr. Tolliver shooting at shadows, snowmen – anything that might resemble the 'wild beast' that ravages his imagination."

But the thing of it is: the sound also loosens a giant shoulder of snow and ice high up in the fog, causing it to tumble down the mountainside, dangerously nearby, and to crash into the deep abyss. Another blast of the shotgun and ... Geez! – I could be buried alive!

I move along as fast as I can. I have to remain on the railroad ties because the pass is so narrow and the snows on either side of the tracks look deep enough to swallow me up. If the passenger train does come along ... well – I won't have any choice, will I? – I'll have to dive for dear life into one of the snow banks, piled up along both sides of the train tracks, and then dig myself out, won't I? But, of course, that's something that I can deal with when – not when – if ... if the time comes for me to scramble from the oncoming train.

After about twenty minutes, the railroad tracks level off. I see ahead a series of bends and turns because the further I move away from the abyss, the less fog there seems to be. And there's something else, too – trees! Tall and leafless, they're the first indication that there's more than just mountains and snow, train trestles and railroad tracks, in this sparse landscape.

I wonder: 'am I still in Christmasville? Or am I somewhere else?'

"Maybe I'm on the outskirts of New York City!" I reply optimistically.

'The city *could* be south,' I think. 'It doesn't have to be east like I thought before, when Brett and I were exploring the woods beyond the sledding hill and I convinced myself that that's where the city lie – in the east, in the direction that I insisted upon going at the moment. The truth is, New York City could be anywhere, in any direction, because I haven't a lick of evidence to suggest any which way it might be. What I only know for sure is what I heard on the radio.'

' *"John F. Kenn ... arriving in New York City ... Jacqueline and the children, shopping along Fifth Avenue"* ...'

'What's a "Resident-Elect" anyway? It must be something important because otherwise they wouldn't have talked about it on the radio.'

I stop to drink a mouthful of juice and then press on. The landscape is gradually changing, the rocky ridges of mountains flattening out into a broad plain. Where there were oak trees before – the leafless poles of trees – now there are spruces and firs, fanning off to my right and my left into a vast, dense forest. A frozen brook, laden with snow, swings serpentine through the woods. Two ravens, winging above treetops, descend to a hidden perch.

It's so quiet here. And peaceful.

'Wouldn't it be wonderful to stumble upon a hunter's cabin and rest? – To nap in the fragrant embrace of this beautiful, unspoiled place? Wouldn't it be nice to live out here? – All by myself, without chores or homework, worries or responsibilities?'

I guess that I'm daydreaming, allowing myself the luxury of being swept away by my daydream. I must be tiring, too, because ... because I hear it in the back of my mind – steel wheels spinning on steel tracks, jets of steam shot from the engine – the sound of it getting louder and louder as it rapidly approaches from behind, as the sound of it gradually transforms the tranquil, pastoral image of a cabin on a hillside into the hardened, metal image of a speeding locomotive.

Snapping out of it, I whip my head around.

Having wiggled through the upward curves of the pass behind me, the train is bearing down on the long, straightened path before it, charging at breakneck speed across the flattening plain. Through the trestles behind me, I see what looks like cloudbursts – a series of fuming, spiraling jets of steam, convoluting, blasting the snow from tracks and banks into wild flurries, each burst shot from the engine a split second after the one before it. It's mesmerizing – watching the bursts from the engine – reminding me of those tiny picture books in the Five & Dime, each burst, a page in one of those tiny picture books that you hold in your hand and quickly flip through so it likes look the pictures are suddenly animated and moving, depending upon how fast ...

I almost slip on the railroad tie before I plunge into the snow bank alongside the tracks.

It isn't the passenger train, but the freight train. When I pull my head out of the snow, I see the locomotive rushing along the trestles above the plain. There is the same steady sequence of cloudburst and snow blast, roiling over the tracks of the passenger train below. Above the engine, a moving pillar of smoke rises, chugging upward, before bending back over the long train of freight cars behind it and dissipating into the cold air.

I get myself back to my feet. Far ahead of the freight train, I see a glint above the tree line. It isn't a light but a reflection of light as it strikes a window or a mirror or a piece of polished metal. I don't know what it could be except that it's something fairly large and raised up high above the ground, on a long, narrow pole that's perfectly straight. It couldn't be natural, something that's part of the landscape. It must be manmade and it looks like the freight train is driving straight for it.

"*Maybe it's a sign!*" I suggest with sudden excitement. "Maybe it's a sign that says, '*Train Station – New York City*'!"

Energized, I clamber out of the snow bank onto the railroad ties, pressing forward.

I start to think now about some of the things that Esmeralda said – not about the thunder and the lightning or the darkness and the falling – but the other stuff, the stuff that I had set aside, reserving it because I wouldn't have to think about it until I actually *arrived* in New York City or wherever it was that I found myself at the end of my journeys.

'Who could the Queen of Swords possibly be? – "*Someone I know but ... but someone I don't,*" said Esmeralda. What kind of crazy riddle is that? And the two figures – statues, I guess – because one is of iron and one is of gold. One strains with an enormous weight upon his shoulders; the other sort of floats in the air, carrying fire. And then there's the tree – "*the Tree of Knowledge,*" suggested Esmeralda – a giant Christmas tree, decorated with bands of ribbon that are red and black, "*revealing things that I want to know, things that I do not*".'

I don't know. Maybe Esmeralda is more 'emotionally challenged' than I. Maybe she's nuttier than a hundred fruitcakes.

'But then, of course,' I counter, 'how do I explain what she said about falling, and the lightning on the sign, and the darkness in the tunnel?'

"Speaking of darkness," I say out loud, looking at my watch. "It's almost three o'clock already!"

'Geez! – Why do I do this to myself? Why didn't I leave the house earlier so I wouldn't always have this problem with not having enough time?'

"Damn it!" I say, realizing that there won't be enough time to get where I'm going and back home again before it's dark.

'How will I cross the rock bridge in the dark? – I didn't bring a flashlight because I broke dad's in the tunnel. And I didn't bother to buy another one. And Mr. Tolliver – did he recognize me? Will he tell mom and dad and everyone else in Christmasville? And if he does, how am I going to explain it?'

I feel myself shudder. No matter what – one way or the other – I'm really going to be in hot water this time.

The train tracks lead into the forest. Before the treetops all but swallow up what I imagine is a sign that says, *"Train Station – New York City"*, I stop for a moment to study it. But the only thing that I can figure out is that the object on top of the pole is big and round and that it looks like ... Yes! – It looks like there's some kind of writing on it!

I drink the last of my fruit juice and look at my compass. 'Due south,' it reads, before I continue along the tracks into the forest.

The lengthening shadows of trees cloak the winding way. The snow, spread taut like sheets along the sides of the train tracks, is already tinted in an evening blue, absorbing it, safeguarding it through the long passage of night, only to return it to the budding wing of dawn as it spreads color and cloud across the brightening sky.

'I wish it was 'D-Day',' I think, trudging along, spotting ahead a dying spike of sunlight as it briefly illuminates a patch of snow in the forest. 'If it was 'D-Day', then I wouldn't have to go back to Christmasville at all. I'd never have to go back,' I add, shivering in the growing cold.

Through the trees, I can see it now! It's not the sign – what must be a sign – but the thick, black pole that supports the sign high above the trees. I start to run. I start to run as fast as I can along the railroad ties, watching the ties glide by beneath me as I run, as I stretch each leg forward, driving each foot toward every other tie in front of me. Gasping for breath, I swing around the last curve.

"There! There it is!" I exclaim, stopping in my tracks, panting, leaning forward to draw quick, cold bursts of air into my lungs.

The huge pole is in the center of a large clearing, stretching up and up and ...

It's a clock tower! Cradled at the very top of the pole is a giant clock, with hands the size of ... but ... but the numbers. They're not numbers at all! They're ... They're letters – an 'I' where the '1' belongs, an 'II' where the '2' should be, a 'V' for the '5' and an 'X' where the '10' ...

"Where's the ... Where's the train station?" I say between breaths, searching the space beyond the clock tower.

It's a huge, flat, treeless circle, its circumference delineated by the double-decker train tracks that start, and end, on the V-shaped track that I'm standing on. At the opposite end of the circle is the passenger train, quiet and idle. Above it – equally dormant – sits the freight train, a wisp of smoke, rising like a gray thread from its cooling engine. Beside the two locomotives is an open staircase that enables the conductor of the freight train to access his engine on the trestles above.

"The trains don't go anywhere," I say with disappointment. "They just loop around the circle, returning the way they had come."

Beyond the perimeter of the train tracks, I have the sense that there's nothing – nothing but jagged, vertical cliffs, fit like the pieces of an unsolvable puzzle into the countless gaps, crannies, nooks ... of nothing.

I look at the clock on the tower, inferring the time by the position of its hands on the clock face.

'Ten after four,' it says, the longer hand on the "II", the shorter one a little past the "IV".

What I see now is a thick cable that's connected to the top of the clock tower. I trace the line of it across the darkening sky, toward an area just to the right of the locomotives. It runs to a log cabin – and no sooner have I distinguished its unmistakable shape and structure from the ring of trees that sparsely populate the outer edge of the circle – than a light goes on inside. Then it's the light by the front door, illuminating the path in front of the cabin.

I shiver once, twice, because the air is rapidly changing, becoming colder and damper as night approaches. My teeth start to chatter. I turn around to look at the tracks behind me.

Darkness, generated in the shadows of the forest, spills across the snow and the train tracks, dragging its thickening fabric over all.

My stomach growls; my canteen, empty – 'What choice do I have?'

Turning toward the cabin, I start from the train tracks, marching straight across the wide, circular plain of snow.

I smell wood burning. Another light goes on in the cabin. The shadow of a figure, passing between the light and the curtains of the window, moves toward another room.

I'm so tired now – and disillusioned – that, instead of blinking my eyes, I close them for five or six steps before opening them up again, insuring myself that I'm not drifting from my path. My arms hang limp at my sides. My legs ache. I reach up to scratch the back of my neck and, wincing, find a bright smear of blood across my glove. I'm bleeding again. I had forgotten about the wound in my neck and I'm bleeding again.

Instead of approaching the door, I go to the window on the left – no one. A fire licks logs with blue and yellow tongues in the fireplace, spitting sparks against the metal mesh. A couch, two chairs, a table with a reading lamp. It looks so cozy and warm.

I move toward the window on the right, closing my eyes for at least half my steps ...

"You're welcome to come in, if you like, Mary Jane."

I freeze in place – from sheer exhaustion rather than by surprise. But I guess what is surprising is the fact that I'm not even startled by the voice behind me, the voice, which I recognize, which somehow, I had expected to hear after discovering the log cabin.

"Good evening, Mr. Bachmann," I say, before turning about.

"Good evening, Mary Jane," he reciprocates. "You've come a long way to see us."

"That I have, Mr. Bachmann. That I have."

I never thought that chicken soup could taste so good – or to smell as good either, the steam rising from the bowl to fill my nose with a hearty goodness.

"Eat up, Mary Jane – we've plenty to go round," Mr. Bachmann says, spreading crackers around a plate of cheese.

"And drink up as well!" says Mr. Lionel, coming in from the kitchen with a teapot in one hand, an extra cup and saucer in the other.

I look at the teapot with suspicion. "It's not going to put me asleep, is it, Mr. Lionel? – Because if it is ..."

"No – it's not that kind of tea, Mary Jane," he says, smiling broadly as he pulls out a chair and sits at the dining room table. "It'll give you some energy – perk you up a bit – for the ride home."

I make a sandwich of the crackers and cheese and bite into it.

"You're taking me home?" I ask Mr. Lionel, between chews. "Like you did last January?"

He glances at Mr. Bachmann, who is seated to his right and who replies with a funny kind of expression that says: 'See? – *I told you so.*'

"I guess I shouldn't be too surprised that you remember," says Mr. Lionel. "That you remember what occurred last year."

He lifts the teapot and pours, filling up the three teacups. I pull the zipper of my coat down, loosen the knot of my scarf without removing it.

"What do you remember of the years before that?" asks Mr. Lionel casually.

I swing a spoonful of soup into my mouth and swallow. I guess it's because I'm tired – physically tired, for sure, but certainly far more tired of keeping secrets, of fibbing, of constantly guarding everything that I say so that I don't reveal what I think, what I know to be true.

"I'm fourteen years old," I reply, staring at a broken cracker on the plate in front of me. "I've been fourteen so long that I don't remember ever being thirteen or twelve or ten, like everyone else does. And I guess what I remember more than anything else is that each year is ... different. But each year is the same, too, because *I'm always fourteen years old* and it never changes."

"I see," says Mr. Lionel, adding a dash of sugar to his tea and stirring before picking up his soupspoon. "Well, as I said before, I'm not too surprised because it does happen on occasion – to a few of us, that is. It's a glitch in the clockworks, you might say."

He slides a spoonful of soup into his mouth, returns the spoon to the bowl.

"But anyway," he continues, folding his arms and leaning on the table in front of him, "to answer your question: No, I did not take you home last January. What happened was: You boarded the train, the train stopped at the precise stroke of midnight – just like it always does on the 31st of January. You fell asleep; I fell asleep; Mr. Bachmann fell asleep. The next morning, which was the first of December, of course, we all awoke in our beds, just like everyone else in Christmasville. The difference, of course, is that you, and me, and Mr. Bachmann here – well, we remember what everyone else in Christmasville does not. And because we remember, because we always remember, we saw the remarkable transformation that had taken place – that always takes place between the night of January 1st and the morning of December 1st. You do know about the transformation, don't you, Mary Jane?"

I guess that I'm staring again – frozen in disbelief – because Mr. Bachmann says:

"You should close your mouth, Mary Jane, or you might catch what the bat missed."

I close my mouth, slowly digesting what Mr. Lionel is saying, what he is revealing, that he's *confirming*. No one – not Esmeralda or Otis Wright – no one – at least, not to my knowledge anyway – ever dreamed or imagined, guessed or speculated what I had known all along.

"Mary Jane?" says Mr. Lionel. "You do know about the transformation, don't you?"

"Everything," I say, snapping out of it, looking up from the plate with the broken cracker on it. "Everything is different on the first of December."

"Yes," says Mr. Lionel. "Everything – almost everything – is different. Homes, stores, churches – they've all been re-arranged. It's as if..."

"... As if someone had taken a map of Christmasville and turned it into a giant checkerboard!" I interject.

"Indeed!" remarks Mr. Lionel, raising his soupspoon up and sliding it into his mouth, swallowing. "But what doesn't change – and some of which you might already suspect – are the train stations and the power station, the train tracks and the clockworks, and my home here, located at the end of the world. These – for whatever reason – never change."

I have a thousand questions, each of them jockeying for position, racing wildly toward the doorstep of my voice box.

"Clockworks?" I ask, vocalizing the first thought in line. "The clock on the tower?"

"Yes," Mr. Lionel replies, "the clock on the tower."

"Why does it have letters instead of numbers? What's it used for?" I ask, lifting my teacup and sipping.

"We don't understand the purpose of the letters on the clock face," replies Mr. Bachmann. "We know that it's very old and that, possibly, it was constructed by the same, ancient race of artisans who built the rock bridge that brought you here."

"As for its use," continues Mr. Lionel, "it's the clock that we consult for the train schedules, the clock upon which all other clocks in Christmasville are set. And although Mr. Bachman and I have, on numerous occasions, attempted to determine it's precise origin and the source of its power ... – Well, you saw for yourself how high it's raised, how difficult it would be to inspect its complex mechanics. It's just impossible to get to. But what we do know is that it never stops, never loses or gains a fraction of time in its long march through all the days and nights of the year."

"But I saw the cable!" I point out. "I saw the cable that runs from the top of the clock to your cabin. It must get its power from here."

Mr. Lionel takes a deep breath, glances at Mr. Bachmann.

"I did warn you," Mr. Bachmann says, addressing Mr. Lionel, "our Mary Jane, here ... well, not only does she remember, but she's smart as a whip to boot – just like I told you."

"And that you did," Mr. Lionel agrees with a sigh.

"It's not the power source," Mr. Lionel explains, pausing to sip his tea. "It's the cable that connects the clock tower to our ... to our radio."

"Then it's an antenna too!" I remark with elation. "Then you've heard it as well! You must have heard it! – The broadcast from New York City!"

" 'New York City'? – But how ... how is this possible?" Mr. Lionel asks, looking toward Mr. Bachmann for an explanation.

Mr. Bachmann scratches his head, shrugs his shoulder perplexedly.

"Have you been there, Mr. Lionel??? Mr. Bachmann???" I ask feverishly, switching from one face to the other. "Have you met John F. Kenn? And Jacqueline and the children – have you met them as well? Have you been shopping along Fifth Avenue?"

Mr. Lionel closes his eyes and bows his head, bringing his hand up to pinch the top of his nose as if, suddenly, he had developed a painful headache.

"I fear we've opened a can of unwieldy worms," he says to Mr. Bachmann.

"How did you find ... How do you *know* about New York City, Mary Jane?" Mr. Bachmann asks.

"Because I heard it on the radio that I bought my dad for Christmas," I reply.

"And does your dad – does anyone else, for that matter – do they know? Do they know about New York City?"

"No – just me," I answer, unsure of the importance that they both, apparently, seem to have placed on the topic. "I was going to tell my friend, Emily, but she can't keep a secret so I didn't."

While Mr. Lionel gets up from his chair and paces, Mr. Bachmann stares at his hands on the table on front of him, twiddling his thumbs.

"Why is this so important?" I insist. "And before – why did you say that your home is at the end of the world, Mr. Lionel, when it isn't? It may be at the end of Christmasville, but it's not at the end of the world."

There's an awkward silence, wrinkled only by the sound of Mr. Lionel's footsteps as he treads across the carpet, by the crackling flames of the fireplace in the other room.

"I don't understand," I say, breaking the silence. "Why are you so concerned? Isn't it a good thing that there's a New York City? – That there's a whole other world out there, waiting to be explored?"

"But that's just the point," Mr. Lionel replies. "It's a whole other world that can't be explored ... that *shouldn't* be explored, even if we could."

"You're going to tell her?" asks Mr. Bachmann.

"I don't think we have any choice at this point," says Mr. Lionel, taking his seat again.

There's that uncomfortable silence again, as each man processes his thoughts separately.

"What is it that you're going to tell me?" I ask, swallowing apprehensively before biting my lip.

"First," says Mr. Lionel, "you must promise us, Mary Jane, that everything that's said in this room will remain here, never to be repeated again."

I look at Mr. Lionel, then toward Mr. Bachmann. "OK," I agree, realizing the serious nature of the request. "I promise not to repeat anything that you're about to tell me."

"Or anything that we've already told you as well," Mr. Bachmann hastens to add.

"That too," I say. "I promise not to repeat anything that's been said or anything that will be said."

"It's not simply important, Mary Jane, it's *absolutely essential* that no one – no one in Christmasville ever realizes what we're about to tell you."

"OK," I say, nodding my head, eager to proceed. "I understand," I add, though the truth is, I don't understand at all.

"All right," says Mr. Lionel, looking down at the table and clearing his throat before he begins.

"For whatever reason, Mary Jane, Christmasville lies apart from the rest of the world. And, from what we can only deduce – Mr. Bachmann and I – is that the world around us operates differently – certainly in terms of time, possibly in terms of space, though there isn't any way that we could ever prove this, or to disapprove it either. And, for now, that's not important. What is important for you to understand is that the world around us is entirely *different* from the world of Christmasville."

"And much to our blessing," Mr. Bachman chimes in.

"Assuredly – much to our blessing," agrees Mr. Lionel. "You see, Mary Jane, what you imagine in the world around us – in New York City, for example – is the world as you perceive it in Christmasville. But the truth is – it's not like Christmasville at all."

"I know!" I interrupt. "It has seasons – two months for spring and two for summer; two for autumn – that's when the leaves fall from the oaks and the maples – and two months for winter. That's where Christmasville's stuck – in winter," I add. "It's because of all the snow that we can never find leaves. It's because it's always winter that we never see the grass in the meadows ... in summer ... and ..."

I suddenly get that weird feeling – like I have two heads or something – because both men are staring at me.

"You should close your mouth, Frank," Mr. Lionel advises Mr. Bachmann, "or you might catch what the bat missed."

Mr. Bachmann glances toward the man beside him, curling his mouth into a telltale smile.

"I remember something on the radio about 'leaves'," Mr. Lionel says reflectively, something about them changing colors before falling. And 'grass'? – I think it's yellow, or maybe green, I seem to recall."

"Grass is green," I state with certitude – as if I had actually witnessed the process of its growth, the miracle of its sprouts rising from the snowless soil of summer.

"You've heard this on the radio, Mary Jane?" asks Mr. Bachmann with a pinch of disbelief.

I bite my lip, a bit embarrassed by my outburst. "Well, no, it's ... it's from my dreams."

"Remarkable!" Mr. Bachmann says.

"Indeed," agrees Mr. Lionel. "But, Mary Jane," he continues, "even though this phenomenon of 'seasons' changing, of 'leaves' falling, and of 'grass' sprouting – even though all of this sounds pleasant and inviting – there's much more to the world around us that suggests ... that *paints* an entirely different picture. It's ..." he explains, carefully choosing each of his words, "It's ... – I don't know how to say this with any degree of tact or delicacy, but it's ... it's a *horrible* place – the world beyond the boundaries of Christmasville. It's a place of hunger and thirst, of countless diseases, and of unimaginable poverty. It's a place of terrible wars and of crimes so wicked, that you would indeed be desperate to venture from the safety of your home – a home constructed more like a jail than a house, a home with doors that must always be locked, with windows protected always by iron bars."

"What are 'wars'? – I don't know what 'wars' are. And 'poverty'? – What does 'poverty' mean?"

"Wars," Mr. Bachmann explains, "occur when a large group of people wants something that belongs to another group. In all cases, it's stimulated by greed and is resolved only when the one group takes, or attempts to take, through physical violence what, by right, belongs to the other."

"Why can't they just share?" I ask, thinking myself naive and childish because I don't understand any of this.

"Because they choose not to. Because the notion of sharing is as foreign to them as the notion of greed is to you."

"Poverty," Mr. Bachmann explains, "is a condition that people live in when they have no food or clothing, no roof over their heads to protect them from the snow and the cold."

"And no one helps them?"

"No one," he states firmly.

I try to imagine a world of 'wars' and of 'poverty', but I can't. I can't imagine it. What's more – although I have no reason to suspect that Mr. Lionel and Mr. Bachmann ... well, that they would fib, that they would deliberately distort the truth – I have difficulty believing that the outside world is as dark and evil as they make it out to be.

"But how do you know all this?" I ask. "Unless you've actually gone to New York City, how do you know any of this?"

"It's impossible to get there, Mary Jane," answers Mr. Lionel.

"But the train! – Doesn't the train take you to St. Valentine's and to Easterville? And beyond – to New York City?"

"There are thousand of cities out there. And I'm sure that, somewhere, there's a St. Valentine's and an Easterville as well. But, no – neither the passenger train, which I of course drive, nor the freight train, which, aside from his duties as stationmaster, Mr. Bachmann drives ... Well, the point is, neither passenger train nor freight train ever wind their roundabout way beyond the boundaries of Christmasville. The trains move in a broad configuration of turns and curves, through tunnels and across bridges, skirting mountains that are insurmountable, an abyss so deep that it is wholly impassable. Where we are right now, Mary Jane – here, this very spot – this is the end of the line. Or the beginning, dependent upon your point of view."

"We only know of the outside world," continues Mr. Bachmann, "by what we hear on the radio. And, as Mr. Lionel disclosed, there are thousands of cities – New York, Boston, Philadelphia ..."

'I've heard of Boston and Philadelphia,' I think to myself, picturing the menu at the diner – '*Boston cream pie* and *Philadelphia cream cheese*. I wonder if there's a "Frenchland," like Otis said...'

"... London, Paris, Hong Kong – cities as diverse as imaginable, but all sharing the same ... the same accursed *blight.*"

I know what the 'blight' is – it's the strange disease that kills grapevines and chestnut trees. Maybe this blight – the one referred to by Mr. Bachmann – is one that kills another type of organism, a kind ... a kind of spiritual organism that grows in our hearts and our souls, that enables us to give and to share, to hope and to dream, that allows us to be somehow far more than what we would be without it. Maybe the 'blight' of the outside world kills what makes people ... what makes them human. It's just that ... I can't believe – I *refuse* to believe that the 'blight', the 'blight' that kills our spirit ...

"But if it is a 'blight', then it can't infect everyone," I insist. "The 'blight' only infects certain things – like chestnut trees, but not spruces and pines, cedars and firs – it doesn't kill them so maybe ...," I continue, taking a breath, "... maybe everyone in the outside world ... maybe they're not as bad as you think. Maybe there's a lot of good people out there – people that you just don't hear about on your radio, people who haven't been infected by the 'blight'."

Mr. Lionel sips his tea and sighs. "If only that were true," he remarks, unconvinced.

"Yes, if only ... What's that on your neck?" asks Mr. Bachmann, leaning to the side so he can get a better view. "Why – you're bleeding, Mary Jane," he says, getting up from his chair.

"Oh – yes," I reply, reaching back without really thinking about it and finding blood on my hand. "I had an accident."

He pulls the collar of my coat down, starts to remove my scarf.

"Ouch!" I exclaim, because part of the fabric is stuck to the wound.

While Mr. Lionel gets a damp cloth from another room, Mr. Bachmann gingerly peels the scarf from my neck.

"A rather serious accident, I would say. How did this happen, Mary Jane?"

"It's a long story, Mr. Bachmann," I reply, standing up to remove my coat.

"I'm sure," he says, before calling to Mr. Lionel in the other room. "You better get the first aid kit, George, and a bandage."

' "George"?' I think, 'Mr. Lionel doesn't look anything like a "George". George Johnson looks like a "George" – he sits behind me in algebra class. And George Morrison, the little boy next door – he looks like a "George". And, of course, Mr. Gabriel – his first name ...'

"I know this is kind of nosy, Mr. Bachmann, but ... What were you and Mr. Gabriel talking about in the pharmacy? You know, on Christmas Eve?"

"Here's the cloth," Mr. Lionel says as he comes back into the dining room and hands it over to Mr. Bachmann. "I'll get the first aid kit from the train," he adds, slipping into his long, black, conductor's coat and leaving.

"You should see a doctor when you get home," Mr. Bachmann advises. "I hate to tell you, Mary Jane, but you may need a couple of stitches for this to heal properly."

"Ouch!" I repeat, but louder, as he swabs the cloth across the back of my neck.

"Sorry," he says, easing up on the pressure.

"What were you saying about Mr. Gabriel?" I ask again.

"I wasn't aware that I was saying anything at all about Mr. Gabriel – nosy, little girl."

"I'm not little," I say.

"No – you're not little."

I try to turn my head so I can look at Mr. Bachmann behind me.

"Don't twist your head like that, Mary Jane – you're making it worse."

I bring my head back, looking forward. "Was it about Mrs. Gabriel and their daughter, Caroline?" I ask, prying again. "Do you think he'll ever find them?"

I can hear him sigh, the breath of his sigh warming the cool dampness on my neck.

"Mr. Gabriel doesn't remember things like you and I and George – Mr. Lionel, that is. Mr. Gabriel doesn't remember things like we do. And because he doesn't remember, he doesn't realize that his wife and daughter ... well – with each 31st of January, with each night of the 31st as it turns into the first of December – Mr. Gabriel imagines that it's only been weeks since they were lost in the snowstorm. But the tragedy – aside from the tragedy of Mr. Gabriel's forever going out into the wilderness to look for his wife and daughter – the tragedy is that January has rolled into December not once, but fifteen? – Twenty times over since Mrs. Gabriel and Caroline were lost in the snowstorm."

Oddly, it never occurred to me. It just never occurred to me that more than twenty years have elapsed since that terrible snowstorm.

"I guess he'll never find them now," I say sadly, though not fully convinced because I picture in my mind the plastic figure of Jesus, glued to the dashboard of Mr. Gabriel's pickup truck. '*FAITH*', it says, at the bottom of the statue.

"Unfortunately, I don't think that he will," says Mr. Bachmann. "Anyway, Mary Jane, what we were talking about in the pharmacy on Christmas Eve was the train. In fact, each year he talks to me about the train, about taking the train to St. Valentine's and Easterville and continuing his search there. And, of course, each year he doesn't remember talking to me about the train the year before. He doesn't remember me convincing him each year, as I must, that he should exhaust his search throughout Christmasville *first* – before he even considers taking the train."

"Because the train goes nowhere," I remark.

"Because the train goes nowhere," Mr. Bachmann repeats. "So, each year, I help Mr. Gabriel in his search, usually on Saturdays – today, for example ..."

The door to the cabin opens and closes, a blast of frigid air rushing in.

"Cold! Cold! Cold!" says Mr. Lionel, smacking the plastic case of the first aid kit down on the table before charging toward the fireplace to warm himself up. "It must have dropped twenty degrees, Frank," he says from the other room.

After my neck is tightly bandaged, we climb into our coats for the train ride home. I have thousands of questions but it's getting late and Mr. Bachmann must attend to his other duties as stationmaster. And then there's the train schedule as well, which requires Mr. Lionel's attention. As for me ... – well, I'm reluctant to leave, to go back home again because I just know that I'm going to find myself in more hot water than I'll ever be able to handle.

'And all because of that ... that donkey ass, Mr. Tolliver!' I think to myself in exasperation.

"I don't think you'll be wanting these," Mr. Bachmann says, holding in one hand, the end of my badly stained scarf and, in the other, my teal gloves, mottled with dried blood.

"No, I don't think so," I reply, before he deposits them in the trashcan in the kitchen.

"Here – you can have this one," Mr. Lionel says, pulling an extra black scarf from the coat rack and wrapping it gently about my neck. "And I've got another pair of gloves in the closet," he adds, fetching them. "They're too large, of course, but they'll do in the meantime."

Of course, I've ridden the passenger train once before – last year, on the last night of January. But the ride in the club car was so short – the train swinging from the station and into the tunnel, slowing down before grinding to a complete halt – that it could hardly be appreciated. But now, tucked inside the powerful locomotive as it streaks through the forest and across the white, frozen plain, the train ride is far more exhilarating than I could ever imagine.

Mr. Lionel mans the controls and watches the tracks ahead for foxes or deer that may stray into the path of the oncoming train. As an added precaution, he pulls the cord of the train whistle every now and then, its piercing blast announcing to all the train's rapid approach.

Mr. Bachmann stokes the fire with coal, resting his shovel only after the flames curl up and around the giant steel belly of the boiler. Then he clamps the door to the firebox shut, sitting on a stool and catching his breath until it's time to shovel again.

Standing on a plastic crate, I gaze through the window of the locomotive. It slows as it winds upward through the mountain pass; accelerates as it dips down and rumbles across the rock bridge. Turning west, the train veers from beneath the trestles of the freight train, drives along the southern edge of the bottomless abyss. Through the trees, on the right, I see the first lights of town.

'*Christmasville,*' I say to myself. '*Beautiful, peaceful, perfect Christmasville ...*

'*But it's not enough, is it, Mary Jane?*' I ask, watching the lights populate through the thinning trees, the lights percolate through the gaps widening between the trees.

'*It's not enough,*' I reply in the silence of my thoughts, my dreams, my secrets.

Elastic Plastic

If I thought that I was going to find myself in a pot of hot water, then I was sadly mistaken. It wasn't a pot at all. And the water? – Well, it really wasn't what you would call 'hot'. No, it was more of a steaming, simmering, scalding *cauldron* of water in which I found myself floundering, thrashing about, sinking – without the slightest hope of salvation – once I arrived at my home on Pine Street.

What happened was this:

It was well after dark when Mr. Lionel pulled his locomotive up to Union Station. Engine hissing, brakes squeaking – it was as if the train was reluctant to stop at all, preferring instead to charge headlong into the tunnel beyond the station and to continue its breakneck run along its winding, circular course throughout Christmasville.

"Mary Jane," said Mr. Lionel, after the train had finally jerked to a stop, "you're always welcome to visit us at my home in the wilderness. But next time – *please* – take the passenger train. Mr. Bachmann will not charge you train fare and you'll find it a much safer, warmer, enjoyable experience than trekking through the hazardous snows along the train tracks. Can we agree upon that?"

"Agreed," I complied, removing the bulky pair of gloves that he had lent me, returning them and shaking his hand.

"And Mary Jane," he added on a more somber note. *"Remember your promise."*

"I'll remember," I replied. "But you must remember something too."

"And what would that be?" he asked, grabbing his brass lantern and igniting it.

"I have a thousand questions, Mr. Lionel."

"Only a thousand!" he replied with the burst of a belly laugh, leading us from the cozy compartment of the locomotive toward the steps. "All in good time, Mary Jane. All in good time. But don't think that I'll have all the answers – because I don't."

When the three of us emerged from the train onto the snowy strip of ground between tracks and station, Mr. Lionel brightened the flame of his lantern. Mr. Bachmann tugged on the chain of his watch until it swung from the pocket of his vest.

"You're running late," he advised Mr. Lionel.

"By nearly four minutes," replied the conductor of the passenger train, turning to begin his inspection of the cars behind the locomotive. "Oh – and Mary Jane," he said, turning about again. "Be sure and have that wound looked after. You don't want it to develop into something far more serious."

"I will," I said, reaching instinctively toward the back of my neck.

"Have a good night, Mary Jane. Sleep well and ... *pleasant dreams,*" he added.

"Good night, Mr. Lionel. Thank you so much for the ride! – And you have a safe trip home."

"All aboard!" the conductor called out, his voice echoing from the train cars.

But no one, of course, came forward to board.

Mr. Bachmann offered to drive me home but I declined. I never realized it before but he actually lives right in the train station. He has an apartment that starts in the office behind the ticket counter, extends into kitchen and living room, bedroom and bath. I guess that's why Union Station is so much bigger than the Oak Street Station – because of the apartment.

Anyway, I'm sure that it's much more convenient when Mr. Lionel picks Mr. Bachmann up for his other job – conducting the freight train round and round, in the same, pointless circle as the passenger train. But at the time, I should have asked him. I should have asked the both of them. 'Why do you do it? – Why do you perform the same, meaningless task, day in and day out?'

Maybe it's because of the train – because of the ride itself, the exhilaration of the ride wholly eclipsing the fact that the freight train, like the passenger train, never really goes anywhere. Maybe it's important, too, to keep up the hoax, to give the impression to everyone in Christmasville that ... – *Sure, you can take the train to St. Valentine's or to Easterville. You can leave anytime that you have a mind to. Sure you can* ... – except nobody ever has a mind to leave Christmasville. Nobody but me.

I didn't want a ride home because mom and dad would get suspicious if they saw the headlights of Mr. Bachmann's car as he pulled up to the front of the house. It would certainly raise questions, which in turn, would surely prompt any number of fibs, on my part, since ... well, I *did* promise not to disclose anything, and there were at least a half dozen other reasons why it was best for everyone concerned if I said as little as possible. And besides – I wanted to stick with my plan, which was to sneak into the back door and tiptoe to my room, climb into bed and pretend that I had fallen fast asleep.

' "Oh! We've had dinner already!" ' I would say after mom or dad or one of the twins wandered into my room and discovered me. ' "Geez! – What time is it anyway?" '

But it didn't go anything like that because, for one, I'm really clumsy sometimes, and two, there was what I guess you could call, "an extenuating circumstance", one which I should have foreseen but didn't.

When I stepped into the darkness of the laundry room, I closed the door silently behind me, listening intently for any noise in the kitchen. I had to go through the kitchen because it leads to the hallway, down to my room. It seemed quiet enough so I moved toward the kitchen door and – that where's the clumsiness part comes in – I walked right into the ironing board, sending it crashing, clamoring, clacking to the linoleum floor.

Mom was the first one in. She snapped the light switch on and – the moment that I saw her face in the rush of fluorescence, flooding throughout the laundry room – I knew that she had been crying. Her eyes were wet and glassy, a red puffiness encircling them.

"Oh, thank God!" she said, bringing her hands up to her face as she burst into another round of tears. She ran forward and hugged me and squeezed me, the heat from her cheek warming the coolness of mine.

"Thank God!" she repeated, over and over.

"But where have you been???" she asked, pulling away from me abruptly, the expression on her face rapidly changing from one of relief to one of anger. "What in God's name have you been up to, Mary Jane???"

How could I say anything? I couldn't fib because it was far too serious for fibbing. I couldn't tell her the truth because I promised. And even then – if I did break my promise, which I wouldn't, and I did tell the truth – they would surely send me off to the psychiatric ward of Christmasville Hospital, my only visitor – the knucklehead, Dr. Sperry.

I looked down at the floor, at the pattern of specks, molded randomly into the squares of the linoleum floor. The specks were gold and yellow and – I never noticed it before but there were bright green specks that suddenly reminded me of ... grass – fire green grass that sways in the summer breeze ...

"Mary Jane!!!! – Where have you been???" mom said, holding me by the arms and shaking me so hard that I thought my head was going to pop off. "Where have you been???"

"Evelyn!" dad said, running into the laundry room and grabbing her.

He was dressed in his heavy coat and snow boots, his cap and gloves.

I guess I really didn't think about it. I know that's a horrible thing to say. But I really didn't think about the consequences of tricking Mr. Tolliver into thinking that I had fallen off the planet. At the moment, I only wanted him to stop following me, and to stop shooting at me. I never thought that he would come to my father and my mother, after tracking my footsteps and blood stains across the snow, across the train tracks, to the edge of the abyss. I never thought that he would come to them and say: *"I'm sorry but there's been an accident. There's been a terrible accident and I'm so very, very sorry and ... I don't know if it was the gunshot or the wild beast that caused Mary Jane to fall into the bottomless abyss ..."*

And it's because Mr. Tolliver did indeed encounter a wild beast – at the train tracks at the end of the woods – the big, furry creature sniffing the trail of bloodstains at the edge of the abyss, scraping its huge claws in the snow, charging Mr. Tolliver when it saw him approach and raise his double-barreled shotgun up, his hands shaking uncontrollably as he pulled the trigger once, twice, the shots going wild ...

' "I dropped the shotgun," he told my parents, *"and ran for dear life all the way back to the old electric building. The beast was running faster than I – almost catching me before I ran up the half-broken, half-burnt staircase, the weight of the beast collapsing the bottom of the steps even as I scrambled from the top ...*

' "I've see the beast in picture books. I've read about it in fairy tales when I was a youngster. It weren't no donkey or wild dog. It weren't no wolf either",' said Mr. Tolliver.' "It was a bear! – A giant, ferocious bear!" '

"Where have you been?" dad asked, his tone of voice far sterner than he had ever taken with the twins.

The three us – dad, mom and I – were seated at the kitchen table. The twins ... I didn't know where the twins were, but – as unlikely as it seemed – I sure wished that they were there, causing a ruckus and getting themselves in trouble, kind of offsetting ... of upsetting the cauldron of water as it started to boil.

"Where have you been?" dad repeated, raising his voice, deepening it. "We're not leaving this table, Mary Jane, until your mother and I get an answer, until you tell us where you were going. And why? *Why did you cross the train tracks when you know that it's strictly forbidden?"*

I didn't want any of this. I didn't want dad and mom to be upset, to be angry with me but ... but what could I do?

"Answer me!" dad demanded, pounding his fist on the table.

"Tom! – Don't!" mom said, reaching out to grab dad's hand, enfolding it tenderly in hers.

I didn't realize that I had started to cry until I looked up from the table, the two of them – dad and mom – distorted by their anguish, wrinkled by the wetness swelling in my eyes, running down my cheeks and falling in big droplets on the table in front of me.

"I can't tell you, dad," I said, my voice wavering. "I'm sorry that I made you angry, that I made you upset but ... but I can't tell you why I crossed the train tracks."

"'Angry?'" dad said. "'Upset?'" he added. "You have no idea, Mary Jane. You have no idea what you've done to your mother and I, what you've put us through. But the thing of it is – how can we ever ... how can we ever *trust* you again? How can we be sure that tomorrow, or the day after that, or next week, you won't wander off again – across the train tracks and into the wilderness – losing you like ... like Mr. Gabriel lost his wife and ... and his daughter, Caroline. How can we ..." he said, breaking off and lowering his head, clenching his mouth with his hand because he was so terribly upset.

Mom draped her arm about dad's neck and shoulder, leaned her face softly against his.

"It's all right, Tom," she whispered. "She's safe now and everything will be all right."

Looking down at my hands on the table, I realized dolefully that I had never seen my father cry.

"What really ... what really *hurts*," dad continued, after composing himself well enough to speak, "is that I'm ... *I'm disappointed in you, Mary Jane. I'm disappointed.*"

That was far worse than anything else he could have said to me.

I leaned my head down, spiraling into a dark, lonely void – a bottomless abyss – which, at the moment, I never thought that I would find my way out of. How could I ever erase the disappointment that I had instilled in my parents? Or replace the trust that I had taken from them? And I was so terribly tired, exhausted, drained, not only by what I had done to my parents, but by the ordeal of my journey and by the stark reality that it had revealed. There was neither road nor bridge, footpath or train track that would ever lead me out of Christmasville. I would never feel the warmth of summer, see the greenness of grass or the changing colors of leaves, falling from the trees in autumn. I would never meet John F. Kenn, or Jacqueline and the children. I would always ... always be a fourteen year old prisoner, sentenced to the endless repetition of life in Christmasville.

"I'm sorry, dad. I'm so very, very sorry that I ... that I disappointed you but..."

It was then that I reached back to scratch my neck. I was bleeding again, the redness smeared across my fingertips and reminding me – oddly – of Willy's tomato sauce, spread across a clump of macaroni on Mrs. Watts' plate.

Mom became hysterical. Dad jumped from his seat and raced around the table, catching me as I leaned to the side and fell toward the floor, fainting.

I didn't have to stay in the hospital. I got seven stitches that will probably leave a scar but at least I didn't have to stay in the hospital again. But the bad news is: I've been sent to my room indefinitely, allowed to leave only for school, for church and for the inevitable trips to the bathroom. But I guess the good news – though maybe it's not really good news after all – is that December 1st is right around the corner, which means, of course, that dad and mom will have forgotten all about my crossing the train tracks. But I won't forget. I'll never forget what dad said before I fainted: *"I'm disappointed in you, Mary Jane. I'm disappointed."*

And I know that it's silly, and childish, and immature, but I have the horrible feeling that never ... never will dad call me "princess" ever again.

Sunday is awful. Confined to my room, I sleep most of the day away, waking every now and then as Roger and Todd run through the house, shouting, banging things, celebrating my imprisonment. The worst thing is being ignored, of passing dad or mom in the hallway on my way to the bathroom, or when they bring my meals into my room. They don't look at me, or speak to me. It's as if I don't exist any more.

On Monday, everyone seems different at school – as if they all know that I had done something wrong. Debbie Lister, seated at her desk three rows over, keeps glancing at me and smirking, her eyes conveying that sort of smug satisfaction she gets when somebody else gets in trouble. At first, I think it's only my imagination, playing tricks on me but ... No – lining up to go to the cafeteria, Debbie, with her cousin, Sally, go out of their way to get in line behind me.

"We decided to celebrate my birthday on Saturday afternoon," Debbie says to Sally, loud enough for me to hear. "I'm having a skating party at the lake! – With a bonfire and toasted marshmallows and hot cocoa and then, afterwards, we'll go up to Link's Pharmacy for ice cream and my birthday cake. That's where I'll open all my presents up. And absolutely *everyone* is coming! Lisa Jenkins and Susan Wilson will be there and ... and Brett Tolliver. His parents said it was all right to come, but only for my party at Link's. It's because of his broken leg and his cast – he really can't go skating."

"Brett's so clumsy that he can't skate anyway," Sally says, giggling.

"I know," Debbie agrees, giggling as well. "He's a real klutz, isn't he?"

The beginning of the line starts off, heading from the classroom into the corridor.

"Oh – I forgot to tell you," Debbie says, starting up again, "Millie what's-her-face is coming too. You know – that funny little girl with the glasses – Millie Thompson."

"You mean Emily – Emily Thompson?" Sally asks. "Why'd you invite her?"

"Mom thought that it would be a good idea because she's the mayor's daughter and the mayor, of course, is daddy's new boss. So I invited her because ... because it's the political thing to do. But it's not like I have to talk to her or anything. I mean, for me – well, it's just another present for me to open, isn't it!"

"That's true," Sally remarks. "Oh – but it'll be such fun, Debbie! How can you stand it? Waiting for Saturday to come?"

"I know. That's the hard part – waiting for Saturday, for my fabulous birthday party!" replies Debbie. "But you know what, Sally? – What could be far worse is ... well, if you were invited to my birthday party, but for some reason or other, found that you couldn't come because you were ... Oh, I don't know – because you were being punished or something and ... Oh, that reminds me," she says.

I hear her fumbling in her lunch pail behind me.

"Mary Jane?" says Debbie, tapping me on the shoulder as we file into the cafeteria. "I have a surprise for you."

Turning, I see in her face the same smug satisfaction that she had expressed in the classroom, only more so – her face beaming in ... in smugness.

Sally looks over her shoulder, biting her lip with amusement and anticipation.

"This is for you," Debbie says, holding out what looks like a page, torn from her notebook and folded in half.

Scribbled in pencil across the top is my name: *Mary Jane Higgins.*

"What is it?" I ask skeptically.

"Why – it's an invitation to my fabulous birthday party! I know we haven't always gotten along but – it'll be so *much* fun and *everyone*, of course, will be there."

But when I reach out to grab the slip of paper, she quickly retracts her hand.

"Oh – that's right. You're being punished," she says, the expression on her face changing swiftly to one of cruel delight. "You won't be able to come after all, will you, Mary Jane? – Because you've been bad and you're being punished. It's such a shame that you won't be able to come," she adds with a false sincerity, crumbling the paper invitation and sticking it back into her lunch pail. "Really – such a terrible shame but ... but we'll be thinking of you, won't we, Sally? We'll be thinking of poor Mary Jane as she sits in her room with nothing to do because she's being punished!"

Laughing, the two of them break from the line and head off toward a lunch table.

I was going to say something about the wild beast – about the bear that Mr. Tolliver encountered – and that maybe he'd show up for her skating party as well, but ... well, they had already scurried away like ...

'... Like two little bitches,' I think, adding: 'Every dog has their day.'

I don't see Emily until lunchtime on Tuesday because she had to go to the dentist on Monday and have a tooth pulled. Her mouth is still sore and all she can eat for lunch is chicken soup and Jell-O. She doesn't talk much and I think it's because of her mouth.

"I know your mouth hurts, Emily, but you're not saying anything."

"I guess I don't have anything to say," she replies, swallowing a spoonful of soup and then glancing around the room uncomfortably.

"Aren't you even curious about my adventure into the wilderness?"

"No," she states bluntly. "I don't want to know anything about it."

"And why's that?" I ask, staring at her. "Why don't you want to know anything ...?"

"Because daddy said ...," she replies, interrupting me again.

She drops her spoon into the soup bowl and quickly brings her hand up, covering her mouth as if she had slipped up, saying what she wasn't supposed to say.

"What did your daddy say, Emily?"

One of her classmates – Sarah Franklin – pulls out a chair next to her and sits down at the table.

"Hello, Emily," she says, clanking her lunchbox open.

"What did your daddy say, Emily?" I repeat, narrowing my eyes in determination.

Emily looks toward Sarah, then back towards me. She glances at the clock on the wall at the far end of the cafeteria, stares down at her plastic cup of red Jell-O.

"Tell me what he said," I insist.

"Daddy said ...," she starts, reaching up to adjust her glasses. "Daddy said that I shouldn't ... that I shouldn't talk to you for a while. He said that I shouldn't frat ... fraterize with you because you're a ... you're a bad influence. And because daddy's the mayor, it might not look good if ..."

I gather up the remains of my lunch and dump it in the trashcan, stepping outside onto the playground. The treatment from Emily is something that I did not expect – not from someone who was supposed to be my friend.

You always pay a price for being different. It's just that ... I don't know if I'll always have enough money because, starting on Wednesday afternoon, the price for being different doubled, tripled, sky-rocketed – the hands of the clock, raking in coins and bills throughout the day, demanding more and more of what I was willing to pay; of what others, I discover, were compelled to pay.

It starts in algebra class. It starts the moment I enter the classroom. Everyone is standing by their desks, staring at me with open mouths.

"What ... What are you all looking at?" I say with annoyance.

Ricky Caterson points toward the front of the classroom. "Up there," he says.

Printed in big, yellow-chalked letters across the face of the blackboard is a long message:

"Mary Jane Higgins is a crazy lunatik person. She's a troublemaker and a dirty rotton comminist too. That's what my parents said. They said she should be kicked out of school and have her head operrated on until she gets normal like everyone else. And she's got dog crap for brains. That's what my parents said. They said Mary Jane Higgins is a comminist ands got dog crap for brains.

Everyone's been warnned!"

I want to crawl away into a corner and hide, but I don't. Instead, I drop my books on top of my desk and march to the front of the classroom. I pick up the eraser.

"Mary Jane?" Mrs. Kelly says, entering from the hallway. "What are you doing?"

I look at the blackboard, then back toward Mrs. Kelly.

"I'm erasing this," I reply without emotion.

She puts her pocketbook and briefcase on top of her desk, moves around to the front row of pupils so she can get a better view.

I start to erase.

"Just a minute, Mary Jane," says Mrs. Kelly, reading.

I stop, staring at the eraser in my hand.

"Who did this?" Mrs. Kelly asks, addressing the class.

I can tell that she is angry.

"I asked you all a question and I expect an answer. Who wrote this nonsense on my blackboard?"

Not a whisper or a cough – there's absolute silence throughout the room.

"I'm not going to ask again," Mrs. Kelly says, raising her voice. "What coward among you wrote this spiteful nonsense on my blackboard?"

Timidly, Ricky Caterson raises his hand.

"It was you!" Mrs. Kelly exclaims, swiftly approaching him.

"No! – No! It wasn't me, Mrs. Kelly!" he says nervously. "I only wanted to say ... – It was already on the blackboard when we came into the room. Wasn't it ... wasn't it already there?" Ricky says, turning to implore his classmates.

Everyone agrees with Ricky.

"Mary Jane?" Mrs. Kelly says. "Please go down to the Principal's Office and ask Mr. Marshfield to come here at once."

My legs feel like maples or oaks – stiff, wooden logs that carry me awkwardly across the room and out the door.

I was excused from algebra class indefinitely. Well, maybe 'excused' isn't the right way to put it because I still had to pick up my algebra lessons at the end of the day and complete them at home. In the time slot that I would normally attend algebra class, I was instructed to go to that arch-nincompoop's office, Dr. Sperry. Lucky me!

Although Mrs. Kelly vigorously objected – "Why should Mary Jane be penalized for the scandalous handiwork of a coward?" she insisted – it was Principal Marshfield who ultimately decided upon "the appropriate course of action".

He's a nincompoop, too – Marshfield – who seemed more concerned with the foul language and the gross misspellings in the message on the blackboard than he was with its meaning.

After school – it's still Wednesday, right before dinner – the twins sneak into my room. They want to tell me that dad was sent home from work because he got in an argument with a customer at the lumberyard. It was Mr. Tolliver.

"Dad was going to punch him right in the kisser," Todd explains, swinging his fist through the air as if he would succeed where dad had not. "It's because dad heard Mr. Tolliver saying nasty things to Mr. Burks."

"Yeah," Roger says. "The nasty things were about you, Mary Jane."

I close my eyes for a moment, wishing that none of this was happening.

"Where's dad now?" I ask.

"He took a ride in the car. He's gotta burn off some steam," Todd says, repeating, apparently, what dad had said.

Todd acts as if he himself was thoroughly familiar with the notion of 'burning off steam'.

It seems, too, that at Cauldwell's Supermarket, mom had experienced her unfair share of difficulties as well. At her cashiering station, customers would wheel their shopping carts into the slot by mom's register but then, seeing her, back themselves up, making up all kinds of excuses for continuing to shop – "Oh, I forgot the pickles!" – or for moving to another check-out lane – "Oh, hello Marge! It's been ages since..."

When Mr. Cauldwell saw mom, standing around doing nothing, he sent her back to the stockroom for pricing.

"Boy! Was mom teed off!" Roger says.

" 'Specially with Mrs. Jenkins," adds Todd. " 'Cause she didn't even have an excuse. She just backed up her cart and left without sayin' nothin'."

I guess it's one thing when I pay the price for my actions. But it's a whole other thing when someone else – my dad and mom, for example – when they have to pay the price, which, rightfully, should only be mine to pay.

That was the beginning of my week – my ninety-six hours of thrashing, struggling, nearly drowning in the cauldron of boiling water.

On Thursday morning, my alarm clock goes off at six o'clock. I had set it a half hour early so I'd have time to think about what I'm going to do today. Of course, today is 'D-Day', which means that finally – *finally* it's the 31st of January.

Maybe I'll be sick today because tomorrow ...

'*Tomorrow*' – What does that mean exactly?

'*Tomorrow*' – A distant speck at the far end of a long bridge, linking the end of January with the beginning of December. It stretches through months and seasons, across the shifting checkerboard of Christmasville. It winds through wet spring showers and summer grass that's fire-green. It spans autumn forests of maples and oaks, their leaves crisping in the chilling air, crinkling in the cool breath, rusting in the cold dew of night – the long and silent night in which everyone in Christmasville ... almost everyone, sleeps deep and dreamless, slowly forgetting what they had once remembered.

'*Leaves, falling from dormant trees ...*

'*Leaves, scattering in the stirring winds ...*

I turn in bed and pull the covers up, staring at the blankness of the ceiling. From a far corner, a tiny spider moves in a serpentine route toward the center.

'*Tomorrow.*'

Of course, it means as well that I'll have to find my way down to the gas station again, wherever it's been re-situated, and get myself a new map of Christmasville. It means that everyone will have forgotten about my crossing the train tracks, and about my being different. There won't be any more prices to pay – not for dad, not for mom, not for me. And it means that I won't be punished anymore. On Saturday I can take the passenger train with Mr. Lionel (Free of charge!), and visit him at his home in the wilderness.

' "*I have a thousand questions*",' I had said.

Maybe we can listen to his radio. Maybe we can pick up broadcasts from New York City! – And find out more about John F. Kenn, about Jacqueline and the children.

I wonder: does anyone beyond the boundaries of town, beyond the mountains and the bottomless abyss, do they know anything at all about Christmasville? Has John F. Kenn – or Jacqueline for that matter – have they ever turned a radio on, adjusted the antenna and found themselves listening to WHYY of Christmasville?

It's funny. It's funny but I never really thought about it before but maybe there's someone outside the boundaries of Christmasville who is trying to get in. Maybe they heard about Christmasville on the radio and they got themselves a map but ... but Christmasville isn't on any of their maps. There isn't any road or bridge. There isn't any train. They could never find their way but then ...

'*Where did the donkey come from?*
And the shepherd boy with his lamb?
Where came the riders of ... camels?
And where did all of them go again?'

On the ceiling, the spider approaches what surely must be an insurmountable obstacle – it's the light fixture and it's situated directly in front of him.

'*Where is the Queen of Spades?*
And the goddess to lighten my way?
Where is the Tree at the end of the road?
And when ...'

Dad taps on my door three times before bringing my breakfast in, setting it on my desk. For a moment, he stares down at the tray of food – the glass of chilled juice, the toasted muffin, the bowl of oatmeal, steaming – then turns away to leave. Stopping, he takes a deep breath and looks through the open doorway, down the empty hallway.

"Are you OK, Mary Jane?" he asks, turning his head to the side but not far enough to look at me directly.

His voice is soft and sad.

"I'm OK, dad," I reply. "Are you OK?"

"I'm OK," he answers, taking a deep breath before leaving.

I stretch my arms out and yawn before getting up to eat. On the ceiling, the spider inches around the circular rim of the fixture, stops, scoots through a little hole where a screw is missing.

I decide to go to school after all. I guess it's because it's the last day before tomorrow and because I refuse to give in. It's because I have that picture in my mind of Otis Wright – when he stood at the helm of his strange contraption as Willy pulled him through the parade on Christmas Eve. He wore that tight-fitting cap and those goggles that made him look bug-eyed. I guess I have that same ... *defiance* – that same ... that same *virtue* of defiance, I guess you could call it, which enables me to say, to shout, to scream *"No!"* in the face of whatever winds might come my way.

That's one of the things that makes me feel good about myself – being my own person. I'm just glad it's the last day that ... well, that I have to continue being my own person all by myself, if you know what I mean.

For obvious reasons, I haven't been taking the school bus. The weather's been mild enough for me to walk and, any more, it's the only opportunity that I have to get some fresh air, to breathe in the luxurious scent of pine trees and spruces. Instead of taking the shortcut through the Thompson's yard (after all, I'm not welcome there, am I), I go toward the end of Pine Street and cut through the side yard of the Rausch's. Then it's under the trestles of the freight train and over to the library at the intersection of Maple and Juniper. While everyone else streams from the buses in the parking lot at the back of the school, I meander through the last of the snowmen – and snow*women* – and enter the school from the front.

And just so you know – in the mild weather, it was the snow*women* who had fared much better than the snow*men* did.

My morning classes go well enough. Nobody talks to me, of course, as I move from one class to the next. But at least there aren't any surprises – nasty messages, scribbled anonymously on blackboards or mock invitations to birthday parties, offered and withdrawn. At lunchtime, I sit by myself at a table in the corner of the cafeteria. Classmates pass by, some of them giggling or laughing, none of them so much as acknowledging my presence. And that's fine because today is the last day of January ... and the hell with everybody else.

I eat my lunch like I normally do, looking down at my food or through the window that overlooks the playground. Outside, the wind is picking up, swinging through the trees, scurrying through the bushes and shrubs on the other side of the window. Wally, the postman, speeds by in his little chipmunk van. He's earlier than usual – and oddly, moving in the opposite direction that he normally goes. I don't know ... maybe he's trying to get more of his route done so he can take his time when he loses his chess match with Mr. Mason at the diner.

When it's time for algebra class – I mean, when it's time for my classmates to go to algebra, but for me, to Dr. Sperry's – I pass through the corridors of the second floor, heading towards his office. Along the way, there's an empty classroom but ... Wait! – Inside, there's a girl with her hand pressed against the window, watching something outside.

She has dark hair – long and straight as a ruler – and a barrette on the back of her head that looks like .... but no – for a moment ... for a moment, the plastic design on the barrette looked like the image of a woman, kneeling, a glass bead sparkling like a star above the woman's head.

Stepping into the classroom, I can see what the girl's looking at now. It's bright blue – and huge! – A great sheet ... a giant flag ... something – something that's flapping wildly in the wind beyond the trees.

"They've been having a hard time of it," the girl says, without turning from the window. "But they seem to be managing now."

I guess she heard my footsteps as I approached the window beside her.

"But what is it?" I ask, watching the commotion of the big blue thing, reeling in the wind over the lake.

"But you already know what it is – don't you, Mary Jane?" the girl says, turning towards me.

The instant I turn to look at Esmeralda, the image of the contraption in Otis' workshop jumps into my mind.

"Oh, my God!" I exclaim. "How could I have forgotten? – It's Thursday afternoon and ... how could I have forgotten?"

Turning back, the huge blue thing billows and furls in the sky above the lake beyond the trees. I see now that construction along Beech Boulevard has come to a full halt as workmen jump from their tractors and dump trucks, rushing to the edge of the roadway to stare in amazement. Directly below, on the front sidewalk of the school, two boys – coatless – race from their classrooms to watch. And there's Mrs. Franklin, followed by Mr. Marshfield, and dozens of other kids.

"I have to go now, Esmeralda," I say, turning from the window to leave.

"Yes, I know," she replies with a smile. "Be careful, Mary Jane – and good luck."

"Well, it's about time!" says Dr. Sperry, blocking the open doorway of the classroom, scowling, his hands perched on his hips in irritation. "But as quick as you go, young lady, don't think that you'll catch the five minutes that you've lost in tardiness. And, as you should very well know by now, tardiness is not something that I..."

"You know what, Dr. Sperry?" I say, interrupting him. "You can just stick it!"

I brush past him and start to run down the corridor. I just don't have time for any of his nonsense – psychiatric or otherwise.

"Well, I never!" I hear him mutter behind me. "You just wait, young lady, until Principal Marshfield ..."

"You can take your tardiness and just stick it, Dr. Sperry!" I shout from the end of the corridor, turning to run down the stairwell.

Tossing my books into my locker, I swing into my coat and scarf, pulling my hat and gloves on as I run toward the front door. Outside, students and teachers are milling around, watching and pointing, shivering their bones as they try to comprehend the large blue object that rises and heaves, that flaps and furls over the lake beyond the trees.

"Mary Jane Higgins!" I hear Principal Marshfield shout, after I snake through the crowd and dash across Juniper Street toward the lake. "Get back here this instant!" he adds.

A couple of other kids run out as well but stop and return, their curiosity stymied equally by the wind and cold – because they haven't their coats on – as by the harsh warning of Principal Marshfield.

"Mary Jane Higgins!" he calls again, the sound of his voice ambushed by the wind through the trees.

Quickly, I cross Beech Boulevard and run toward the lake. I see that the big blue thing is getting organized into a definitive shape – a titanic teardrop that's bobbing and weaving, buckling and bending above the tree line. It's becoming rounder and fuller, its surface flattening out as it swells into shape.

When I get to the little finger-islands that protrude through the surface of the lake, I stop to catch my breath. Out on the ice, ahead of me, a large group of people form a half-moon around what looks like ... well, it looks like an oil truck or a cesspool cleaning truck that's off to the left because its got one of those long flexible hoses that extends all the way from the tank of the truck, up and into the bottom of the ... the great ... blue ...

"It's a balloon!" I shout. "Oh my God! – It's a great blue light bulb of a balloon!"

Running as fast as I can, I see – to the right of the tanker truck and directly beneath the balloon – the strange, wooden contraption that Otis constructed in his workshop. His pickup truck is chained to the platform that's supported by the two long tubes. But his truck! – His truck has been so radically modified that it hardly looks like his truck at all! While the cab is still there – I can see the tiny dot of Otis seated inside it – the entire bed of the truck's been removed. In its place is a box, a metal compartment – it's a tank that's similar to the one on the truck with the hose and rises up higher than the top of the cab. From the top of the tank is a cone-shaped nozzle that reaches up and into the balloon, just like the hose from the bigger truck does.

I can just about make it out – fastened across the side of the tank on Otis' truck – is the sign: *"Frenchland or Bust!"*

As I push forward across the frozen lake, I see now that there's a dozen or so heavy ropes that tether the great balloon to metal clamps along the wooden tubes. When the wind gusts, it pushes the balloon up, lifting Otis and his contraption two or three feet above the ice. It rocks and turns, hovers and tilts for as long as the wind blows, then plunks down, back onto the ice again.

What holds Otis' contraption from blowing off, or from sliding along the frozen lake, is a network of ropes, laced across the top of the tubes, or over the tank, or across the cab and hood of the truck itself. The ends of the ropes are anchored by long metal spikes that have been driven into the ice. That's Willy's job – his and Mr. Atkinson's. They scramble around like a couple of spiders, quickly weaving their nylon web, replacing ropes that have snapped by the force of the wind as it briefly lifts the contraption upward.

"That's all we've got!" Willy shouts to Mr. Atkinson on the other side of the contraption. "We've used up all the rope!" he adds, kneeling a knee down onto the ice to catch his breath.

Mr. Atkinson waves back in acknowledgment, leans over to catch his breath then trots off toward the tanker truck. That's when I notice the sound of the pump, filling the balloon up with ... I don't know – filling it up with something.

When I arrive on the scene, everyone that forms the half moon on the far side of Otis's contraption is mesmerized, staring at the great blue balloon as if were a figment of an impossible dream. Eyes widened, mouths open, they stand frozen in place, transfixed by the huge object that hovers above them, that sways back and forth like a giant pendulum. I see Mr. Mason and ... and Tolliver – Mr. Tolliver, that is – though I have another name that I call him now. But at least he doesn't have his shotgun so he won't try to shoot me – or the balloon. And there's Wally, the postman – that's why he was driving his little van the other way! To see the balloon!

"Mary Jane!" Willy calls out. "Don't move any closer! The ropes – they're going to snap!"

Quickly, I move backwards about ten paces. Willy rises to his feet and jogs over.

"Ya see, Mary Jane," he says as he approaches. "It's a 'float' after all – just like you said."

I look up at the great, blue light bulb, hovering in space. "But it isn't a float for any parade, is it, Willy?"

"No. It's a real 'float' – one that floats in the sky."

There's a lapse in the wind. Unimpeded, the balloon stands perfectly erect over the contraption, the surface of the balloon smooth and expanded, without a wrinkle or furrow.

' *"Elastic plastic"*,' Otis had said in his workshop.

"When we first came up with the idea for the contraption – for what eventually became the 'float' – we were going to build wings and attach them to the top of the truck," Willy explains. "Of course, we couldn't make the wings flap – like birds do, when they lift themselves up and into the air, pushing themselves forward and away. So, what we decided instead was that Otis would drive his truck across the lake as fast as it would go until the wings lifted it up. To keep the contraption in motion, after it was airborne, we made some modifications to the motor in Otis' truck. There's a switch on the dashboard, which enables him to divert the power from the back wheels of his truck to what we call, the 'propeller'. Can you see it?" he says, pointing to the back of the truck. "It looks like two paddles connected to each other at their ends."

Sure enough, extending from the back of the truck, between the two wooden tubes that support the platform, is what Willy calls, the 'propeller'.

"We added a couple of flaps that drop down into position after the truck is airborne. They're connected to the steering wheel and allow Otis to control the direction of his flight. But the biggest problem with the original configuration," Willy continues, "was the propeller. We didn't think that it would generate enough thrust to keep the truck airborne. And even if it did ... well, there was the whole business of getting Otis and his truck safely back on the ground again once, if ever, he got himself up there.

"Of course, everything changed," Willy adds, turning around because he hears the sound of the wind whooshing through the far trees behind him, "when you came into the workshop and asked if it was a 'float' for the parade. That's when we decided to keep the propeller and steering flaps but to scrap the whole idea of the wings and to go with the balloon. That's when we renamed it, too – you know, 'giving credit where's credit's due' – changing it from *'The Wright Brother's Flying Skymobile'* to *'Mary Jane's Cloud Racer'*."

The giant balloon leans in the flurry of wind that races across the lake. One, two, three ropes snap as the float lurches upward, tugging on the remaining ropes before plunking down onto the ice again.

Willy moves us back another ten paces.

"Willy!" Mr. Atkinson shouts from the tanker truck. "The tank's empty – it's outta helium!"

"OK, Tom!" Willy shouts back. "I'll tell Otis to switch to his tank! Then we'll cut the ropes and let him loose!"

In a wide circle, Willy starts to run toward the front of the float but stops, turning about. "Mary Jane!" he shouts, waving his arms. "Move back a ways!"

The pump from the tanker truck stops and that's when I hear it coming again – the wind, charging through the trees behind me, streaming across the frozen surface of the lake. Willy hears it, too, because he stops and turns, then runs forward again, signaling to Otis inside his truck.

It's a tug of war now as the wind lifts Otis and the float up off the lake, plunks it down again, drags it a bit across the ice as a half dozen ropes stretch and snap, the float rising, dropping, the remaining ropes, barely holding.

The flexible hose that extends from the tanker truck up and into the bottom of the great balloon suddenly snaps away from its fitting, the end of it smacking the top of Otis's truck with a thunderous clank.

It's the sound of it – compounded with ropes snapping, winds blowing, and the wild movements of the balloon and the float – that suddenly awakens the crowd. Several women scream in fright. Men begin to shout to each other, each pointing at a different thing, in a different direction.

Willy runs off toward his pickup and the trailer, which hauled the float all the way from their workshop to the lake. Fifty yards off, it lies directly in the path of the float as it starts to hopscotch towards it.

I look at Willy, running. I glance at Mr. Atkinson – he's reeling in the flexible hose, securing it in its compartment on the side of the tanker truck as fast as he can. I see Otis, bobbing in mid-air – up, down, boom! The two wooden tubes, which support the float, strike the surface of the lake so forcefully that I hear the ice crack, feel the lake shiver beneath my feet. I look at all the people on the other side of the float, the half-moon of them receding further and further back.

' *"I see at least three journeys in front of you"*,' Esmeralda had said. ' *"At least three"*.'

Without a second thought, I run as fast as I can toward the float. I see it rise up about three or four feet over the lake, causing another rope to snap, another to loosen one of the metal spikes on the far side of the float and to zing it back, dangerously close to my head.

"Otis!" I shout, running. "Otis! – Wait!"

The float plunks down in front of me – I feel the ice quake beneath my feet. I hear it splinter and crack, the pressure of the float grinding against the surface beneath it.

The thick ropes that tether the float to the balloon, sag down – I could reach out and almost touch ...

"Mary Jane!" Willy shouts.

Pulling his truck and trailer a ways off, he must have seen me. He jumps from his cab – leaving the door open, the truck continuing to roll forward – and runs toward me.

"Mary Jane!" he calls again, running.

The ropes to the balloon tighten, lifting the float slowly upwards.

"Move away, Mary Jane!"

But it's Mr. Atkinson this time – he must've heard Willy shouting. Dropping the end of the hose, he breaks into a run, but slips and falls, sliding awkwardly on his shoulder across the ice.

In front of me now, there is one other person who is racing towards me. With the float raised up – and rocking – about seven feet over the lake, I see him break from the receding crowd and run with all his might. He's shouting as he dashes forward but, with the wind blowing into his face, with the wind tossing his cap away and pulling his hair back, with the wind gathering up his cries and propelling the sound of them over his shoulder and away, there is only a single word that I can hear. It's the word, *"princess"*.

From the trees far behind me, I hear a long roar of wind as it sweeps through branches and glides out across the frozen expanse of the lake. In the lull – in the fleeting lull – the float sinks down, gently, hovering about a foot above the surface of the ice. Quickly, I reach out and grab the handle of the truck door, pulling myself up onto the wooden tube. I yank the door open.

"Mary Jane!!!" Otis shouts from inside the cab. "No! – Don't!!! Don't! Mary Jane!"

He's wearing his tight-fitting cap and those crazy, bug-eyed goggles.

I hear the wind coming ... I hear it arriving as it smacks into the side of the truck and tilts it, causing my feet to slip from the wooden tube. I feel the weight shift rapidly from my legs to my arms as I reach and grab, the float lurching upwards, jerking, the last of the ropes snapping, the sound of the wind – the force of it pushing against my body that's half-in, but half-out ...

"Otis!" I shout, digging my hands into the fabric of the seat, my legs dangling wildly from the open door.

"Mary Jane!" he shouts, leaning across the seat and, with one hand, grabbing my arm and dragging me into the cab of the truck.

The float swings upward, sinks, veers off to the left and then begins to steadily rise. Below, I see the crescent of people backing away – some of them running, some of them moving slowly back, stopping, as if they're mesmerized again. Almost directly below us, the speck of a figure stands on the ice, waving his arms.

For a second, I think about saying, *'Good...'* – But no! – I will not say it. I will not think it.

We're rising quickly now, the winds helping us ascend. Near a far shoreline of the lake below, is the handiwork of Stark, the Iceman. The holes scattered across the ice are frozen, freezing, or unfrozen – the groups of them forming an indecipherable inscription, a message, a salutation, scribbled in a language that I don't understand. Beyond the lake, I see the twin plumes of locomotives – the freight and passenger trains – driven by Mr. Bachmann and Mr. Lionel through the winding zeros of train track. I see the first lights of Christmasville, twinkling distantly. The dark half-moon of people, who have lingered against the white sky of the icy lake far below, begin to fade like ... *like memory* ... like the memory of all in Christmasville, who, in climbing into their beds – tonight, the 31st of January – will sleep long and dreamless, slowly forgetting what they had once ...

'*Remember me, dad,*' I say to myself, a sudden tear, swelling along my lower eyelid, streaking across my cheek. '*Please ... Please dad, mom ... Please remember me.*'

In the east, night rapidly approaches, its black licorice fingers weaving the shadow that covers all things. Off to the west, great glaring flashes of lightning splinter the gloaming sky into jagged fragments, the growing storm racing to catch us. Once – and only once – the float plummets downward at such tremendous speed that I think ...

Recovering, dislodging my stomach from the narrow passage of my throat, and breathing again – I suddenly picture the face of Esmeralda in the library on First Night.

' "... *Darkness!*" ' she said.

' "... *Lightning!*" ' she added, and then moments afterwards, her head snapping forward, her eyes opening widely ...

' "*Falling.*" ' she cried.

With the winds settling down, Otis turns the key to the ignition of his truck, starting up the 'propeller'. He pushes a lever by the steering column, causing the flaps to drop. He turns the wheel slowly, aiming the float towards a single star in the east.

Epilogue
A Remarkable Discovery

It took him over an hour to jockey the furniture and the boxes around, re-arranging them until he was satisfied that everything was in order. The large volume of Christmas decorations – comprising twenty-two crates, boxes and containers – were moved to a space near the attic entry, making it far easier to carry them down when the next yuletide arrived, the first weekend after Thanksgiving.

Adjacent to the Christmas decorations is an empty space that he had reserved for the Easter boxes. Although they were big and bulky, there were only two of them – and they were lightweight – containing wicker baskets and Easter grass, cardboard cutouts and the hollow, plastic figurines of Peter Rabbit and the like. He had dragged them from the far end of the attic, beneath the air vent, to the edge of the entry steps where he would carry them down once he was finished.

Next to the space that he had left for "Easter", he stacked four, square boxes – labeled "Halloween" – followed by several shopping bags of St. Patty's Day and Fourth of July decorations.

The most difficult task – and most time-consuming – had been the furniture, sliding each piece across the warped wooden planks to the opposite end of the attic. An awkward and unwieldy process, he had crawled on his hands and knees, pushing each piece ahead of him until he discovered its niche on the other side with his flashlight. His knees had paid the highest price, striking, on occasion, the unforgiving protrusion of a raised nail head.

Opposite the holiday decorations – neatly arranged across the floor joists like the tidy squares of a calendar – are the boxes of record albums and photographs, curtains and baby toys, summer clothes and ice skates, mittens and ear muffs.

Sweaty and exhausted now, he lay back across the wooden planks of the center aisle and stretches his legs out. He wipes the sweat from his forehead, breathes in the dust-ridden air. His knees and lower back ache from his efforts.

"I'll rest for just a minute," he says, satisfied with his accomplishment, cognizant of the fact that only two chores remain.

The weight-lifting set: it would be foolish to move it at any great length of distance. Instead, he had carried two thick sections of plywood up from the garage and laid them across the floor joists behind the leaden discs and steel rods that made up the set. All he need do is to transfer them to the plywood, which, being out of the way, would prevent any of the discs from falling again, from puncturing another hole in the ceiling of a room below.

The Easter boxes and the mattress and crib: he had to carry them down because Easter, of course, was this Sunday. And two weeks afterwards was the due date for his wife, Caroline.

'Twins!' he thinks with much anticipation, mixed with a modicum of apprehension. 'With the addition of twins to the family – nothing will ever quite be the same!'

He must have dozed off because when he opens his eyes, the beam from the flashlight is conspicuously waning.

'I should have turned the darn thing off!' he admonishes himself – a futile warning since the beam has all but faded from the rafters above him. 'Brand new batteries, bought only this morning! – I should have turned it off,' he repeats, snapping the flashlight off.

It's then that he hears the voices – two voices from one of the rooms below.

"... No. I mean the pin on your blouse."

"Oh – my brooch," says his wife, Caroline. "My father gave it to my mother a long time ago for Christmas. It's kind of silly but ... well, my father used to shovel snow from walkways and driveways to make extra money for us. Jokingly, mom would call him the 'King of Spades' when he returned from his work. It lifted his spirits, eased the aches in his bones. That's why dad had the brooch made – and why it looks like the Queen of Spades. 'Every king needs his queen', dad said to mom when he gave it to her."

In the attic, he rolls onto his stomach and crawls quietly toward the hole that he had made in the ceiling of Maddy's closet last Christmas. That's where the voices are coming from – not the closet, but Maddy's bedroom.

He's curious for two reasons. First, he had never heard Caroline tell that story about her parents before. And secondly, the other voice – it isn't Maddy's. It's someone else.

"Where's your mom and dad now?" the other person asks.

'It's the girl next door,' he says to himself, recognizing the sound of her voice though he had heard it only once before. 'It's the girl next door – Mary ... Mary Jane – the one who moved into the Johnson house with her uncle.'

He thought her a bit odd because, when she was moving in, he had asked her: ' "Where did you live before?" '

She had bitten her lip, glanced around the front yard of the Johnson house as if she would discover the answer behind a bush or up in the branches of a tree.

' "Do you know where ... where China is?" she asked.'

' "Sure. I know where China is," I replied.'

' "Well, that's where we're from," she said. "Otis – my Uncle Otis and I – we're from China." ' '

In the bedroom below, his wife replies: "My mom passed away six years ago."

"I'm sorry to hear that," says Mary Jane.

"As for my dad," continues Caroline, "I haven't see my dad in more than twenty years. He lives in a place that's far, far away," says Caroline.

The sound of her voice is imbued with the distinct flavor of sadness, of loss.

"But don't you visit him?" Mary Jane asks. "You could take the train to see him, couldn't you? – The trains go everywhere."

"No," Caroline replies. "It's so far away that ... No – there aren't any trains that go there because ...

She breaks off, struggling with the notion of discussing her father, whom – as she said

– she hasn't seen in more than twenty years.

"The trains don't go there because ... because he lives in China, Mary Jane. And you do know where China is – don't you?"

There is a long silent lull.

It's as if he's still dozing on the attic floor, dreaming of this strange conversation between his wife, Caroline, and the girl next door – the strangeness emanating from what was becoming a magical, almost mystical notion of ... *China*, and by a growing disbelief ... – *'Why hadn't Caroline ever told him before about her father ... about her father in China? Or about the brooch that belonged to her mother?'*

He puts the flashlight down and inches forward until he's directly above the hole in the ceiling. Peering down, he sees the back of Maddy, sitting on the floor near the closet, quieting listening to the conversation between her mother and the girl next door. Behind Maddy, spread across the floor of the closet, she has constructed a tiny village of sorts. It's composed of an unusual medley of items: several plastic houses that she would assemble each year and put on the train platform; chalkware figures from the Nativity set – a donkey and camels, the three wise men, Mary and Joseph and the shepherd boy with his lamb. Mixed between the houses and the figures – items that normally would have been packed away with the Christmas decorations – is the animal set that Santa Claus brought. There's a grizzly bear and two deer, chickens and cows, a spotted Dalmation that Maddy called, "Tucker" ...

"I know where China is," Maddy says, breaking the silence.

"I know you do, dear," Caroline says. "You dream about China all the time, don't you?"

Maddy gets to her feet, carefully protecting the wrist of her right arm, which is wrapped in a sling because she had broken it when she fell down the steps.

"I know about Mary Jane, too," Maddy says. "Because I dreamed about her in the liberry."

"*The library?*" Mary Jane says. "That's where I read about you, Maddy!"

"Mary Jane," Caroline says. "Why you haven't changed one little bit! You haven't changed at all ... Mary Jane Higgins!"

'Higgins?' he repeats to himself in the attic. *'But I thought ... I thought that her last name was Wright? And if it isn't Wright, then how would Caroline know otherwise?'*

"You don't remember me, do you, Mary Jane?" asks Caroline.

"No," Mary Jane replies. "I don't remember – I'm sorry but I don't remember you."

"Well – I know that you'll find it hard to believe but ... well – I'm Caroline," his wife announces. "I'm Caroline Gabriel."

"But ... but you're alive!" Mary Jane stammers. "You're alive and you're all grown up!"

"Yes – I'm all grown up now," Caroline says. "I know it's difficult to understand, Mary Jane, but I'm all grown up now because ... well, I know it sounds impossible but ... it's been more than twenty years since mom and I were lost in that terrible snow storm."

There's another silent lull, broken only by the sound of a car horn on the street in front of the house.

"But you were only ... seven? – seven or eight when ..."

"I was eight years old then," Caroline says.

"But how did you ... How did your mom and you..." Mary Jane says, rambling. "I have a thousand questions, Caroline."

"I'm sure that you have, Mary Jane – just as mom and I had after we stumbled blindly through the wind and the snow, pushing on and on until we could go no further, finding ourselves ... But that's another story, Mary Jane. For now ... – well, for now, don't try to digest everything all at once. You'll have plenty of time for that. And, of course, Maddy and I can help you. Won't we help Mary Jane, Maddy?"

"We'll help you, Mary Jane," replies Maddy.

He puts his hand up to his forehead. 'This doesn't make any sense!' he says to himself.

' *"Wind and snow? ... Pushing on and on"?* ... And if Caroline was only eight at the time and that was ... that was more than twenty years ago and Mary Jane is ... – Geez! – It doesn't make any sense because Mary Jane would have to be thirty- ... thirty-five or six and ... *and she wasn't even born more than twenty years ago* so how could she...'

There's another honk from the car horn out front.

"Oh," Mary Jane says, having gone to the window, apparently, and looked out front. "That's Otis – my Uncle Otis."

"Mary Jane," Maddy advises. "You have to look at mommy when you talk so she can read your lips."

"I'm sorry, Maddy ... Caroline," she says, repeating what she had said before.

"Oh, yes – 'Uncle' Otis," says Caroline. "And how's your other 'uncle' doing? You know – your 'Uncle' Willy?"

In the attic, he's not at all sure how Caroline could possibly know about Mary Jane's 'other Uncle' – her 'Uncle Willy'. And he's utterly confused as to why Mary Jane finds Caroline's question so amusing. Nevertheless, the girl next door – the *odd* little girl next door – breaks out with a laugh, replying:

"Willy's just fine!" she replies, still laughing. "He's fine."

"I'm so glad to hear that!" states Caroline. "And ... and – I guess I'm reluctant to ask but..."

"Your father's doing well," Mary Jane says, anticipating her question. "That is – as well as could be expected, under the circumstances ... – You know, after losing you and Mrs. Gabriel ..."

From the room below, there's a muffled, sniffling sort of sound.

"I'm sorry," Caroline says, blowing her nose. It's just that ... well, I really miss them – dad and mom, that is."

"I know," says Mary Jane. "I miss my dad and mom too."

"It's all right, mommy," Maddy says, comforting her mother. "Someday we'll find a way for you to see your daddy again."

"Maybe, sweetie," Caroline says. "Maybe."

"Well," says Mary Jane. "I guess I better be running along for now – Otis and I are driving into New York City today. We're going shopping on Fifth Avenue!"

"Oh – what a fun time you'll have of it, Mary Jane. Is this your first trip into the city?"

"Yes. We've never been to New York City before."

"Well – be prepared, Mary Jane, because there's a much different scale of things than what you're used to."

"Don't forget your ice skates!" Maddy says.

"My ice skates?" Mary Jane says. "Why would I need my ice skates, Maddy?"

"To go skatin' at Rockafella Rink, silly!"

"But that's only at Christmas time, Maddy," explains Caroline. "It's Easter time now and they've taken the skating rink apart, carted away the big Christmas tree behind it."

"A Christmas tree?" asks Mary Jane.

"It's a really, really big one," Maddy replies. "It's the biggest Christmas tree in the whole wide world! It's got millions of lights and ornaments and pretty ribbons that are red and ... – And there's a big gold man that floats in front of the tree and watches all the skaters! That's 'Rockafella'! daddy says, because – if you squint your eyes like this," Maddy explains, "and move your head like this," she adds, "the gold man looks like he's dancin' to the music. 'Rockafella!' – That's what daddy calls him."

"And the big iron man? – Is he there too, Maddy?" asks Mary Jane.

"He's around the corner, I think. But he isn't gold and he doesn't float in the air and dance like 'Rockafella' does."

In the attic, he hears their footsteps as they leave the bedroom and enter the hallway, circling the foot of the ladder.

"I wonder what's taking your father so long at the store?" Caroline says, the sound of her voice rising through the attic entry. "All he needed was batteries."

Running from the house – across the grass that's greening in the warm breath of spring – Mary Jane jumps into the pickup with Otis.

"Ready to get started?" he asks.

"Ready," she replies, eager to go into the city, bursting to tell him about her remarkable discovery.